THE
CAPTIVE
HEART

BOOKS BY BERTRICE SMALL

THE BORDER CHRONICLES
A Dangerous Love
The Border Lord's Bride
The Captive Heart

THE FRIARSGATE INHERITANCE
Rosamund
Until You
Philippa
The Last Heiress

CONTEMPORARY EROTICA
Private Pleasures
Forbidden Pleasures
Sudden Pleasures
Dangerous Pleasures

THE O'MALLEY SAGA
Skye O'Malley
All the Sweet Tomorrows
A Love for All Time
The Heart of Mine
Lost Love Found
Wild Jasmine

SKYE'S LEGACY
Darling Jasmine
Bedazzled
Besieged
Intrigued
Just Beyond Tomorrow
Vixens

THE WORLD OF HETAR
Lara
A Distant Tomorrow
The Twilight Lord
The Sorceress of Belmir

MORE BY BERTRICE SMALL
The Kadin
Love Wild and Fair
Adora
Unconquered
Beloved
Enchantress Mine
Blaze Wyndham
The Spitfire
A Moment in Time
To Love Again
Love, Remember Me
The Love Slave
Hellion
Betrayed
Deceived
The Innocent
A Memory of Love
The Duchess

BERTRICE SMALL

THE CAPTIVE HEART

 NEW AMERICAN LIBRARY

New American Library
Published by New American Library, a division of
Penguin Group (USA) Inc., 375 Hudson Street,
New York, New York 10014, USA
Penguin Group (Canada), 90 Eglinton Avenue East, Suite 700, Toronto,
Ontario M4P 2Y3, Canada (a division of Pearson Penguin Canada Inc.)
Penguin Books Ltd., 80 Strand, London WC2R 0RL, England
Penguin Ireland, 25 St. Stephen's Green, Dublin 2,
Ireland (a division of Penguin Books Ltd.)
Penguin Group (Australia), 250 Camberwell Road, Camberwell, Victoria 3124,
Australia (a division of Pearson Australia Group Pty. Ltd.)
Penguin Books India Pvt. Ltd., 11 Community Centre, Panchsheel Park,
New Delhi - 110 017, India
Penguin Group (NZ), 67 Apollo Drive, Rosedale, North Shore 0632,
New Zealand (a division of Pearson New Zealand Ltd.)
Penguin Books (South Africa) (Pty.) Ltd., 24 Sturdee Avenue,
Rosebank, Johannesburg 2196, South Africa

Penguin Books Ltd., Registered Offices:
80 Strand, London WC2R 0RL, England

First published by New American Library,
a division of Penguin Group (USA) Inc.

Copyright © Bertrice Small, 2008
All rights reserved

ISBN: 978-1-60751-120-5

Set in Goudy
Designed by Ginger Legato

Printed in the United States of America

This book is dedicated with love and great respect to the two women who unknowingly started me on my career. The late Ivy Bolton, aka Sister Mercedes from the Anglican community of Saint Mary's, a wonderful author of children's historical novels, who encouraged my passion for history; and the late Miss Frances Anderson, the best English teacher any girl ever had. God bless you both and thank you!

THE CAPTIVE HEART

Prologue

MARCH 29, 1461

The screams of the dying men could hardly be heard over the howling wind. Foe was indistinguishable from friend amid the heavily falling snow that swirled about the combatants. It was bitterly cold as only an early spring in Northumbria could be. The king and his few remaining advisers huddled on the edge of the battlefield until one, braver than the others, reached out to take the bridle of the king's horse and lead it away. Then those who were with them followed. It was the end of an era. The end of a reign.

The wiser among them knew it. Understood it. They considered now how best to retain their heads as well as their fortunes with a new king in a Yorkist regime. They thought of the enemies and the friends that they had among the now favored. Which of those men would have influence enough to save or destroy them? The loyalists, however, were painfully aware that they now faced exile. They silently prayed for the safety of their own families, whom they might never see again in this life.

"Is it over?" the king asked softly. His eyes were beginning to lose their focus. It was a sure indication that one of his attacks of madness was approaching.

"Yes, my liege, it is over" came the quiet reply.

"Have we won?" the king inquired hesitantly.

"I think not, my liege, but until the snow stops we cannot really tell," the man said candidly as they rode away.

1

"Where is the queen? The queen will know if we have won. The queen always knows what is happening," the king said anxiously. He was still with great effort managing to cling to his sanity.

"I am taking you to her now, my liege," the man responded, "but we must hurry lest the Yorkists catch us." *And before one of us decides to turn you over to them to save his own skin*, the king's companion thought to himself. He noticed three or four of their party had already disappeared. Well, good riddance to them, the traitors!

"They will kill me," the king said fatalistically. "They have to in order to justify what they have done. And they must kill my son though he be just a lad, for he is the true heir to England's throne after me. But if I know my wife, Margaret will fight like a tigress to protect our child." Henry VI had not yet released his hold on his sanity. But the few men left to accompany him knew it was but a matter of time before he was once more hurled into his private hell. His mind was simply not strong enough to manage this terrible change in his fortunes.

They hurried through the fierce storm to reach Queen Margaret and the little prince, who were sheltering in a nearby farmhouse. They would have to get deep into the borderlands before the storm ceased. Only then would their king and his family be truly safe, and then only temporarily. Sir Udolf Watteson, who now rode with them, would give them all shelter. At least for the few days it would take for the outcome of the battle to be known down in London, where the new king resided. Until the order was given, and came north for the arrest of Henry Plantagenet, his wife, and his son. The Lancasters were done. At least for now. Perhaps forever.

Chapter 1

The queen knew all was lost. At least for now. Perhaps forever, but no! Not while there was breath in their bodies and their son remained healthy and strong. *They* would not steal Edward Plantagenet's inheritance from him. Not while she lived. No! It was unthinkable that Edward of York would supplant them.

"Madame, we must go now," Sir Udolf Watteson said to the queen.

Margaret of Anjou nodded. "*Oui*" was all she said. She did not look about her. The others would be ready because it was their duty to anticipate what was to come. It would not do to be caught now, and besides, if they were, what was to become of their few remaining retainers? Their loyalty to her deserved better than to be caught and murdered by a pack of Yorkist traitors. The queen drew her heavy fur-lined cloak about her and pulled up its hood. "*Allez!*" she said as she stepped through the farmhouse door.

It was still snowing steadily. Fifteen-year-old Alix Givet followed her mistress, her arm about her physician father. "Are you certain you are warm enough, Papa?" she asked him softly, her hazel eyes concerned.

"I am fine, *mignon*," he told her. "You worry too much."

"You are all I have left, Papa," Alix said as a man-at-arms helped first her father to mount his horse and then boosted her into her saddle. The girl rode astride, for it was easier for her in their flight.

"We will have at least several days of rest before we must move on again," Alexander Givet replied. "I just need a little time to be dry and warm to recover, *ma petite*. This ride will be the worst of it, I promise."

"Where will we go then, Papa?" Alix asked him as she gathered her reins into her gloved hands. "We are being driven from England."

"The queen will ask sanctuary from her distant relation Marie of Gueldres, who is Scotland's queen. It will be granted, and then we shall probably take flight for France. You will finally see Anjou, *ma petite*," he told her. "We still have family there, and I shall make a good match for you, Alix, so you will be safe after I am gone."

"I do not want to marry, Papa. I want to remain with you," the girl told him.

The physician chuckled as they began to move north into the storm. "It is your duty to marry, *mignon*, so your papa may have a warm place by the hearth in his old age," he teased her. "Unless, of course, you wish to enter a convent."

"Nay, Papa, I am not meant for the church," Alix assured him.

"Then we must find you a good and generous husband who will take us both in," Alexander Givet said. "Or perhaps I could find a nice wealthy widow who would have us. But two women in a household is rarely a good thing. And besides, I could never marry again after all my years with your mama."

"Oh, Papa," the girl responded, "why did Mama have to die?"

"Her heart was not strong in these last years," the physician told his daughter. "The strain and the tension surrounding the royal couple over the past months were finally too much for her, Alix. I would have taken her home to Anjou, but she would not hear of it. She loved her mistress, and they had been friends since they were girls. Loyalty to each other was something that both the queen and your mother possessed in abundance." He sighed gustily. "I miss her greatly, *mignon*. Blanche de Fleury was the only woman for me." The tone of his voice was sad, and trembled just slightly as he remembered.

Alexander Givet had met Blanche de Fleury at the court of the
Count of Anjou. It was a busy court forever on the move, for Rene,
the count, who was also the titular king of Naples and Sicily, and his
first wife, Isabelle, the Duchess of Lorraine, were sovereigns without
a real throne. The youngest son of minor Anjou nobility, Alexander
had become a physician. Brought to the court by his father to gain
a place among the count's retainers, he quickly found himself assigned to the household of Yolande of Aragon, the count's mother,
who was raising his second daughter, Margaret. He was twenty-two
at the time.

Negotiations were already underway for Margaret of Anjou to
marry the young king of England. Blanche de Fleury was one of the
young girls who had grown up with Margaret of Anjou. She had
been brought to the Count of Anjou's court at the age of six. Her
mother was dead, her father remarrying, and if the truth be known,
she had been considered an encumbrance by her surviving parent.
She was three years older than Margaret, but the duchess thought
that Blanche de Fleury had beautiful manners and would make a
suitable companion for her daughter, Margaret.

At first Blanche was like an older sister to Margaret. But as the
young girl grew, the two became friends. When Margaret was sent at
the age of twelve to her paternal grandmother to be trained to be a
queen, Blanche went with her, as did the young physician, Alexander Givet. But before they departed for Yolande of Aragon's household, it was decided that the young physician should be wed. The
count's mother looked among her granddaughter's companions and
concluded that the fifteen-year-old Blanche de Fleury was a sensible
choice. She sent to the girl's father for his permission, although it
was actually no more than a formality since the count approved the
match his mother was proposing. It was, Alix's mother later told
her, a fortunate match. She was acquainted with the young physician, and like most of the girls in Margaret's circle, Blanche thought
Alexander Givet handsome. She was not unhappy to find herself
his wife.

Her new husband was, at twenty-five, ten years her senior. And to her surprise, he was interested in what she thought and what she wanted. And Blanche did indeed know what she wanted. She wanted to remain with Margaret of Anjou. In this her husband concurred, for to go to England among the household retainers of its new queen was quite an honor. So Blanche took the potion her husband fed her each morning to prevent any children from being born, and she told no one, not even her confessor. And if the wise Yolande of Aragon suspected, she said nothing. Blanche de Fleury was an excellent influence on her granddaughter, and it was Yolande who made the decision that the physician Givet and his wife would be among those accompanying Margaret to England.

But once in England Alexander and his wife began to long for a child. Perhaps a son who would grow up with their queen's children. But their only child, a daughter, was born to them in April of 1446 while Margaret of Anjou remained childless until 1453. The English king was devout and shy of his young bride, who was acknowledged to be a beauty. Intelligent and vital, the young queen realized her husband's weaknesses at once. Henry was not suited to rule. Still, she became fond of him, and allied herself with the Beaufort-Suffolk faction at court to see her husband's position was protected by his competent relations while he pursued his religious and scholastic leanings, founding Eton College and King's College in Cambridge.

But Henry Plantagenet's weaknesses finally proved too much. His first bout with insanity occurred shortly after the birth of his only son, Prince Edward. In the year that followed, the next man in line for the throne following the king and his infant son, the Duke of York, reigned as Protector. Upon the king's recovery a year later, the queen and Edmund Beaufort, the Duke of Somerset, grew all-powerful. Almost immediately, rivalries between the Lancaster and York factions broke out. Edmund Beaufort was killed at the first battle of St. Albans in May of 1455.

A rough peace of sorts was made, but four years later the hostilities broke out once again. King Henry was captured at Northampton in the summer of 1460, and forced to accept the Duke of York as his heir, eliminating his own son, little Edward Plantagenet. Furious at this attempt to exclude her child from the succession, Queen Margaret rallied the Lancastrian forces and five months later won a victory at Wakefield, where the Duke of York was slain. Two months later the queen's forces won the second battle of St. Albans, freeing the king, who had been held captive by the Yorkists since the previous July.

But the king's victory over his rivals was brief. The Duke of York's heir was crowned King Edward IV two weeks later in London, formally deposing Henry Plantagenet. The new king then went on to drive the old king and his family up the length of England until they reached Towton, where the final battle had taken place. Now Henry Plantagenet, his wife, his son, and their few remaining followers rode north into the borders as the early spring snows swirled about them.

They were relying upon the hospitality of Sir Udolf Watteson, a Northumbrian baron of minor family and no court connections at all. Their brief presence in his home was unlikely to ever be noted by the powers that be because Sir Udolf was one of those unknown factors, being an unimportant man who, until the battle of Towton, had never even laid eyes on King Henry. He had little but his lands, which were rugged and not particularly arable, a stone house of no distinction, and nothing of value that would appeal to anyone. How did you punish a man like that even if those now in power down in London learned of his part in sheltering Henry Plantagenet? But it was unlikely King Edward would ever learn of Sir Udolf Watteson or that he sheltered the former king and his family. In the important scheme of things, the unknown baron didn't matter at all.

The snow fell steadily as horse followed horse. Nose to tail was the only way they were able to keep from getting lost in the storm. At their head, Sir Udolf led them onward until, finally, after almost two hours in the bitter cold and freezing winds, they saw the faint outline of a house ahead of them. Coming to a stop, they waited briefly, but Sir Udolf jumped from his mount and pounded upon the door of the dwelling. It opened, and the faint light of the interior beckoned to them.

"Come in! Come in!" the baron called to them.

And then there were several boys coming to take their horses to the safety of the barns. Alix Givet dismounted from her small mare, patting the beast to comfort it. Its dark mane was frozen stiff. She went to her father's side. He was being helped down from his own gelding and could barely stand. "Lean on me, Papa," she said softly.

"I am rigid with the cold," he murmured quietly, and then came the ominous cough that had been worrying her these past weeks. He balanced himself a moment, his hand upon her small shoulder as he began to walk towards the house with his daughter.

Once inside, they were brought to the hall, where a hot fire was burning in the large hearth. The queen was already warming her hands over it, the little prince by her side. The king had been seated in a high-backed chair near the warmth, and there was quickly a goblet of wine in his hand. His eyes were closed, and Alix could see he was shaking ever so slightly.

"Welcome to my home!" Sir Udolf said. "I have instructed my servants to prepare a place for you. Your Highness," he addressed the queen. "My house is not grand, but you shall have the best I can offer you. My own apartment is yours."

"*Merci*, Sir Udolf," Margaret of Anjou said softly. "Is there to be food soon? The king needs to eat, and then he must be put to bed to rest. This has been a terrible day for him, and he is not well, as you know."

Seeing the expression of distress upon their host's face, Alix spoke up. "Madame, perhaps it would be best if the king were made comfortable first, and a warm supper brought to him," she suggested quietly.

"Ah, *ma chérie* Alix, that would indeed be best," the queen said, sounding relieved, for she herself had suddenly realized that Sir Udolf's cook would not be ready for guests. Margaret of Anjou went to her husband's side. "Henry," she said, "let us go now to our chambers, and Alix, will you watch over little Edward? I see his nurse has fallen asleep, poor woman. She is too old for all this excitement." The queen helped her husband to stand, and then following Sir Udolf's steward, the royal fugitives walked from the hall.

"This is terrible," Sir Udolf said when they were gone. "That the king should be driven from his lands. He is a good man, and she a good queen. I am glad now more than ever to be a simple man. To have so much power that others would covet it is frightening." And he shook his head, sighing.

"I must agree with you, sir," Alexander Givet said from his place near the fire. "But once King Henry's court was a pleasant place to be. He is a learned man."

"What place had you among it all?" Sir Udolf asked, curious.

"I am the queen's physician. I came with her from Anjou many years back with my late wife, who was one of the queen's ladies. The young girl playing now with the prince is our daughter, Alix. My name is Alexander Givet."

"I, too, am widowed," Sir Udolf replied.

"Have you children?" the physician inquired.

"A son, Hayle. He is twenty. His mother and I were wed several years before he was born. Audrey was not strong. She died when Hayle was four, birthing our daughter, who lived but a day. I married again eight years ago, but she turned out to be a nag. I was not unhappy when she died three years later of a winter ailment. I have a farm wife now, who satisfies my manly urges when I need her. I do not need another wife."

Alexander Givet chuckled. "I am widowed two years now, and I have no need for a wife. My daughter takes good care of me, and we are content in the queen's service."

"Tell me, physician," the baron said, "how am I to house the royal party? My house is not large, but I would not stint on anything or appear inhospitable."

"The king, the queen, and their two remaining servants will

share your apartment, Sir Udolf. If there is a chamber for the little prince; Edmee, his nurse; and my daughter, the rest of the party will sleep wherever you have the space for us."

"You must have the bedspace nearest the hearth," Sir Udolf said. "You are not well, physician. I hear the rattle in your chest."

"It has been cold for spring," Alexander Givet said.

"The season can be cruel here in Northumbria," the baron admitted. He waved to a servant, who came to stand by his master's side. "Ask the cook when the dinner will be ready, and bring this gentleman more wine," Sir Udolf said. It was pleasant having another man with whom he could talk. He had had some small education in his youth, but his son could not even write his own name or read. Hayle had not wanted to learn, and could be neither forced nor cosseted into doing it. He was not a man to sit talking of a winter's evening. He preferred the company of his little mistress, Maida.

The servant returned to say, "The meal will be ready within the hour, my lord."

Sir Udolf nodded his acknowledgment. "Go upstairs and tell the queen," he said. Then, turning to the physician, he said, "The meal will be simple compared to what you have at court, I fear."

"The king will be content with a good soup and some bread," the physician surprised his host by saying. "He has never been a man to enjoy a heavy, oversauced meal, Sir Udolf. Sauces often hide spoilage of the meat. The king prefers light meals. Watch what the queen eats when she comes to the high board, and you will see her preferences. She has a delicate belly, and always has."

Sir Udolf nodded and gave the orders to his servant. The queen returned to the hall just as the steward announced that the dinner was served. She and her son joined Sir Udolf at the high board while the others took their places at the trestles below. Edmee and the queen's tiring woman, Fayme, sat with Alix and her father. The physician had more color in his face now that he was warm again.

"The queen was pleased with the food they brought the king,"

Fayme confided to the others. "A nice thick hot soup, fresh bread, butter, and a baked apple. We were able to get him to eat it all. I did not believe in a place so rough there would be good food."

"We're fortunate to have a place at all tonight to lay our heads," Edmee remarked. "My poor wee princeling being robbed of his rightful place and his heritage. Well, if those Yorkist pretenders believe they can hold on to their stolen goods, they're wrong. You mark my words, the queen will see to it, and we'll be back in London before you know it." She popped a piece of meat pie into her mouth. Edmee was an old woman now, at least sixty. No one knew for certain. A hot meal had restored her spirits.

"I do not think that we will be back in London quite so soon," Alexander Givet said quietly. "I know for a fact that the queen means to send to Queen Marie of Scotland and ask for refuge once the storm has stopped. She means for us to shelter in Scotland. Queen Marie must give her refuge, for their shared blood demands it, but she will be able to do little more than that. Her own child has only recently become king, and he is near our prince in age. It will take time to rebuild our king's forces. She might even send her son to Anjou for his own safety. He and his father will now be hunted down with an eye towards killing them both."

"Mary, Jesu, have mercy!" Edmee cried, and she crossed herself. "They would not kill a child, would they?"

"Every moment Henry and Edward Plantagenet live, they present a danger to King Edward of York," the physician answered. "The father they will kill outright when he is caught. The boy will suffer a tragic accident. It is the way of our world, old woman."

Edmee and Fayme crossed themselves again.

"Papa, do not frighten us," Alix said.

"I do not mean to frighten you," Alexander Givet answered her. "It is the truth."

"What will happen to us?" Edmee quavered.

The physician shrugged. "Who knows," he said. "The queen has been leaving many of our retainers behind as we moved north.

They were fortunate to be put with other noble families who will weather this storm. We are the last. Who knows what will happen to us, but I suspect nothing. We will take refuge in Scotland, and probably in the end return to Anjou. We three came with the queen when she was brought to England. It will not be so bad to go home again, eh?"

The two women smiled tremulously and nodded.

"She will not cast you two aside," he assured them.

"But maybe the king will be restored," Alix said hopefully.

Her father shook his head. "Perhaps" was all he said. Alexander Givet was a realist. Henry Plantagenet had, since his son's birth, been subject to fits of madness. Some lasted as long as a year. Others but a few days or weeks. But he had never been a successful ruler, and now his condition made it impossible for him to rule at all. The rivalries at court had contributed to his downfall. That and his queen. The nobility did not like having a strong queen who was England's actual ruler. It had been inevitable that the king would be dethroned eventually, but the Duke of York's high-handed methods had rubbed Margaret of Anjou and her allies the wrong way. The past few years had been chaotic, and the chaos had but contributed to the king's fragile mental state. Alexander Givet would not say it aloud, but he very much doubted if Henry VI would ever again sit upon his throne. A madman could not rule England, or any other land.

Sir Udolf had taken the physician's suggestion. While he and his guests sat eating, his servants were cleaning up two small rooms to house the little prince, his nursemaid, and Alix. The young boy was so exhausted by the day he had lived, he fell asleep at the high board. One of the baron's servants carried the lad to his bed, old Edmee following in their wake. After thanking their host, the queen and Fayme departed. Alix remained behind to see her father settled for the night.

"Nay, *mignon*, I am quite capable of putting myself to bed," Alexander Givet assured his daughter. "The baron and I plan to drink a bit more wine and play some chess," he chuckled, patting her small hand. "Go and rest yourself."

The king's body servant, John, came into the hall on his way to the kitchens for his meal. He had been watching over the king while the others had eaten. "Mistress Alix," he called to her. "The queen needs you to sing to the king."

"Go," the physician said. "I am fine."

Placing a kiss upon his cheek Alix hurried from the hall.

"She sings to the king?" Sir Udolf looked quizzically at Alexander Givet.

"When the king is restless and the dolor comes upon him, my daughter sings to the king the songs that his mother used to sing to him. It calms him."

"She is a pretty girl," the baron said, "and both faithful and true not just to her parent but to her lord and lady, as well I can see. You are truly blessed in your daughter."

"Your son," the physician said. "He was not in the hall tonight."

"Hayle had many things to do for me, and he is devoted to Wulfborn," the baron answered. "Ah, here is the chessboard all set up for us now. Will you play black or white, my good doctor?"

"White," Alexander Givet said. "Wulfborn?"

"The name of our estate. This is Wulfborn Hall. Our distant ancestors were Vikings, or so the legend goes. Hayle looks very much like I would imagine a Viking warrior would look," the baron said. "He is tall and blond."

The two men sat down to play at chess, talking, sipping at their cups. The hour grew late, and after each man had won, the baron suggested they retire for the night. A servant helped the physician to his bedspace, which was made up with a feather bed and a goosedown coverlet. It was, as the baron had promised, the bedspace nearest the hearth, and the walls were warm. Alexander Givet settled himself comfortably, relieved. He was truly warm for the first time in days, and he prayed they would not have to move on too quickly. These past weeks had been hard on them all.

The king had slipped away into himself by morning, and was unresponsive to all, and everything about him. The queen put on a brave front, but she was frightened more for her husband and son than for herself. Sir Udolf, however, reassured her that the royal fugitives were more than welcome to stay at Wulfborn Hall. He reminded her that his home was isolated, and near enough to the Scots border for a quick escape should one be necessary. Margaret of Anjou was grateful.

"I wish," the queen said, "that there were some way in which we might repay you, Sir Udolf." They had been sheltering in his home for two weeks now, and it was mid-April. The snows had vanished, and the longer days were almost mild. "But as you know, we are little better than beggars now."

"Madame, I am honored to have you as my guests," the baron replied gallantly.

She nodded graciously, but then she said, "My lord, you have a son, do you not?"

"I do," he acknowledged.

"But he is not wed," Margaret of Anjou continued. "Why is that?"

The baron sighed deeply. "He is a good lad, madame, but to be most candid with you, Hayle is a bit odd. We have few neighbors, but those with daughters will not agree to any match with my son."

"What makes him odd?" the queen asked.

Again the baron sighed. "He was a sweet-natured little boy, but when he was four he almost drowned in my mill pond. After his recovery he changed, becoming impatient, determined to have his own way, and subject to terrible tempers when he did not get it. He has a mistress. The miller's daughter. He says he wants no other woman but Maida. I have told him he must have an heir. But there is no suitable bride for my son. I do not know what I will do. I cannot accept the child of a miller's daughter as my son's heir. But if I die before he weds, Hayle will have his way, I fear."

The queen's beautiful face was devoid of expression, and then she said, "Perhaps I may be of help to you, my lord."

He looked at her questioningly. "Madame?"

"As fugitives who will soon have a price upon our heads, we must travel quickly. The fewer in our party the less difficult it will be to find sanctuary. We have not traveled in some months with the royal dignity due us. At the homes of various nobility I have had to leave our servants and beg for their safety." The queen paused briefly, and then she continued. "Alexander Givet and his wife came with me from Anjou when I married the king. Blanche grew up with me. I am their daughter's godmother. Alix is fifteen going on sixteen. Her parents come from noble families in Anjou. Minor nobility to be sure, but then you too, Sir Udolf, are counted among the lesser nobility here in England. The physician is a younger son. His wife was put in my father's care when she was six. Their daughter was born in England. She would make a very suitable wife for your son, and I would know my godchild was safe."

"Would her father accept such an arrangement?" Sir Udolf asked the queen.

"Ah, my lord, there is the small difficulty. If you would have my goddaughter for your son, you must give her father a home too. My doctor is not well, and hasn't been in some time. He can travel no longer, I fear. The cough he had when we arrived has barely subsided in these few weeks despite Alix's vigorous nursing. He misses his wife greatly, and has lived for their daughter. Once he sees her safe and settled at Wulfborn Hall, I suspect he will die at peace."

"I will be happy to have him here," the baron said generously. "I am enjoying his company in the evenings. Very well, madame. If Alexander Givet will let his daughter wed my son, we have a bargain."

"How will you coerce your son into obeying you?" the queen wanted to know.

"He will obey me after much argument," the baron said in a hard voice.

"I do not want my godchild abused," Margaret of Anjou replied. "You must give me your word, my lord, that Alix will be treated with the respect due to the lady of this house. As much as I seek her safety, my conscience will not allow her to be put in jeopardy, my lord. Will you give me your guarantee?"

"I will, Your Highness!" the baron said. "I swear you my oath to treat Alix Givet with kindness and respect. She shall not be harmed in my care."

"Thank you, Sir Udolf. I will speak with my physician on this matter, then," the queen said, and she left the baron to find him.

He was seated in a sunny corner of the hall's small garden. Alix was with him. Reaching them, the queen smiled and said, "*Non! Non!* Alexander, do not rise. Tuck the coverlet back around him, *ma chérie* Alix. Then go and relieve Edmee of her duty. I would speak privately with your father."

Alix did as she had been bid, and then hurried off back into the house.

Margaret of Anjou sat next to her physician upon the small stone bench. "Well, *mon ami*, we have come to the end of our travels together. You are not well enough to go on, and I cannot let you die by the wayside."

Alexander Givet nodded. He, his daughter, Fayme, Edmee, and the king's servant, John, were the bare remnants of what had once been a large royal household. "I will take Alix home to Anjou," he said. "My brother will see my daughter married to a good husband, Highness. It has been my honor to serve you all these years." Then he began to cough, struggling to control the spasms that racked his thin body.

"You have not the strength to reach Anjou," the queen said gently when her physician's coughing had subsided. "And traveling alone with a young girl would be much too dangerous for you in your condition and especially for Alix."

"Then what, Highness, am I to do?" Alexander Givet asked his mistress.

"Sir Udolf has a son who needs a wife. If you will agree to give your daughter in marriage to Hayle Watteson, you will both have a home and a place," the queen said. "Sir Udolf likes Alix, and has given his oath that she will be treated with kindness and respect as his son's wife and the mother of his grandchildren."

"The son is odd at best," the physician said. "He has a mistress to whom he is devoted, madame. Sir Udolf himself has told me his son is prone to unreasonable anger when he cannot gain his own way. I am not certain my daughter would be safe as his wife, especially as he so dotes on this miller's child."

"The girl cannot wed Sir Udolf's son. Her birth is low. Her children, should she have any, cannot be heirs to Wulfborn. Hayle Watteson must have a wife who is suitable," Margaret of Anjou said to her physician. "His heirs must be got on the body of that wife, and no other. This is a good solution, Alexander. You will live far longer safe here at Wulfborn, and you will be here for Alix. And Sir Udolf is a good man. The son will obey his father. Many a marriage has begun like this, between two strangers, as did my own. Yet I came to love my husband, and Alix will learn to love Sir Udolf's son. But should she not, at least they may come to have respect for each other. That is far more common in marriages among our kind than is love."

"Blanche and I loved each other," the physician replied softly.

"I know," the queen said with a small smile of remembrance. "It was your love for each other that gave me courage and hope when we came to England."

"Ahh, so many years ago now, it seems," he answered her.

"You can negotiate your own marriage contract for Alix with Sir Udolf," the queen told him gently but firmly. "Satisfy yourself that Alix will be well cared for by this family. But do not delay, *mon ami*. In another few days, when my messenger returns from my cousin of Gueldres, we will have to move on into Scotland in order to be completely safe from the Yorkists."

Alexander Givet sighed. "I know if there were another choice, madame, you would give it to me," he said.

"Better she wed here in England than Scotland," the queen said. "I am told the Scots are a wild and uncivilized people. I have always been surprised that the Duc de Gueldres allowed his daughter, Marie, to be sent to their king in marriage."

"I will speak with Sir Udolf this evening while we play chess, as has become our custom. He is a bit rough, but I believe him honest and fair," the physician said. "But if I am gone, madame, who will care for you?"

"I must care for myself now, Alexander," the queen answered him. "Fortunately, you have been careful of my health, and I have learned a thing or two from you over our years together. I will manage, for I must." Then she rose from her seat. "Come," she said to him, "the air is growing chill again, and the sun has gone behind those clouds." She helped him to stand, and together they walked back into the hall.

That evening Alexander Givet and Sir Udolf Watteson sat separated by a game table as they discussed a union between their only children. "My daughter is not penniless," the physician said. "She will come to your son with a dower portion of five gold pieces and ten of silver. Unfortunately, her dower trunk with her linens and her feather bed had to be left behind at Windsor. But she has been raised in the queen's household, and knows all there is to know about running a nobleman's hall. And, of course, she is a virgin. She is modest, obedient, and devout. Your son cannot be dissatisfied with her."

"Your wife had but one child," Sir Udolf noted.

"Blanche chose to have one child because her service to the queen came first. There are ways to prevent conception, though the church might not approve," Alexander Givet told his companion. "Blanche's mother had several healthy children. It was my wife's birth that was her undoing. I am one of nine."

Sir Udolf nodded. "Then I see no impediment to a match between Hayle and Alix," he said. "I will have the priest draw up the betrothal agreement. And, Alexander, you will have a home here at Wulfborn too. You have my word on it."

The physician nodded. "I am frail now, it is true, but I am still capable of performing my trade. One thing concerns me, however, Udolf. Your son does not want a wife. Can you force him to the altar? Will he hate Alix for it and be cruel to her? Will he keep his mistress?"

"I will be candid with you," Sir Udolf said. "He will wed with your daughter because he knows I will never allow a miller's daughter to birth my heirs. And despite his determination to have his own way, he knows he needs legitimate heirs. His loyalty to Wulfborn is strong, for he is a proud man. But he will keep his mistress, and I will not dissemble with you over it, Alexander. I am sorry, but even to gain Alix for Hayle, I will not lie to you, my friend."

The physician nodded. "Your honesty means much to me," he told his companion. "Now I will be honest with you. Were there any other choice, I should take Alix and return to Anjou. But I will never again be well enough to make that journey. I will die within a year or two. I need to know my daughter is safe, if not with a man who will love her, at least with a good family who will appreciate and respect her. If you will guarantee me that, then you may call your priest and we will draw up the contracts."

"I swear to you on the Blessed Virgin that my son and I will always take care of your daughter, Alexander. If I should die, he will honor my wishes," Sir Udolf said.

"Then I will speak to my daughter," the physician said.

Alix was not pleased to learn the future that was being planned for her. "Why can I not just serve the queen as Mama did?" she wanted to know.

"The queen is no longer honored as England's queen," her father answered her. "There is no court or royal household in which we may serve. I am too weak to take you home to Anjou, Alix. You do not wish to devote your life to God. There is no other choice open to you but marriage."

"But who will help old Edmee if I am not with them? Who will sing to the king when the dolor is upon him if I am not with them?" Alix demanded to know.

"There is no other choice," her father repeated.

"Have I ever seen this man you propose to wed me to, Papa?" she asked.

"He is the tall young man in the hall with the white-blond hair," the physician said. "He is there in the evenings sometimes."

"I do not recall such a man," Alix answered her father, "and I am in the hall every evening. Wouldn't he sit at the high board? Yet only the queen and the little prince sit with Sir Udolf. The king eats in his chambers."

"I have seen the lad," Alexander Givet responded stubbornly. "Look more closely this evening, *mignon*. Perhaps if you did not gossip so much with Fayme and Edmee you would pay more attention to the high board."

"We speak of bygone days," Alix told her father. "They miss their old life greatly. I do too, and I miss Mama."

"That life is gone for us all," he replied. "And you will not spend your days at court, *ma petite*. You will live out your life here in the north as mistress in your own hall. It is not a bad future, *mignon*. Your mama would be pleased by what I have done."

"You are marrying me to a stranger," Alix said unhappily. "At least you and Mama knew each other a little bit when the Count of Anjou approved your match."

"Aye, Hayle Watteson is a stranger to you, but I will be with you, *mignon*. And Sir Udolf likes you, and I suspect already thinks of you as a daughter. The queen wants you safely wed, and I concur."

Alix sighed sadly. She might protest, but the truth was there was no other choice for her. The queen could no longer keep them, and her father grew frailer with each passing day. At least this marriage she was entering into would give her father a safe haven for whatever time he had left upon this earth. Alix was a sensible girl, and she knew her father's days were numbered. Aye. Her mother would want this both for Alix and for Alexander Givet. And she had to marry sooner than later, didn't she? Sir Udolf was a kind man. He always had a twinkle in his eye, and Alix suspected if she ran his household well, and gave him grandchildren, he would treat her with great kindness and respect. Although she honestly could not recall having seen his son, he certainly couldn't be a terrible person. Not with such a father.

"There is one thing you must know about your intended," her father said, breaking into her thoughts.

"What, Papa?"

"He has a mistress he holds dear. He will not give her up even for a wife," Alexander Givet said, looking closely at his daughter for her reaction.

"Many men have mistresses they will not give up. I care not as long as I am treated with the respect due the wife of the heir to Wulfborn," Alix said sanguinely, surprising her father. "Perhaps Hayle and I will come to love each other. Perhaps not. But as long as he is kind and my place is secure, it matters not to me."

"For a maid born and raised in England, you speak like a Frenchwoman," the physician said with a small chuckle. "I suppose it is being influenced by French women all your life that has made you such a practical girl."

"When is the wedding to take place?" Alix wanted to know.

"The contracts must be drawn. Then they will be signed, and we will adjourn immediately to the church for the priest's blessing," her father said. "A few days, *mignon*. No more than that."

"Am I to meet my betrothed husband before that day?" Alix wanted to know.

"Indeed, you should," he agreed. "I will speak with Sir Udolf."

Alix dressed carefully before she came to the hall that evening. Her gown was simple, of dark green jersey with a high waist, gathered sleeves with cuffs trimmed in a thin skim of brown marten that matched the trim around her neckline. She wore a gold chain to which was attached a small jeweled cross. A slender pretty girl of medium height with long hair the color of dark honey that she wore loose to denote her unmarried status, she had fair skin and hazel-green eyes.

Entering the hall discreetly, she let her gaze sweep about, seeking out those who were already there. Her father and Sir Udolf were sitting by the hearth drinking and talking. Alix was glad that they liked each other. It would make her father's last days pleasant to have a friend. And then she saw him. A tall boy, and yet he was said to be twenty. Still he had a boy's face. His hair was the lightest blond she had ever seen, and he wore a sullen look upon his almost pretty face. Was he to be her husband? Swallowing hard, Alix walked across the hall to greet her father and Sir Udolf. She curtsied to them.

"Ah, Alix, here you are," Sir Udolf said with a smile. Then, turning his head, he beckoned to the young man. "Hayle, come and meet your bride-to-be."

The young man sauntered from his place at the end of the room to where his father sat. He looked Alix over with a bold eye, causing her to blush. "Her breasts are small," he pronounced. "Maida has breasts a man can pillow his head upon."

Alexander Givet drew a sharp breath.

"Hayle," his father remonstrated, "some thoughts we keep to ourselves. Greet Mistress Alix politely now, and ask her pardon for your rudeness."

Hayle Watteson looked at Alix with a hard gaze. "She's pretty enough, and seems biddable. Are you obedient, mistress?"

"I try," Alix said. What kind of man was this who spoke in such a fashion to the girl he was about to wed?

"She'll do, Father, but you know my conditions for this marriage," Hayle Watteson said. "See she understands them. How long do I have before I must wed her?"

"My name is Alix," Alix said sharply. "And I greet you, my lord."
She curtsied politely to him.

He looked startled, but then he bowed from the waist.

"Take Alix and walk her about the hall, my son," the baron instructed. "It is a good thing to get to know the woman you are marrying before the contracts are signed."

"They will be signed nonetheless whether I will or no," Hayle
responded to his father. "But I will obey you, sir." He offered his arm
to Alix. "Come," he said.

Alix took his arm, and they walked away from their fathers. "You
are not happy about this marriage," she said. "Would it surprise you
to know that neither am I?"

"You don't want to marry me?" He was surprised. "Why not? I am
most eligible, and I am said to be pleasing to the eye, wench."

"I am not a wench," Alix told him. "I am a lady. The queen is my
godmother. My mother served the queen as one of her ladies. My
father is her physician. I had hoped to spend my life at court in the
queen's service."

"The queen is brought down, as is our mad king," Hayle replied.
"You have no court in which to serve. You must either wed, or enter a convent. Those are the choices open to a respectable woman.
Since your father has decided to barter you in marriage so he may
have a warm hearth in his old age, you are to be married to me."

"The queen proposed this match to protect us," Alix said angrily.
"If my father's health were better, he would take me back to Anjou. Papa loves me, but you are near to correct in your assumptions.
However, it is I who agreed to wed you so my father would have a
safe place to live out the rest of his days."

"I have a mistress whom I love," Hayle said. "I would marry her
if I could, but my father would not accept any children of such a
union as his heirs."

"What is wrong with her?" Alix asked, curious in spite of herself.

"She is of low birth," he answered.

"Then your sire is right in the matter, I fear. My blood is more than equal to yours, and so we will wed. I to protect my father, and you to please yours. There is the long and the short of it, my lord."

"You are a hard girl," he told her.

"Nay, I am a practical girl," Alix replied. "If you treat me with respect, I will be a good wife to you, my lord. I will keep the hall, honor our fathers, bear your children, and care for all within my realm as chatelaine of Wulfborn Hall. Keep your mistress. I will not complain, but do not flaunt her publicly, I pray you."

"I am accustomed to doing as I please," he told her.

"That is a child's excuse. You are not a child, my lord. You are a man," Alix said to him. "Once you take a wife, you must act like one."

They had reached the end of the hall, and Hayle suddenly pulled Alix into a dark corner. Pushing her against the hard stone wall, he said, "You will belong to me as my dogs, as my horse belongs to me. I will do with you as I please." He pressed himself against her, his hand grasping one of her breasts and squeezing it hard. "Do you understand that, *wench*?"

Alix gasped with shock. "Take your hand away," she half whispered.

In response, he tweaked her nipple sharply. "No," he said, and he kneaded her soft flesh with cruel fingers. "Are you a virgin?"

Alix flushed. "Yes! Of course! Why would you think otherwise?"

"I thought nothing. I merely wanted to know," Hayle told her. He leaned forward and pressed his lips to hers.

I am going to swoon, Alix thought as his mouth ravaged hers. She had never before been kissed, but she sensed the anger in him.

He lifted his head from her. "You don't know how to kiss, do you? Well, it matters not. All I need to do is get you with child. Then I shall not have to be bothered with you for a while." And releasing his hold on her, he began to walk them back to where their fathers sat by the hearth.

Alix's legs felt wooden as she walked by his side. She was in shock. Would this coldhearted man ever care for her? Did she even want him to? Could she even marry him now? She had to, and tears pricked the backs of her eyelids. There was no other choice. Her father had to be protected even at the cost of her own happiness.

·

Chapter 2

*I*t would be a few days before the contracts were signed. To her credit, the queen did attempt to comfort her goddaughter. "I would not do this but that your father is ill and can travel no farther," Margaret of Anjou said to Alix. "And it is easier for us to find shelter with just one body servant each. The day after your wedding we will depart here. Only the isolation of this refuge has kept us safe, but we cannot take the chance of remaining for much longer. Sooner than later the Yorkists will scour the countryside most thoroughly, and we will be found."

"I understand," Alix said dully.

"He is an attractive young man," the queen noted.

"He wants to marry his mistress," Alix replied.

"Pah!" the queen exclaimed. "All young men want to wed their mistresses, but mistresses are not for marrying. Be dutiful to your husband, and he will eventually outgrow his mistress. This is a good match for you, *ma chérie*. The family is respectable, and the baron likes you. If your husband misbehaves, go to him, for Sir Udolf is the head of the family, and I suspect he will live to be a very old man. But most important, your papa has a safe refuge now. I could not desert him for the sake of your dear mama, who was always so good to me. Think of her, Alix. When my grandmother and father decided she was to marry your father, she did what she was told. Can you do any less?"

"No, Highness," Alix replied. *Think of your mother*, the queen said. Alix was thinking of her. A day did not go by that she did not remember Blanche Givet. Her mother had been so beautiful. Many said that Alix resembled her, but while their coloring was the same, the daughter thought her mother far more lovely. Blanche was French to her fingertips. Elegant and quick. Charming and diplomatic with the most difficult of the queen's high-born English companions. Everyone had loved Blanche Givet. But especially her husband and her daughter.

What would her mother say about this match that Margaret of Anjou had made for Alix? Would she have made it had Blanche been alive? Alix wanted to believe that if Blanche had lived, she and her husband would have returned with their only child to Anjou to live out their lives. But no. Blanche would have never deserted Margaret of Anjou. Especially not under these circumstances. Alix sighed. But if her mother had lived, she was certain this marriage would have never been proposed.

Her mother's death had come as a complete shock to everyone who knew her. It was sudden, and totally unexpected. It was Alexander Givet whose health had begun to fail. But Blanche, up until the moment of her death, had appeared healthy and vibrant. And yet she had gone to her bed that fatal night and never awakened again. Oh, she had complained of being tired that last day, but was that so unusual for a queen's lady who was always kept running?

Alix felt the tears coming, and she brushed them away impatiently. From the moment they had told her that her mother had died she had attempted to remember the last words Blanche had said to her, but she never could. Her father had tried to comfort her, telling her the conversation was obviously not that important that she would have remembered. But shouldn't you remember the last words your mother said to you? Still, if you didn't know they were to be her last words . . .

Alix sighed sadly.

But she did remember standing by her mother's grave and promising her that she would take care of her father. Alix knew that would have been the one thing Blanche would have asked of her had she been able to ask it. So now here they were in the wilds of Northumbria, and she was about to marry a man who didn't want her so that her father could have a home, a place to die. The tears flowed silently, and she bit her lower lip to keep from sobbing. *I have kept my promise to you, Mama*, she said silently.

She considered Hayle Watteson. There was something not quite right about him that she could not quite put her finger upon. He was very childish. A spoiled child who must have his own way. He had made his dislike of her quite clear. He didn't want her, but he would accept her as his wife to please his parent. He would sire children on her to please his father. She would be nothing more to him than a broodmare would be.

The tears came faster. It wasn't that she was feeling sorry for herself, but it seemed so unfair. Her mother had loved her father. Margaret of Anjou had come to love her royal husband. But her father had been happy to have her mother for a wife. And Henry Plantagenet had, for all his shyness, been welcoming of his bride. And while she knew that many men had mistresses, neither the king nor her father had ever taken another woman to their bed. And now she was facing marriage to a man who not only had a mistress, but loved her, intended to keep her, and had nothing but hostility for the girl he was to marry. Every instinct she possessed told her to run, but Alix would not listen. Her father needed a home, and Wulfborn Hall, despite its surly heir, was a good place. She would marry Hayle Watteson, and if he didn't love her, their children would. She would honor the promise she gave at her mother's graveside.

Alexander Givet was feeling stronger having been able to rest these past few days. "You do not have to wed this man if you do not wish to," he told his daughter. "I am better for resting. I will take you back to Anjou, *mignon*."

"Nay, Papa," Alix told him. "You are better for a warm hall, a warm bed, and regular hot food. On the road we would have none of these things. The queen goes to Scotland. She has no means to reach the coast, and neither do we. And if we did manage to get there, what guarantee do we have that we could find a ship to take us to France? And if we found a ship, and reached France, how would we get to Anjou? The journey is too long and too difficult for a sick man. You would not live to get there, and then I should be left alone."

"I do not like this man you are to wed," the physician admitted.

"I do not like him either," Alix agreed. "But his father is a good man, and it is he who is the lord here. Not Hayle. Sir Udolf likes us both, Papa. All the Wattesons want of me is children. I will give them what they want. Sir Udolf will dote on his grandchildren and honor me as their mother. I have agreed not to interfere with Hayle and his mistress as long as I am treated with respect."

Alexander Givet shook his head. "That my daughter should have to barter herself to protect us pains me. I feel so helpless, *mignon*. Forgive me!"

"There is nothing to forgive, Papa," Alix assured him. "I am content with this." She lied with a smile, and she kissed his cheek.

He knew she lied, but what other choice did they have? Alexander Givet silently cursed his body's weaknesses that had put his beloved daughter in this situation. But while his pride had made him give up half of his small hoard of coins to provide Alix with a very respectable dower portion, he had kept back an equal amount, which he would see Alix had in her possession before he died. She would be a woman of means if it ever became necessary for her to leave Wulfborn.

When they had fled their last royal sanctuary those many weeks back Alix had been able to take very little. Her camises were either lawn or silk. They took up little space, and so she had packed half a dozen of them as well as two batiste shertes she kept for night garments. But she had only three gowns: two jersey—one green, the other nut brown—and a violet silk. She had a pair of boots for outdoors and a pair of sollerets for indoors; a wool cape, the hood lined in rabbit fur; and two lawn veils. Her father had given her the jewelry that had belonged to her mother: a strand of creamy pearls; two gold chains, one with a jeweled cross; and five gold rings, each with a gem stone. One had a large pink pearl, another a garnet, another a small sapphire, the fourth an amethyst. The last was of red Irish gold, with a green tourmaline. She kept her jewelry in a small pale blue silk bag with a drawstring.

On her wedding day, Alix decided she would wear her best gown, the violet silk. At her request, an oak tub was brought up from the kitchens, and she bathed in it, taking the time and care to wash her hair. A serving woman of undetermined age who said her name was Bab helped her.

"The old lord said I am to serve you, for you will be mistress here," Bab informed Alix. "You are pretty, but not as pretty as Maida."

Alix was startled by the reference to Hayle's mistress. "Do not speak to me of that wench," she told Bab. "It matters not to me if she is pretty."

"You do not care that your husband futters her, and will continue to do so?" Bab asked boldly as she helped Alix into her bath.

"No," Alix said. "I do not." She began to wash herself.

"Yet you bathe yourself so you may please him. You'll never please him, mistress. It is Maida he wants."

"I bathe to please myself, Bab, and Maida is his for eternity. She matters not to me. I will be Hayle's wife, the mother of his legitimate heirs. Now, I have asked you not to speak of this wench. Cease, or I will be forced to beat you."

Bab sent Alix a surprised look, but she stopped speaking, helping her new mistress to dress when Alix had come from the tub and dried herself off. Then, unable to help herself she said as she slipped the camise over Alix's head, "Maida has more meat on her bones than you do." Then she cried out as the girl's hand made sharp contact with her fat cheek. "Oww!" Her own hand reached up to soothe the stinging flesh.

"Are you slow-witted that you did not understand me, Bab? You are not to speak of my husband's wench to me." Alix glared hard at the woman. "I will be lady in this hall very shortly. The household is mine to command. If you wish to remain in my personal service, you will obey me when I instruct you. Do you think because I am young I can be intimidated by you or your chatter about that wench? I was trained in my duties by a queen, Bab. And I have learned well."

"Indeed you have, *ma chérie*," Margaret of Anjou said as she entered the chamber that was now Alix's. She gave the serving woman a scornful glance in passing. "I am so sorry I have nothing of value to give you on this day. Were things as they once were, I should have gifted you with a gilt saltcellar, or a dozen silver spoons. Your husband would have been given hunting rights in the royal forests. But alas, things are not as they once were, so I have brought you this." The queen then clasped a gold girdle studded with small gemstones about Alix's hips. "There! Now that gown looks perfect." Taking the girl by her shoulders, the queen kissed her on both of her cheeks. "I must speak to you now, as your mother is not here for you." She turned. "Get out!" she said to Bab. "You will be called when you are needed."

The serving woman scurried out, realizing as she went that the bride, whom all had thought soft and weak, was not. She hurried to tell the other servants and to see that her niece Maida knew that the new lady would not attempt to usurp Maida's place in Hayle Watteson's heart. But she wondered what the lady would think when she learned that Maida was with child.

Margaret of Anjou had waited until the servant was gone. "I must explain the wedding night to you," she said.

A small smile touched Alix's lips. "Papa has explained it all to me," she replied.

The queen looked shocked. Then she laughed. "Of course," she said. "He would not want you totally unprepared, and so Alexander would carefully tell you all the physical elements involved. However, his is the masculine viewpoint. I will give you the feminine side of the equation. You can experience passion even when you feel no love for your partner. Love, however, turns passion into a great wonder, Alix. I know that right now you and your husband are strangers. I am aware he has a mistress. But it is my belief that your sweetness and loyalty will overcome his baser nature eventually. Watch what will happen when you give him his first son. He will love you then. Now, be aware that some men are rough in their loving. Still, you need not be afraid. Just let him have his way, and be gentle in return with him."

"Thank you, Highness," Alix replied to the queen's speech. "I am grateful for your words and your wisdom." She wasn't going to argue with the queen, or tell her that Hayle Watteson would never love her. The queen had done what she believed was her best by her ailing physician and her goddaughter. Let her go off to whatever fate awaited her believing all was right.

"I am pleased that this solution presented itself for you and your father. I will leave tomorrow knowing that my dearest Blanche's husband and daughter are safe. Now, ma petite, I believe they are waiting for us in the hall. Shall we go?"

Alix drew in a deep breath and asked, "How do I look?"

The queen smiled tenderly. "Beautiful, and far too good for this baron's son, but hélas! We must be grateful to God and his Blessed Mother that they have been given to us, ma petite." She reached out to settle the gold girdle on Alix's hips, and touched the girl's long wavy hair that had been unbound to signify her virginity. "Allez!"

Together they descended into the hall where Sir Udolf, Alexander Givet, and the bridegroom awaited them with the priest. The two fathers were garbed in long dark furred robes. The bridegroom, however, wore a dark green tunic that came to his knees, and black breeches beneath. The king was present, silent in a dark heavily furred velvet robe that touched the stone floor of the house. The young prince was by his side. He gave Alix a mischievous wink that made her smile.

The priest, Sir Udolf, Alexander Givet, and the bridegroom all stood at the high board upon the dais. Alix came slowly to join them.

"The contracts for the marriage between Hayle John Watteson and Alix Margot Givet have been drawn up and approved by Holy Mother Church as well as Sir Udolf Watteson and Alexander Givet, the parents of the parties involved. It but remains for the bridal couple to sign the agreement," the priest said, and he held out the quill to the bridegroom.

Hayle Watteson took it, placing a careless X where the priest pointed. Then he returned the quill to the cleric, who handed it to Alix.

Taking it, she carefully wrote out her name, *Alix Margot Givet*. It was neat and quite legible. She handed the quill back to the surprised priest.

Both fathers and the queen stepped forward to sign as witnesses, adding their names on the parchment document. When they had all finished, the priest sanded the signatures. "It but remains for us to adjourn to the church now so this couple may be properly blessed, and their union may be formally sealed." He rolled the parchments up, binding them with a small strip of leather. Leaving them upon the high board, he led the bridal party from the hall.

They left the house, which was at one end of Sir Udolf's village of Wulfboro, and walked to its other end, where the small church was situated. The village street was lined with silent villagers who stood watching them as they passed. Inside the empty church, Alix and her husband knelt before the altar. The priest blessed them, and then he celebrated a short Mass. When the Mass had been concluded, he pronounced them husband and wife. They departed the church and returned to the house. The street was empty now.

"They hate you for taking Maida's place as my wife," Hayle told her cruelly. "She is with child. It was her wedding gift to me. Maida will bear my first son."

Alix felt as if her spirit was being crushed by his words. "Could you not at least be civil to me on our wedding day, my lord? It is not my fault that your lover is of low birth. You know I should not have married you at all were it not for my father."

"You are no better than a whore," he told her. "Maida loves me. She asks nothing of me in return but my love, and I gladly give it to her. But you have whored for your place here. You had best prove quickly fruitful so that my sacrifice not be in vain."

"*Your* sacrifice? What of mine?" Alix demanded of him.

"Whore!" he said coldly.

Sir Udolf had arranged a feast for the entire village, and his hall was filled when they returned. The beer was already flowing freely. Alix sat at the high board numb with her misery. She watched as her husband danced with the villagers, quickly realizing that the lovely dark-haired girl whose side he never left was his mistress, Maida. The baron was obviously shamed by his son's behavior, but Alexander Givet was furious.

"Have you no control over your offspring that you would allow him to embarrass my daughter?" he demanded of the baron. "And on their wedding day too."

"What can I do?" the baron said helplessly, and he turned to Alix. "Forgive him, my daughter. He is young, and he is a fool to boot. It will do no good to lock him up, for his resentment towards you would be even worse. Give me a grandchild, and I will protect you as long as I live."

"I should never have allowed my daughter to marry your son," Alexander Givet said furiously. "God forgive me! God forgive me!"

"It's all right, Papa," Alix tried to reassure him. "Hayle is behaving like a child because he did not get his own way. But I am his wife, and I shall be the mother of his heir. Then all will be well. I don't want you to worry." Privately, however, Alix was not pleased with her new husband's behavior. He did behave like a child. A ten-year-old. What was the matter with him, anyway? He had agreed he would not shame her publicly, but then she recalled he hadn't agreed. She had asked it of him, but he had never agreed. Was she to be subjected to this sort of behavior forever because he couldn't have his own way? She sighed softly, letting her eyes go to where he danced with his mistress. His whole face was different than the one he usually presented. It was soft and kind. Alix knew, looking at her husband, that he would never present such a face to her.

"Alix is wiser than you, Alexander," the queen murmured. "Be still, *mon ami*."

When the evening came, the villagers departed and Hayle with them. Sir Udolf took Alix aside, sitting with her by the blazing hearth. "Do you remember that Hayle spoke of certain conditions for agreeing to your marriage, Alix?"

She nodded. "I do, but you have never told them to me."

"I must tell you now." He looked unhappy. "My son feels coupling with you is a betrayal of his mistress. Therefore, while he knows he must lay with you if he is to have a legitimate heir, he does not wish to see you while he does his duty by you and by the family. You will be prepared for bed and then left in a totally darkened chamber. And whenever he comes to your bed, the room must be dark. The shutters will be closed and the draperies drawn tightly. I am sorry, but those are his conditions, and I was forced to agree with them else he would not have made this marriage."

Alix shook her head. "His mistress is with child," she said. "Did you know that, my lord? He told me as we returned from the church."

"Forgive me, my child!" the baron begged her. "In time I am certain he will relent and you will warm his heart."

"He will never relent," Alix said despairingly, "but I will do my duty, my lord. You need have no fear of that." No. For her father's sake she would let Hayle Watteson have her virginity, and she would bear him children. And with Sir Udolf's aid, she would raise her sons to be true gentlemen like her father, like the poor king. She would teach them kindness, respect, and duty. Once she had her children about her, she would be safe even after her father and Sir Udolf were gone.

"Do not go to his bed!" her father said desperately. "I should rather die in the cold than have you suffer that man a moment. Call the priest and have this union annulled." And then Alexander

Givet began to gasp with his distress. He coughed so hard that his whole body was convulsed, and he collapsed back in his chair.

"Papa!" Alix was immediately by her parent's side. The physician held a napkin to his mouth, and she saw the flecks of blood staining the linen. "It's all right, Papa. I am content with this marriage. Do not distress yourself any more. I need you and Sir Udolf here with me. You must not fret yourself." She put the wine cup to his lips now that his coughing had subsided.

Alexander Givet sipped slowly. He was pale, and he felt so weak that he could hardly move himself even to sit up. "I can't let you do this, *mignon*," he murmured softly.

"It is done," Alix told her parent. She signaled to a young serving man, who came immediately to her side. "Take my father to his bedspace, and see he is made comfortable for the night. Then sit with him until he sleeps."

"Yes, mistress," the young servant said. He had a pleasant face, and did not seem hostile to her as so many of the servants did.

"What is your name?" Alix asked him.

"Wat, mistress" came the reply.

"I will speak to the steward, Wat, for I should like you to look after my father, to be his body servant," Alix said.

"Thank you, mistress," Wat answered her. Then he helped Alexander Givet from his chair. "Lean on me, sir. I am strong."

"When you are settled, Papa, I will come and bid you good night," Alix told her father. Then she turned to Sir Udolf. "He cannot continue to sleep in the hall," she said. "He must have his own chamber. Since your son must now share my bed, I shall take his room for my father. If Hayle needs another place, let him make it somewhere else."

"Should you not go to your chamber now to await your husband?" Sir Udolf ventured quietly.

"I will go nowhere until I see my father properly settled for this night. Besides, your son is with his mistress. He is in no hurry to bed me."

The baron looked unhappy, but he said nothing, for he knew that Alix was right. She sat at his left hand with a stony face looking out over the hall, which was now empty. The queen quietly departed, taking her son with her. The king's body servant had come for him during the dancing and taken his master away. Finally Wat came to tell Alix that her father was settled within his bedspace next to the large hearth.

Alix went to him and kissed her parent's brow. "Tomorrow I will prepare a chamber for you, Papa. You will no longer have to sleep in the hall."

"There is still time," he said softly to her.

Alix shook her head. "Remember what Mama always said? You must make the best of a bad situation no matter how you may feel. While I may scorn Hayle Watteson in my heart and mind, I will always treat him respectfully in public. From his behavior today, I suspect I will see him but infrequently."

Her father reached out, and in his hand there was a small pouch. "If you are determined to go through with this travesty, *mignon*, then you will need extra strength of both body and mind for your ordeal. Put a pinch from the contents of this bag into a cup of wine tonight and drink it. Then take a pinch of it in wine or cider each morning. I will give you more when you need it." He put the pouch in her hand, grasping her wrist and saying, "Promise me you will take it, Alix. *Promise me!*"

"If you believe it will help me, Papa, then yes, I will take it tonight, and each morning as you have prescribed." She bent and kissed his cheek. "*Bon soir*, Papa."

"*Bon soir, mignon*," Alexander Givet replied. "God keep you safe this night."

Alix left him, and without even a word to Sir Udolf, departed the hall, going upstairs to the chamber she was to share with her husband. Bab was waiting for her. "Fetch me a small goblet of wine," Alix told the serving woman.

Bab did as she was bid, setting the goblet on the table next to the bed. Then she helped Alix disrobe. "He'll want you naked," Bab informed Alix, who now stood in her chemise washing her face and hands.

"Then I will be naked," Alix responded. She felt numb, and she was cold. Perhaps the wine would help to warm her. "Be careful with my gown," she warned Bab. "It is my one good one." And while the servant folded the violet silk with meticulous care, Alix took a pinch from the contents of the little pouch, put it in her wine, and drank it down. She must remember to ask her father what it was. She didn't want Bab to see the pouch, and so she tucked it discreetly beneath the bed's mattress until she was alone and could find another hiding spot. "Has my husband returned yet?" she asked Bab, knowing the serving woman would be aware of Hayle's whereabouts.

"Not yet," Bab replied sourly. "Get into bed and sleep. He'll awaken you when he comes. I hope for your sake there is blood on the sheet come morning. He won't like it if you aren't a virgin."

Alix climbed into the bed. "Good night, Bab" was all she answered. Then she watched as the servant snuffed all the candles but the one she carried, and departed the chamber. The room was cold, Alix noted, but then, of course, since Hayle would want total darkness there was no fire to keep her warm. The bed smelled fresh with lavender. The pillows were plump behind her. She drew up the coverlet and closed her eyes, but she could not sleep. As she lay there alone and in the dark Alix considered what was to come. She knew what to expect. Her husband would stuff his manhood into her female sheath and expel his seed. With good luck he would get her with child quickly, and she would be quickly quit of him. He would futter her to get the son to please his father. There was nothing more to it. She wished he would come and get it over with, for she was tired and wanted to sleep. Would he remain with her? Would he do it more than once? At court she had overheard two women in the queen's apartment speaking of one of their husbands. He had fucked her, the first told the second, three times in a night, and the two women had giggled like girls. How many times did it take a man to get a woman with child? Alix wondered. That was not a part of her knowledge.

Finally the door to the chamber opened, and she saw him in the light from the hallway torch, hesitating a moment before coming in. "Do not speak," he told her as he shut the door behind him.

Alix remained silent, as bidden. The bed sagged as he sat upon its edge. She heard his boots hit the floor as he removed them.

He pulled back the coverlet, saying as he did so, "Spread your legs open wide, whore," and when she had, he climbed atop her. "Now put your arms above your head," he further instructed her. "You will make no move to impede my actions." Reaching out, he squeezed one of her breasts, pinching the nipple hard. "At least your skin is soft," he noted as he ran his hands over her body, "and you smell of flowers."

Alix felt him adjusting his position. She felt his bare buttocks against her thighs as he leaned forward, his fingers and hand seeking. And then she felt *it* as he found the opening to her woman's sheath. As he leaned forward, she realized he was wearing his tunic robe and had just hiked it up so his male parts would be free. Alix felt she should be doing something, but she didn't know what. He thrust into her, and it hurt. She bit her lip to keep from crying out as he kept pushing himself into her. But then he thrust hard, and Alix could not prevent the scream that tore from her throat as a sharp pain engulfed her. She began to weep.

"You didn't lie to me, whore. You were a virgin," he said as he began to piston her in earnest, grunting with each stroke of his cock until she felt him stiffen above her and groan with the sound of pleasure attained. Then, climbing off of her, he said, "I'll be back in the early morning to fuck you again. And I'll keep fucking you each day until you ripen with my child. Then we can be quit of each other." He sat on the edge of the bed once more, pulling on his boots, and then left her.

Alix began to cry in earnest. He had not kissed her, or been kind at all. He had behaved like a stallion brought to stud. Surely this was not the way all men and women behaved with one another? She remembered her mother's face once when she had come from the bedchamber that she shared with her father. It had been soft and dreamy. Alix remembered saying to her mother that she looked particularly beautiful at that moment and Blanche responding that when a woman was well loved she glowed.

"You will understand one day, *ma petite*," her mother had told her, smiling.

And had the queen not said that a woman could feel passion even if she did not love a man? But all Alix had felt was pain and degradation. She suspected it was all she would ever know from Hayle Watteson. Alix pulled the coverlet back over her cold body. He was a cruel and stupid creature. She was going to pray to the Blessed Virgin that he got her with child quickly, for the thought of having to bear his cruel attentions night after night was too terrible to even contemplate. Alix instinctively knew that her husband would never treat her any other way than he had treated her tonight. Hayle hated her for being what his beloved Maida couldn't be. And he would continue to punish her for it.

He came again just before the dawn, when Alix could see just the faintest sliver of light beginning to creep along the edges of the shutters, but the room was still in darkness. He woke her roughly, shaking her hard. "Take the position you were taught earlier," he ordered her. "Legs spread, arms about your head. Do not speak, and this time make no noise at all, whore. I know you could not prevent your earlier scream, and I forgive you for it. But I will have no sound from you." He penetrated her once again without further ado, riding her until the inevitable conclusion. Then he left her, telling her, "I will be back tomorrow night."

When she was certain he was gone, Alix crept from her bed and went to the small hearth. There in a little round container was a live coal. She put it into the midst of the wood kindling and blew upon it until a small flame leaped up to catch at the wood. Soon the fire was blazing merrily and the chill was leaving the chamber. Alix placed the earthenware pitcher of water into the edge of the hearth to warm. Then she climbed back into her bed to sleep for a short while more.

Bab awoke her at dawn, opening the shutters to allow the light of day into the room. Alix took the now-hot water from the fireplace and bathed herself thoroughly.

"Well, he did his duty by you, I see," Bab said, yanking the sheet from the bed. "The old lord will be pleased, mistress."

"Yes," Alix said. "He will be pleased, I'm certain." She pulled on a clean camise, and then her nut-brown jersey gown. After pulling on a pair of woolen socks, she put her feet into her sollerets. Then, sitting on the edge of the bed, she took up her hairbrush and brushed her hair out, plaiting it into a single thick braid and tying off the end of it with a bit of white ribbon.

"I'll be in the hall seeing to the meal and the royal departure," Alix said to her servant, and then she left the chamber. She found her father up and in the company of Sir Udolf. Alix greeted them pleasantly, avoiding their questioning looks, and then sought out the steward. "Donald," she said, "have you told the cook to prepare food for the royal party's trip today? And send to the stables to make certain their horses are ready and that the creatures' feet are healthy. It will not do for them to be caught on this side of the border by the Yorkists."

"The cook has been advised, and I'll go to the stables myself, mistress," he told her. The steward was no kin of Maida's and was loyal to Sir Udolf.

"And will you see that a chamber with a hearth is prepared for my father today? He cannot continue to sleep in the hall," Alix continued.

"I will, mistress," the steward replied with a small bow.

"Thank you," Alix said.

The queen came into the hall prepared for travel. Her little son was with her. He ran to Alix and put his arms about her waist. She embraced him, tousling his hair and smiling down at him. "So, my lord Edward, you are leaving us," Alix said to him. "You are going into Scotland today."

"King James is a boy like me," Edward Plantagenet replied. "Do you think he likes to play, Alix?" His small face looked up at her. "I will miss you so much! You are much more fun than Edmee. She never lets me do anything, and is always running after me. I wish she had married the baron's son. Then you could come with us."

I wish she had married Hayle too, Alix thought silently to herself. Then she said, "Well, I had to marry Sir Udolf's son because poor Papa cannot travel any longer and needs a good home. And the baron needed a good wife for his son. So we are both well served, my lord Edward. Ohh, what a fine time you will have in Scotland!"

The young prince sighed. "I liked it better when my father was king of England."

"Your father is England's king," Alix said quickly.

Edward Plantagenet looked at her with eyes that were far older and wiser than he was. "My father has been dethroned, Alix. Edward of York now sits in his place. We must go to Scotland so they cannot kill my father and me," he said to her as if explaining it to a child. "My mother says she will not let them take my inheritance, but my mother has no army with which to fight the Yorkist pretender."

"If anyone can raise an army, my lord Edward," Alix answered him, "it is your mother." She loosened his grip upon her. "Now go to the high board and eat your meal. You have a full day's ride ahead of you." Turning him about, she sent him off.

Margaret of Anjou came to her side. "You are all right? It went well?" she inquired softly.

"The deed is done, madame," Alix answered.

"But it went well?" the queen pressed her.

Swallowing back any outward sign of anger, Alix said to the older woman, "He will not have me but in a totally darkened room. I am not permitted to speak, but must spread myself open to him and not touch him. He came twice last night, mounted me, and did what was necessary. Nothing more. Not a kiss or caress. I can only pray to the Blessed Mother that I am quickly with child so I may be done with him, madame."

"Ahh, *m'fant*," the queen cried softly. "What have I done to you?" Tears sprang into her eyes. "But for the Yorkists, none of this would have happened!" Briefly she looked genuinely distraught.

"You did what was necessary to protect Papa and me, madame," Alix said quietly, feeling guilty that her anger had permitted her to tell the queen of her misery. "Sir Udolf is good to both Papa and me. All I need do is give him a grandchild, preferably a lad. Pray for me, madame, as I will pray for you, the king, and Prince Edward." Alix brushed away the tears that now stained Margaret of Anjou's face. "Your husband and son are at the high board now, madame. Let us go and join them. Your day will be long."

Alix oversaw the meal expertly. The cook had served up oat stir-about with bits of dried fruit in it. There were hard-boiled eggs, a small ham, half a wheel of hard yellow cheese, newly churned butter, a pitcher of heavy cream, and freshly baked bread. "Donald, the steward, has seen to food for your travels. The blacksmith has given the horses new shoes, and they stand ready for your departure," she told the royal couple.

The king suddenly spoke. "You have done well, mistress. Your hospitality has been gracious, and we will not forget you when we come again. We are traveling to Windsor today, you know."

Alix smiled. "God travel with Your Highness," she told him, and he nodded. Poor man, Alix considered. He knows not where he is, or where he goes. What will happen to them? And for the first time since Blanche Givet had died her daughter was glad, for at least her mother did not have to witness the fall of Henry VI and Margaret of Anjou, whom she loved. God help them, Alix thought, for who else will?

Their meal eaten, the royal party prepared to depart Wulfborn Hall. They were accompanied by the fifteen loyal retainers left to them, and their three servants. Edmee and Fayme hugged Alix, both weeping copiously as they were boosted onto their horses.

Alexander Givet gave the king's body servant, John, the few remedies left to him that would ease the king's anxiety or help him to sleep. He bowed to the king, who nodded vacantly, shook hands with the little prince, and finally he came to the queen.

"So, madame, we come to the end of this long road we have traveled together," he began as he took up both of her hands and kissed them reverently. "I would continue on if I could, but while my daughter continues to deny it, I am dying."

Margaret of Anjou nodded. "I know, Alexander," she replied. "You have been the loyalist of the loyal and I am not unaware. I fear, however, I have repaid you and Blanche ill by arranging this union for Alix. Yet if she will give the baron a grandchild her place in his house and heart will be safe. The son is a *couchon*, but the father is a good man. Alix will not suffer in his care."

"I will be here for my daughter as long as I can be," the physician said. He kissed the queen's hands again. "Go with God, madame. Leave England to the Yorkists for now, and take the prince home to Anjou, where he will be safe and live to reclaim his kingdom one day. I know you are hurt, and angry, but take my counsel in this, madame."

"I cannot desert my husband," the queen said.

"The king, God protect him, will never rule again," Alexander Givet told her. "Save yourself, madame, and save the little prince. You have never in all the years I have known you failed in your duty, Highness. Forgive me if I speak candidly, but it is the privilege of a dying man."

She squeezed the two hands holding her. "My duty is first to my husband, Alexander. Do not fear for me. It will be God's will that prevails in the end."

He kissed her elegant gloved hands a third and final time. "*Le bon Dieu* and his Blessed Mother protect you all," Alexander Givet said, his eyes wet with his tears. "Farewell, my beloved lady."

Margaret of Anjou nodded silently and quickly turned away from the physician lest he see her own tears. A servant helped her to mount her mare. The captain of the little troop raised his hand and called out, *"Allez!"* The small royal party began to move off, down the narrow dirt track that led north. The weather was fair. The hills beginning to green up. The queen turned but briefly in her saddle to raise a hand in farewell to Alexander Givet and his daughter.

Around her everyone went back to their duties. Her father was helped into the house by Wat, but Alix stood silently before the hall watching until the riders were no more than specks on the road, finally disappearing over the horizon. The life she had known was almost entirely gone. Only her father remained. Yet for how long? How long until she was entirely at the mercy of Hayle Watteson, who loved not his wife but the miller's daughter, who would bear his first child. If he truly loved the girl, she couldn't blame him for resenting the wife foisted upon him. Still, it wasn't her fault, was it? She turned and reentered the house. *I will not allow him to punish me because of something neither of us can help*, Alix thought. *I will be strong for my father. For Sir Udolf, who is good to us. For my husband, who is a child.*

It startled her to face that realization. Hayle Watteson was a child in a man's body. A mature man would have realized his wife had to be of equal blood to him. He would have wed such a woman and kept his mistress discreetly in the background. If his mistress bore him children, he would provide for them, but he would never force his lover or their children into his wife's realm. His wife's children would be his heirs. Perhaps in such a rural setting as she now found herself her husband's children would know one another, but they would all keep their place.

She knew this wasn't going to happen with her husband. Hayle Watteson would crow and boast when Maida delivered her child. If it was a male child so much the worse for them all. And if Alix did not give him a strong legitimate son, he would blame her alone. And if Sir Udolf should die what would happen to her? Alix grit her teeth. If anything happened to her father-in-law she would flee Wulfborn Hall as quickly as she could. She would not remain to be hated by a peasantry who didn't even know her, and a husband who was little better than a brute. She had agreed to this marriage for her father's sake, but although she would not admit it aloud, Alix knew that Alexander Givet would not live for very long. He would stay as long as he could for her sake. But one day even that would not be enough, and he would die.

In the days that followed the royal family's departure Alix found those who served her doing so with a grudging respect. They had expected someone associated with a queen to be high-blown and arrogant. Alix, however, was gentle-spoken and patient. She knew exactly how her household should be managed, and she guided her servants with a firm hand but kind words. Sir Udolf managed his poor lands carefully, attempting to teach his son who would one day inherit them, but Hayle had no forbearance for planting schedules, haying, harvesting, counting sheep or cattle. He wanted nothing more than to spend his time riding the hills hunting, or being with Maida.

And each night, but for when her courses were upon her, he visited Alix's bed in his attempt to sire a legitimate heir upon her. Alix hated that brief hour each night, but she bore it, for it was just about the only time she ever came in contact with her husband. But as Maida's belly swelled Hayle began to become impatient that Alix showed no evidence of being with child.

"I have been given a barren whore to wife," he mocked her one evening.

"Children should come from love, or at least respect. You neither love nor respect me," Alix responded coldly.

"If you cannot give me an heir, what good are you to me?" he snarled.

"Perhaps it is you who are barren," Alix snapped back at him. "Are you so certain the child *that* woman carries is yours? I have seen your Maida. She is very fair, perhaps even more so than I. Are the village lads so blind to her beauty that they leave her in peace? And was she a virgin when you first mounted her as I was, or had she taken lovers before you, sir? Perhaps if you showed me the tiniest bit of kindness, if you were gentle with me, I would conceive. But you are cruel, and you are hateful! It is not my fault that you cannot have the woman you love to wife. I treat you with respect, and ask nothing more than you do the same with me. But you are constantly flaunting your mistress before me. Always berating me because I am Alix and not Maida. If it were not for my sire I should have never agreed to this marriage. Be warned that when he dies, I will flee you at the first opportunity, Hayle Watteson. And you will never find me. You will not know if I am alive or dead. The church will not allow you to remarry without proof of my demise. And the law will not allow your bastard to inherit. Wulfborn will be brought down even as you will be brought down!"

He swore at her in the darkness, reaching out to grasp her long hair. "Have I not warned you, whore, that you are never to speak to me when I come to your bed?" Then he began to beat her, but Alix pulled from his grip and quickly jumped from the bed before he could do any damage, hiding in a corner where he could not see her. With a violent oath, Hayle arose from the bed and stormed from the chamber. He did not return for several nights, much to her relief. But when he did, it was the same as it had ever been. Alix put him from her mind but for that one hour each night when she was forced to bear his company in the pitch-black silence.

Her father had encouraged her to revive the old herb garden they found in the larger walled garden of the hall. "Look," he said that late April day when he had spied it, "lavender, rosemary, sage, peppermint, and rue, *mignon*. You must begin to supply your apothecary. You will be responsible for your people should illness strike the hall or the village. Have you not learned from me the remedies necessary for caring for the sick?"

"And how to bind and heal a wound," Alix replied. "And to sew a cut."

"My physician's bag with its tools is yours, Alix," her father told her. "Now, let us see to this little garden."

She worked with young Wat beneath her father's supervision to bring the garden into full flower by early summer. And she walked out into the fallow fields gathering flowers, seeds, and grasses that held medicinal value, digging up certain roots. And each day when she returned to the hall she would go first to her father, telling him of what she had found, listening to his advice, learning more about what she had found. One afternoon she showed him the seeds of the wild carrot she had found. "These are what you give me for strength," Alix said with a smile.

Alexander Givet sighed. For her own sake she had to know the truth before he could no longer tell her. "They are not for strengthening," he said. "They have another use, *mignon*. They are to prevent conception."

Alix paled. "Papa! What have you done to me?" She was horrified by the revelation. "You know I must have a child."

"*Non!*" he said in a hard voice such as she had never before heard him use. "You must never have your husband's child. If you do not give him a son but rather a daughter, he will berate you for it. If you do give him an heir, he will try to take the child from you and make your life even more miserable. Sir Udolf is in his prime, and hearty in his health, but what if an accident befell him? You would be left with his son and none to protect you, *mignon*."

"Papa, he has already called me barren. If I do not have a child I am of no use to him, and even Sir Udolf will see that. What will happen to me then? My very life is in peril and especially if Maida has more children."

"Wait at least until I am gone," her father begged.

Alix sighed. "I will wait," she said.

The summer passed, and autumn arrived. No one had come to Wulfborn Hall seeking King Henry. It was obvious that the new king had more important matters to attend to, and Sir Udolf was relieved. Loyal he might have been to Henry Plantagenet, but now his loyalty must belong to the Yorkist king should he be queried.

Isolated though Wulfborn was, the lord of the Northern Marches was not above paying him a visit.

On a gray, oddly warm day in mid-October Maida went into labor with her child. And it was on that same day that Alexander Givet chose to die. He had been fine in the morning. Alix had left him seated by the warm hearth as she departed to seek any useful plant that she had earlier missed in her harvesting. There had been a hard frost, and Sir Udolf told her it but portended an early winter. Hayle had run into the hall as she was leaving to announce that his mistress was in labor with their child, and he smirked at Alix. She shrugged and walked past him.

The warm weather after the past cold days was strange. The ground had thawed enough for her to dig some roots she had missed. She found a patch of wild carrot, and carefully snipping the flower heads, shook the seeds into her pouch. She felt no guilt at doing so now. Hayle's behavior had hardened her heart even more. She had meant what she had said to him. When her father was gone and buried she would go. She could not remain in a loveless marriage. But where she would go she had no idea. She couldn't return to the queen. The queen would send her back to Wulfborn and to Hayle Watteson. She would have no choice.

Alix walked though the village as she returned to the hall. She passed the house where Maida lived with her mother. She could hear the laboring woman's howls and groans as she walked by. The girl's little sister stood in the open door watching her as she passed, and unable to help herself Alix made a rude face at the child. The child turned and fled back into the cottage. Alix laughed, feeling better at being able to make this simple gesture of defiance towards her husband and his mistress.

Entering the house, she went immediately to her little apothecary and set aside her pouch. She would sort everything out later. Hurrying to the hall she found her father as she had left him, but he was now sleeping. "Papa, I'm back," Alix said, bending to kiss his brow and kneeling by his side. It was cold, and Alexander Givet did not move. "Papa? *Papa!*" Her heart began to hammer in her chest. *"Non! Non! Mon Dieu! Mon Dieu!* Papa, do not leave me," Alix sobbed, and then she began to weep wildly.

The servants coming into the hall saw her grief and quickly realized what had transpired. One of them ran to find Sir Udolf, who hurried quickly to Alix's side.

"My child! Ahh, my poor lass. He is gone, is he?"

Alix looked up at her father-in-law and nodded. Then she said, "Why was no one with him? Why was he left to die alone, my lord? Where was Wat?"

Wat stepped forward. "I brought him wine when he asked me, mistress. Not more than an hour ago. He drank some and then said he would rest for a while and dismissed me. I went to his chamber, for he had a robe that needed repair, and my mother said she would do it. I brought it to her and waited. I was not gone long, I swear it!"

Alix looked at her father. His body showed no signs of distress. His face was at peace. Indeed, there was a small slight smile upon his lips. It was obvious to her that he had just gone to sleep. "There is no blame to be had here," she finally said. "Wat, go and fetch the priest."

"He will be buried on the hillside with our own family," Sir Udolf said. "I am so sorry, Alix. He was a good man even as his daughter is a good woman."

Alix rose to her feet wearily. "Thank you, my lord," she said.

Hayle did not come to her that night, and Alix was relieved. She could not have born his cruelty right now. She felt vulnerable and alone. In the morning she learned that Maida was still in labor. She briefly felt pity for the girl. The priest had come the night before and blessed the body of the physician. Alix and two of the women servants had bathed his frail body and dressed him in his best dark blue damask silk robe. His body had been carried to his chamber, and now with morning the men brought a coffin into the house. Alexander Givet was put into it and carried to the church at the end of the village, where a Mass was said for his soul. He was then buried on the hillside, Alix, Sir Udolf, and Wat following the coffin to the graveyard.

Alix remained by her father's grave for much of the day. The winds had begun to blow from the north, and she was glad for her heavy wool cape with its furred hood. Finally, with the red slash of the setting sun burning through the gray clouds on the horizon, Alix arose from her sire's grave and returned home. Passing Maida's cottage once again, she heard shrieks from within and the roar of her husband's voice as he protested something that did not please his childish nature.

Alix went to her bed, for she was exhausted from her sorrow and her weeping. She had never felt more alone in her life. And then in the morning Bab came into her chamber filled with the latest gossip.

"Good morrow, mistress, and it is certainly a good morning for you. Maida has died, and her babe with her! It was a lad. A great big creature like his father, and it almost split the lass in two birthing it. When it came out the cord was about its wee neck and its face was blue. And then she began to bleed and it couldn't be stopped, so she died, Maida did."

"Why was I not called?" Alix asked Bab. "Perhaps I might have stopped the girl's bleeding. There are herbs."

"*Call you?*" Bab laughed harshly. "Why would we call you? You hated our Maida. Why would you help her? She was the lass your husband loved. You probably wanted her dead. Her sister, Nora, says you made a wicked face as you passed the cottage yesterday. Did you spell our Maida?"

"I stuck my tongue out at the brat," Alix said. "She looked rudely at me."

"He's mad with grief," Bab said. "Aye, he is."

"I am sorry," Alix replied, not knowing what else to say. She had seen Maida several times, but she had never spoken a word to her, nor had the girl addressed her. As for Hayle, he would undoubtedly find another girl to love, for like any child who loses a toy he would want it replaced. It would not, Alix knew, be her, but maybe before he found another she might soften his heart long enough to conceive a child. And it would not be done in the dark. She would have no more of that foolishness, Alix decided. As soon as Hayle's grief had eased, she would cease taking the wild carrot seeds her father had prescribed. She would attempt to win him over enough to give him a child. A child who would not be overshadowed by Maida and her son. She would try to make peace with him for both their sakes, and for Sir Udolf, who so desperately wanted to know that his son had a legitimate heir to follow him.

It would not be easy, Alix knew. But it was her duty. Both her mother and the queen would be pleased that she was attempting to make things right. Had they both not taught her that a woman had a duty to her lord and must honor it? She couldn't run. There was no place to go, but she would do her best to be the kind of lady that Wulfborn Hall deserved. And surely her husband could be brought around even if only temporarily.

Chapter 3

At first Hayle Watteson would not allow them to either prepare for burial or bury his mistress and her infant. Only when Sir Udolf pointed out to his son that he was endangering Maida's immortal soul were the women in the girl's family allowed to wash and dress her. They laid her out in the gown that her lover had given her. It was a simple yellow jersey, but no woman in the village had anything nicer. They braided Maida's long black hair with the yellow ribbons he had given her to match the dress. The dead child they wrapped in clean swaddling clothes. The priest would not bury her, for by her actions she and her child were both damned souls. And so Maida was sewn into her shroud with her son and carried to her grave by her family.

Hayle Watteson did not go to see her buried. The thought of them placing his mistress in the ground and covering her with the earth was too painful for him to watch. But when she had been interred he went and sat by the grave for almost a week while he wept and called her name. He would not eat and he would drink but little. His heart was broken by his loss. Finally Sir Udolf went to his son, and with the help of two men they pulled Hayle from the graveside.

"You must come home," the baron told his only child. "Maida is gone, and your mourning will not bring her back."

"I want to be with her" came the dull reply.

"You have a wife," Sir Udolf snapped angrily. "And she has been more than patient with you. You have a duty to me, to her, to Wulf-born."

"The whore cannot conceive!" Hayle cried. "I have plugged her almost every night since you forced this marriage upon me. My seed does not take root in her womb. She is useless to me, to us, to Wulf-born. If you had but accepted Maida, Da." And Hayle began to weep inconsolably.

"Maida is gone," Sir Udolf repeated. "Neither she nor the lad she bore will come back to you. Nothing will be the same ever again, my son. Cleave to your wife, and do not again call her whore. Alix is a good girl. She will give you a son in time." He nodded to the two men holding Hayle's arms. "Bring him home, lads."

"Let me be!" the distraught man cried out. "I want to stay with my Maida!"

The two serving men, however, did their master's bidding, and half carrying, half dragging Hayle, brought him to the house. There servants forcibly removed his clothing and bathed him. When the candles and lamps were lit they escorted him to the hall where he was seated at his father's right hand while Alix sat on Sir Udolf's left. The meal was brought, but Hayle Watteson would eat nothing, and he only sipped at his wine. Sir Udolf conversed with his daughter-in-law, attempting now and again to bring his son into their light conversation, but Hayle Watteson would not speak to them.

When the food had been cleared away Alix arose and curtsied to the two men. Then, without a word, she departed the hall.

"You will go to her tonight," Sir Udolf said. "And you will treat her with kindness, for she has done you no wrong, my son."

"She allowed the queen and her father to make a marriage with me," he said. "She did not love me, and she knew I did not love her. She wanted a place for her father. She is little more than a whore, for she let herself be used by others. And she is barren."

"She is a good lass, my son. You have not given her a chance because of your overwhelming passion for your mistress. But now Maida is dead and buried. Alix has behaved well since your marriage. She has kept the hall, and the house servants have come to respect and like her. You would like her too if you would but cease this unreasonable behavior. You must have an heir. You have a wife. Do your duty!"

"Mount her yourself!" his son snarled angrily.

The baron's face grew crimson with his anger. "I have spoiled you," he said in a suddenly hard voice. "I saw no harm in your taking a mistress. It is what a man does, but you do not behave like a man. You behave like a child. Must you be put to your wife like a stallion to a mare? Will you shame her so? She has done you no ill, Hayle. Why do you persist in punishing her?"

"She is not Maida" came the stubborn reply. "Why can you not understand that? Your grandson, my heir, died with Maida. There will be no other, damn you!" And Hayle Watteson stormed furiously from the hall.

"Go after him," the baron ordered his servants. "And then take him to his wife." He reached for his goblet and drained it, nodding to a servant to refill the container.

In her chamber Alix had drawn the draperies wide, and an autumn moon shone through the glass, spreading a wide beam across the floor. She had dismissed Bab, for the serving woman's constant chatter and her lack of respect irritated Alix. Eventually she was going to have to find a servant who suited her better. She would wait until she was with child, for she knew Sir Udolf would give her anything at that point. Alix undid her long wavy hair and began to brush it out. Her mother had said its color was that of dark honey—rich and deep gold. The brush slicked down its length again and again and yet again. It was silky to the touch, Alix thought, as she plied her brush. Suddenly she heard a commotion in the hallway, and her door was flung wide and Hayle Watteson virtually thrown in by two husky male servants. Alix jumped up as he landed at her feet.

"Master said to bring him to you," one of the men said with a half leer. Then they were gone, pulling the door closed behind them.

He got to his feet slowly. Between the moon and the candles, the chamber was well lit. He stared at Alix in her simple batiste night garment, her long dark gold hair framing her heart-shaped face, hanging about her shoulders. "You aren't Maida," he finally said. His eyes were dull, showing no emotion.

"No, I am your wife, Alix, my lord," she answered quietly.

"You aren't Maida!" he repeated more forcefully, and began to become agitated. "My darling is dead, yet you live. You do not deserve to live!" He took a step towards her, his hands reaching out for her.

Frightened suddenly, Alix screamed a piercing cry. The blank look in his eyes had now been replaced by a mad fury. She shrieked again, falling back upon the bed.

He fell upon her, his hands wrapping themselves about her slender neck. "I will not allow you to live if my Maida is dead," he said in a cold voice. His hands began to tighten about her throat, his thumbs pressing into the soft flesh.

Alix clawed at those hands, loosening them enough to scream again and yet again. "Help me! Help me! He is trying to kill me!" she cried as his hands again closed about her flesh. She fought the madman, struggling to sit up, scratching his face, yanking at his hair as he sought to choke the life from her. And then, to her vast relief, the door to her chamber flew open again as the two serving men rushed in, pulling Hayle Watteson from atop Alix. Sir Udolf stood, staring with shock and dismay at the scene before him.

Alix reached up to stroke her bruised skin. The marks of his fingers were bright scarlet on her creamy flesh, and she was gasping for air. She tried to stand, but her legs would not hold her. And then, without warning, Alix began to cry.

Her husband, restrained by his father's servants, stared at her, and then with a shout he broke away from his keepers and ran from the room.

"Take him!" Sir Udolf roared. He was furious and dismayed all at once. "Alix, my child, I am so sorry," he began. "In my eagerness for a grandchild I forced him to come to you, and it was too soon.

I see that now. Forgive him. Forgive me." And then the baron departed the chamber following the sound of his son's pounding feet and those of the servants pursuing Hayle. The madman moved up the stairs of his house, to the attics where his servants slept. There was a narrow corridor on that top floor, and reaching it, Sir Udolf saw his son standing in the open window at the hall's end. For a brief moment he thought that his heart had stopped, but no. It was beating rapidly. The two serving men seemed frozen where they stood.

"I'm sorry, Da. I have to go to my Maida," Hayle Watteson said in a clear, calm voice. And then he flung himself from the window's ledge.

"Jesu! Mary!" one of the serving men cried, and they both crossed themselves.

Sir Udolf stared at the open window. His son. His son had stood in that window but a moment ago, and now he was gone. The baron turned and ran with all possible haste downstairs, trying as he ran to remember which side of his house the attic corridor window was located. Two men from the stables came running, shouting, pointing. He followed them in the dusk of evening. Hayle Watteson lay sprawled upon the earth, his neck twisted at an odd angle. Sir Udolf knelt by his son's body.

"He's dead, my lord," someone said.

"Killed himself, he did," came another voice.

"Him and our Maida are together now for eternity," someone else murmured.

Sir Udolf was numb with his grief. He brushed a lock of his son's hair back from his forehead and rose to his feet. "Take him to the hall," he instructed to no one in particular. "I must tell his wife." Then the lord of Wulfborn turned away and walked slowly back into the house. His son was dead. He had no heir, and he was past forty. Finding his way upstairs to Alix's chamber, he entered without knocking.

"My lord?" Alix looked up from her place on the bed where she was sitting. "What has happened?"

"My son is dead," Sir Udolf said slowly as if tasting the words. "My son has killed himself, but I shall deny it to the priest. Hayle must be buried by the church."

She grew pale with shock. "Why? How?" And then a sense of great relief swept over her. She would never again have to bear his company in a darkened room.

"He loved her," Sir Udolf said in a tone tinged with surprise. "And he threw himself from a high window to be with her. He *really* loved the miller's daughter. She was a peasant, but a few generations removed from serfdom. Yet he loved her though she was not suitable. A man marries for wealth, for station, for land, but not for love."

"My parents loved each other," Alix said quietly.

"Your father told me the Count d'Anjou made the match between him and your mother. That your mother and he barely knew each other. They were fortunate that love came afterwards. Hayle's mother was a good woman, and I had great respect for her, but I did not love her. She brought me land as a dower. It was land that matched mine. It was a good bargain," the baron replied.

"Yet I brought you nothing," Alix responded.

"Nay, lass, you brought gold and silver. You, too, were a good match. My son should have been grateful to have you as a wife. You were a far better bride than he might have expected. You are pretty. You know how to manage a household. You are devout and mannerly." The baron sighed. "I have done you an injustice, Alix, for I did not realize the depth of my son's passions for the miller's daughter."

"You gave my father a home in his dying days, my lord," Alix said, "and for that I will always be grateful. With your help I will now follow after the queen. Under the circumstances, she will surely give me her protection, if only for my parents' sake."

"You would leave Wulfborn?" He seemed surprised.

"My husband is dead, my lord. There is no place here for me now," Alix said.

"Is there any chance you might be with child?" Sir Udolf asked hopefully.

Alix shook her head. "Your son could barely stand to use me even in the darkened chamber he seemed to need. He said my scent was not Maida's, and he could not convince himself even in the blackness that I was she. While he entered my body, more times than not he did not spill his seed. And he had not come to my bed in the past few weeks. My courses came and went in the last week. I am sorry, but my womb is an empty one, my lord. There is no child of your son's to be your heir."

Sir Udolf nodded.

"I must go and prepare my husband's body for burial," Alix told her father-in-law.

Again he nodded. "I will leave you so you may dress," he said and, turning, he was gone from her.

It was sad, Alix thought, that Sir Udolf had lost his only child. But I am free now! she exulted silently to herself. Certainly Sir Udolf will give me escort to the queen, and someone will know where she is. She will take me back and all will be as it was. My parents would want it this way. She pulled her brown jersey gown over her night garment, stuffed her feet into a pair of house slippers, and hurried to the hall.

Hayle Watteson lay upon the high board, his head lolling to one side. He had been a handsome man despite the petulant twist of his lips and his round, childish face. No one had bothered to close his watery blue eyes and so now Alix did. "Bab," she called, knowing the woman would be lurking nearby.

Bab hurried forward. "He died to be with his Maida," she said, looking from beneath her eyelids to see what kind of a reaction she would get from Alix.

"Aye, he did," Alix agreed. "Does he have anything better to wear?"

Bab nodded.

"Then go and fetch it. He should be buried as befits his station as

59

Wulfborn's heir." She turned to the other women servants who were standing in a knot nearby. "Go bring water and clothes, lasses. We must bathe him before he is dressed in his finest."

The serving women scampered off to do her bidding. Bab had already gone.

Alix looked at the body upon the high board. She felt nothing for it, but then why should she? Hayle Watteson had treated her badly. He had neither loved nor respected her. She had done her best to please, to be a good wife. He had felt no such compunction to respond in kind. She had no regrets, and she would shake the dust of Wulfborn from her shoes as quickly as she could. To have remained to publicly mourn him would have been hypocritical. The winter was close, and she needed to find Margaret of Anjou quickly before travel would be too impossible.

The women returned, and together they stripped the clothing from the dead man's body. Then they carefully washed him. They giggled and rolled their eyes at the sight of the young man's genitals. "No wonder our Maida was so happy," one said, and Bab cackled knowingly. A sharp look from Alix silenced her and prevented any further remarks. The older woman had brought a dark blue velvet robe whose sleeves were edged in gray rabbit fur. They dressed him in it, and Bab combed his hair before placing a strap of linen around his head and beneath his chin. His head straight now, Hayle did not appear so odd. They sewed him into his shroud, leaving only his head visible.

Alix called for candle stands to be brought and beeswax tapers to be lit. The frost had killed the last of the flowers, and so there were none. "Tell the village they may come on the morrow to pay their respects. We will bury him at noon."

"Where is the grave to be dug?" Bab asked.

"That is Sir Udolf's decision, not mine," Alix answered her.

"He'd want to be next to his Maida," Bab persisted.

"I care not, but it is still Sir Udolf's decision," Alix told the woman.

"The priest will not bury him. He killed himself," Bab said.

"You are mistaken, Bab, and if you spread such a rumor Sir Udolf will see you driven from Wulfborn, and winter is almost upon us. My husband fell when he attempted to dislodge a stuck window, and it opened suddenly, throwing him off balance. This is a tragic accident. Do you all understand that?"

Bab nodded, and suddenly there was a grudging respect in her eyes for Alix.

Another woman spoke up. "Why should he be given the church's blessing when our Maida was not?"

"Because he is the lord's son and was heir to Wulfborn. Maida was merely a miller's daughter. Will your family thank you if I have you driven from this place?" Alix's voice was soft, but there was definite menace in it.

"Shut yer gob, Molly," Bab said. "She's right, and shows more loyalty to Sir Udolf than you are showing. Listen to me, all of you. The young lord's death was an accident, and any says otherwise will be sorry they did."

The serving woman threw Alix a sullen look but said no more.

"You are dismissed, all of you, with my thanks," Alix said. She watched as they went from the hall, several of them whispering among themselves. Bab remained. Turning to her, Alix said, "Thank you. Now go and fetch Father Peter for me."

"At once, mistress," Bab replied respectfully. Then she hurried off.

Sir Udolf came into the hall, and walking over to his son's body, began to weep.

"I have told all who helped me prepare him that this was an accident. He fell trying to open a window in the attics. They will be silent, for I have said that any who says otherwise will be driven with their families from Wulfborn."

The baron looked at her with grief-stricken eyes. "You are clever," he said slowly. "It was a kind thing to do."

"I have but attempted to repay your kindness to me and to my

61

father," Alix replied. "I hope you will forgive me if I do not remain here to mourn, my lord. You will surely understand why I cannot."

"In the morning I will send a messenger to Queen Margaret telling her of this tragedy," Sir Udolf said, brushing his tears away.

"Will you tell her I am returning to her service?" Alix asked him.

"I will tell her of my son's death, and then tell her I am sending to the archbishop in York for a dispensation to marry you," Sir Udolf said.

Alix grew pale with shock. "My lord! The church will never allow you to marry your son's widow. It is an unnatural thing! Besides, I do not wish to wed. I seek only to serve my queen in her exile. I am certain the reason she left me at Wulfborn was only for my father's safety. She will surely take me back."

"For whatever reason, you did not give my son an heir and now my son is dead. I need an heir for Wulfborn. I am still young enough to sire one, Alix, and I shall not be cruel to you as was my son. We already know each other. The queen has no place for you, I fear. You must have a husband, and I am in need of a wife."

"The church will never approve such a dispensation," Alix said stubbornly.

He smiled a little smile and, rubbing his thumb and his forefinger together, said, "The church is not above certain persuasions, Alix. Surely, having been raised at court, you understand that. Anything is possible given the right circumstances. I will have my dispensation by the spring, and you will be my wife as soon as I do. Until then, I will respect your place in my house as my son's widow and Wulfborn's chatelaine."

She had no time for further protest, for Father Peter came hurrying into the hall. "I have heard of young Hayle's death, my lord, but two tales reach my ears."

"My son fell from an attic window trying to dislodge it," Sir Udolf said. "It was an accident, Good Father." He sighed sadly.

"A terrible tragedy indeed, my lord. I shall, of course, bury him on the morrow," the priest replied.

"At noon so the Wulfborn folk may pay their respects to their heir," Alix said.

"Of course, lady, and to you I offer my condolences. Despite the trials you have suffered in recent months, your example to all women is exemplary. I shall pray for Hayle, and for his father, and his wife," the priest told them.

"We are grateful, Good Father," the baron answered.

"I must go to my chamber, my lord, Father," Alix said.

"Of course, my dear," Sir Udolf responded. "This has been a terrible day for us all, and in seeing to the preparation of the body you have done your duty. It is late."

Alix curtsied to the two men, and forcing herself not to run, went from the hall. She was horrified by Sir Udolf's plans, but right now she wasn't certain what she could do about them. But she did know she had no intentions of marrying her late husband's father. And now her plan to rejoin the queen was blocked. She couldn't flee to her godmother, for it would be the first place Sir Udolf would look for her, and if he could indeed obtain a dispensation from the church to marry her, Margaret of Anjou would probably agree. As much as she hated admitting it even to herself, Alix knew that the queen in her desperation had matters more important to her to consider than her godchild for whom she had already made provision. She was alone. Truly alone for the first time in her life. She was a widow. Her family was gone, and she had no intention of permitting Sir Udolf to make decisions for her. She would make her own decisions.

When the morning came, Alix sat in the hall with her father-in-law as the Wulfborn folk came to pay their respects to them and view Hayle's body. She had dressed herself in her only good gown, the same violet damask silk she had worn on her wedding day almost seven months ago. The villagers shuffled by the body, but none, Alix noted, shed a tear. Hayle, despite his devotion to Maida, had obviously not been well liked by them. His father, however, was another thing. The loving respect they showed to Sir Udolf was touching, and the tears shed that day were for him.

She had never paid a great deal of attention to him, but now she studied him surreptitiously as they sat together. He was taller than his son and heavier set. But where Hayle had had blond, almost white hair, Sir Udolf's pate was a bald one. He had but a fringe of grayish brown hair that ringed the back of his head. Where Hayle's light eyes had been emotionless, Sir Udolf's blue eyes were emotion filled. Alix believed him a good man, but the thought of marrying him repelled her. He was certainly her father's age, and while she knew many young women wed with older husbands, the thought of his coupling with her was horrific. She did not like coupling. It was distasteful to her.

The noon hour came and before the six serving men came to take her husband to the small village church. Alix arose, took the needle and thread Bab handed her and, drawing the shroud over Hayle's head, completed the sewing of the funerary garment. The heir to Wulfborn was then placed upon an open cart, which was driven through the village to the church where Father Peter said the Mass. Then the body was placed again upon the cart and taken to the grave.

"This is not hallowed ground," the priest said as he saw where Hayle Watteson was to be buried.

"He would want to be buried next to Maida and his son," Sir Udolf said. "What difference does it make, Good Father? Is the ground cursed?"

The priest raised his hand and blessed the open grave. "Not now," he said.

The body was lowered into the ground. The prayers were said, and then the grave diggers moved to fill the grave. They waited until the mound of earth had been raised, and then turned away, making their way back to the hall. Sir Udolf took the priest aside and began speaking to him earnestly. The priest listened, but no sign of what he might be thinking showed on his ageless face. When he turned briefly to look at Alix, she quickly lowered her eyes. Surely Father Peter would dissuade Sir Udolf from his plans.

But to Alix's shock, the priest came to see her several days later. She brought him to the fire in the hall and offered him a cup of cider. "Thank you, my daughter," he said as he settled himself, pointing his sandaled feet to the fire. "Has the lord spoken to you of his desires, lady?" the priest inquired gently.

"I am not certain to what you refer, *mon père*," Alix replied.

"Your modesty becomes you, daughter," the priest responded. "Sir Udolf wishes to obtain a dispensation so he may wed you. He is in need of an heir now, and still filled with vigor. You are young and, it is to be hoped, fertile. You need a home. This would seem a good solution to the problems that you both face."

"I would think a father attempting to wed his son's widow would be an anathema to Holy Mother Church," Alix said slowly. "And how can I think of Sir Udolf as a proper husband when I already think of him as a father? Would I not be committing the sin of incest, Good Priest?"

Father Peter looked briefly troubled, but then he said, "There is no blood link between you and Sir Udolf, for you did not give his son a child."

"But his son's seed entered me. Now you would ask me to accept the father's seed? Surely that cannot be right!"

"We must leave these weighty matters of philosophy to the archbishop's counsel in York, my daughter," Father Peter said. "As a woman, you are not competent to make such decisions. They will decide what is best in this matter, but as you are an orphan and there is no blood between you and Sir Udolf, it is possible the archbishop's counsel will decide to give him the dispensation, especially given the circumstances of your marriage. They will consider the fact that your inability to keep your husband by your side may have led to his unfortunate demise."

"But his death was an accident!" Alix insisted.

"Given the circumstances surrounding his death, the archbishop's counsel may have *certain* doubts," the priest answered her smoothly.

"But he was involved with Maida before I ever came to Wulfborn Hall," Alix said, in an attempt to defend herself.

"Still, as his bride, the church will believe you should have been able, by your good example, to bring him to your side and away from that of a wicked woman. And if it is thought that Maida lured him from beyond the grave, and you did not prevent it, the church will consider that you are in part responsible for the death of Sir Udolf's only heir, that you owe him a debt that can only be paid in kind. As the good daughter of the church I know you to be, lady, you will obey the directive of our Holy Mother Church," Father Peter concluded with a nod of his head. "Will you not?"

Alix swallowed hard. The priest reasoned skillfully, especially for a country cleric. "I will do what is right, Good Father," she told him.

He smiled at her. "I know you will, my daughter," he told her, "which is why tomorrow I will travel to York myself carrying Sir Udolf's request along with my own recommendation that the dispensation be given. Such permission will have to be discussed and is not likely to be given before spring, so I will return quickly, for Wulfborn should not be left without its priest. There is much sin here, I fear. In the meantime, your presence as our lady will be a comfort to the folk." The priest arose from his seat. "I must return to the church, for it will soon be time for evensong and vespers. Thank you for your hospitality, lady. I am comforted to know that you are a sensible girl." And he hurried from the hall, his brown robes flapping about his scrawny ankles.

Alix shook her head. There was nothing for it but that she would have to flee. And soon. She knew Sir Udolf would be going hunting shortly so that the winter larder would be full. He had told her he would be away two days. The priest's trip to York as well as his return would take far longer. It would be several weeks before he returned. But how could she keep the nosy Bab from learning that she was gone? Alix suddenly knew. When Sir Udolf rode out she would say that she would spend the time he was off hunting praying and fasting in her chamber for Hayle's soul. She was not to be disturbed for any reason. Her strength of will after her husband's death had impressed Bab, and the serving woman was now treating her with grudging respect.

"When do you plan to hunt?" Alix asked Sir Udolf that evening as they sat at the high board for the light evening meal.

"A few days before Martinmas," he told her, taking her hand in his. "Is it possible you will miss me, my lass?" He kissed her hand, but did not release it.

With effort, she let him hold her hand and did not snatch it away. God's wounds, but he was attempting to play the lover! Alix fought back a shudder. "There is something I wish to do, but I did not want to deprive you of my company, my lord."

"And what is that, my sweet?" he asked her, smiling directly into her eyes.

Alix made her mouth turn up in a small return smile. "Father Peter has suggested that by not being able to comfort Hayle in his distress I might in part be responsible for his unhappy death, my lord." She cast her eyes down.

"That is ridiculous!" he responded, dropping her hand. "The priest is an old fool, Alix. He knows nothing of love and the lengths to which it can drive you."

"Still, my lord, it cannot hurt if I spend two days fasting and in prayer for my husband's soul," Alix replied. She sighed. "What can we know of God's will, my lord? We are but mere mortals. It can surely not hurt any if I take the time to do this. And prayers for a husband from his wife will certainly be of help, considering his sin against me, my lord."

"That you can forgive him!" the baron cried softly. "Ah, Alix, now I know I am right to make you my wife. What an example you will be to our children. I rue now that I did not wed you myself instead of giving you to my son. His lust for his mistress blinded him to your goodness and your beauty. I regret a long winter must pass before you will become mine." His look was an ardent one.

Alix blushed, for she could not help it. "My lord, there is no guarantee that the church will give you a dispensation for a marriage between us," she reminded him.

Sir Udolf smiled broadly. "Do not fret, my sweet lass," he told her. "Father Peter carries a generous gift with him for whoever can help me attain such an indulgence. The priest will know the proper person to choose. You are safe at Wulfborn, Alix. It will always be your home, and if God favors us, you will be with child, *my child*, by this time next year." And for the first time she saw a lustful look come into his eyes. "We should not have to wait," he murmured almost to himself. He squeezed her little hand.

"Should we not mourn Hayle a good year?" Alix said, pulling her hand away.

"Nay. When the dispensation is given, you and I will marry without delay. I am no stripling, my sweet, although I promise to be a vigorous lover to you," Sir Udolf told her. Leaning forward, he attempted to kiss her lips.

"Please, my lord," Alix responded, drawing back so that his mouth did not touch hers. "Your son is not even cold in his grave. Your tone is too intimate. Your manner even more so." Her tone had become scolding. Her look one of stern disapproval.

He was immediately contrite. "Forgive me, Alix," he said, genuinely remorseful.

Alix nodded graciously at him and arose from the high board. "I will go to my own chamber now, my lord," she told him.

"When we are alone together will you call me Udolf?" he asked her, rising too.

"If it would please you, my lord . . . Udolf," Alix answered him. Then she said, "You did not tell me when you plan to hunt, *Udolf*."

"Not tomorrow, but the day after. The weather is getting colder, but there are no signs of a storm on the horizon," he told her. "You will find I am a good provider."

"From the moment I entered this hall I have never wanted for anything, Udolf," Alix responded. Then she left him. This evening had helped her to make up her mind. She must leave Wulfborn, and she must go the moment he was gone hunting. She could not wed him, and she did not think he could keep his growing desire for her in check until a dispensation arrived. What if he got her with child? Then she would have no choice but to remain. She knew that many would consider her actions foolish, but she had to go. Sir Udolf was old enough to be her father. Had become her father's friend. The thought of being his wife, of being mounted by him, repelled her, made her nauseous.

The following day she prepared her chamber for prayer and fasting. She told Bab of her plans, saying, "I must not be disturbed while my lord is away. He has sent the priest to York, for a dispensation for he wishes to wed me himself and get an heir on me. Before I can be at peace with such a thing I must discharge a final duty to my husband. I will fast and pray for his soul while Sir Udolf is gone."

"Why, the wicked old devil," Bab said, grinning. "We all knew he needed a new wife. He should have taken one years ago, after the second one died. He has not even taken a mistress, although now and again I know he satisfies his naughty urges on one or two widows in the village. But they can't give him an heir. Only something young and juicy like you can give him what he wants. And you, being orphaned, are content, I suppose, to have him for a husband. Well, you're strong enough to manage him, lady. And old men always dote upon their young wives, especially them that gives them bairns."

"Of course I will do what is right," Alix said. "Now, do you understand that once I enter my chamber tonight I am not to be disturbed?"

Bab nodded. "Aye," she responded. "Say your prayers and clear your conscience, lady. I cannot fault you for that."

"No, you cannot," Alix replied sharply.

Bab cackled with laughter. "You look all soft and meek, but you are not," she noted. "I'll tell all to keep away. Shall I come to you when the master returns?"

Alix nodded. To do otherwise would have aroused Bab's suspicions. But where was she to go? She had had no family in England but her parents, who were now dead. The queen would—could—not take her back, and besides, Margaret of Anjou being a practical woman, would side with Sir Udolf. Perhaps if she could reach the coast she could take passage for France and then make her way to Anjou to find her father's family. It would not be an easy journey. Indeed, for a young woman traveling alone without even a servant it could be dangerous.

In the days before her father had died he had surprised her by giving her a pouch containing an amount just slightly in excess to the dower he had paid Sir Udolf. "A woman alone should always have her own wealth for emergencies," Alexander Givet had told his only child. "Sew these coins into the hems of your gowns and your cloak. And tell no one, my daughter."

Alix had followed his instructions, sewing at night in her chamber when she was alone. There had been eight gold coins and almost twenty of silver. She had put two gold and five silver pieces into each of her two jersey gowns. The remaining four gold and ten silver coins she had hidden within her heavy wool cloak, some in the hem, and others in a secret pocket she fashioned within the folds of the garment. She had put nothing in her silk damask gown, for it was too fine.

Alix had eaten the evening meal with Sir Udolf, who was now attempting a more intimate relationship with her. She managed to keep him at bay beneath a guise of shyness and propriety. It seemed to delight him and he praised her decorousness while attempting to kiss her now and again, chuckling when she fended him off with a scolding. Alix finally decided it was time to make her escape from the hall. She stood, but at the same time so did he. "I shall not come to table on the morrow, for I will at first light begin my prayers and fasting," Alix said, attempting to move away from him.

His arm reached out to clamp about her waist and he drew her to him. "Give me a little kiss for luck, sweet lass," he said to her. His other hand fumbled at her breast.

"My lord! Udolf!" Alix cried softly. "This behavior is most inappropriate. Let me go at once! Ohh, how can you shame me like this?" she protested to him.

"Forgive me, sweet lass," he said, but he did not release his hold upon her, and he could not resist giving her small round breast a little squeeze before he took his hand away. "From the moment I realized you were to be mine, I grew as eager as a lad with his first love," he admitted. "The thought that you will be my wife has made me alive again! My son was a fool, Alix. You are fair to gaze upon. You are sweet-natured. I am a man long grown, but I cannot seem to resist you. I do not know how I will wait the winter long to possess you." And then he kissed her mouth.

It was not an unpleasant kiss. More eager and excited. Indeed, almost boyish and sweet. Nothing at all like that first cruel kiss she had received from Hayle. Alix gasped, surprised, and pulled away from him. "Shame, my lord!"

"I will not apologize," he said almost defiantly, but he made no further move to touch her. "I will be a good husband to you. And I mean to kiss you and court you the winter through, sweet lass. You might as well know it now and be accepting."

Alix let a little smile touch her lips. She couldn't help it. Then she grew serious. "You must respect me, my lord," she told him sternly, "even as I respect you." Then she curtsied to him prettily. "Good hunting, Udolf."

He nodded. "Thank you, my lady love," he replied as politely. "I will see you upon my return, and prepare to be kissed then."

Alix hurried from the hall. Aye, it was time to go before the baron's newly discovered romantic nature aroused itself any further. Once a man's lust was engaged, he could not be stopped until he had attained his goal. She had seen that happen at court, and it seemed to be the same wherever men and women went. He was a good man, but she could not wed him. She did not want to ever wed again. But what would she do? She could not remain in England. The baron might come after her, and a man's word was always taken over a woman's. And as part of the queen's entourage her entire life until recently, she could be considered a traitor. She had overheard those who remained with King Henry until almost the end talking about how to save themselves and their families. Alix knew that association was often enough cause for guilt. No. She must leave England. She must go north, as the queen had done, into Scotland.

And what will you do in Scotland? the voice in her head asked her. That was a fair question, but also a conundrum. Perhaps she might seek out the widowed Scots queen, Marie of Gueldres, and ask for a place in her household. She would tell that queen her history, and say Margaret of Anjou no longer had a place for her now that she was widowed. Certainly the Scots queen would take pity on her. She had skills to offer. She was good with children. She had certain medical knowledge learned from her father that could make her useful. Aye! That is what she would do. She would make her way to wherever the Scots court was currently residing.

Alix prepared the soft chamois pouch her mother had always carried when the court traveled. At its bottom she lay her father's few surgical instruments and several small containers of medicinals that she had made along with some bags of herbs. Sadly, she could not take her violet damask silk gown with her. She would wear one of her jersey gowns. The other she folded and put into the bottom of the pouch along with her camises, and two night garments. A smaller silk pouch held her few bits of jewelry. She stuffed it at the bottom of the larger bag amid the folds of her gown. She would leave the sollerets, she decided, as she laid her leather house slippers atop her camises. They would only add weight to the pouch, and as long as she had her boots on her feet and her slippers, she could manage. She took two pairs of knitted stockings and stuffed them into the sack. Then, bathing her face and hands and brushing her long hair, Alix went to her bed. Who knew how long it would be before she slept in a clean soft bed again? Whispering her prayers, she asked God to protect her.

It was her habit to always wake early. Arising, she dressed quickly in two camises, one of lawn and the other of flannel. She pulled a pair of woolen stockings onto her feet along with her worn leather boots and drew her brown jersey dress over her slender form. Sitting upon the edge of her bed in the half-dark, half-gray light before the dawn, Alix braided her long hair into a thick plait. Then, lifting the strap of her pouch, she put it over her head to rest against one side of her body. Picking up her heavy wool cloak with its fur-edged hood and her gloves, Alix slipped from her chamber.

The house was completely silent. She knew that very shortly one of the servants would come to start the fires for the day. The cook would arrive in the kitchen to begin his preparations for the day. Alix hurried downstairs, and slipping into the pantry near the kitchen, took a loaf of day-old bread and a wedge of cheese. She tucked them into the top of her pouch and then filled the small stone flask she carried with watered wine. She listened, but the quiet was still deep as she crept quietly towards the kitchen door, which was rarely barred, even at night. It opened as her hand touched the latch. She quickly hurried outside and looked about her, but there was no one in her view.

If she took her horse from the stables they would know that she was gone. Reluctantly, Alix set off walking, hurrying away from the house as fast as she could. The sky was getting a little lighter with each passing minute. She didn't look back for fear she would see someone. Alix followed the track that led north. The very same one the queen had taken. She prayed that Sir Udolf would not come this way with his hunting party, but if she heard horses she would hide herself in a ditch. Then she laughed softly to herself. The lord of Wulfborn would go across the fields. He would not come upon the road that wound its way north. To her surprise, a weak sun rose as she walked. It was cold, but not unbearably so for November. There was little wind at all and it was at her back, coming from the southwest.

Alix walked for several hours and then suddenly realized that she was hungry and thirsty. Stopping, she sat herself in the grass on the side of the road. Reaching into the pouch beneath her cloak, she pulled a piece of bread from her loaf and bit off a large chunk of cheese from the wedge. She ate slowly, and when she had finished she opened the flask and drank several swallows. She would remember to add water to the flask when she came to a stream. She had already crossed one narrow little brook this morning, stepping from stone to stone to keep her feet dry.

Arising, she started on her way again. The track she was traversing was getting narrower and narrower, becoming more difficult to follow, but she trudged on, watching the feeble sun as she moved to keep her direction correct. The sun was already beginning to lower itself towards the horizon by early afternoon. It was almost winter, and the days were shorter now than at any other time of the year.

As she traveled Alix began to look about for a spot in which she might shelter for the night. She hadn't seen a living soul the day long, although once she had seen an antlered stag on a nearby hill. And then, as the sun was almost ready to set, she spied what appeared to be the remnants of a stone wall. Or perhaps, she considered, it was a cairn raised in memory of some long-dead warrior. She stopped and, looking about, decided it would be as good a place as any to spend the night, especially as the sun now sank behind the horizon. Clearing some stones to make a place for herself, Alix sat down.

About her the silence hung heavily. What had she done? she asked herself. She was in the middle of nowhere, and night was upon her. She had no means to start a fire, and there obviously wasn't a living soul, man or beast, for miles. Reaching into her bag, she tore off a chunk of her bread and bit off another bit of cheese. She ate slowly as the sunset faded and the night closed in about her. She didn't even know where she was. Had she already crossed the border into Scotland? The light breeze of the day had gone, and above her the skies were cloudy. Not a star shown in the dull firmament.

It was cold, but not unbearably so. Alix pulled her cloak close about her, drawing the hood tightly about her face. She began to pray. She would either survive the night or she wouldn't, but anything was better than being forced into marriage again. And with a man old enough to be her father. A man with a bald pate. Sir Udolf's son had been a lustful man, although his lust was not directed towards his wife. Last night she had seen where that lust had come from, for the father was equally, if not more, lustful. Alix had not a doubt he would have been in her bed before the week was out. And he would justify it because he was meant to marry her. She would have had a big belly at her wedding, and she was certain Sir Udolf would have been delighted.

Drawing her legs up, she tucked her skirts about her and put her gloved hands under her armpits for more warmth. Her back against the stones, Alix fell asleep, and she slept for several hours before awakening briefly only to sleep again. When she opened her eyes again the gray half-light was lightening the skies. Arising, she moved stiffly away from her sleeping spot to pee, lifting her skirts high so as not to splash them. The morning air was cold on her buttocks. Then, sitting back down again, she ate more bread and cheese and drank a few more swallows of the watered wine, now more water than grape.

Finally she arose, and she began to walk again. She passed several more piles of stones and decided that she surely must be in Scotland by now. As the morning wore on, the skies above her grew gray, and the wind began to rise, coming from the north. By late morning a light snow had begun to fall, and Alix knew if she did not find serious shelter and some warmth she could be in trouble. But the countryside about her seemed as deserted as it had been yesterday. Alix didn't dare stop to eat. She simply kept walking. The path was virtually obscured now. She couldn't be certain which way she was going. The wind began to rise and the snow grew heavier.

Alix hunched down into her cloak, pulling it closely about her. Her hands were cold despite her fur-lined gloves. Her feet were icy in her wool stockings. It was growing darker with each passing minute. There wasn't a bit of shelter in sight. And then ahead of her she saw what appeared to be large mounds in the heath. Approaching them carefully she found herself walking among a herd of great horned shaggy cattle. There had to be at least two dozen of them, legs folded beneath them, settled down to ride out the storm. Their hides were already well dusted with snow.

She could go no farther. For a moment Alix stood stock-still. This was the end. She was going to die. She would freeze to death out here in the borders. Her legs gave way and she slipped to the grass half wedged between two of the great shaggy dark beasts. Laying her head against one, she began to weep softly, and then suddenly it dawned upon her that she felt warmer. The two creatures were sheltering her with their big bodies. Alix pushed herself firmly between the two cattle. Aye! She was warmer. Warm enough to perhaps survive the long night ahead. She lowered her head and pulled her hood up as far as she could. The creatures made no protest, and their quiet, even breathing shortly lulled her into a deep sleep. If she died, Alix thought, she would be with her mother and father again. And she would not have to wed Sir Udolf. Despite her circumstances, it was a very comforting thought. And if she survived this night it would be a sign that she was not meant to marry Sir Udolf. She would never marry again, Alix decided. She would never again be at any man's mercy.

Chapter 4

"*D*a! Come quick!" the young herdsman called to his father. "Over here!" The two border collies with him were barking wildly and dancing about.

The Laird of Dunglais's head herder, one Jock by name, moved across the field in the early dusk of the morning. The wind had thankfully died, and while a light snow still fell, the worst of it, he thought, was over. Now all he wanted to do was to get his master's cattle out of the weather on the moor, away from predators and nearer home. They were the last of the herd in the summer pastures, and had been caught by the sudden unexpected weather, but fortunately it hadn't been a bad storm. "What is it, Robbie?" he asked his son as he joined the younger man.

"Look!" Robbie pointed to the still figure between two shaggy beasts.

"Jesu! Mary!" Jock exclaimed. " 'Tis a lass." So small and delicate a form could be nothing else, he realized. He bent and brushed the snow from the girl's cloak. "Are ye alive, lassie?" he inquired, shaking her gently.

She moaned faintly, but did not move.

"The poor creature was probably caught in the storm," Jock said. "We must get her back to the shelter. Can you carry her, Robbie? I'll want to get the cattle up and moving. This snowfall will continue for a few more hours though 'tis light now. Here, Shep, here, Laddie," he called to the two dogs. "We have work to do."

His son nodded and, pulling Alix up, he took her into his arms and walked off. Behind him his father and the two border collies began to rouse the cattle from their comfortable positions in the heath. It was over a mile to the small shelter on the moor, but Robbie walked doggedly along, carrying Alix as if she were a child. She did not stir, and were it not for her faint breathing, he would have feared her dead. It was a miracle she had survived her night on the moors, but then huddled between the two big cattle she had been saved from freezing. Still, the poor thing was cold.

Reaching the small shelter, he kicked the door open with his foot and laid the girl down on the single cot there, covering her with the sheepskin. Then he stirred the embers of the fire that had burned through the night, coaxing it alive once again. He added more wood from the store near the hearth. He and his father had come to fetch the cattle when the storm had caught them. Arriving at the little hut, they had sheltered for the night. Even inside with a fire it had been cold. The fact the girl was alive at all was a miracle. Swinging the iron arm from which a kettle hung, he added a bit of whiskey from his flask to the water in it and warmed it over the fire.

He turned as a weak voice said, "Where am I?"

Pouring some of the hot liquid from the kettle into a little tin cup, he put an arm about the girl, helping her into a sitting position, and put the cup to her lips. "Drink some of this, mistress, but take a care. 'Tis hot," he advised her.

Alix sipped, coughed, but sipped again. Then, pushing the cup away, she repeated her query. "Where am I?"

"Yer on the lands of the Laird of Dunglais," Robbie answered her. "My name is Robbie, and I'm one of the laird's herders. My da and I found you out on the moors huddled between the cattle. They saved yer life, they did, mistress."

Alix took the cup from him more to warm her hands than to drink the harsh brew he had given her. Aye. She had thought she was going to die when she had fallen between those two great beasts. Yet they were warm, and she fell asleep thinking about her mama and her papa. The Laird of Dunglais. Then she was in Scotland. Alix sneezed.

"Take more of the whiskey and water, mistress," Robbie said.

"I'm so tired," Alix told him, but she sipped until the cup was empty. Then, falling back against his supporting arm, she closed her eyes.

The young herder slid his arm from beneath her, and going to the fire, added more wood. Then he stood by the hearth, waiting for his father to come and tell him what to do next. After some time had passed, the older man entered the shelter, shaking the snow off of him, going to the fire to warm his hands.

"How is she?"

"I gave her warmed whiskey and water, Da, and she fell back to sleep," Robbie replied.

"Who is she? Did she tell ye her name?" the chief herder wanted to know.

The younger man shook his head. "I dinna ask, and she dinna say."

"I've got the cattle outside." He looked over at Alix. "The lassie looks like she'll sleep for several hours. There's plenty of wood, and I'll leave one of the dogs with her. But we've got to get the cattle home, and the laird should be told about the lass. He'll know what to do. She isn't strong enough to come with us, and you canna carry her all the way to Dunglais Keep. Leave yer oatcakes and some whiskey. If she awakens she'll know we haven't deserted her, especially if the dog is here. Shep, stay!" he commanded the younger border collie. Then he left the small shelter.

Robbie followed his father's instructions, pulling the stool near to the cot, leaving two oatcakes and his flask. The girl was sleeping heavily, and as his father had said, probably would for many hours. She was very pretty, he thought. Then he hurried to join his father, and together the two men drove the herd of shaggy Highland cattle the several miles through the still-falling snow into the safety of their winter pasturage.

While his son secured the beasts, Jock went to find his master, who was seated in the hall of his keep breaking his fast. His small daughter was with him, and the laird was smiling. Jock could not recall having seen his master smile in years. He made his way through the hall, stopping to stand before the high board and patiently waiting for Malcolm Scott to recognize him.

"Did you bring the cattle in safely, Jock?" the laird said in his deep, rough voice.

"Aye, all are accounted for, my lord," the herdsman replied.

"Good," the laird responded, turning his attention to his little daughter again.

"My lord, there was something out on the moor that you should know of," Jock began, and when the laird looked up, his dark gray eyes focusing directly on the herdsman, he continued. "We found a lass, my lord."

"You found a lass? Where? Out in this storm?" the laird asked sharply.

"I cannot say for certain, my lord, but it would appear that the lass was traveling alone on foot and was caught unawares by the storm even as we were. She was clever enough to secrete herself between two of the cattle. It kept her from freezing to death. Robbie and the dogs found her when we went to fetch the cattle home."

"Where is she now?" the laird wanted to know.

"Robbie carried her to the pasture shelter where he and I had spent the night. He heated some whiskey and water and gave it to her. She fell back asleep, but after a night in the open she is, I suspect, very ill. We built up the fire, left food and water, and one of the dogs with her. We had no means to transport her, my lord, being on foot ourselves."

"Who is she? Did she tell you her name?" the laird asked sharply.

The herdsman shook his head. "Nay, my lord. The poor lass was barely conscious at all. If my son and I might take the cart and fetch her to the keep."

"*Here?* Why not your cottage, where your wife can nurse the wench?" the laird said. "She's probably some tinker's lass who got lost or separated from her people."

"Nay, my lord, I believe her to be a lady," Jock quickly responded.

"Why would you think a lady would be traveling alone and on foot across the moors?" the laird wanted to know.

"Her clothing, my lord. 'Twas not poor stuff. Her cloak is an excellent heavy wool, its hood edged in fur, its closure polished silver. She had good leather gloves upon her hands. I will wager they are lined in fur. I caught a glimpse of her gown beneath her cloak. Jersey of the best quality, and she carried a fine leather pouch strapped about her. She is not tinker's brat, or servant. She is a lady, my lord, and must come to the keep."

"Fiona, my angel, go and find your nurse," the laird instructed his little daughter. He kissed her cheek, and with a smile at him the little girl ran off. The laird turned back to Jock. "We'll ride out," he said, and then he called out that he wanted two horses saddled immediately. Standing up, he came down from the high board and, with Jock following in his wake, he hurried to the stables.

Malcolm Scott was a big, tall man with coal-black hair and eyes the color of a stormy gray sky that looked out from beneath a tangle of dark, heavy eyebrows. His thick wavy hair, which was longer than fashion dictated, was held back by a strip of leather and gave the appearance of being undisciplined. But the look in his eye bespoke a stern, strong man not easily moved. Everything about him appeared long. His straight nose. His thin mouth. The shape of his face with an oddly neat, squared chin that had the faint imprint of a dimple in its center.

As they entered the courtyard of the keep, a stableman ran forward with two horses. The laird mounted the large dappled-gray stallion while Jock clambered aboard a roan gelding. They clattered out and across the moor, heading toward the summer pastures and the pastures' small shelter. By horseback the distance was traveled more quickly, and they soon had the little structure in sight. No sooner had they dismounted than the dog inside began to bark.

"Hush, Shep!" the herdsman said as they entered. He was relieved to see that the fire in the tiny hearth was still burning. The oatcakes and the flask lay as they had been left. And the girl was still half conscious, half sleeping.

Malcolm Scott strode over to where Alix lay curled tightly up. He took her gently by a shoulder and rolled her onto her back. "She's flushed," he said, and put his hand upon her smooth forehead. "And feverish. We had best get her back to the keep." The herdsman was right. The lass was no tinker's get, cottager's wench, or servant girl. The high, smooth forehead, the dainty straight nose, the rosebud of a mouth, told him whoever she was she was not lowborn. "I'll carry her outside and take her up with me on my horse," the laird said to Jock. "You get the fire out and secure the shelter."

"Aye, my lord," Jock responded.

Malcolm Scott picked up the girl. Her head fell back from her hood against his arm, revealing a tangled mass of honey-colored curls. She was really quite lovely, he thought, but then the beautiful ones were always troublesome. Whoever she was, he would wager she was running away, but from whom? A husband? A father? He'd see she was made well again, and then he'd send her back from wherever she had come. Outside he handed the girl back to Jock briefly as he mounted his stallion, reaching back to take her up into his arms. She murmured softly as her cheek pressed against his leather jerkin, snuggling against him in a manner that made him oddly uncomfortable. He wasn't her savior, but she would soon know that. Urging his horse forward, he rode off towards the keep while behind him Jock closed up the shelter, then followed his master.

Alix finally awoke to find herself in a large bed. The sheet smelled of lavender. The coverlet was down, and she was not flea-bit. Opening her eyes fully, she saw a small hearth directly across from the bed blazing merrily. Next to the fireplace was a chair in which a woman dozed. "Can you tell me where I am?" she called out.

The woman woke immediately. She arose and came over to stand by the side of the bed. "Ahh, lassie, you're finally awake," she said in a soft voice. She was small and plump. Her hair was snow white yet her youthful round face held snapping blue eyes, a turned-up nose, and a broad mouth that now smiled at Alix. "I'm Mistress Fenella, the laird's housekeeper. Yer at Dunglais Keep."

"How long have I been here?" Alix asked softly.

"Ah, lassie, 'tis six days now since you were found out on the moor. Yer a very fortunate lass too that Jock and his lad found you. You might not have awakened at all if they hadn't. 'Twas canny of you to put yourself between the cattle for warmth." She turned. "I'm going to go fetch the laird now. He'll want to know that yer awake." Mistress Fenella bustled out of the room before Alix could question her further.

Alix pulled herself up, stuffing the pillows behind her. She was in one of her own night garments. Her eyes quickly swept the chamber. There was a trunk at the foot of the bed. To her right was a large window draped with a homespun linen and shuttered. Her bed was hung with the same linen. It was a natural color with a pattern of blue. To her left was a small table with a taper stick. Was it day or night?

The door to the room opened and a tall man strode in. "I am Malcolm Scott, the Laird of Dunglais," he said brusquely. "What is your name, mistress?"

"Alix," she answered him, startled. "Alix Givet, my lord."

"You are English," he noted almost scornfully.

"My parents came from Anjou," Alix said, stung by his tone.

"Where are your parents, mistress?" he asked.

"They are dead, my lord," and Alix crossed herself piously.

"And from whom were you running when we found you half-frozen out on the moor?" he demanded to know. "Who will sooner than later come pounding at my door insisting upon your return? Or are you being sought after by the local warden of the Marches and his sheriff?" He fixed her with a stern look.

"I am not a criminal, my lord. I have stolen nothing, nor broken any laws of which I am aware. I am a widow, and having been left with no means, set out to find my old mistress who has come into Scotland from England with her family. I hoped to be taken back into her service once again," Alix explained.

"You are no servant," he said. "The quality of your garments, the small bits of jewelry in your pack told me that."

"Where is my pouch?" she asked him nervously.

"In the chest at the foot of your bed, mistress. I have no need to steal," he said softly. "Why were you on foot? And how long had you been walking?"

"I was on foot because I would not take what was not mine from my father-in-law's stable," Alix said.

"You did not take a horse because you did not want him to know you were going," the laird responded. "Did the old man lust after you?" He chuckled.

"I had been walking for two days when the storm caught me," Alix said, ignoring his query. He didn't need to know why she had left Wulfborn. She had done nothing wrong, and she certainly wasn't going to put herself in the position of being forced back.

Malcolm Scott noted her avoidance of his question, but the truth was it didn't matter. As soon as the lass was fit, he would send her on her way. Of course he would give her the loan of a horse and have her escorted to her old mistress, wherever the woman was. Having rescued the girl from death once, he wasn't about to put her in harm's way again. No one had come seeking for her in the few days she had been at Dunglais. And winter was about to set in anyhow. If she had been truly wanted, they would have.

"Have I been ill?" Alix asked him, breaking into his thoughts.

"Aye. You were unconscious and ran a high fever for several days. Fenella thought you would pull through, and she's usually right," the laird told her.

"I'm hungry," she said softly.

He chuckled. "Then you are indeed on the road to recovery."

"What are you going to do with me, my lord?" Alix asked him.

"Do with you?" He looked puzzled by her query. Then he said,

"When you are well enough, I will help you to reach your old mistress."

"Oh."

She did not, he noted, appear happy by the news. But now was not the time to continue his interrogation of her. Fenella had said he was not to exhaust the lass, and if truth be known, she looked paler than when he had entered the room. "I'll go and see that you are brought something to eat."

"What day is it, please, my lord? And is it day, or is it night?"

"It's two days after Martinmas, and 'tis afternoon," he replied. Then he turned and was gone from the chamber.

Alix lay back against her pillows. She was safe. But for how long? Would Sir Udolf come riding over the border to demand her return? And if he did, would the laird turn her over to him? She somehow thought that he would. She had unwittingly intruded upon his life, and Alix suspected he wasn't a man who liked being imposed upon even unintentionally. He was very handsome, but his face was a stern, hard one. This was a man used to being obeyed and having his own way.

The door opened again, and Mistress Fenella bustled in with a young girl who was carrying a tray. "Here's a nice hot meal for you, lassie, and this is Jeannie. She'll be looking after you now that you seem to be on the mend. I didn't fill the trencher full. You may be hungry, but your belly will only be able to take a little food at a time. Eat what you can. Don't make yourself sick, lassie. And there's a cup of nice red wine for you. I've mixed an egg in it. It's strengthening."

"Thank you, Mistress Fenella," Alix said to the housekeeper.

"I'll leave you with Jeannie, then," Fenella responded, and hurried out.

"Can you eat by yourself, or shall I feed you?" Jeannie asked, setting the little tray down on Alix's lap. She took the serviette from it and tucked it in the neck of the girl's gown. "It's nice lamb stew with leek and carrot."

"I can feed myself, but thank you," Alix said. The stew in the round bread trencher smelled wonderful. She dipped her spoon into it. "Ummm, that's good!"

"It's the one dish Mistress Fenella won't let the cook prepare. She does it herself," Jeannie said chattily. "Did they tell you how lucky you were? The cows kept you warm. Robbie said you were near death when they found you."

"Robbie?"

"He's one of the two cowherds who discovered you wedged like a winkle on a rock between two of those big cattle. The laird brought you home himself," Jeannie said.

Alix tried to remember. She vaguely recalled the storm getting worse and then finding herself amid some cattle. But the rest of it was gone. "I can't recall anything," she told Jeannie. "Does he ever smile?"

"Who? Oh, the laird. Rarely except with his little daughter. Not since his wife ran off with her lover and broke his heart, poor man," Jeannie informed Alix. "But don't say I said such a thing. Mistress Fenella says we shouldn't gossip about such a tragedy."

Alix slowly spooned the lamb stew into her mouth. It was really quite delicious.

"She was a Ramsay, his wife," Jeannie continued on, ignoring her own words. "They found the body of the lover out in the heath. He was the laird's older half brother, and had never been well liked. They say he died with his sword in his hand. A better death than the traitor deserved."

"What happened to the laird's wife?" Alix wondered aloud.

"Some say the devil took her to breed his own bairns upon. He would need her body for that. Others say that it's obvious the laird and his half brother fought. When she saw her lover was getting the best of it, she rode off, and the laird didn't care enough to follow after her. She didn't go back to her family. Some months later the body of a woman was found, but there was no way of really identifying who it was. The garments were hers, but rotted away, and the body was half eaten by beasts, but they think it was her."

"How terribly sad," Alix said. "Especially for the little girl."

"The laird went to her family to tell them what had happened. Neither the Scotts nor the Ramsays wanted a feud over the lady's bad behavior," Jeannie explained.

"But if the body could not be identified, how can you be sure?" Alix asked.

"It had to be her. To this day no sight of her has ever been seen," Jeannie replied.

Alix scraped some of the bread from the trencher and ate it. "Do you think that the laird might have killed her and hidden the body for another to find?" she asked.

"He's capable of it, aye," Jeannie replied, "but he swore an oath to the priest that he didn't harm her. The Laird of Dunglais is noted among the border folk for his honesty. He's often called upon to settle disputes among the local clans because of it. They all know he can be trusted and that his word is good."

An interesting fact to have, Alix thought to herself.

"If you're through, I'll take your tray," Jeannie said. "Would you like me to come back and keep you company later? I can see yer tired now."

"I am," Alix admitted. "Aye, come back later," she said. Then she lay back. She felt warmer now, and her belly was full of hot food. She had gained some interesting information from young Jeannie. But despite the girl's reassurances, Alix couldn't help but wonder if the laird had indeed killed his wife for her betrayal of his honor. Still the man hadn't remarried. Perhaps his wife was still alive. Her eyes beginning to feel heavy, Alix fell asleep again. She awoke at the sound of her chamber door opening, and looking across the room, she saw a little face peering at her. She smiled.

Immediately the little girl stepped into the room. "My name is Fiona," she told Alix. "What's your name? My da said you were found on the moor. Why were you there? Were you lost?"

"My name is Alix, and aye, I suppose I was lost," she told Fiona. The child was very pretty with her father's black hair and inquisitive blue eyes. The blue eyes were not the laird's. "How old are you, Mistress Fiona?" she asked the little girl.

"I will be six come the fifth day of December," Fiona answered Alix. "How old are you, Mistress Alix?"

"I'm sixteen this August past," Alix answered her.

"Sixteen is old," Fiona observed, "but twenty is very old, I think."

Alix laughed aloud. "I suppose when you are to be six on the fifth day of December," she said, "sixteen does seem old, and twenty older yet."

"Do you know any stories?" Fiona asked.

"I know lots of stories," Alix replied.

Fiona trotted around the door, and crossing the room, climbed up into the bed with Alix. "Tell me a story," she said.

"Shall I tell you about a prince?" Alix inquired.

"Oh yes! I should like a story about a prince!" Fiona exclaimed, snuggling next to Alix, her small dark head on the older girl's shoulder.

"Once upon a time," Alix began, "there was a prince named Henry. He was only a baby when his father the king died and the prince had to become king of his land. They unofficially crowned him with one of his queenly mother's gold bracelets, for being a baby his little head was very small. He was the youngest king ever crowned, and presided over his lords sitting in his mother's lap. One month before his eighth birthday he was officially crowned king of England. And two years later he was crowned king of France."

"He was king of two lands?" Fiona asked, her tone disbelieving.

"For a time, yes, he was. He gained France through his mama," Alix said.

"Who was she?" Fiona wanted to know.

"A beautiful French princess named Katherine," Alix answered her.

"Are you English?" Fiona said.

"I was born in England, aye, but my parents came from Anjou."

"What happened to the prince who became king?" Fiona inquired.

"He married a French noblewoman. Her name was Margaret," Alix said.

"Did they love each other?" Fiona wondered. "My papa loved my mama. My mama is dead, you know."

"Kings cannot always marry for love," Alix explained. "But to answer your question, King Henry did grow to love his queen. And she came to love him. A prince was born to them. His name is Edward, and he is just eight years old."

"Will he be king one day?" Fiona wondered.

"I do not think so," Alix responded.

"Why not? Doesn't he want to be king?"

"Aye, he wants to be king, but another king overthrew his father. Now that man rules in England. It is unlikely that Edward Plantagenet will ever rule," Alix said. "Poor King Henry was ill, and his enemies took advantage of him to steal his throne."

"What happened to King Henry? Did they kill him?" Her blue eyes were curious.

"They tried, but he fled with the queen and their son," Alix replied.

"Where did they go to hide?" the little girl wanted to know.

"Right here in Scotland!"

Fiona giggled. "Here? Are they near Dunglais?"

"I don't know where they are now, but they are in Scotland," Alix told her.

"How do you know?" Fiona said.

"Because I was with them until several months ago," Alix answered.

"Did you lose them out on the moor?" Fiona inquired.

"Nay, somewhere else."

"Fiona!" The laird stood in the open door. "Everyone has been looking for you. You must not disturb Mistress Alix. She is still not well."

"Alix has been telling me a story," Fiona said as she scrambled down off the bed. "It was about a prince who became a king not just of England but of France too! And princesses and a prince who is just eight years old, but will never be a king. And they're hiding here in Scotland, Da! Could we go and find them tomorrow?"

"Not tomorrow," the laird said, "but perhaps another day. When Mistress Alix is well, so she may go with us."

"Oh, I would like that, Da!" the little girl cried as she practically danced to his side. "And can I come back to see Alix so she can tell me some more stories?"

"I would like that!" Alix said quickly before he might say nay.

The laird's mouth quirked with his amusement. "As long as you do not tire Mistress Alix, Fiona, you may visit her again. But you must tell your nurse where you are going when you do. She was very worried."

"She was asleep," Fiona said. "I could not tell her. She sleeps all the time, Da. And she treats me like a bairn. I'm not a bairn. I'm almost six!"

"You are?" The laird feigned surprise. "I did not know that."

Fiona giggled again. "Oh, Da, you did know."

"Six is a grand age," Alix noted.

Malcolm Scott looked across the bedchamber at Alix, and their eyes met for a brief moment. Was it sympathy she saw there? Then he nodded his head. "Aye, lassie, six is a very grand age." Reaching down, he took his daughter's hand. "Come along, Fiona Scott. We must let Alix get some more rest if she is to be well again."

Alix watched them go, Fiona turning about to wave at her. Alix waved back. Over the next few days Alix grew stronger with the good food she was being fed. After two days Mistress Fenella let her get up and sit for a time in the chair by the fire. Jeannie kept her company. The girl was full of chatter about the keep and its inhabitants. And then came the day that Alix stood up and began to walk for short distances about her chamber. She was feeling so much stronger. Better actually than she had in months.

November ended with a fierce blizzard that raged for almost two days. Alix was now joining the laird and Fiona in the hall. She began to teach the little girl how to sew properly. The housekeeper was delighted to have Fiona out from underfoot. The child's nurse was an old woman who should have been sent back to her cottage years ago.

"It isn't that she doesn't love the bairn, for she does," Fenella said to Alix one morning. "But she is too old now to watch over such an active little girl. And she cannot teach the child to be a lady with a lady's manners. A laird's daughter shouldn't be a hoyden. She needs to know how to sew fine stitches and direct her servants. She should be able to make soaps and perfumes. To know how a household should be managed. If the laird had remarried, his wife would teach Fiona those things, but he hasn't remarried."

"Why not?" Alix asked, curious.

"Robena Ramsay was the love of his life," Fenella said. "When she betrayed him, she broke his heart, but to betray him with his half brother was a terrible treachery. Black Ian was the bastard of the laird's father, born when the old laird was scarce fifteen. His mother was a cotter's lass. The old laird had a daughter by her too. But then he fell in love with a Bruce, married her, and was faithful to her the rest of his life. Oh, he acknowledged his bastards, but after his legitimate son was born things were different. Black Ian was almost grown by the time our laird was born, but he never forgave his father for favoring and putting his legitimate son first. Everyone knew that was how it should be," Fenella said, "but Black Ian would not accept it. He was the firstborn. Whenever he got the chance, he was cruel to his half brother, although never in sight of their father. One day, however, our laird's mother caught him throwing stones at her child, who was just four at the time. The lady took a stick to him, and when he dared to fight her back, she screamed at the top of her lungs. The old laird came running, saw his bastard attacking his wife and child, and beat him almost senseless. For Black Ian that was the final straw. He turned outlaw. Our laird grew up knowing about his half brother, but he didn't remember him, not having seen him since that fateful day."

"How did the laird's half brother get involved with the lady Robena?" Alix asked.

"Black Ian had been gone from here for several years. In that time his father had died, his brother became Laird of Dunglais and took a bride. Fiona was just a year old when it began, although no one knows how they met. Or even why the lady Robena betrayed her husband. But Black Ian made certain that our laird knew his wife had run away with him. And of course, the laird being an honorable man, had no choice but to go after his wife and avenge his honor. He killed his half brother, but the lady Robena ran off when she saw her lover would lose. They found her body months later. No one knows how she died, but when they found her she had been ravaged by wild beasts."

"So Jeannie told me. A terrible end nonetheless even for a bad woman," Alix murmured. "Jeannie says the laird swore an oath to her family that he didn't kill her."

Fenella nodded. "He did, and he would not have killed her. He couldn't. He loved her in spite of it, and she was the mother of his child. Malcolm Scott is an honorable and a good man, Alix," the housekeeper said. "It wasn't right that he be so wounded by his wife, but then she wasn't as perfect as he believed."

"You did not like her?" Alix was surprised.

"Some girls are suited for marriage at fourteen and motherhood at fifteen. Robena Scott was not," Fenella replied. "The laird fell in love with a beautiful young girl who fit his ideal of perfect womanhood. He was sophisticated. She was not. He was a friend of our late king and had been to court. She expected he would take her to court when they married, but he did not. Like all men, he wanted an heir first, but she birthed a daughter and the lady was angry at the child. She would hardly touch her, would not nurse her, and sulked. So to cheer her up, the laird took her to court, introducing her to the king and the queen. I am told she had a fine time.

"When they returned, he wanted her to give him his son, an heir for Dunglais. But she kept him from her bed, wept most of the time, and still showed little interest in Fiona. She wanted to go back to court. It was then she took to riding out alone. That must have been when she met Black Ian. Suddenly she was in a state of high excitement much of the time. The laird became suspicious, of course, for he is no fool. One day as he watched her ride out, the lady's tiring woman came to him and told him that she had watched her mistress take her jewelry from its box and secret it upon herself.

"The laird immediately called for his horse and rode after her. Even a man in love knows a woman who rides off with her jewelry is up to mischief of some kind. He found her, of course, with his half brother. What transpired between them that day only the laird is left alive to say. The fight ensued. We know that because the laird brought his half brother's body home to bury. Black Ian bore the Scott name, and the laird is both respectful and proud of it."

"Was Black Ian's mother still alive?" Alix asked, curious.

"Aye, and while she mourned her son, she knew that if Malcolm Scott killed him he had just cause," Fenella said. "The old laird was always good to Black Ian's mother, and after he died our laird treated her and his half sister, Moire, with kindness."

Alix absorbed all the information that both Fenella and Jeannie imparted to her. For the time being she knew that with the weather already wintry it was unlikely the laird would send her off. He was a good and honest man, but she suspected that once she told him more of her history he would be unlikely to allow her to remain at Dunglais once it was possible for her to travel. Nor would he trust her.

And Alix had decided that she wanted to remain. Dunglais was isolated. It was unlikely that if Sir Udolf bothered to seek for her that he would find her here. But the laird would need a very good reason to permit her to stay, and Alix had that reason. With no wife, mother, sister, or suitable female relation in residence, little Fiona had no one to teach her what a young lady would need to know. *But*

I can teach her, Alix thought. *And the sooner I broach the subject with the laird, the better.*

That evening, with Fiona tucked into her bed, Alix approached Malcolm Scott as he sat by the great hearth in the hall, a half-emptied goblet in his big hand. "May I speak with you, my lord?" she said in a quiet voice.

He looked up. Christ's bones, he thought, but she was a pretty lass. He nodded, and gestured towards the chair facing his. "You are feeling better," he said.

"I am, my lord, thanks to you, Fenella, and Jeannie," Alix answered.

"Good! Good!" His gaze drifted away from her.

"My lord, I thought that perhaps you would wish to know more of my history," Alix began, and his eyes cleared, fixing their steady look on her.

"I should very much like to learn more of you, Mistress Alix."

Alix gave him a small, amused smile. "My name, as I have told you, is Alix Givet. My parents, who are deceased, came from France with Margaret of Anjou when she wed King Henry. My father, Alexander Givet, was the queen's personal physician. My mother, Blanche, one of her ladies. Both were the children of minor nobility in Anjou. I was born in England and raised in Queen Margaret's household. My mother died over two years ago. My father and I fled with the royal household when the Yorkists overthrew King Henry.

"At a place called Towson, King Henry's forces were defeated a final time. The royal family, with their few remaining retainers, fled into the English border country. They sheltered with one Sir Udolf Watteson preparatory to coming into Scotland. During the weeks of our flight, Queen Margaret had reluctantly come to realize it was easier to beg sanctuary if your retinue was smaller than larger. She left behind most of her servants with friends and others who were willing to take them in." Alix paused briefly, then continued. She was surprised by the emotions she had begun to feel with the retelling.

To her surprise the laird offered her his cup. "Take some wine" was all he said.

Alix took two hearty sips and handed the vessel back to the man across from her. "Sir Udolf had a son for whom he sought a wife. The queen, with my father's permission, made the match between us. She is my godmother, and wanted a safe place for me and for my father who was ill. I should not have agreed to the match but for my father's health. He could no longer travel, and needed a home where he might live out his final months in peace.

"Sir Udolf is a good man, but his son was an odd, childlike creature. He had a mistress upon whom he doted. He wanted to marry her, but her birth was low. Sir Udolf would not have it. I knew all of this, but while I knew my husband would not love me, I asked only for his respect. But he would not give it. He punished me for marrying him, and for not being Maida. Still, I was a good wife, keeping the hall while caring for both my father-in-law and my father.

"Then poor Maida died in childbed, and her son with her. It was the same day in which my own father died." Alix crossed herself. "My husband was devastated. His mind had never been strong. During the next few days he went completely mad. He attempted to throttle me, but Sir Udolf and the servants saved me from what would have been a certain death. Then, as the servants attempted to restrain Hayle—that was my husband's name—he broke free of them and fled to the top of the house. For the briefest moment his sanity returned. He told his father he could not live without his Maida, and while Sir Udolf looked on helplessly, Hayle flung himself from an attic window to his death below." Alix crossed herself again.

"So you fled," the laird said. "Why? You did not kill the poor man. None of what happened was your doing, or your fault. Surely Sir Udolf did not blame you."

"Nay, Sir Udolf is a good man. But I knew I could not remain at Wulfborn. I told him so, and decided to find my godmother, the queen, here in Scotland. I hoped that she would take me back into her household. But Sir Udolf said that as his only son, his heir, was dead, he would have to remarry and father another son."

"God's blood!" Malcolm Scott swore immediately, seeing where Alix's tale was going. "He wanted to marry you!"

"I could not, my lord! I simply could not wed him. I pointed out to him the church would not give him a dispensation to marry his son's widow. He said the archbishop could be bought, and he would get his dispensation, and I would give him his heir. I thought at first that I might with time dissuade him, but he began to approach me in a manner with which I was not comfortable. I told him I wanted to return to Queen Margaret. He said he would ask her permission to wed me once he had his dispensation and that she would give him that permission. I suspected he was right. I knew then that I must escape Wulfborn and its lord. I waited until he planned a two-day hunting party with his men and it was then I fled. I never expected a snowstorm."

"The weather here in the borders is changeable," the laird said.

"I was fortunate you found me," Alix replied.

"If you cannot go to Queen Margaret, what will you do?" Malcolm Scott asked.

"I would remain at Dunglais, my lord. Please, I can be of service to you."

"Indeed," the laird replied, cocking one of his thick black eyebrows. "And just how would you *serve* me, Alix Givet?" He let his glance move slowly over her form.

Alix blushed at his open scrutiny. "Your daughter is growing up, and her nurse is too old. Fiona needs to learn the things that only a lady can teach her. You have no wife, or other female relation here at Dunglais, my lord. How do you expect to prepare your daughter for the marriage she must make one day?" she boldly demanded to know.

He looked surprised. "What would you teach her, then?" he said.

"Fiona must learn to read, to write, to do simple sums so she can be certain her steward isn't stealing from her. She needs to study French, for she might go to court one day. She should learn how to sew and embroider. Her table manners are terrible and must be corrected. She needs to know all manner of household matters, and how to treat large and small illnesses that will afflict her servants and her Dunglais folk. Her old nurse cannot teach her any of these things, but I can. And I am skilled in certain healing arts, having learned them from my own father. Until Fiona is old enough to manage your hall, you need someone like me." She looked at him hopefully.

The laird was thoughtful for several long moments and then he spoke. "You make a good case for yourself, Alix Givet," he said. "And I have seen you already with my child. Fenella says that Fiona likes you. But can you be content to remain here? I am a simple border lord, nothing more. You will find no excitement at Dunglais. Your life here will be most circumspect."

"I can be content here, my lord," Alix assured him.

"Twelve silver pennies a year to be paid at Michaelmas then, material for two gowns and two chemises, the loan of a mare to ride. You will keep the bedchamber that you have and eat at the high board. This in exchange for your service to me. Is it suitable, Alix Givet?" he asked her.

"It is most acceptable," she replied without hesitation as relief swept over her. She was safe! And it was unlikely that if Sir Udolf ever got his dispensation that he would find her here in the isolated place. "I will take up my duties tomorrow, my lord."

"Go to bed, then," he told her, and he watched as, with a curtsy, she left the hall. Alix had given him pause for thought. She had been perfectly right when she said Fiona needed her, or someone like her. He didn't intend marrying ever again. Once had been more than enough. If only Robena had been unique in her behavior, but he knew she was not. He had seen women like her at court whose only passion was for their own pleasure. Alix was in a difficult position, he knew. He thought it rather brave of her to speak so boldly to him, pointing out that he was not doing all he could for his child.

Fiona was his heiress. And any husband he found for her one day would expect her to be fully capable of managing her hall, her servants, and her Dunglais folk. His servants, even Fenella, could not teach her what she needed to know as a laird's only child. Clever of Alix to assess the situation and take advantage of it. But, of course, by taking advantage of his need she had assured herself of a home. But would a girl raised in a royal court be truly happy at Dunglais? Only time would tell.

The Christmas season was upon them. The countryside about Dunglais's dark stone towers was white with snow. Fiona was now spending her mornings at her studies. He was amused by her excitement at learning French. Now she would greet him each morning with a cheerful *Bonjour, Papa!*, and because he did speak French he would return her greeting with an equally bright *Bonjour, ma fille. Bonjour, Mademoiselle Alix.* And Fiona would giggle delightedly.

The first time it had happened, Alix had said, "I did not know you could speak French, my lord." And she was indeed surprised.

"I was educated in my youth," the laird replied. "And I have spent time at court. It always pleased Queen Marie to be addressed in her own language."

"What did you do at court?" Alix asked him, curious.

"The little king's father and I had similar interests," he responded. "I was his friend, and with him when he was killed."

"How did he die?" Alix asked.

"He was preparing to fire a cannon. It exploded, and he was killed," Malcolm Scott said. "We were, as usual, fighting the English. As soon as the queen heard, she came with the little king to rally the troops, and we triumphed in the fray."

"What interests did you share?" Alix queried.

"Guns, good whiskey, and beautiful women" came the reply. He looked directly at her. "Has anyone ever told you that you're a very pretty lass, Mistress Alix?"

"She is, isn't she, Papa?" Fiona piped up. "I think Alix has the most beautiful hair. I wish mine were that dark gold and curly."

"Your hair is glorious, *ma petite*," Alix told the little girl. "It has the ebony sheen of a raven's wing, and is thick and wavy. Curls can be *très difficile*."

The laird smiled. It pleased him that Alix was so thoughtful of his little daughter. It was as if she really cared for the child. "I think you both have glorious hair," he said.

An enormous Yule log was dragged into the hall and hoisted into the fireplace on St. Thomas Night. Alix took Fiona out to gather branches of pine and holly with which to decorate the hall. She had the child watch as she directed the servants in their placement of the greenery. "Next year I shall expect you to do this," she told her. Together the young woman and the child set scented beeswax candles about the hall.

Fenella had, at Alix's request, made patterns of the laird's chemise and a shirt. Then, with Alix aiding her, she cut pieces for the two garments. The chemise was the easier garment to sew, and little Fiona set to work under Alix's guidance to complete the garment while Alix sewed a new shirt for the laird. The child's stitches were not small, nor were they as neat as they might be, but the knee-length chemise was made with love.

"They're like mother and daughter," Iver, Dunglais's steward, observed to Fenella.

"Aye, they are," Fenella said softly.

"Don't even consider it," Iver responded. "He'll not wed again. Not after *her* betrayal. He no longer trusts women, if indeed he ever did."

"He fell in love," Fenella responded.

"A foolish error in judgment on our laird's part," Iver noted dryly.

"Not all women will betray a man. If that were so, where would humankind be today? You're a sour lad this day."

"Don't expect him to wed the wench," Iver warned. "She's a good lass, even I can see that—but he'll not make the same mistake twice."

"He needs an heir," Fenella said.

"He has an heiress, and is content," Iver answered.

"Perhaps," Fenella remarked. "But I think every man wants a son."

Iver chuckled. "You will have your own way in this matter, lass, won't you? Well, go ahead and dream that the laird will fall in love with the little English girl and make her his wife. Maybe he will. I wouldn't object, nor would any other at Dunglais."

"It could happen," Fenella replied stubbornly. "A man needs a soft companion."

"Then he takes a mistress," Iver said with a mischievous grin. "I'll wager he's thinking about it too. Have you seen the way he looks at her of late? There is budding lust in the laird's eye, Fenella."

"It could begin that way, but if it does it will end with Alix having a ring on her finger and the laird having one through his nose," Fenella said with a throaty laugh.

The steward laughed too. "We'll watch together," he replied.

Chapter 5

On Christmas Day Fiona Scott presented her father with the chemise she had made for him. She had, with Alix's help, wrapped the garment in a piece of red Scott plaid, tying it with one of Alix's green hair ribbons and decorating her parcel with a small bit of pine. "For you, Da," she said. "I wish you a happy first day of Christmas." Then she curtsied prettily as Alix had taught her and smiled up at him.

"Why, Fiona, what is this?" The laird was genuinely surprised.

"I made it myself!" Fiona told him. "Alix showed me."

The laird carefully unwrapped his gift, untying the ribbon, unfolding the fabric. He held the garment up, admiring it.

"It's a chemise!" Fiona crowed excitedly just in case he might not recognize it.

"It is indeed," Malcolm Scott said. "And a finer one I will never own. Thank you, Fiona. And to think you made it yourself. I did not realize you could sew. I have some socks in need of darning." His gray eyes, usually stormy, were twinkling.

"Oh, Da, I don't know how to darn a sock," Fiona told him.

"But you will learn, *ma petite*," Alix said, "just as you are learning to sew." Then she handed the laird her own parcel. "For you, my lord. A happy Christmas, or, as my mama used to say, *joyeux Noël!*"

He took the gift she offered him, and opening it, discovered a new shirt. It was exquisitely made, and her stitches were so tiny as to be invisible. "Thank you, Alix Givet," he said to her. "This is most kind of you." Their eyes met briefly, and then she looked away, color flooding her cheeks. The laird spoke again. "Girls who give gifts must receive them as well," he said in a light, teasing tone. He stood up. "Come, both of you. Come and see what I have for you both." He led them from the hall, Alix signaling to Iver to bring cloaks for herself and little Fiona.

They moved outside, following the laird across the keep. Reaching the stables, they were greeted by the head stableman, who, nodding to his master, disappeared back into the building, returning several moments later leading a pretty roan mare with a white star upon her forehead and a dappled gray pony with a dark mane. He brought them to a stop before the laird, awaiting further instructions.

Malcolm Scott took the pony's reins and handed them to his daughter. "For you, my Fiona," he said. "Since you have now learned from me how to properly ride, you should have your own beast. Happy first day of Christmas!"

The six-year-old girl squealed with delight. "Oh, Da, thank you! Does my pony have a name? Or may I name her myself?"

"What would you call her?" the laird asked his daughter.

"Stormy," Fiona said. "Her coat is the color of a blustery sky."

"Then Stormy she shall be," the laird responded with a smile. "Now talk to her, Fiona, so she may get used to your voice. And walk her about the courtyard so she begins to know your touch."

The little girl stood on her tiptoes and whispered into the pony's alert ear for a moment or two. Then she grasped the animal's bridle firmly and began to walk it.

As Fiona moved away from her father and Alix, Malcolm Scott turned to the young woman. She had a small doting smile upon her face as she watched the child. Then, suddenly aware his eyes were upon her, Alix focused to meet his gaze.

"You could not have given her anything better," she said. "Fiona loves to ride out. Until the spring permits her to do so again, her new pony will keep her very busy right here in the courtyard. And it will certainly help me to keep her mind upon her studies, for until they are done, and done well, there will be no riding."

"You are a hard taskmistress," he remarked.

"Queen Margaret and my mother taught me that you complete your duties first. And when you have done them well, then you may take your pleasure, but not before. It is not really a difficult lesson to learn. Fiona will be a much better chatelaine knowing it, my lord. Her hall will always be neat and fresh. Her husband will be content, too, surrounded by an orderly household and well-trained servants."

"You are a very serious lass for one so young," the laird noted. The horse by his side danced impatiently.

"Teaching a child well is a serious endeavor, my lord," Alix answered him. "I have a duty to both Fiona and to you in this."

"Happy first day of Christmas, Alix Givet," Malcolm Scott said. "The mare is your gift from me. She is yours, and when you decide to leave Dunglais, as you eventually will, you will take her with you. Her name is Darach, which means 'oak' in the Scots tongue. She is a delicate beauty, but she is deceptively strong even as you are." He handed Alix the mare's reins.

"My lord, this is too generous!" Alix said, but she was already stroking the mare's nose with gentle fingers.

Malcolm Scott was enchanted by the picture they made. Alix with her hood fallen back from her face to reveal her honey-colored curls as she lay her head against the roan mare's dark coat. He had offered her a most extravagant compliment in addition to the horse, but she had not even noticed, so much was her delight in his gift. Most women would have twittered and demurred over his words. They would have taken what they considered an opportunity to flirt with him, to lead him on, but Alix had not.

Now she looked up at him. "I will not leave Dunglais as long as Fiona needs me, my lord," Alix told him. "You have my word on it. If you remarry then of course I would go, for it would not be seemly for me to remain when you had a wife to watch over your daughter." She rubbed the mare's nose again. "She is beautiful, and I have never had a finer horse. I had to leave my beast behind when I departed Wu . . . my former home. You were right when you said I didn't want them to know I was going." She began to walk the mare about the courtyard following little Fiona's pony.

"Why didn't you want them to know?" he asked her softly.

"As I have previously mentioned, my deceased husband's father wished to marry me as he had no wife and no other heirs. The very thought was repellent to me despite the fact he is a decent man. I know he would have been good to me, but I thought of him more like a parent than a husband. How could I lay with a man who had been a father figure to me? How could I couple with him and give him a child?" Alix shuddered. "I told him the church would not allow it. But he said he could get a dispensation since there was no blood involved between us. When he sent the local priest off to York with his request and a pouch of coins to expedite that desire, I knew I must flee. I waited until he planned a two-day hunt to stock the house larder for the winter, and then I made my own plans. I told everyone that I would fast and pray for two days while their master was gone, and I was not to be disturbed. And early in the morning, before my father-in-law was even gone off to hunt, I made good my escape. I did not take my horse, and it was mine not his, because I did not want it known I was gone."

"It was a very brave thing you did," the laird told her, "but where did you plan to go when you left? Why did you come north instead of remaining in England?"

"I was afraid to stay in England for fear someone would recognize me from King Henry's court. The Yorkists are not kind to their enemies. I hoped at first I might return to Queen Margaret, but then I realized that would be the first place Sir Udolf would seek for me. And I knew that with his honorable offer of marriage the queen would send me back to him." Alix sighed. "I thought then that if I could reach the Scots court your queen might take me into her service, and I would be safe."

"But would not Queen Marie wonder why you did not return to Queen Margaret?" the laird asked Alix, curious.

"Your queen will give mine sanctuary, but nothing else. It is unlikely they will ever meet. Poor King Henry will never regain his throne, I think, and Scotland must deal with England. While a slim thread of blood connects these two queens, it is not enough for Queen Marie to endanger her own child's throne by antagonizing England's new king. And that king may bluster and blow, but he will not start a war over such a trifle. Henry of Lancaster is finished. Eventually he will be seduced into venturing back into England, where he will be captured and killed. If the queen and the prince travel with him their lives will be forfeit too," Alix told the laird.

He was surprised by her grasp of the situation, but then he thought he shouldn't be. She had been raised in a royal court. She was intelligent and understood the dynamics of the situation. "Aye," he agreed with her. "You are correct, Alix Givet."

"I want nothing to do with this situation," Alix continued. "I never wanted to be a creature of the court like my mother. And in the end I suspect my father, except for his deep loyalty to his countrywoman, would have been content to settle in a quiet village somewhere and live out his life in peace. I would have liked that too." She sighed.

They had traversed the courtyard several times now. Arriving back at the stable, Alix gave Darach's reins back to the head stable-man. "I will exercise her daily," she told him with a sweet smile.

The man nodded. "She'll be ready for you, mistress," he told her.

"Fiona," Alix called to her little charge. "Come now and bring Stormy back. She needs to go into her warm stable."

The child obeyed, but both the laird and Alix could tell she was reluctant to leave her beloved new pony.

"You are good with her," the laird noted. "She already loves you."

"I love her," Alix responded. "She is a dear little girl." Then she said boldly, "Her blue eyes. Are they her mother's?"

"Aye," he said tersely.

"I thought as much, but everything else about her is you, my lord. No one would mistake her for anyone else's daughter," Alix remarked.

"Can I ride out with Stormy tomorrow?" Fiona asked, coming up to her father. She handed the pony's reins to the head stableman. "Can I, Da? Can I?"

"There is too much snow on the hills right now, Fiona," the laird answered.

"Daaa!" Fiona stamped her little foot.

"Fiona, your father has spoken true. There is too much snow outside the gates. And hungry wolves, and badgers too just waiting for a fat pony and a sweet little lass. We will ride in the courtyard," Alix told the child. "And please do not stamp your foot again at your father. It is disrespectful."

"But, Alix, I can't gallop in the courtyard," Fiona protested.

"We don't have to ride at all," Alix responded calmly.

Fiona's lower lip formed itself into a pout. Her blue eyes were mutinous.

Alix took the child's hand in hers. "Come, and let us go in now. I have it on the best authority that Cook is serving baked apples and sugar wafers today."

The laird almost laughed aloud as the rebellion disappeared swiftly from his daughter's eyes and the pout was replaced with a wide smile.

"I *love* baked apples and sugar wafers," Fiona said as she trotted obediently by Alix's side back towards the keep.

"Has a way wi' the bairn, she does," the head stableman remarked, and then he disappeared into the stable with Fiona's pony.

The laird chuckled. Alix did manage Fiona very well. Everyone noted it. Fenella and Iver in the hall, and now the stableman. He was almost jealous at the lovely English girl's way with his child, but he knew he couldn't handle Fiona; and her old nurse, now happily ensconced in a cottage in his village, had not been able to since

Fiona began to walk. It had been a miracle the child hadn't done herself a serious mischief. It was a great relief to have his daughter in such good and capable hands. Now maybe everyone would cease their nagging about his lack of a wife. Fiona was his heiress, and that was that.

He had a young uncle, Robert Ferguson of Drumcairn, who had been responsible for bringing Robena Ramsay to his attention and helping him to arrange the match between the Scotts and the Ramsays. Ever since Robena's betrayal of her husband, his uncle had been desperate to correct what he deemed his error in judgment. He was always riding over from his own holding to Dunglais, and each visit brought with it a new candidate for his nephew's hand. And the more the laird refused, the harder his uncle tried. Malcolm Scott tolerated his uncle because he was his late mother's much younger half brother, and she had loved him well. But he had no intention of remarrying and being made a fool of again by any woman.

Twelfth Night passed, and a hard winter set in with at least one snowstorm every few days. It was all the Dunglais folk could do to keep a path shoveled from the keep proper to the stables, the cow shed, the poultry house, and the granary. The laird's cattle were brought into the cattle barns. His flock of sheep milled in a pen that had been built within the courtyard. The days were cold, and as he watched Alix with his daughter the laird began to find the nights colder and longer than he could ever remember them.

The English girl filled his hall with warmth and laughter. He noticed his servants deferring to her, going to her for instructions. He suddenly realized she was nursing the sick among them. Each morning they would come to wait outside of the small chamber Fenella now told him was Alix's apothecary.

"She would make a good wife," Fenella ventured one day when the laird had noted Alix's busy day. "Everything is better with her here."

"You ran the household well enough," Malcolm Scott replied.

"I do it better with her instruction," Fenella said dryly. "You need a wife, and your uncle would be pleased to see you take one and sire a son. Are the Scotts of Dunglais to die off because a Ramsay broke your heart? Broken hearts heal, my lord."

"You forget yourself, Fenella," the laird growled at her.

Fenella laughed at him. "We're blood kin, Malcolm Scott. My mother may have been a cotter's daughter, but my father was your own grandfather. I have always spoken my mind, and I always will. If it displeases you, I will gladly take myself back to my mam's cottage."

"If you didn't look so much like the portrait of the old devil in the gallery," the laird told her, "I would doubt your paternity, as did most in the village when you were born. The lusty old devil had to be near seventy when he put you in your mam's belly. Nay, Fenella, don't leave us, but cease your gab. I have my uncle to bedevil me about taking another wife, but I'll not do it. Robena Ramsay killed my taste for married life."

"Yer as lusty as your father and your grandsire, my lord. How long has it been since you've bedded a woman? There is no gossip in the village. Mistress Alix is a lady born. She does not appear to me to be flighty as was your wife. And see how well little Fiona has come to love her."

"I'd bed her," Malcolm Scott told his housekeeper, "if she were of a mind. She's pretty, and sweet-natured. I will admit she tempts me of late. I should not object to taking a fair mistress, Fenella. A mistress can be disposed of, but a wife cannot."

Fenella sighed deeply and audibly. But as she left the laird she considered that if he took Alix for his mistress the young woman might become with child by the laird. He wouldn't want his son born a bastard, she was certain. Fenella smiled. Aye. He'd take her to wife then, but he would be content with Alix, she was certain. She was the total opposite of Robena Ramsay.

Robena had been high-strung and childish, but she had also been incredibly beautiful, with snow-white skin, bright blue eyes, and long, dark auburn hair. Malcolm Scott had been dazzled by her.

And in the beginning Fenella believed that Robena had loved him back. But then, as the laird's desire for an heir grew, Robena's wish to go to court increased. There were none at Dunglais to admire and flatter the laird's beauteous wife. She needed a larger stage, but then Robena found herself with child. Furious, she sulked her way through her confinement. When little Fiona had been born she was beside herself with anger that she had birthed a daughter and not the longed-for son. She refused to nurse the infant and would not hold her.

And then Robena fell into a deep depression. Nothing the laird did could console her. He brought her little gifts. She would look at them, sigh, and turn away. There were days when she could not arise from her bed, and she wept inconsolably. Finally Malcolm Scott told his wife that if she could not recover from her melancholy he could not take her to visit the court. Within three days the laird's wife had recovered from her unhappiness. She grew more excited each day with the anticipation of their visit to court.

And it was, Robena told Fenella upon their return, everything she had imagined, and even more. She had been admired, flirted with, and courted by important men. The king himself had kissed her, and not upon the hand or cheek. But upon her lips, she giggled. She had wanted to stay, but her husband had grown jealous of all the attention paid her, forcing her back to Dunglais, Robena said. He wanted a son. But another child would spoil her body for certain. She would be unattractive to other men. And it was then the laird's wife began to deny him her bed.

He was patient at first, Fenella admitted to herself. And even when she began riding out alone, he tolerated her behavior because she seemed so nervous and skittish. But her mood seemed to soar from another near depression to a near hysteria of excitement that grew with each passing day. Fenella suspected that the laird's wife harbored some secret, but because she wasn't certain, she held her peace.

And then came that fatal day that Robena Scott had ridden out, and the girl who served her came to Fenella to tell her she had seen her lady taking her jewelry and secreting it on her person before she had gone. Fenella sent the girl to the laird with this news, for she did not want to bring it herself. The housekeeper now knew her suspicions had been correct. Robena Scott had a lover and was now planning to run away with him.

And Malcolm Scott had ridden out to return with his bastard brother's body to be buried. His wife, however, was never seen again. Fenella did not believe the body found months later out on the moor was Robena's, but the laird had sworn to the Ramsays that he had not harmed Robena, and Malcolm Scott's word was good in the borders. Still, there were times these past four years when Fenella wondered that if the laird had not harmed his wife he knew what had happened to her.

Was she still alive? Somewhere. Was that the true reason for his obstinate refusal to marry again? Nay. Malcolm Scott would have followed Robena to the ends of the earth if for no other reason than to finish their alliance properly. The bishop of St. Andrew's was not above helping a gentleman end a bad marriage and especially if the wife could or would not give her lord a son. Nay. Robena Ramsay was dead, and good riddance to her. Now Fenella decided she must manage to get sweet Alix into her kinsman's bed. The lass needed a husband every bit as much as the laird needed a wife. And besides, little Fiona was already thinking of her as her mother.

January drew to an end and February promised more snow. The laird's ewes were birthing their lambs in a small hay-filled barn where they would remain safe from predators who now and again managed to creep into the keep's courtyard in the dark of the night to steal a tender lambkin. Each time the dogs set up a barking the laird's men would take up their staffs and lanterns to patrol the keep, making certain all was secure, and the thieves, both two and four-footed, remained on the other side of the keep's stone walls, not within them.

The laird could not help but watch Alix as she moved about his hall directing his servants, as she sat by the great hearth carefully instructing Fiona in her writing, or when she sat by his side at meals. Her fragrance was elusive. Sometimes a hint of wild rose. Sometimes the fresh scent of a wind across the fields. He would survey her delicate hand as she reached for the cottage loaf on the table. His eyes caressed her graceful form as she came towards him, smiling, a welcoming goblet held out to him.

Malcolm Scott struggled to keep his lust in check, but it was a losing battle. What in the name of all that was holy had made him believe that a lovely young woman in his household would simply be another Fenella? He had been without female companionship for far too long. Longer than any could imagine. Unlike most men who found it simple to casually bed a woman merely to satisfy their lust, the Laird of Dunglais did not. Oh, in his youth he had been like other men, rollicking and wenching. But then Malcolm Scott had fallen in love with Robena Ramsay, and lust satisfied upon the body of someone you loved, he discovered, was far more satisfying than mere lust satisfied.

But he would never love again. And his needs had to be met, didn't they? He did, of course, now and again visit one of the village women. She was a pleasant, clean widow who had no illusions about why her master was using her body, and was grateful for the silver coin he always left her, the brace of rabbits, or the game bird that always came to her afterwards. Her children were well clothed and fed because of it, and she frankly enjoyed his visits. But no one would have called her his mistress.

A mistress lived in her lord's house and met all her lord's needs. Unlike a wife, she could be cast off when her lord became bored with her or brought a new wife into the house. But the Laird of Dunglais would not be bringing another wife into his house. And if he managed to make Alix his mistress he still needed her to be there for Fiona until his child was grown. What if she did not please him in his bed? Once he had taken her, their relationship could never again be the same even if he had her only that one time. She wasn't a virgin, and had been taught the sensual arts by another man. Malcolm Scott paused for thought. She hadn't been wed that long. She could be retrained like any intelligent creature, couldn't she? Yet what if he did not please her, or she did not wish to become his mistress? He shrugged. Did it really matter? She would lie like all women lied, and she would be content with being in his favor.

Alix had become increasingly aware that the laird was contemplating her in a different manner than he had before. Raised at a royal court she had watched the byplay between lustful men and the women they sought to seduce. The interest in Malcolm Scott's eyes as he watched her bespoke a hunter stalking his prey. She began to avoid the hall as much as she might, departing for her own chamber immediately after the evening meal. And sometimes Alix would make an excuse not to sit at the high board at all, and eat in the kitchens with the other servants. She wanted no man, and she certainly did not want him to mistake her growing love and care of little Fiona for anything else than what it was. She certainly did not want him to believe her kindness stemmed from a desire to attract him to her bed.

Then one night his hand touched hers as she reached out to cut herself a wedge from the half wheel of cheese upon the board. "Let me do that for you," he said.

Alix flushed, pulling her hand quickly away from his. "I can do it," she said.

"But I should like to do it for you," he responded. "There is much I should like to do for you if you would let me, Alix." His gray eyes locked onto her green ones.

"I need nothing more than I have, my lord," she quickly told him, the blush on her cheeks now receding as she grew pale with the shock of his words. All along she had hoped it was her imagination playing tricks upon her where the laird was concerned, but now she knew her instincts had been right all along. He had begun to lust after her. What was she to do? How could she remain at Dunglais if he forced himself upon her? What would happen to little Fiona? What would happen to Alix Givet?

Malcolm Scott cut a slice of the cheese, holding it out to her on the tip of his knife. A faint wintry smile touched his lips but briefly as he let his eyes linger a moment on her. "Here," he said softly.

Alix took the cheese. To refuse when she had been attempting to cut it herself would have been inelegant. Her fingers plucked the offering from his knife. "Thank you, my lord," she whispered, and quickly looked away.

He laughed softly. A cruel sound. A knowing one. The battle had been engaged, and she was wise enough to know it. How long would it take him? he wondered to himself. How long until he could bed her? Her honey-colored hair looked soft. Was it? Her breasts beneath her simple brown jersey gown were nicely rounded. His fingers itched to fondle those sweet globes. To suckle upon their nipples. To his surprise he felt his manhood tightening in his breeks. It had been a long time since he had thought such thoughts, had his member behave in such a way.

Alix ate her cheese, but suddenly it was tasteless in her mouth. Jesu and his holy Mother Mary help her! What was she to do? Reaching for her goblet, she took a long drink of her wine. She recognized lust on a man's face, in his eyes, when she saw it. Unable to help herself, she arose quickly from the high board. "If you will excuse me, my lord. Fiona. I find I am suddenly unwell." Then she fled the hall.

"Poor Alix," his daughter said sympathetically. "She works very hard, Da. We must be kinder to her, I think."

"Indeed, my daughter, I have been thinking exactly that," the laird agreed with his child. "I will send Fenella to make certain she is all right." He called for his housekeeper and instructed her to go to Alix and see if she needed anything.

Fenella departed the hall. She knew she would find Alix in her bedchamber, but when she reached it the door was barred to her. "Alix, are you all right?" she called through the door, rattling the handle as she did.

"I am not feeling well," Alix said.

"Let me in," Fenella said in a firm voice.

The door opened to reveal a pale-faced Alix.

Fenella entered the chamber, closing the door behind her. "What is the matter, Alix?" she asked. "The laird was worried when you left the hall."

"I should not have left it were I not afraid of him," Alix replied.

"*Afraid?* Why would you be afraid of the lord? You have certainly never before been afraid of him. What has he done that you fear him?"

"His attitude has changed towards me," Alix said, and she sat heavily upon her bed. "He looks at me when he believes I do not notice, but I do. I have seen men look at women like that before. I do not want him to look at me like *that!*"

Fenella sat down next to the young woman. "He cannot help himself," she said. "Dunglais has been without a woman in residence ever since his wife ran away."

"Are there not women in the village for him?" Alix replied.

"Aye, there is a widow, but he visits her only when he must," Fenella said.

"I do not want another husband," Alix said. "I am content as I am."

"And the laird does not want another wife, or so he says," Fenella surprised Alix by saying.

Alix grew even paler. "Then what does he want?" But she already knew the answer to her own question. "Oh! It is unkind that he would insult me in this way!"

"You are offended that he would take you for his lover?" Fenella inquired. "But if you do not want a husband, and you do not want a lover, what do you want?"

"I want everything to be as it was. I want to take care of little Fiona and see to her education. Nothing more. I want no man, Fenella!" Alix cried, and she began to weep bitterly. "If the laird cannot understand that then I must leave Dunglais as soon as the snows are gone and I can travel in safety."

"Did you love your husband so much, then?" Fenella said. "I did not think it so."

"I despised Hayle! He didn't want me for his wife. He wanted his mistress. A miller's daughter, but his father would not have it. I knew that when I agreed to wed him, and I did so only that my poor father could have a safe place to lay his head in his last days. Still, I was willing to take this man for my husband, keep his hall, bear his children. I did not ask for him to love me. I asked him to respect me, to respect my position as his lawful wife. But he hated me, and took every opportunity to show it. Hayle killed himself, you know. Oh, his father and I told the priest it was an accident, but even the priest knew it wasn't, although he said naught. My husband killed himself when his mistress and their son died in childbed. He was not able to accept my sympathy, to at least try to begin anew with his wife. He wanted to be with her, and because he loved her that much I could not fault him. But his death, and that of my own father, freed me. I will never again allow any man to have dominion over me." Her tears had stopped now with the recitation of her tale. "Tell your master that he must treat me with respect, Fenella, or I will go. You are his friend. He will listen to you."

Fenella drew a deep breath and then she spoke. "Was your husband cruel to you in your bed?" she asked candidly, and she looked directly at Alix. "Is that why you fear a lover? The laird is a kind man, Alix. He would never be cruel."

Alix's face had gone white at Fenella's words. "Will you pander for him?" she gasped in shocked tones.

Fenella arose from her place by Alix's side. "I will tell the laird of your distress," she said stiffly, and then she left the bedchamber.

Alix followed after her, barring the door once again.

Returning to the hall, the housekeeper took the laird aside. Fiona was playing contentedly with the dogs by the hearth. "Her marriage was an unhappy one," she said.

"I had assumed that," Malcolm Scott answered.

"Not just the situation in which she found herself," Fenella responded. "The husband was cruel to her in their bed. When I asked her about it, she grew as white as the snows outside the hall windows and accused me of pandering for you. I should have been offended but that her pain was so strong it was visible, my lord."

"Ahh," the laird said, "then she must be wooed gently." He smiled.

"I am not certain that she can be wooed at all, my lord," Fenella said. "She told me to tell you if you cannot treat her with respect she must leave Dunglais. You cannot let her go, for that would break Fiona's heart. The wee lass has had enough sadness in her life without losing the only mother figure she knows or can remember. You must satisfy your manly urges somewhere else," Fenella concluded.

"Nay, I will have Alix," he replied softly, "but when I do, she will come to me willingly. I would not harm my daughter's happiness, but I will not deny myself the prize I want."

"Offer her marriage," Fenella suggested wickedly.

"If her distaste for carnal union is as strong as you say it is, that would but terrify her further," Malcolm Scott said. "Nay, kinswoman, Alix needs to be wooed with kindness and gentleness, for she has never before been wooed."

"Be careful, my lord," Fenella cautioned him. "If not for Alix's sake then for Fiona's. She has come to love her companion well."

At that moment the little girl came to join them. "Is Alix well now, Fenella?" she asked innocently.

"She will be on the morrow, lass," Fenella said. "But 'tis your bedtime. I will take you since Alix cannot. You will see her in the morning." She took the child's hand and led her from the hall.

Malcolm Scott went to the sideboard and poured himself a dram of his own whiskey. Then he went to sit by the fire and consider what Fenella had told him. What the hell was the matter with a man that he would treat his wife cruelly in their bed? And what cruelty had he inflicted upon her? She was a beautiful young woman of respectable breeding who had been given to the Englishman as a bride. Could he not have enjoyed her favors as well as that of his mistress? Was it necessary to punish her for not being the wife he wanted? Most men never got the wife they wanted. They got the wife who was given to them. He had taken the wife he wanted, and look how well that had turned out. But he could not imagine being cruel to any woman. He had certainly never been cruel to Robena. If he could have saved her, he would have. *I will go slowly with Alix,* he told himself. She deserved to know how sweet passion can be when it is shared between two consenting parties. *I will win her over, and sooner than later.*

In the days that followed, the laird's behavior returned to that which it had been before he had revealed his desire for Alix to her. She was wary of him, but as February ended and March began she grew less so. And then one evening as she returned to the hall to oversee the closing up of the house for the day he called to her.

"Fetch a goblet, Mistress Alix, and sit with me by the fire," he invited.

Alix did not know why she accepted his invitation, but it seemed more the plea of a lonely man in need of a friend than it did a lustful man attempting to seduce a female. She poured some wine into a cup and came to sit with him. "I smelled spring in the air today," she said with a small smile. "And the lambs in the paddock are more frolicsome."

"Spring has not failed us yet," he agreed. "I would apologize to you, Alix."

"Apologize? For what need you beg my pardon, my lord?"

"Some weeks back I frightened you, and for that I am sorry," the laird said.

Alix stiffened. "My lord, I am so happy as Fiona's companion and teacher. I would want nothing to spoil that."

"I will not spoil it," he promised her. "But I would have you tell me why you would find my attentions so repellent."

Her first thought was to leave him then and there, but she did not. Alix realized the laird, like most men, had been puzzled why she would not want his favors. He was a handsome man, a propertied man, all the things that women were supposed to admire in a gentle-man. "My marriage, as you know, my lord, was not a happy one," Alix began. "I am not unhappy being without a husband."

"And I am not unhappy being wifeless," he admitted.

"Yet you would have had me in your bed were I willing," Alix responded.

He nodded. "Aye, I would." The laird smiled a small smile.

"You are insulted that I refused you," Alix said.

"I am curious why you refused me," he answered her. "Will you tell me why?"

Alix considered his request. He was, she suspected, the kind of man who would not be content until she had told him the truth. But if she told him the truth then he was apt to leave her in peace and seek his pleasure elsewhere. The shame in what had happened between her and Hayle Watteson was not her shame. It had been her husband's. Alix sighed, and then she began to speak.

"He hated me for not being the girl he loved. Maida was her name. Because it was necessary, he bedded me else the marriage be annulled, because that would have displeased his father mightily. He used me as a man uses a woman. But there was no kindness in it. The room was always in total darkness because he felt guilt at what he believed was a betrayal of his Maida. He did not want to look upon me in those brief moments. He took my virginity quickly, cruelly, then left me alone in that black chamber. And each time our coupling was swiftly accomplished so he might depart and re-turn to the woman he loved. I am only fortunate I did not conceive his child." Alix did not bother to tell the laird how her own father had protected her from that disaster. "I found our time together un-pleasant, and I did not like the coupling. My father told me that it is beautiful with someone you love, but I do not think I will take the chance of being hurt and degraded again. I don't want to be any man's wife again."

Malcolm Scott nodded. The shock of what she had just told

him actually hurt him. As he had previously thought, her husband was a fool. She was young, beautiful, and eager to be loved. The man's treatment of her had been nothing short of barbaric. "I believe I might change your outlook of passion between a man and a woman," he began slowly, "but I should certainly not force myself upon you."

"I know naught of passion, my lord," Alix replied.

"And there is the tragedy," he told her as he engaged her eyes with his. "Can you give me your trust, Alix? Can you believe I will not harm you if I say it?"

"What do you want of me, my lord?" she asked him, realizing suddenly she was no longer afraid of him even though it was dangerous ground upon which they trod.

"To show you how sweet passion can be," he said. Then, "Give me your hand."

Alix complied with the simple request, curious as to what he would do.

Malcolm Scott took the elegant little hand in his own big one. He admired it with his eyes. He raised it to his lips and slowly kissed the back of it with a warm kiss. Then he turned her hand over, exposing the palm, and placed his lips upon the open flesh moving with a lingering motion to the delicate skin of her wrist.

Alix's heart leaped within her chest at the touch of his lips upon her hand. She had never before experienced anything like it. Indeed it was startling to say the least.

His eyes met hers. "And that, Alix, is but the beginning of passion," the laird told her. "I hope that you did not find it distasteful."

She did not break his gaze, saying, "Nay, I did not find it unpleasant, my lord."

"Your husband had to have been a fool to have treated you so unkindly," he said.

"I think he was more like a spoiled child," Alix responded. "He wanted what he wanted, and disdained whatever else was offered him."

"With your permission I would like to introduce you to passion, Alix," Malcolm Scott told her. "I believe you will find everything I can offer you pleasant."

"Ah, my lord, now I see you have not been deterred in your desire to seduce me," Alix said. "Is it so difficult to understand I never enjoyed the coupling?"

"There is more to passion than just coupling," he replied. "Let me show you. I will force nothing upon you, Alix, but I cannot allow someone as beautiful as you are, someone with such a warm nature and kind heart, to be denied the delights of passion. Your husband was cruel. I have never even used a whore as he used you."

"But if I am to continue to educate your daughter, is it right that we should become lovers, my lord?" she asked him.

"My daughter must one day go to the marriage bed. Should it not be you who instructs her in its delights and pleasures so her lord will be well pleased? And how can you do that if all your memories are of a husband who hated and abused you?" he countered.

Alix had to laugh. "It is an excellent argument you make in your wicked efforts, my lord. Have you studied the law, perhaps?"

Now it was the laird who laughed, but he grew sober again when she spoke.

"*If* I should allow you to demonstrate some of the aspects of passion to me, then you must do so discreetly. I will not have the servants gossiping, or Fiona distressed by what she might hear. I must continue to command respect in this hall or my usefulness to you, to your daughter, is finished. I am not certain this is a good idea, but since I can see you will not be satisfied until you have made your point, I will succumb to your blandishments provided that if I say nay, you will accept it."

"Agreed!" he quickly answered her.

Alix arose from her place by the hearth. "Then I will bid you good night, my lord," she said curtsying to him.

He stood. "Wait but a moment," he said, reaching out with one hand to cup her face as he stepped near her. "We must seal our bargain with a kiss, Alix."

Her eyes widened. He gave her no time to think or even protest. His mouth descended upon hers in a deep, warm kiss that sent a shiver down her spine right to her toes. She had never been really kissed. Hayle's few attempts had been nasty, and his father's kiss repellent to her. This kiss was neither. Her eyes closed. Her lips softened as he plundered them tenderly. She felt his arm go about her waist and was grateful, for she wasn't certain she could stand on her own much longer. She sighed deeply as his kiss slowly concluded.

Then, as he put two firm hands upon her shoulders and gently pushed her back, Alix's green eyes flew open. "I like your mouth," he said softly.

"I did not know a kiss could be so delicious," Alix told him honestly.

"Neither did I," he admitted. The sweetness, the innocence of her, had surprised him. He could have kissed her again and taken her here before the fire, but he did not. "Go to bed now, Alix," he said. "It is enough for today."

She nodded and, turning, departed the hall. It had been enough for a lifetime, Alix thought as she climbed the stairs to her bedchamber. If she died in the night she knew now that his kiss would sustain her through eternity. She had not known! She had not known how wonderful a man's kiss could be. How good it felt to be held against a man's hard body and cherished tenderly. And she had learned that all with just one kiss! Flinging herself upon her bed, she wept with both happiness and sorrow. She was filled with sadness that her virginity had been so brutally squandered by Hayle Watteson. If a small kiss could bring about such emotions within her, what would giving herself to this Scotsman be like? Would it be heaven?

Alix sat up. Was she mad? Had the sweetness of his kiss wiped away her memories entirely? Nay, it had not! She shuddered as she recalled her husband mounting her without a word. Jamming his cock into her body with no care for the pain he caused her. She believed he enjoyed giving her pain, enjoyed punishing her for daring to be his wife when he had not wanted her. He had practically said as much one night as he thrust back and forth atop her while she pleaded with him to stop for he was truly hurting her. Her passage was dry, and his movement did nothing to improve it.

"Get yourself with child, you bitch," he had snarled at her, "and I shall gladly forgo your bed. But until you do I am bound to fuck you and waste my seed in your ugly body." And he had renewed his efforts, putting his hand over her mouth to stifle her cries of pain when she could bear no more of him.

That was what she knew of coupling. Would being in the laird's bed be any different? And yet his kiss had been different. Alix swallowed hard. How could she ever consider coupling with a man after what her husband had done to her? The pain and the humiliation he had inflicted upon her. And yet if the kiss had been different, might not the other be as well? Still, to give herself to a man not her husband made her no better than a common whore. Yet the ladies of the court had dallied with men not their husbands. Wouldn't her sin be less for not deceiving a husband? She was a widow.

Alix took off her jersey gown, and taking the pitcher of water from the coals, she poured some into the little stone basin, washing her hands and face, cleaning her teeth with the little bristle brush that had been her father's last gift to her. After climbing into her bed, she said her prayers and then tossed restlessly before finally falling asleep. When the new day dawned she was no more near answers to all her questions than she had been the night before. What was she to do?

Fiona was excited with the longer days that were growing milder. Finally the laird gave his permission for them to ride outside the gates of the keep as the snow was almost all gone from the moors. He even decided to ride with them. Escorted by four men-at-arms they left the keep one midmorning. The laird's daughter was ecstatic when she was finally allowed to gallop her pony, her father's horse keeping pace with her. Her dark hair blew loose from its red ribbon, which blew across the moor, one of the laird's men cantering after it to retrieve it. He brought it to Alix and she thanked him.

Finally, as the horses all slowed to a gentle walk, they were approached by a small party of riders coming over a hill.

"God's nightshirt!" the laird swore softly. " 'Tis my uncle the Ferguson of Drumcairn. He'll have another candidate for my hand, to be certain. Perhaps two as he has not been able to get over the moor since the snows set in."

As Alix looked puzzled, Fiona explained, giggling. "My da's uncle wants him to remarry and sire sons. But Da loved my mother so greatly he wants no other wife. Whenever he comes to Dunglais, he brings with him the suggestion of another lass for my da to wed. He is very persistent, as you will shortly see."

"He looks too young to be your father's uncle," Alix said.

"He was my grandmother's half brother, born the very year she married my grandfather. His mother was stepmother to my grandmother. He is just five years older than Da," Fiona explained.

"He behaves as if he were fifty years older," grumbled the laird as the Ferguson riders approached. "Uncle! You have survived the winter, I see," Malcolm Scott greeted Robert Ferguson jovially. "What brings you to Dunglais this fine spring day?"

"Nephew," Robert Ferguson responded, but his eyes quickly turned to observe Alix. "And who is this lovely lass?" he asked, smiling at her.

Had she not known he was the laird's uncle, Alix would have never thought them blood related. The Ferguson of Drumcairn, while a big man like the laird, had a shock of bright red hair, a freckled face, and sharp blue eyes that were hardly discreet in their curiosity and admiration of the girl riding with his nephew.

"This is Mistress Alix Givet, Uncle. She is Fiona's companion and instructor in all things the daughter of the Laird of Dunglais should know if she is to be a proper wife and chatelaine one day. She came to us late last autumn."

"*Vous êtes Francaise, mademoiselle?*" Robert Ferguson asked.

"My parents were from Anjou, sir, but I was born in England," Alix answered him. So this border lord was educated, she thought, interested.

"How on earth did you find the lass, nephew?" his uncle asked.

"I didn't find her, Robert. She found us," the laird replied with a grin. "Come along now and let us return to the hall, where I will satisfy your insatiable curiosity." He turned his great dappled gray stallion about, and they returned to the keep.

The Ferguson of Drumcairn was off his mount quickly and by Alix's side, reaching up to help her from her mare. His hands lingered about her waist a moment too long, and while she said nothing she glared indignantly at him. With a grin, he released her, watching as she turned to take Fiona by the hand and enter the house. "Indeed, Malcolm, I shall look forward to hearing the story of how you came into possession of that spirited little wench. She's more than just pretty."

"Remember you have a wife, *Uncle*," the laird reminded him as they entered the hall and found places by the blazing fire. Alix and Fiona were nowhere to be seen, but the servants hurried to place goblets of wine in their hands.

"Aye, and a fine woman my Maggie is, but it doesn't keep my eyes from seeing. Is she your mistress, Malcolm? You'll have to put her somewhere else when you take a wife, y'know. Maggie's niece is now sixteen, and ripe for marriage."

"How many times must I tell you, Robbie? I have no intention of marrying again," the laird said to his uncle.

"And how many times must I tell you that you owe it to the Scotts of Dunglais to remarry and sire a son? If I had known how wild Robena was I should have never suggested her to you as a bride, Malcolm. We will be most careful with the next wife you take, but take another wife you must."

"Nay, Robbie, I do not have to take another wife," the laird said heatedly.

"Is your daughter's *companion* your mistress?" his uncle asked again.

"Nay, she is not," the laird answered.

"What is it that prevents you from making her so?" Ferguson wanted to know. "She's lovely, and certainly can be no virgin at her age. How old is she?"

"I don't know," Malcolm Scott replied. "But she is a widow, so nay, she is no virgin. Her marriage was an unhappy one. She says she seeks no husband or lover."

"But you have begun to campaign to change her mind, haven't you?" His uncle chuckled. "Well, perhaps after you have enjoyed the pleasure of having a woman in your bed again you will consider your duty and take a wife. Maggie's niece is too tall anyway. The wench has legs like a stork and watery eyes. At least you wouldn't have to worry about her taking a lover, but still you would have to bed her." He drank down half his goblet of wine. "Ahh, the chase is always the best part of it, Nephew, isn't it?" He chuckled again. "And here is the subject of our conversation now."

"My lord." Alix curtsied to him respectfully. "I thought perhaps that Fiona and I would have our meal in the kitchens so you and your uncle might visit more comfortably with each other this evening."

"Nonsense!" the Ferguson of Drumcairn said before the laird might reply. "A lovely woman at the board adds much to the meal, Mistress Alix. Tell her she must sit with us, Malcolm. 'Tis your hall, not mine. Still, I would enjoy her gentle company."

"The decision is Alix's to make," the laird said, giving her a small smile.

"Then you will excuse me," Alix replied quietly. "Fiona is still quite excited by her ride and needs the calm of the kitchen table, not the excitement of the high board with a guest present, my lord." She curtsied again.

The laird nodded. "I bow to your judgment," he told her.

Alix then turned and hurried from the hall.

"You would indulge her and let her believe she is free when the truth is you are slowly tightening the bonds about her," Ferguson noted. "You are sly, Nephew."

"How long do you intend to stay with us?" the laird asked, amused.

"Your hall offers more peace than mine does," Robert Ferguson admitted. "I have been cooped up all winter with my Maggie and our offspring. She is breeding again, Malcolm. This will make an even dozen. I but look at the wench lasciviously and her belly swells. Well, maybe this time it is the hoped-for heir. Eleven daughters are more than a man can bear. Other men breed on their wives, lose them in childbed, or lose the bairns. My wife is as strong as an ox and our daughters stronger. God only knows how I shall find husbands for them all, Nephew, and even the church requires a dower."

"I'm sure eventually you will offer me one," the laird teased his uncle.

Robert Ferguson laughed. "If you are not wed by the time the eldest is marriageable, which will be in another two years, I probably will. I have to get rid of them somewhere, and Maggie agrees with me. We must keep praying for a son. All men want sons, Nephew."

"I have an heir in Fiona," Malcolm Scott said stubbornly.

"If you manage to get that pretty wench who now mothers your daughter into your bed," the Ferguson of Drumcairn said, "you are certain to get her with child. Will you let your son be born a bastard?"

"I only managed to get a daughter on Robena, and if I do indeed entice Alix to my bed, she bore no child to her husband. It is unlikely she would bear me one."

"Then she would be the perfect mistress," his uncle noted, "if all she gave you was pleasure but no encumbrances. 'Tis a rare occurrence, but I have heard of such."

"You have not answered my question, Uncle. How long do you mean to stay?"

"A few days, a week, perhaps," the Ferguson answered. "I should be ready to face my wife and daughters again by then. The new bairn isn't due until autumn."

"You are welcome as always, Uncle, provided you do not speak of marriage again," the Laird of Dunglais said.

"I will hold my peace for now," Robbie Ferguson said with a grin. "You have my word on it, Malcolm."

Chapter 6

In August of 1460 James II of Scotland had been killed when a cannon misfired during the siege of Roxburgh Castle. A special salvo had been arranged to greet Queen Marie, who had arrived to view the proceedings. The cannon, however, had been overcharged with gunpowder. It exploded and a piece of the metal had shattered the king's leg as he stood nearby. He died almost instantly, and once again Scotland was faced with a child king. James II had been six years old when his father had been murdered. James III was eight.

Queen Marie took no time to mourn. Instead she hastened to fetch her eldest son, James. Bringing him before the commanders of Scotland's armies she asked them to make her husband's death not a defeat, but a victory for Scotland's new king, James III. Encouraged by her bravery, Scotland's army responded to the queen's words and the sight of their young boy king standing proudly before them. Within a few days Roxburgh fell, and the new king was crowned at nearby Kelso Abbey on the tenth day of the month.

The queen mother quickly took charge of the situation. The bishop of St. Andrew's, Bishop Kennedy, was out of the country when the king was killed. This allowed Queen Marie to put her own people into place, much to the bishop's annoyance when he returned. Still, the bishop's powerful family was amenable to compromise. So was the queen. Although she had given sanctuary to her kinswoman, Margaret, and her mad husband, King Henry of

England, she quickly saw the way the winds were blowing to the south. While she would do nothing to harm the English fugitives, she would do nothing to help those who would pursue them either. Still, she made a long-term peace with the new English king, Edward IV, who was being tempted into supporting a war against Scotland in order to partition it. The south would be held by the exiled Earl of Douglas, and the north by the MacDonald Lord of the Isles, both of whom would rule as vassals of England's king. Queen Marie's signature and that of her son's on a document put a stop to that treasonous plan.

The Douglas family had been a thorn in her husband's side since his youth. The fifth earl of Douglas had been governor of the realm when James II was a child, but he had proved a poor one. His weakness had allowed two lesser lords, Sir William Crichton, keeper of Edinburgh Castle, and Sir Alexander Livingstone, keeper of Stirling Castle, to seize the king. When Lord Douglas died, Crichton and Livingstone took the opportunity to murder his sons in the presence of the ten-year-old James II. It was believed the young Douglases' uncle, known as James the Gross, who now inherited the title, was involved.

James II learned a lesson that terrible night when he begged for the lives of the two Douglases. And ten years later, encouraged by his queen, he finally asserted his authority, executing several of the Livingstone family and destroying their power. The Douglas family, now headed by James the Gross's eldest son, William, however, was a more difficult problem. The Douglas earl had immense holdings in the borders. But when James II discovered him involved in treasonous dealings with England, and that he had formed a traitorous alliance with the Lord of the Isles, he called the Earl of Stirling and ordered him to repudiate his alliances and reaffirm his allegiance to Scotland's king.

William Douglas refused, and after two days of negotiation James II lost his temper and stabbed the earl in his throat. The men with the king joined the fray. Considering that the Douglas earl had insisted on a safe conduct before coming to Stirling to see the king, the murder was a breach of the medieval code of honor. James II moved quickly, however, to shore up his defenses in the matter. Moving his pregnant queen to the bishop's palace at St. Andrew's, he quickly gained the support of his earls by a means of various reassurances and rewards for their loyalty. And considering that William Douglas's brother, the new earl, arrived at Stirling with a large force of armed men, crying for vengeance, and then burned the town in their defiance of James II, who had already departed Stirling, the king's actions were suddenly considered reasonable. The Douglases had obviously grown way too powerful in too short a time.

James II went to war against the Douglases. Fascinated by the new science of gunnery, he systematically battered down the walls of the Douglas strongholds with his great cannon, Mons Meg, which he had acquired from his wife's uncle, the Duke of Burgundy, and which had been brought from Edinburgh Castle. Defeated at the battle of Arkinholm, James, the ninth Douglas earl, escaped to England. Of his two remaining brothers, one died at Arkinholm and the other was captured and executed.

In England at that time the War of the Roses had broken out, and James Douglas allied his fallen fortunes with the Yorkist faction. The king of Scotland, however, chose to support the Lancaster side of the quarrel. And then James II proved himself a worthy successor to his father, reestablishing the rule of law in Scotland. His patronage of his nobility extended to creating several new earldoms, namely Rothes, Morton, Erroll, Marischal, and Argyll. Then, having stabilized his domestic affairs, the king devoted himself to foreign diplomacy, including arranging the marriage of his eldest son, James, with Margaret of Denmark.

In 1460 war broke out again as James II thought to strike a blow for his ally, King Henry VI, laying siege to Roxburgh Castle, which was currently held by a Yorkist governor. Roxburgh had always been hotly contested between England and Scotland, but it had been in English hands since the reign of David II of Scotland, over a hundred years previously. And while the Scots regained Roxburgh that summer, they lost a capable king and once again found themselves ruled by a regency in the name of James III.

Although the Highlands were fraught with disorder, Scotland remained basically at peace, thanks to Queen Marie and Bishop Kennedy. Even the borders were quiet but for a small raid now and again.

At Dunglais, Malcolm Scott continued to pursue Alix. And Alix was finding it more difficult to resist him. Her experience with the Wattesons had left her wary of men. She had felt nothing for her husband, for she had not really known him. She had liked her father-in-law's company as a friend until he had attempted to debauch her, and then she had felt revulsion.

She was not naive enough to believe all marriages were like her parents'. Alix knew better from her childhood at court. But did that elusive something called love really exist? Could she find it? Or was what she was suddenly feeling for Malcolm Scott the more common and forbidden emotion that was known as lust? Why did her first sight of him at the beginning of a day make her heart race? Why did the touch of his lips on hers, or his hand in hers, render her weak with longing? Longing for what?

Since the early spring the laird had found himself courting Alix. He fully intended to seduce her into his bed, but for some reason he could not explain, he did not want to rush her. When the moment came, he wanted her to desire it as deeply as he did. They rode out daily, with little Fiona accompanying them on her pony. In high summer they took bread and cheese with them, picnicking on the heathered hillsides. One afternoon as the child lay sleeping on a blanket, her companions found themselves lying together nearby.

Alix was only slightly startled when Malcolm Scott loomed over her. She smiled up at him. "The sky is so blue today," she said. "I do not think I have ever seen so blue a sky even in England."

"I want you," he said softly, and he bent to brush her lips with his.

"I know," she responded as softly. "I have no experience with a lover, but I would be a total fool not to realize, to sense, how you feel, my lord."

"Then why . . ." he began.

"I am afraid," Alix answered him simply.

"Of what?" he asked, surprised.

"I did not like coupling with my husband. What if I do not like it with you? Worse, what if you find me displeasing? Do we—can we—go back to the way things were, my lord?" Alix wanted to know. "I think not. And then I must leave Dunglais and my sweet Fiona. I do not know if I am brave enough to take this chance you are asking me to take, my lord." She reached up and touched his face with delicate fingers. "And yet . . ."

"I cannot imagine you would not please me, and I swear I will please you," the laird said. Then he bent, kissing her deeply, the tip of his tongue stroking her lips, encouraging them to part, and when they did his tongue plunged into her mouth, found hers and caressed it ardently.

In the few weeks during which they had been exchanging chaste kisses he had never invaded her person as he was now doing. Yet it was exciting, and Alix arched against him, her own tongue stroking his and heat suffusing her body. She reached up to wind her fingers into his thick black hair, kneading his scalp with a need that surprised her greatly. She protested softly as he raised his head from her, but he put a single finger over her lips to silence her.

"Hush, lambkin," he told her. "Let me have my way now, and I promise you that you will not regret it."

"Fiona," Alix said.

"I will do nothing that will awaken my daughter," he promised. Smiling into her hazel-green eyes, he slowly undid the little horn buttons on the doeskin jerkin he and Fiona had given Alix on her birthday in April. Then he unlaced her shirt while she watched him nervously. Pushing the fabric aside, he gazed down for the first time upon her naked breasts. "God's foot," he murmured. "You are perfect, lambkin. Absolutely perfect!"

Alix blushed, suddenly shy, for no man had ever before looked upon her breasts, and his compliment surprised her.

The laird continued to stare for a long moment at the two sweetly rounded breasts that reminded him of two ripe peaches. Her nipples were small, the color of dusky rosebuds. They puckered beneath his ardent look. He brushed the fingers of one hand around the curve of the firm globe, tracing its delicate shape. She trembled beneath his touch. "Don't be afraid, lambkin," he said softly. "I am not like *him*. I will never hurt you. I want to make love to you the way a woman should be loved. Tenderly, and with unrestrained passion. You must never fear me, or fear my passion." He bent his dark head again and kissed her nipple. Then he began to lick it, slowly encircling it with the tip of his warm tongue.

Alix gasped softly with surprise. The only time Hayle Watteson had touched her breasts was to squeeze them hard and mock their delicate size. Maida had big breasts where a man could pillow his head, he always told her. Hayle had never touched her gently as Malcolm Scott was doing. She gasped again. And he had certainly never fondled her breast and sucked hungrily upon it as the laird was now doing. A little cry escaped her. "Oh! Oh!"

He looked up and into her face now. "Do I please you, or distress you, lambkin?" he asked her quietly.

"I never knew . . ." she began, and then, "Yes, my lord. You please me muchly."

He lowered his head and began to pay court to her other breast while she sighed with her obvious pleasure at his renewed devotion. Her scent—or was it the heather about them?—filled his nostrils, making him almost giddy with his rising desire. He felt his cock growing harder and harder in his breeks. But he knew this was not the time. Not with his daughter sleeping so innocently but a few yards away from where he lay with Alix. Finally he forced himself to raise his head from her breasts. He laced her shirt back up.

"We can go no further here with Fiona nearby us. But make no mistake about it, Alix Givet. I want you in my bed. I have never taken a mistress, but I think you would have me, lambkin, as I would have you."

"But what if I should disappoint you in the coupling, my lord?" she asked him once again. "The man to whom I was wed put me on my back that first night and thrust himself into me so cruelly that he hurt me. I could not see his face in the pitch black of the room. And after that whenever he came he would make me kneel upon my bed, for he said I was no better than a bitch hound and should be fucked as a bitch is fucked. I quickly came to dislike the act, my lord. What pleasure is to be had in it?"

Malcolm Scott felt himself filled with anger as he listened to her. How could a man brutalize a woman so cruelly? "I will show you the pleasure in the coupling, Alix. And you will give me pleasure with your fair body as I will give you pleasure when we are joined as one. You will never displease me, lambkin. I can only hope I will not disappoint you." He brushed her mouth with his.

She nodded. "I will trust you, my lord, but remember I want no husband who will have dominion over me. I will be your mistress, but I do so of my own free will, not because you force me to it." She sat up and began to rebutton her jerkin.

"And I want no wife, although I ask one thing of you, lambkin. Never deceive me with another man. If the time comes that you want someone else you have but to tell me and I will let you go, but do not betray me, Alix Givet."

"I will not ever mislead you, my lord," she responded. "I swear it!" He was thinking of his wife, Alix thought. "But you must make me the same vow. If you decide you wish to have another for your mistress, or a wife, you will tell me in order that I not be shamed."

"If that day should ever come I will indeed inform you, and I will provide for you as well, lambkin. I know my responsibilities."

"I ask nothing of you but courtesy," Alix quickly said. "My father left me provided for, and I have the wherewithal to make my own way if I must, my lord. I am no whore to be cast off and paid for services rendered you other than my compensation for educating your daughter." There was a proud tilt to her little chin.

"It is not a matter we are faced with, so why should we argue over it?" he replied. Her stubborn pride pleased him well. Robena had wanted everything of him.

"I will awaken Fiona, my lord." Alix stood up and brushed her skirts off. Then she went to gently shake the little girl awake.

They rode back to Dunglais in the late-afternoon sunshine, listening to the now-rested Fiona chatter about how she wished to ride all the way to Edinburgh one day to see the king. "Do you think he would marry a girl like me?" she wondered aloud.

"Kings usually marry great ladies," her father told her.

"Are you not a great lord, Da?" Fiona wanted to know.

Malcolm Scott laughed aloud. "Nay, lassie, I'm just an insignificant border lord with a herd of cattle, a flock of sheep, and an old stone keep."

"But you were the old king's friend. Can't you be the new king's friend too, and ask him to make you a great lord?" Fiona wanted to know.

"Our new king is a little boy, Fiona. He's just two years older than you are. And his days are spent very much like yours are, learning his lessons and learning how to be a good king of Scotland like his father and his grandfather were. And he is already betrothed to little Princess Margaret of Denmark. His wise father did that for him before he was killed, God assoil his soul," the laird told his daughter.

"Am I betrothed?" Fiona wanted to know.

Malcolm Scott chuckled. "I am not certain yet that I ever want to let you go," he said with a smile at his little daughter.

"Oh, Da!" Fiona replied, but they could tell she was pleased.

As they sat afterwards at the high board when Fiona had gone to her bed, Alix asked the laird, "How did you know the king, and were you really his friend?"

"Jamie Stewart and I were educated together," Malcolm Scott said. When King James the First was murdered and his eldest son became king, his mother, Queen Joan, sought for a few lads his age who were not involved with either the Douglases, Lord Crichton's family, or the Livingstones to be companions to the boy king. Jamie had been the survivor of twins and he bore a rather harsh birthmark. Half of his face was the color of an amethyst. In the streets he was known as James of the Fiery Face."

"Oh, how sad!" Alix noted.

"Because of it he didn't like great public shows or spectacles where he had to show himself. He was intelligent, inquisitive, and preferred companions like himself. He had nothing but scorn for old Douglas, and as for Crichton and the Livingstones he but bided his time until he could take control of his kingdom, for there was a ruthless streak in him. It was shortly after he married Marie of Gueldres, the Duke of Burgundy's niece, that he exerted his influence. Many thought she was behind it, and while I am certain she encouraged her husband, Jamie was his own man. We learned to like bad women, good whiskey, and guns together. Of course, I went back to the borders right after he married. He didn't need me then. My father had just died, and a border holding not strongly held by its owner is apt to be taken by another."

"Were you with him at Roxburgh?" Alix asked.

"Aye," the laird replied grimly. "I said that damned cannon was ill loaded, but he was so anxious to show off for his queen. He loved her, you know, and got four sons and two daughters on her. She has not just the little king to worry about, but the other five as well. Hers is not an easy task, but she was a good wife to Jamie, a good queen, and she is proving stronger than anyone anticipated as the queen mother."

"So in a way you were brought up at a court too," Alix remarked.

"Not really," the laird replied. "We moved from place to place. We were always on the go. There was no real court as you would know it. The idea was to keep the king safe and alive. To get him educated to take up his duties. Most of the other boys fell away in the furor between all the factions trying to control the king's person. But he would never go anywhere without me, and I even slept in his bedchamber most of the time. We were bedded by the same whore for the first time when we were fifteen," Malcolm Scott chuckled as he remembered. "Livingstone was a prig, but Crichton arranged it for the king, and if the king did it then I had to do it. Jamie Stewart would have it no other way."

"And after that you never looked back," she teased him.

"Nay, I never looked back. And now I am looking forward to a new adventure, lambkin." He took her hand and kissed it, laughing softly when she blushed.

"You are so bold," she said softly. "You frighten me, and yet I trust you. 'Tis odd."

"I don't want you frightened of me," he told her earnestly. "But I believe once we have become lovers in every sense you will not be afraid of me, Alix. At least I hope not." He still held her hand in his, and now, turning the palm up, he placed a kiss upon it.

He excited her. She had never before felt excitement for a man, but Malcolm Scott excited her. His touch set her pulses racing. "My lord," she whispered, looking into his handsome face. And he was indeed handsome to her eye.

He smiled a slow smile. "May I come to you later?" he asked her softly.

Alix's heart thundered in her chest. For a moment she wasn't even certain she could breathe. She was actually considering what it would be like to be naked in his arms. But what if his gentle words were just that—words? What if Hayle's treatment of her was the way all men behaved with women? But it couldn't be! Her mother could not have loved her father had he been such a brute as Hayle Watteson. Nor could Queen Margaret have loved her husband if he had been so cruel. But both her mother and the queen were devoted to their men. And she would never know the truth of men and women if she did not take this one chance. And if it was awful? Well, then she would flee Dunglais.

"Alix?" His deep voice penetrated her thoughts.

"Aye," she whispered. "You may come to me, my lord."

"Colm," he said. "If we are lovers, Alix, then you must call me Colm."

She stood abruptly, pulling her hand from his. "I must go to my chamber now, my lord," she told him and fled the hall.

I must bring some wine with me, he thought. *My lambkin is yet frightened, but struggles to be brave. I will give her time. Perhaps I shall even let her sleep a brief time.* Coming down from the high board he seated himself by the fire, gazing into the crackling, leaping flames as they burned. "Wine!" he called out to no one in particular. And after a brief time a goblet was placed in his hand. "My thanks," he said, looking up to see Fenella by his side. "Sit," he invited her.

"You were in deep conversation with Alix earlier," Fenella noted.

"She will be mine before morning," the laird said. "She has agreed to it."

Fenella nodded. "Be kind, my lord. Be gentle. Alix has suffered at a man's cruel hands, and while she may have agreed, she will still be frightened."

"She is to be my mistress," he said.

Fenella nodded again. "Better you took her to wife, my lord."

"I want no wife and she wants no husband," Malcolm Scott answered his kinswoman. "It is an excellent arrangement. We have agreed to be open with each other should we find another who pleases us more. She will be the perfect mistress."

"And what kind of an example is that to set for your daughter?" Fenella asked candidly. "Fiona believes you loved her mother so much that you can love no other."

"Fiona is young, and will not see the change in the relationship between Alix and me," the laird declared. "And she loves Alix, who is like a mother to her."

"Fiona loves you. If she discovers you have taken Alix to your bed she will assume you love her," Fenella pointed out.

"Have you not been nagging at me to take a woman?" the laird grumbled.

"I want you to take a wife, and Alix Givet is the wife for you. She is young enough to give you sons. She is educated and sophisticated enough to keep you from becoming bored with her. But she has also learned the lessons of loyalty to a husband, to clan, as Robena Ramsay did not. Alix will never betray you, my lord. She will never shame our name. She deserves better than to be your mistress."

"Hush your mouth, Fenella. I want no wife, and Alix declares she will have no husband to hold dominion over her. She has agreed to my coming into her bed. The bargain has been struck!" He emptied his goblet and stood up. "I will bid you good night, kinswoman." And he strode from the hall.

"I told you you wouldn't get your way in this, my pretty schemer," Iver chuckled, coming forward from the shadows to join Fenella at the hearth.

Fenella laughed. "Oh, yes, I will," she said. "He will show her she has no need for fear, and she will respond to his passion. And then, Iver, they will fall in love, for they are two people who are meant to be together. They are already half in love, though neither knows it yet. But once he admits to loving her he will want her for his wife, for the thought of another having her will drive him mad."

"We shall see." Iver grinned his lopsided grin. "What else do you know will happen for certain, Fenella? Do you know you will soon be my wife?"

"Of course I do," she surprised him by answering. "But only when the laird takes Alix to wife, Iver, my lad, will I take you for my husband. Now come and give me a kiss to seal our bargain."

He pulled her up and kissed her heartily, a hand fondling her bottom as he did.

"Ah," Fenella said, laughing again, "I can see you'll be a lusty mate, which pleases me well, for we Scotts are lusty people, as I'm sure our lord is now proving."

When Malcolm Scott had left the hall he went to his own

bedchamber, where he stripped off his boots, his breeks, his leather jerkin, and his camise. Naked, he bathed himself with the water he poured into a small basin. Then, wrapping a piece of plaid about his loins, he left his chamber, walking down the narrow corridor to where Alix was probably now sleeping. There was an empty bedchamber next to his, and he would as soon as possible install her there as it had a connecting door.

Putting his hand on the door latch to her chamber he entered the room, barring the door behind him. There was a fire burning low in the hearth. He added wood to it so that the blaze burned brightly now. Then, walking to her bed, he tossed the plaid aside and climbed in next to her. She stirred as he drew her into his arms and kissed her lips gently. "Wake up, lambkin," he murmured into her ear.

Alix slowly opened her eyes, and seeing his face before her, realizing she was being held in his arms, her heart leaped in her chest. "My lord!" she whispered.

"You did say I might come," he reminded her.

"I know I did," Alix answered.

"But now that I am here you are reconsidering," he said.

She didn't answer him, so he continued.

"This will not be rape, Alix," the laird told her. "But you will never overcome your fears if you do not face them. You are a brave lass, for only a brave lass would have fled England in a blizzard. Now be brave for me, lambkin."

"I don't know what to do. What I should do," she admitted.

He smiled warmly into her hazel eyes. "You will do what your body desires," he said, "and you will let me guide you into the paths of passion, Alix. And you will not be fearful of telling me if something displeases you. Now, let us rid you of this garment you wear and then we will begin."

"You want me naked?" she said nervously.

"I am naked," he replied.

Alix's eyes widened. What was the matter with her? Of course he was naked. Could she not see his smooth chest, his broad shoulders, and his sinewy arms? "Aye"—she nodded, feeling foolish—"you are, aren't you?" Alix pulled her little night chemise off over her head and dropped it to the floor.

"Now," he said, "we will become familiar with each other's bodies."

"How?" Her voice trembled.

He drew the coverlet back. "Like this," he said as his eyes swept over her fair young body. The sweet breasts he had earlier caressed were even fuller, more beautiful, he thought to himself. Her waist was slender, but her hips were broader than he had imagined. Her plump mons was free of growth, to his surprise. Garbed she gave the appearance of being delicate, but seeing her naked he realized she was quite a sturdy lass. She would not break beneath his desire, which was beginning to exert itself. Her thighs were rounded and firm, as were the calves on her slim legs. "You are quite the loveliest lass I have ever beheld," he told her.

While he had perused her so thoughtfully Alix had examined a male form for the first time. The chest, the strong arms, his shoulders she had previously noted. His torso was long, his belly flat, and beneath it a tangle of thick black curls that surrounded his manhood. Alix swallowed as she beheld *it*. It was pale in color, veined in blue, and long. But it lay quietly, seemingly innocent of any wickedness. She forced her eyes away from it to view his long hairy legs and large feet.

"Am I pleasing in your sight?" he asked her mischievously.

"I think I am prettier in form," she answered him and he laughed.

"Aye, a woman's form is fairer, I will agree, lambkin," the laird said.

"What do we do now?" Alix asked him shyly.

"Sit up," he said, "and undo your hair for me. When you are alone the plait will do, but when we are together as lovers I would enjoy your long hair."

Alix sat up against the pillows and began to unbraid her honey-colored curls.

"Why is your mons like a little girl's?" he asked her.

"The women of the court are taught to keep that part of their bodies hairless," Alix explained to him. "Only peasant women have bushes to tend. I did not know men did."

When she had finished undoing her long hair, he inquired of her, "Where is your hairbrush, lambkin?" and when she told him, he fetched it. Then, climbing back into the bed, he began to brush her hair with long, slow strokes of the brush.

She had not had anyone brush her hair since she had been a child, Alix thought. She had quite forgotten how pleasant it was and found herself almost purring. She did not see his smile as he finally laid the brush aside. Pressing her back, he spread her hair over the pillows, admiring it for a moment, then kissing her soft mouth slowly, deeply. Alix's lips parted beneath his. Immediately his tongue darted into her mouth, sweeping about it, seeking her tongue to tease it with his. Alix was so mesmerized by the two intertwining digits she didn't notice at first that one of his hands was caressing her belly until his fingers touched her mons and began to play with her nether lips.

"What are you doing?" she cried, breaking off their kiss, her head spinning with the sweetness she had been receiving.

"I want to touch you there," he told her. "You need to be prepared to take my manhood within your sheath, lambkin."

"*Prepared?*" Now she was puzzled. Hayle simply had her assume the position he desired and thrust himself inside of her. What preparation could the laird possibly mean? "I don't understand," Alix told him.

"You are a tender creature, and you cannot easily receive my manhood until you are ready to receive it. Your husband used you like one animal would use another. He wished to harm you because you had wed him. I will not do that to you. Men do not, lambkin. You have love juices, and they must be encouraged to flow for me.

Now be quiet, Alix, and trust me to give you pleasure. Can you do that, lambkin?"

Alix nodded. It was suddenly all very exciting, and it was certainly very new for her. He began to kiss her again, slowly, slowly, their mouths almost melting into each other's. She sighed with delight when his mouth went to her breasts again as they had that afternoon. When he tugged upon her nipple, she felt a corresponding throb in the secret place between her legs. "*Yes!*" she heard her own voice whispering. She struggled with herself not to cry out and leap from the bed when his fingers gently played with her nether lips, when one finger pressed between them. To her great surprise she seemed to be wet. She flushed. Had she peed in her excitement? But no. As his finger played between her nether lips the moisture felt almost creamy in its consistency. And the finger suddenly touching a most sensitive spot, teasing at it, made her feel wonderful, not fearful at all. She sighed audibly.

He was hard. God help him! His cock was as firm as he could ever remember it being. He kept the sight of it from her, for he didn't wish her to panic, which she surely would have. He was longer than he had been earlier and far thicker. Gently he moved his finger to the opening of her sheath and pressed it forward into her. He felt her stiffen and murmured against her ear, "Nah, nah, lassie, 'tis all right. Do I hurt you?"

Alix thought a moment. No. He was not hurting her. "Nay," she whispered.

He moved the finger back and forth so that she would get used to the rhythm, and after a few moments she gave a little cry of surprise as she experienced a first burst of sweet pleasure from that finger.

"*Oh!*" Alix exclaimed softly.

He laughed quietly. "You see?" he told her, and he withdrew the single finger, quickly replacing it with two fingers, which he moved back and forth once again.

"*Oh! Oh!*" Alix cried out.

She was ready and while she tensed as he covered her body with his own, he soothed her with little kisses as he prepared to sheathe himself inside her. The laird positioned himself and pushed his cock forward. The portal gave way as he slid deep. Beneath him Alix was hardly breathing as she waited for the pain to engulf her. But there was no pain.

"Put your legs about me," he instructed her.

Then she gasped, for when she did he moved deeper into her. And there was still no pain. He filled her full, but there was no pain even when he began to move upon her. The fingers of their hands were intertwining as his rhythm grew faster and faster. Alix's eyes closed and pure instinct arched her body up to his every downward thrust. She found herself reveling in the sensations he was engendering within her. Her breath was coming in short hard pants, and she suddenly realized that she was experiencing pleasure. She had never before enjoyed such feelings as were now sweeping over her.

Alix cried out. "Don't stop," she begged him. "Oh, please don't stop, my lord! I am in heaven!" And then, as the hard core within her began to burst, she sobbed, "Oh, sweet Holy Mother, I die!" And she shook with her pent-up release as his love juices exploded within her exciting body.

The laird rolled off of his lover, panting with his exertions. For a moment he couldn't catch his breath, but then he did. Reaching out, he gathered the girl who had just given him such pleasure into his strong arms. To his distress Alix began to weep. She huddled against his chest, sobbing and sobbing and sobbing. Disturbed, he asked, "Did I hurt you? You should have told me! I said I would not harm you, lambkin."

Hearing the distress in his voice, Alix quickly reassured him. "Nay, my lord. It was wonderful! I did not know! I never imagined! Now at last I am beginning to understand my mother's love for my father, the queen's devotion to the king." She hiccupped, and her sobs began to abate.

He kissed the top of her head, relieved, and stroked her long hair as much to soothe himself as to soothe her. There was that elusive fragrance of hers again teasing at his nostrils. "I gave you pleasure," he said simply. "I am glad."

"Will we lie together every night now?" Alix asked him shyly.

"Except those nights when your moonlink is broken," he told her. "I am going to move you into the bedchamber next to mine. It is larger, and there is a connecting door to my chamber. We are less apt to attract my daughter's attention that way. You must be no less attentive to Fiona now that you are mine," he said.

"Never, my lord! I love the child," Alix answered him.

"Colm," he said. "I am not your lord when we lay together. I am Colm, and you are my Alix," the laird responded. "Let me hear my name upon your lips, sweet Alix."

"Malcolm, my dear lord," she said softly. "Colm! And again, Colm!"

He laughed joyously, and Alix realized that she had never before heard him utter such a happy sound. In fact, he was laughing and smiling more of late than anytime since she had come to Dunglais. "I will leave you now, my lambkin," he said. "And you will no longer be afraid of the coupling, will you?"

"Nay, I will not, Colm," she promised him.

He arose from her bed and wrapped the length of plaid about him. Then, bending, the laird kissed her and bid her a good night. Unbarring the door, he departed, and Alix lay awake for some minutes reliving the first passion she had ever known. The passion she had shared with Malcolm Scott. She had been so afraid although she had concealed it well, she knew. While she had enjoyed his kisses and his hands upon her body when he had mounted her, she had waited in silent terror for the cruel pain that would shortly tear into her. But there had been no pain. None at all! He had used her gently and he had given her the first pleasure she had ever received from a man.

She wept again briefly as she considered how sad it was that her husband could not have given her that pleasure. That he could not have loved her as sweetly as Malcolm Scott had made love to her. And Alix wondered if Hayle Watteson had not hated her for not being his beloved Maida, would their marriage have been a fruitful and happy one? But he had hated her, and there was no changing the past.

But there was the future to consider. She was lying with a man not her husband. She had agreed to be his mistress. Alix knew that both her mother and the queen would have been shocked, would have been disappointed by her behavior. But if she had not allowed the laird to become her lover she would have never known the delights of passion. And tonight, Alix suspected, was but the beginning of her education in the amatory arts. Tonight the laird had opened the door for her, and Alix found that despite the less than suitable situation in which she found herself, she was eager to know what else lay on the other side of that wonderful door. Had Hayle Watteson been an exception to the rule? Were all men like Malcolm Scott? She didn't care as long as she might be in his arms, his delicious kisses rendering her dizzy with delight.

The following day the servants moved her few small belongings into the bedchamber next to the laird's. When Fiona asked why, for she was a curious child, the laird told her it was because then Alix would be closer to her, for Fiona's bedchamber was on the other side of the laird's.

"We shall be like three little buglets all in a snug row," Alix added.

"I like that!" Fiona enthused and Alix actually felt a tiny twinge of guilt for beguiling her small charge.

The border was quiet that year, and as the summer waned the Laird of Dunglais found his lust for Alix Givet burning brighter with each day. It was not enough that he shared her bed each night now. They rode out one day alone while Fiona remained behind with Fenella, learning how to stuff a mattress, an absolute necessity for any lady, Alix assured her, and the housekeeper agreed.

On a hillside Alix and the laird sat watching his cattle grazing peacefully. She lay back and looked up at the sky, where clouds scudded back and forth sometimes blocking the sunlight, sometimes letting it blaze bright down upon them. She saw the lust in his eyes as he looked down upon her and held open her arms to him. In no time at all Alix found her skirts about her waist and her lover vigorously fucking her. Her legs about his torso, she ran her nails down his broad back as he brought her quickly to pleasure and then did it again as her cries echoed about them.

"I did not know you could share passion on a hillside," she told him.

"Passion can be shared at any time, in any place," he assured her.

He proved the point again several days later when he found Alix in the stables brushing her mare's roan coat to a fine shine. Standing behind her, he played with her breasts as she worked and her breath began to come in quick pants. Then, as there was no one about, he put her down upon her back on a fat bale of fresh hay and entered her.

"I am your stallion," he told her as he used her vigorously, and then he put his hand over her mouth to stifle her cries, for her arousal was very great.

"You are a wicked man," she said afterwards, but she was smiling.

He laughed at her admonishment. "You enjoyed it every bit as much as I did," he teased her wickedly, pulling a bit of straw from her hair.

In early autumn a rider came to Dunglais wearing the badge of Queen Marie. The directive he bore commanded the Laird of Dunglais to come to her castle of Ravenscraig in Fife as soon as possible. The laird sent the queen's man back with a message saying he would be honored to wait upon her and would bring his little daughter to meet Queen Marie. "You will come with us," he told Alix as they lay abed that same night.

"You would bring your mistress to meet the queen?" she asked him, slightly shocked. "I am not certain that is right, my lord."

"You are my daughter's companion and a former member of Margaret of Anjou's household," the laird said. "I would hardly introduce you as my mistress. But Fiona will need you, and it is an excellent opportunity for her to see how she needs to behave among her own kind. And meeting Queen Marie may be of benefit to you, lambkin."

"Then it is fortunate that I have just made two new gowns from the material you gave me at Michaelmas," Alix responded. She had to admit it. She was excited about going to court, but of course there would not necessarily be a court such as the one she had grown up in around the Scots queen mother; her young son, the king; and his siblings. And they were going to Marie of Gueldres's own castle, not Stirling or Edinburgh, or even Falklands.

"How long are we to be gone?" Alix asked the laird.

"I cannot say, but I doubt it will be long. There is no reason for the queen to desire my company unless it has something to do with guns," Malcolm Scott said. "And we will want to be back again before the weather turns."

"I must have a few days to prepare," Alix said. "I am not certain Fiona has the proper garments. She's a country lass. Her clothing is reflective of her simple life."

"This won't be the court as you know it," the laird responded. "Ravenscraig is the queen's private home. Jamie bought it for her the year he died, and set his royal stone mason, Henry Martzioun, to make the repairs needed and fortify it."

"Nonetheless you can hardly allow your daughter to meet the king's mother looking like a tinker's brat," Alix told him. "You do not know who will be with the queen, or who will see your child. Remember you will eventually have to make a match for Fiona. As your heiress she will be considered to have a certain value. But if she displays well, her value will increase, my lord."

"God's foot, lass!" the laird exclaimed. "Your years at court have taught you well. Three days, and no more."

Fiona was beside herself with excitement. "I am going to meet the queen!" she singsonged over and over again as she danced about her father's hall. "Will I meet the king too, Alix? Will I?" she asked, twirling about the older girl.

"Stand still, you little minx!" Fenella said irritably. "How am I to take your measurements if you persist in prancing about? You can't meet Queen Marie in your chemise, lass."

"Fiona! Do what you are told," Alix said sharply.

The little girl suddenly stood quiet. "I'm sorry, Alix, Fenella. I am just so excited to be going to court."

"It isn't really court," Alix explained. "We are going to visit the queen in her own home. She wishes to speak with your father on some unknown matter. He is taking us so you may meet the king's mother. And aye. You may meet the young king."

"Does he have brothers and sisters?" Fiona wanted to know. "I've always wanted brothers and sisters, but unless Da will take another wife I don't suppose I'll ever have them," she said with a sigh.

"But if your da remarried and had a son, you would no longer be the heiress to Dunglais," Alix said to the little girl.

Fiona looked up at the older woman with wise eyes. "Alix, whether I am the heiress to Dunglais or no matters not a whit. I will be matched and married one day. And if I am the heiress my husband will take over Dunglais when Da dies. It isn't really mine, and never will be. Either way I will have a good dower portion. I'd just as soon Dunglais remain in the Scott family, and in order for that to happen Da must wed again."

Alix was astounded that her young charge had such a firm grasp of the situation. Her eyes met Fenella's, and the housekeeper shrugged, but a small smile played about her lips. It told Alix that Fenella was Fiona's font of information.

"Maybe the queen will have a nice lady for your father to wed," Fenella said wickedly, and her eyes danced with mischief.

"Nay," Fiona said. "I want Da to marry Alix."

"*Fiona!*" Alix turned scarlet. "Your father has been quite clear that he doesn't want another wife."

Fiona sighed dramatically. "I know my da loved my mother, but my mother is dead, and my da is still young enough to have a nice wife. And I like you. Da wouldn't marry anyone I did not like, Alix. Wouldn't you like to marry my da?"

Alix could feel her face burning. What was she going to say to the child? She couldn't say she hadn't liked being married. Fiona should not be swayed from the path chosen for her. But the truth was in the few months since she and the laird had become lovers she had begun to consider that a life with Malcolm Scott by her side would not be a bad thing. Fiona was looking at her expectantly, and so Alix finally said, "It isn't up to a lady to decide whom she will wed, little one. It is the gentleman who must want to marry, and your da does not."

"But would you marry my da if he asked you?" Fiona wanted to know.

Oh yes! Alix thought to herself. But then she said to the little girl, "A lady never reveals her heart until the gentleman has, Fiona. Remember that when you are grown." And Alix was shocked by what she had suddenly come to learn about herself. She had fallen in love with Malcolm Scott! *"Le bon Dieu aidez moi,"* she whispered to herself. It was impossible! From what Fenella had said, the laird no longer trusted women because of his wife's betrayal. He had been willing to take a mistress who could be cast off if necessary, but he wanted no wife. And Alix found herself surprised to realize she wanted no other man but Malcolm Scott.

Two new gowns were quickly made for Fiona. One was a bright scarlet red that complemented the child's coloring. The other a medium blue that was particularly flattering with Fiona's lovely blue eyes. The gowns were carefully packed. Alix saw to her own wardrobe. When she had first come to Dunglais almost a year ago the laird had immediately noticed the paucity of her wardrobe. He had instructed Fenella to let Alix choose some material for two more gowns. She had chosen some velvet for a more elegant gown, and a practical jersey. And then just a few weeks ago at Michaelmas he had given her her wages for the year, and she had been invited to choose materials for two more gowns from the peddler who came each early autumn with his wares. She had been unable to resist a lovely deep green velvet and another velvet brocade in a dusky orange.

And Alix had quickly set about fashioning her new gowns. The peddler had told her that the fashions were changing. Sleeves were now more closely fitted and necklines were much lower. Alix made her new garments to reflect what the peddler had told her. And among her clothing she packed the small silk pouch with her few bits of jewelry. She might not be a great lady, but she had learned from Margaret of Anjou and her own mother that less, especially if it was of the best quality, was far more impressive to the eye of the beholder.

"Such a great fuss over such a brief visit," the laird grumbled as they finally departed on a clear autumn morning.

"But, Da, we must look our best before Queen Marie and the king. Perhaps when he sees me he will decide a good Scots lass is more suitable than that foreign princess he is to wed," Fiona said with great confidence.

"I think the king will honor the commitment his good father, God assoil his soul, made for him, Fiona," Alix said. "Kings must always keep their word. But the king has three brothers. One is a duke and the other two are earls. Perhaps one of them will suit you." And she smiled over the child's head at Malcolm Scott, who smiled back at her.

Their trip took them three days, but the weather held and was pleasant. They avoided the city of Edinburgh with its great castle and bustling streets by adding a few more miles to their travels and skirting about it. Big cities were rife with many dangers and illnesses. The Laird of Dunglais had twenty men-at-arms with him, but traveling with a woman and his beloved child, he sought no difficulties if he might avoid them.

Queen Marie and Bishop Kennedy between them had as firm a

grip upon Scotland as any regency might have. The lowlands and the cities were peaceful. In the north the Highlands were a law unto themselves, but most of their difficulties were between feuding clansmen. As long as those local troubles did not spill over into the few towns there, or into the south, the government was content to allow the local lords to hold sway over their people.

And as for that great enemy, the English, they were too busy with their own problems, the least of which was a deposed king who had fled to Scotland. But as Queen Marie had switched sides, moving her tacit support from the House of Lancaster to the House of York, the new Yorkist king, Edward IV, was content to leave things as they were. And besides, he was too busy solidifying his support in the south to be bothered with what was happening in the north as long as the north would not prove a threat. Henry VI was a toothless old lion and was unlikely to ever reign again. And Scotland's king was a child unlikely to lead his armies over the border.

Each night of the first two they traveled, they stopped at a monastery where they were welcomed in a guesthouse, the men in one, the females in another. They were served a simple meal each evening and again in the morning before they departed. The Laird of Dunglais would leave a donation in keeping with his station, but one that erred more on the side of generosity in order that when they returned they might be welcomed back.

"We will reach Ravenscraig today, late," Malcolm Scott told his companions as they set off the third morning.

"Where exactly is this castle, my lord?" Alix asked him.

"In the region called Fife. It overlooks the Firth of Forth to the south. The king bought it from the Mure family, I believe. The owner had no heirs, was old, and had little wherewithal to keep it up. He died shortly thereafter."

"Is it a great castle?" Fiona wanted to know.

"It is a small castle," her father told her.

"Oh," the little girl said, sounding disappointed. "Shouldn't a king have a great castle, Da?"

The laird chuckled. "Kings have both great and small castles," he told her.

And then in late afternoon, even as the sun was hurrying towards the western horizon, they came in sight of Ravenscraig. While Malcolm Scott had said it was a small structure, he had not told them how impressive a castle it was. And upon its battlements the queen's banner was visible, announcing to all that Marie of Gueldres was in residence. Their party approached it slowly, showing the men-at-arms upon the walls that the visitors were friendly. The banner of Clan Scott with its great stag and the clan's motto, *Amo*, embroidered upon it, went before them, announcing their arrival.

Chapter 7

Ravenscraig Castle sat on a low rocky promontory set between two dark shingle beaches overlooking the Firth of Forth. Two rounded gray stone towers greeted the visitors approaching from the land side of the castle. A drawbridge lay over a water-filled moat at the gate entrance. The tower to the west was the oldest part of the castle, but the tower to the east had a deeper foundation where steps led down to an underground stable. The queen resided in the West Tower. Their party clopped across the oak bridge, beneath an iron portcullis, and into the courtyard between the towers. They were met by a captain wearing the queen's badge.

Malcolm Scott dismounted, saying as he did to the man, "I am the Laird of Dunglais, here at the queen's command. My daughter and her companion travel with me."

"I am David Grant, the queen's captain at arms," the soldier replied. "Aye, you are expected, my lord. If you and the ladies will follow me, I will take you to Her Highness." He turned to the Scott men-at-arms. "You men stable your mounts and then you may come to the great hall to be fed. You'll sleep with your horses. Ravenscraig isn't a large dwelling." He signaled to a soldier at arms, who came immediately. "Show the Laird of Dunglais's men where they are to go and then bring them to the hall."

"Aye, sir!" came the quick reply, but David Grant was already hurrying away with the guests.

"Your trip was an easy one?" the captain inquired pleasantly.

"Good weather always makes a trip smoother, especially when you travel with a woman and a child," the laird answered as they entered the tower, following the captain up a flight of stairs to a second level into a great hall.

Another man wearing the queen's badge hurried forward. He had an air of self-importance about him.

"This is the Laird of Dunglais and his family," David Grant said to the man. Then to the laird, "This is Master Michel, the steward of Ravenscraig Castle. He will see that Her Highness knows you are here." He bowed neatly to them and left.

The steward nodded to the laird and waved a servant to his side. "Go and tell Her Highness that her guests have arrived from the borders." As the servant dashed away, Master Michel said, "I have a bedspace for you, my lord, here in the hall. The ladies must share a small chamber." He signaled to another servant, who dashed to his side. It was obvious that those who served Master Michel were well trained. "Please take these two ladies to their assigned chamber," he told the serving woman who had come in response to his silent demand.

"Da! He called me a lady," Fiona said excitedly.

"Fiona," Alix admonished, but she saw the steward's quick brief smile out of the corner of her eye. "Come along now." And taking the little girl's hand, she followed the servant from the hall.

They were led up two flights of stone stairs to a narrow hallway. Down the dim corridor the woman trotted, finally stopping before a small door. She opened it and ushered Alix and Fiona inside. "You've a hearth," she said proudly. "Her Highness likes her guests to be comfortable. I lit the fire earlier. There's wood and peat both. Ah." She turned at the sound of footsteps. "Here's your trunks. Put it there at the foot of the bed, Finn, and you, Gordie, place yours beneath the window."

The two servants did as they were bid.

"There's water to wash the dust of your journey off," the serving woman said. "Shall I wait, or can you find your own way back to the hall?"

"We'll find our way," Alix said. "Thank you so much for your kindness."

The serving woman gave her a quick smile. It wasn't often guests thanked her. She departed the small chamber, closing the door behind her.

"We will bathe and change our clothing. We do not want to meet the king's mother dressed in our travel garments," Alix said to Fiona.

"I liked it when they called me a lady," Fiona told her companion. "They did it three or more times!"

Alix smiled. "I always felt special when I was your age and someone would refer to me as 'my lady.' I wasn't, of course, but everyone in the household knew it pleased me. My father began it," she remembered with a smile. "We must hurry now, *ma petite*."

They quickly removed their travel clothing and bathed their hands and faces in the warm water they found in a pitcher in the hot ashes of the hearth. Then Alix helped Fiona into her scarlet velvet gown, and, after brushing the child's long dark hair, outfitted it with a matching ribbon with tiny freshwater pearls about her forehead. She made Fiona sit upon the bed while she quickly dressed herself in the green velvet gown she had made. Brushing her hair out, she confined it in a delicate gold caul. She found the little chamois bag and took two thin gold chains from it, putting them over her head. The gold took away from the severity of the deep green of her gown. She then pulled out her rings, slipping them onto her fingers. Rings were an important accessory, and many women wore them on every finger, and the most fashionable wore several rings on each finger, fitting them onto each joint. Alix had five rings. She wore three on one hand, and two on the other. They had been her mother's but for one that her father had given her.

"I wish I had jewelry," Fiona sighed wistfully.

Alix reached into the bag and drew out a long strand of pearls.

"These were my mother's," she told the child as she looped them twice over Fiona's head. "You may have the loan of them only, but they do show nicely on your red velvet."

Fiona flung herself at Alix and wrapped her little arms about the older woman's neck. "Oh, Alix, I do love you! I wish you were my mother! Thank you!"

Alix hugged the little body against hers back. "I love you too, Fiona," she said. Then she untangled them, saying, "We must return to the great hall. The queen will certainly have come by now, and your father will be wondering what happened to us." Taking Fiona's hand in hers, Alix led them downstairs and back to the hall.

Marie of Gueldres was already there and in light conversation with the laird. She was a lovely woman of medium height who still retained a good figure despite the six children she had born her late husband. Her complexion was a light olive in tone, and her hair was jet black. She had fine amber-colored eyes. She was known to be intelligent, educated, and devout.

Alix led Fiona to where the queen and the laird sat. Then she waited politely to be acknowledged. The widowed queen did not wait. She turned almost immediately, smiling at them. The laird came at once to his feet and drew his child forward.

"Madame, this is my daughter, Fiona," he said.

Fiona curtsied prettily as Alix had taught her.

"What a lovely child she is, my lord," Marie of Gueldres said. "Welcome to Ravenscraig, Fiona Scott. We are pleased to see you."

"*Merci beaucoup, madame la reine,*" Fiona answered easily.

"*Vous parlez Français, m'enfant?*" Queen Marie smiled.

"*Oui, madame, un peu,*" Fiona said.

"*Très bon!*" the queen replied, and then she laughed.

"And my daughter's companion is Mistress Alix Givet," the laird said.

Alix curtsied a deep court curtsy.

"You did not learn to curtsy like that anywhere but in a court,

Mistress Givet," Queen Marie noted, curious. "In what court were you raised?"

"In the court of King Henry and his good queen, Margaret of Anjou," Alix replied politely. She realized the laird had said nothing of her background to the queen, leaving that up to her. Alix was grateful for his thoughtfulness.

"And what brought you there?" Queen Marie wanted to know.

"I was born there, madame. My mother was a lady-in-waiting to Queen Margaret, who is my godmother. My father was the queen's personal physician. They are both now deceased, God assoil their souls," Alix said, crossing herself piously.

The Scots queen crossed herself as well in a gesture of respect. "But how came you to the household of the Laird of Dunglais?" she asked Alix.

"I had traveled into Scotland and became lost upon the moor. The laird's men found me and brought me to him. As he has no wife and his daughter's nursemaid was elderly, the child needed to be educated in a manner befitting her station as the laird's heiress; he asked me to remain at Dunglais and care for Fiona. I am recently widowed, madame, and to be candid, his offer was the answer to my prayers. The husband my godmother had seen me wed to had died but seven months after our marriage was celebrated. I was planning to find her, but the truth is in her current condition she would not have been able to take me back into her household. That is why the laird's offer was such a blessing."

"But why would your husband's family not give you refuge?" The queen was curious and surprised.

"My husband's father had no other heirs," Alix said. "He sought to marry me himself, madame, which is why I left. He is a good man, but he was my husband's father. I felt it went against the laws of the church and of nature that he desired such a thing of me. But he sent the house priest to the archbishop at York for a dispensation. When I told him the archbishop would certainly not grant it, my husband's father said he had sent a large purse with his priest as a bribe. That is when I knew I must leave, and so I did."

"And you were perfectly just in doing so!" Queen Marie said. "Desperate men, however, will do desperate things, I fear, Mistress Givet. You are most welcome to Ravenscraig."

Alix curtsied again, and knowing she was dismissed, moved away with Fiona.

"She's lovely," the queen noted.

"She is good for my daughter," the laird answered.

The queen smiled a small smile but said nothing further.

"Tell me, madame, why have you called me to you?" Malcolm Scott inquired. "There is certainly nothing I have that can be of value to you or our young king. I am nothing but a simple border lord."

"You have a knowledge of guns, my lord," the queen said. "I wish to fortify this castle and arm it. Sitting on the edge of the Firth of Forth, it is vulnerable to attack."

"There are others who have a greater knowledge of cannon than I do," the laird replied modestly.

"But I know I may trust you completely, for you were my husband's old and good friend, my lord. My position is precarious now, for my son, the king, is only a little boy. You know what happened to his father in a similar situation. I stand between him and the horrific childhood his father had. Bishop Kennedy has his own agenda, and only I can keep him at bay, making certain his loyalty remains with my son. But there are those among the earls and other lords who would kidnap the king given the opportunity and use him for their own power base. That is why I would make Ravenscraig impenetrable to any who would attack it. And you can tell me what weaponry I will need, for I know for a fact that you have no loyalties other than to yourself, my lord."

"And to Scotland, madame," the laird murmured softly with a small smile.

She returned the smile. "And to Scotland," she agreed. It was silently understood between them that Scotland meant the young king, James III.

"I will advise you as best I can," he told her.

"Good! My uncle of Burgundy has agreed he will have the cannon I need cast and delivered here to the beach below the castle. He will also send men to install the cannon."

The Laird of Dunglais nodded. "Has Martzioun built you battlements?" he asked.

"Aye, he is constructing them now," the queen answered.

"I will want to inspect them to make certain they are sturdy enough to hold the guns you will need," the laird told her.

"Tomorrow is time enough," Queen Marie said. "In the meantime, let us pretend I have simply asked my husband's old companion for a visit because I am feeling nostalgic. I have all the children here with me. Your daughter must meet them. How old is she?"

"She will be seven in December," the laird said.

"My son Alexander is eight, and his brother David is six. They will need wives one day, my lord."

"And you will need greater names for them than mine," he replied with an amused smile. "You can do better for them than a border heiress." She did not need to bribe him. He would help her for the friendship he had had with her husband.

"You must wed again and have sons," Queen Marie said.

"So my housekeeper tells me." The laird chuckled.

"Your daughter's companion would make you a good wife. Her bloodline is respectable," Queen Marie noted thoughtfully. "And your daughter loves her, or perhaps you had not noticed it. However, seeing how well she does with your daughter I wonder if she might not make a good addition to my own household. My daughters are still babies, but Mistress Givet is just the sort of young woman I would want in their nursery influencing them. And her French is excellent, of course. Still I would repay you ill if I stole her away from you, my lord." Queen Marie smiled mischievously.

"I need no wife as long as I have Fiona," Malcolm Scott responded stubbornly. Nay. He needed no wife. Why would he need a wife? He had an heiress for Dunglais, but Alix was testing his reserve of late. She had become a passionate lover under his tutelage. He had thought that that would be enough, but suddenly the queen's teasing banter was making him wonder what his life would be like without Alix. He had lived without her before, hadn't he? And then he realized with a sharp sudden clarity that he didn't want to live without her now.

Was he in love? Aye, he was in love! Yet what he felt now was nothing like what he had felt for Robena. It had been time to take a wife. Robena was beautiful and exciting. Her dower was generous. Her family a good one. Malcolm Scott had approved the match his uncle wanted to make, and married the Ramsay lass. He hadn't been quite certain on their wedding night she was a virgin, but she had seemed at first to be loyal. But he realized now he had never loved her. And when she had betrayed him it was his pride, his honor, that had been hurt. She had gone from his life as easily as she had come into it, and he hadn't cared.

But it was different with Alix. He didn't want her to go away. He didn't want her to marry another one day. She was his! He loved her! And if he loved her then she deserved better from him than to be his mistress. She should be the wife he had been so certain he did not need. Fiona loved her too.

"My lord." Queen Marie broke into his thoughts.

"Madame?" He was immediately alert.

"May I present Eufemia Grant, my captain's wife, to you? Eufemia, this is Malcolm Scott, the Laird of Dunglais."

"Madame." The laird bowed over the elegant white hand that was offered.

"Eufemia is a member of the Stewart family, my lord. My late husband saw to her marriage several years ago," Queen Marie explained.

Eufemia Grant was a tall woman with an arrogant carriage. She had rich auburn hair and large breasts that almost spilled from her dark blue gown. "My lord," she greeted him in a husky voice, her bright blue eyes assessing him as a feline would a particularly plump mouse. The tip of her tongue snaked quickly across her lips. "You have traveled far?"

"From Dunglais in the borders," he answered her.

"I know it not," she replied. As the queen moved away to greet another gentleman who had just entered the hall, Eufemia Grant moved closer to the laird.

"There is no reason you would know Dunglais, madame." Jesu! Her scent was overpowering, and he had to refrain from pulling away when she slipped her arm into his.

"Is Dunglais beautiful?" she murmured so quietly he had to bend his head to hear her, and in doing so was treated to a fine display of her bosom, which he realized was exactly what she had intended.

"It's a simple border holding. Pretty to some, but not all," he answered her.

Across the hall Alix saw the laird bending low over the beautiful woman. Her heart contracted in her chest as if someone were squeezing it. Who was the woman? And why was she clinging to the laird in such a proprietary manner? Alix felt something akin to anger welling up in her. She wanted to go over and scratch the woman's eyes out. But she remained where she was until Fiona, noting the woman with her father, pulled away from Alix and headed straight for the couple.

"Da!" she said, hurrying up to him.

Eufemia Grant looked down at the little girl disdainfully.

"Qui êtes vous?" Fiona said, looking up boldly at the woman.

"What is she saying?" Eufemia Grant wanted to know.

"Vous êtes laide," Fiona continued. *"Je ne vous aime pas."*

"Fiona!" Alix hurried up. "I am so sorry, my lord."

The laird's mouth was twitching with amusement.

"Are you her servant?" Eufemia Grant demanded to know. "Take the brat away! I do not like children, especially those who chatter in a rude tongue. Having to dodge the queen's brood all the time is more than enough for me."

"I am hardly a servant, madame," Alix answered icily. "I am Mistress Alix Givet, goddaughter to Queen Margaret of England."

"Take your child away, then, Mistress Givet," Eufemia Grant said. "She is annoying us."

"She does not annoy me," the laird said, and reaching down, he lifted Fiona up into his arms. "She is my daughter, madame."

"I don't like her, Da," Fiona whispered to her father. "I will be very angry if you want to marry her."

"Mistress Grant has a husband, Fiona," her father reassured her.

"Then why is she clinging to you and showing you her tits?" Fiona demanded.

"Fiona, Mistress Grant's gown is the height of fashion and I am quite jealous," Alix said in an effort to smooth things over. She saw the laird was close to laughter, and so was she. Poor Eufemia Grant looked so outraged, for Fiona's whispers were quite plainly understood.

"Your daughter's manners lack gentility and delicacy, my lord," Eufemia Grant said and, turning, she stalked away.

Malcolm Scott chuckled, unable to restrain his amusement. Alix was caught up in a frenzy of giggles. Neither could help themselves. Fiona looked between them, and deciding that they were not angry at her, grinned.

"Praise God and his Blessed Mother that the woman didn't speak French," the laird said. "Fiona told Mistress Grant she was ugly."

"She is," Fiona said. "And she smelled beneath all that perfume she had bathed herself in, Da. She obviously does not wash regularly like Alix and like me. I did not like her. Why was she hanging on Da that way?"

"She is part of Queen Marie's household," Alix told the girl. "I think she was just attempting to make your father feel welcome."

"Precisely!" the laird agreed.

"I did not like her," Fiona repeated.

It was at that moment the queen returned, escorted by a handsome gentleman. "My lord, have you met Adam Hepburn? Adam, this is the Laird of Dunglais, Malcolm Scott."

Adam Hepburn was a tall, big-boned man with rich auburn hair and light eyes that seemed to waver between green and blue. He held out his hand to the laird, shook it, then smiled at Alix and Fiona. "And who are these two fair ladies?" he asked.

"My daughter, Fiona," the laird said, "and Mistress Alix Givet, who is her companion."

"Mistress Givet is my kinswoman of Anjou's goddaughter," Queen Marie said.

"And how did an English queen's godchild end up in Scotland?" the Hepburn lord asked, curious.

"I will tell you the story later, my lord," Queen Marie murmured.

"Have you seen the battlements yet?" Adam Hepburn asked Malcolm Scott.

"Nay," the laird answered.

"Tomorrow," the queen said quietly. "The laird's visit should be considered social, my lord. I do not wish to draw the attention of others to its real purpose."

"Forgive me, madame," Adam Hepburn quickly replied. "I am as anxious as you to hear his opinion. I forget that even here at Ravenscraig we are not entirely safe from prying eyes and sharp ears."

The queen smiled a tender smile at the Hepburn. "Always be here to watch over me, my lord," she said quietly.

Malcolm Scott caught Alix's eye. He saw the faintly surprised look upon her face. "Tell me," he said, turning the subject, "is the captain of your guard aware of his wife's nature, madame? Forgive me, but I am not used to being approached so boldly."

Adam Hepburn laughed heartily. "I believe Eufemia Grant has feline blood in her veins. She seems to stalk naturally. So far she hasn't caused a scandal, and so far her husband hasn't killed her."

The laird joined in his laughter. "He probably will have to eventually," he remarked. "She quite put my little daughter out."

"Eufemia doesn't like women of any age," Adam Hepburn said.

"My lords," the queen gently admonished them. "David Grant is most loyal."

A group of children suddenly entered the hall and came to where the queen stood. The eldest of them was a handsome young boy between nine and ten with an olive complexion, dark hair, and fine dark eyes. It was obvious who he was.

"Jamie!" the queen said, and she curtsied, as did Alix and Fiona. The two gentlemen bowed to the young king.

"Michel said we had guests, Mama," the boy said.

The queen presented the laird, Alix, and Fiona to him.

"Would you like to come and play with me?" the king asked Fiona. "I like chess. Do you like chess, my lady Fiona?"

"I have never played," Fiona said, cast down. Then she brightened. "But I am learning French, Your Highness."

"But I shall teach you!" the king told her. "And you will practice your French with me. My mother spoke French in her homeland. I speak very good French."

"I should like that, Your Highness," Fiona told him.

"Come along, then," the king said. "You don't want to play with my brothers. They are much too rough for a fine young lady as yourself."

"Jamie plays with lasses," Alexander, the eight-year-old Duke of Albany said with a sneer, and his two brothers, David, the Earl of Moray, and John, the Earl of Mar, snickered and punched each other.

"My lords, the king seeks to make a guest welcome," Adam Hepburn said. "You might learn from him."

"I know what you are and what you do," the young Duke of Albany said with a leer. "There are no secrets, my lord."

"Alexander!" the queen admonished her second-born son. "Apologize to Lord Hepburn at once."

"Your pardon," the boy said with a sneer, and then he led his two younger brothers off across the hall.

"He is jealous," Adam Hepburn said softly. "He thinks he should be king."

"My lords and my ladies," Michel, the queen's steward, called, "the meal is served."

"You will sit at the high board with us," the queen told the laird.

Alix moved discreetly away, but the queen called to her.

"Nay, Mistress Givet. You will sit with us. I know it is two years since you have seen my kinswoman of Anjou, but you must tell me what you know nonetheless."

The meal was served quickly and efficiently. Alix was surprised at the simplicity of it. There were prawns that had been broiled in sweet butter and wine with a sauce of mustard and dill. There was a fish she could not identify, which the queen proudly told them was caught fresh that morning. It too was broiled, filleted, and served upon a bed of crisp cress with pieces of lemon. Alix hadn't seen a lemon in several years, although they were always available at the English court's kitchens. Fat capons roasted golden and sauced with oranges and raisins came next along with ham and venison. There was a potage of vegetables, peas, carrots, leeks, and beets in a cream sauce tasting of rosemary. The bread was fresh. There was butter and several cheeses. How long had it been since she had seen a Brie? Alix asked herself. At Dunglais there was hard yellow cheese. It was tasty but it wasn't Brie. She indulged herself shamelessly until she caught Adam Hepburn grinning at her. Alix blushed, and he chuckled.

"The fare in the borders, I know, is hardly grand," he said.

"Fenella does well enough for us," Alix replied, "but growing up in my godmother's court I grew to love the different cheeses that were available to us."

"It must seem strange living such a rustic life after the life you have lived," Adam Hepburn said. "Yet you seem happy, Mistress Alix."

"The last few years were so chaotic," Alix told him. "The king's bouts of madness grew worse. The Yorkist faction jockeyed for precedence over the king's men. Battles were fought back and forth, and we were never certain that we were safe. The queen was particularly frantic for Prince Edward's safety." She sighed. "And then my mother died. She was one of the queen's ladies and had been with her since they were both girls in Anjou. She had always been so hearty, but suddenly she was tired all the time. My father knew that even if he could take us back to a quieter life in Anjou she would die sooner than later. All those years of looking after her mistress had taken their toll upon her health. She died just before we were finally forced to flee north."

"I am sorry," Adam Hepburn said. "It is always the women and children who suffer in these wars we men create. Your father is gone now too, and you have become orphaned. You had a husband, I am told, and he too is dead."

"Gracious!" Alix exclaimed. "When you put it all together, and I am the only one left standing . . ." She looked momentarily distressed.

"You are a survivor," he told her. "There is nothing wrong with being a survivor, Mistress Givet. Better to survive than not. Have you become your laird's mistress?"

"*My lord!*" Alix's fair skin grew quite pink with her blushes.

Adam Hepburn laughed. "You are a survivor," he repeated.

"I am not that kind of woman," Alix began, but the Hepburn lord shook his head.

"Nay, you are not. I can see that. You love him, but being a wise woman you have said nothing. He loves you, you know. His eyes follow you everywhere."

"Oh no, my lord!" Alix said. "He was cruelly betrayed by his wife. He will not love or trust again any woman."

Adam Hepburn laughed softly again. "What a charming innocent you are, Alix Givet. Your laird loves you, and eventually he will admit to it. Will that make you happy, *ma petite?*"

"*Mais oui*, my lord," Alix whispered.

The meal over, the queen's musicians began to play from a little gallery at one end of the hall. The music was sprightly, and Alix found her foot tapping to it.

"Madame, shall we dance?" Adam Hepburn asked the queen.

Marie of Gueldres smiled and clapped her hands. "What a lovely idea!" she agreed, and arose from her place at the high board. She led them to the floor, and clasping hands, they made a circle. David Grant and his wife joined them. Together they circled first one way and then another to the music. Then the circle broke briefly as they paired and danced as couples. At first the queen danced with Adam Hepburn while the Grants made a couple, and Malcolm Scott took Alix in hand. The gentlemen bowed. The ladies curtsied. The women were twirled several times and then lifted up to shouts from the men-at-arms seated at the several tables in the hall.

They joined hands again, circling, broke apart as pairs once more but this time with different partners. The laird partnered the queen while David Grant danced with Alix, leaving Adam Hepburn with Eufemia Grant. Alix was flushed and laughing as the queen's captain lifted her up to the shouts from his men-at-arms. They circled a third time and then danced together again, Alix with Adam Hepburn now. Finally the music ceased and the dance was ended.

Malcolm Scott made his way to Alix. He took her by the arm, and while the others began to chat among themselves, the laird took her from the hall. His face was dark with his anger. "I thought you were different from other women, but you are no better, Alix Givet!" he snarled at her.

"What is the matter, my lord?" Alix cried softly. "What have I done to offend?"

"Do you think I would not notice you shamelessly flirting with both Hepburn and Grant as you danced with them?" the laird demanded. "Did you think I did not see you at dinner with Hepburn, your two heads together? You swore to be honest with me, Alix!"

"And I have been. I am," Alix responded. "I was not flirting as I danced. I was having a happy time much like I had at my godmother's court. Did you expect me to put on a dour face when I danced with others? Am I only to smile at you, my lord?"

"Aye, damn it!" he almost shouted, and then he was kissing her hungrily, pushing her up against the stone wall of the corridor in which they stood. "You are mine, Alix! *Mine!* Both Hepburn and Grant were admiring you with their eyes. I saw it!"

Alix, reaching out, caressed his handsome face. "Colm, I am yours. I want no other, and that is the truth. I cannot stop other men from admiring me, and it is pleasant to be admired. But I do not encourage any man but you, my lord, and you know that to be a truth. I am not Robena Ramsay," Alix told him boldly. He was jealous! She almost laughed aloud at the revelation. He was jealous! Did he love her? Or was it simply that he thought of her as his possession? She would never know until he told her. "Let us go back into the hall, my lord, before we are missed. The queen has not ended the evening yet, and we cannot depart until she does."

He groaned low, pulling her against him. "I need you, Alix," he told her.

"As I need you, my lord," she reassured him, "but it is not to be until we return home to Dunglais. Now let us return to the hall."

Malcolm Scott slept restlessly that night. So *this* was love. The desperation. The longing. The frustration. The burning need. He wasn't certain he liked it, and yet he seemed to have no choice in the matter. Alix had been correct, of course. She had not been flirting; and both Hepburn and Grant had simply been having a good time as any man dancing with a pretty girl would have. Yet seeing her with other men had enraged him. He had never felt that way with Robena. He had always enjoyed watching her and seeing the effect she had on others.

It was not the case with Alix. He understood now he had married Robena Ramsay because he had believed it was time to take a wife. He had liked her at first for she seemed a pleasant enough lass. But he had not loved her. Not like he loved Alix. When she had run off with his half brother it had been his pride that had been hurt, not his heart. But if he ever lost Alix he knew it would kill him. He loved her. God and his Blessed Mother help him. *He loved her!* Now what the hell was he to do?

When the next day dawned the Laird of Dunglais had his duty to the queen to consider first and foremost. He ate oat stirabout, hard-boiled eggs, bread and cheese with Adam Hepburn, who then took him to see the fortification work now in progress.

"Our Jamie meant to fortify all of the shoreline of the Firth of Forth," Hepburn informed his companion. "Since it opens to the sea it opens Scotland, particularly Edinburgh, to any enemy seeking to invade."

"It's an entry to the lowlands as well," the laird noted.

"Aye, it is," Hepburn agreed.

They climbed to the stone battlements that were now being finished and connected the east and west towers of Ravenscraig.

"You need at least two cannon openings on the land side as well," the laird said.

"There are four facing the water as you will see," Hepburn told him.

"The queen will have to set up a foundry here in Scotland. She cannot rely on her uncle entirely. He may cast her first weapons, but she will need to be independent of him eventually. If he dies, if he decides not to aid her, she must be able to fend for herself. She must be able to make her own ammunition. You need a reliable supply of ammunition. You can't control the quality if you don't make it," Malcolm Scott said. "And you'll need a goodly supply of saltpeter, sulfur, and charcoal for it. Saltpeter will be the most difficult to obtain, as it is in short supply. But large stones, the rounder the better, can also be used as ammunition."

"I never knew any of this," the Hepburn said.

"Jamie loved his guns, and frankly so did I," the laird said.

"Is your keep armed?"

"Dunglais? Nay. I don't have the means for it, but if I did I wouldn't bother. I have no neighbors for miles, and the only conflict we see is nothing more than ordinary border skirmishes," the laird told his companion.

"Six cannon are enough artillery for Ravenscraig?"

"Why would you need more? Especially if you build up other cannon forts along the coastline," Malcolm Scott said.

"It will be some time before they can be finished," Hepburn said.

"Scotland is at peace for now. The English prefer coming over the border and have no navy of any size with which to attack us. And they are too busy with their own civil strife to be bothered by us unless, of course, we poke the lion. The French are our allies. Who else is there? I'm a practical man, my lord. But the queen will make her own decisions in this matter. These battlements are well and strongly constructed. They will hold your artillery. I would see that sturdy wood shutters are made for the cannon ports to conceal them. I would not set my cannon on trestle benches like many do. Have good stone mounts in which to set them. I have heard that of late some are experimenting with wheels. It requires fewer men to move the weapons. The queen would have to ask her uncle, and he would have to speak with his foundry master." The laird looked about. " 'Tis a fair land, our Scotland," he said, gazing out over the Firth of Forth and its surround of green hills.

"Aye," Adam Hepburn agreed. Then he said, "The queen should be ready to receive us now. It is her custom to break her fast each morning in a small private chamber with her children. She worries about her lads. Alexander is the wild son, and unfortunately David and John follow his lead rather than young James."

"They are braw lads," Malcolm Scott said. "Jamie was proud of them." He didn't ask how the Hepburn of Hailes knew all this. The rumor had it that Adam Hepburn was the queen's lover. Well, if he was, she was entitled to a bit of comfort. It didn't stop Bishop Kennedy from attempting to discredit her, however.

Coming down from the battlement and reentering the great hall, they found the queen and Alix in conversation. The laird's heart leaped at the sight of her. Seeing them, the queen waved them over and the two men joined her.

"Malcolm Scott has given me an excellent assessment of what you will need, Your Highness," Adam Hepburn reported.

"I would say one or two more things," the laird interjected. "They are beginning to cast cannons with cast iron now as well as bronze. Cast iron is stronger. Have at least half your supply made from it. And do not use serpentine powder. The sulfur and the saltpeter fall to the bottom of the barrels, leaving the charcoal on top. It means the powder has to be remixed on site. It can be dangerous."

"Why does that happen?" the queen asked him. "How can it be prevented?"

"Saltpeter and sulfur are heavier elements than charcoal," the laird explained. "The newer method is called *corning*. All of the ingredients are mixed wet and then spread out and formed into a cake, which dries hard. The cakes, when broken up into granules, have the advantage of staying dry and are easier to transport. It offers more firepower using less." The laird did not tell the queen that the cannon that had killed the king had been loaded with too much corning. Its disadvantage was in making those loading the weapons understand they did not need as much. It was a better method nonetheless, and the king had approved it.

"The laird has suggested we set up a factory of our own to make the ammunition that you will need. And a foundry to cast our own cannon should your uncle's help not be readily available to you," the Hepburn of Hailes told the queen.

"You have been an enormous help to us, my lord," Marie of Gueldres said.

"Madame, I will always be ready to aid you and the young king," Malcolm Scott said. "I am honored you called upon me."

"It was better that others not be aware I intended carrying out my husband's plans to fortify the Firth of Forth," the queen told him.

"Then if my service to you is done, madame, and with your permission, I will begin my return home on the morrow," the laird said.

"It is but midautumn, my lord. Bide with us for a few more days," the queen said. "I am enjoying muchly the company of Mistress Alix, and my son the company of your little daughter. She is a lively and outspoken lass. The king is not used to such." The queen smiled a mischievous smile at Malcolm Scott.

Alix giggled. "She told the Duke of Albany this morning to mind his manners, which she thought no better than a cowherd's when approaching his king."

The queen laughed. "Alexander was mightily taken aback and equally offended, but the king was quite delighted to have a small defender."

The invitation to remain had not been a request. It had been a command, and the laird knew it. He had bowed and acquiesced, but he wanted to go home. They hunted in the hills surrounding Ravenscraig over the next few days. The young king was not a particularly good horseman. Though he strove to hide it, he was afraid of the great black horse upon which they seated him. His three younger brothers took every opportunity to spook the animal, laughing as their older sibling clung to the beast. One morning, just as they had started out, the king fell off of his horse. He lay still for a moment or two.

"Is he dead?" Alexander Stewart wanted to know. "If he is dead then I am king!"

"I am afraid Your Grace is doomed to disappointment this time," Adam Hepburn said dryly as the king groaned and sat up.

"What an unpleasant child," Alix murmured to the laird as they rode back to the castle, for the accident had shaken the king, and their hunt that day was over before it even began. "How he covets his brother's place."

"If young James grows up, his brothers will give him nothing but difficulty, I fear," Malcolm Scott replied quietly. "Come and walk with me on the beach, lass."

She smiled a slow smile of assent and nodded.

When they had dismounted within the castle courtyard the laird took Alix's hand, and they quickly departed across the drawbridge. The queen, seeing them go, raised a questioning eyebrow at the Hepburn of Hailes.

"I believe she is his mistress," Adam Hepburn said softly. "They have been gone from their home for over ten days now, madame. I believe he misses her company."

Marie of Gueldres laughed low. "He misses her body, my lord."

"I do not enjoy being separated from you," the Hepburn said quietly.

"Hush, my lord," she told him. "In public we must both remain circumspect. As it is Bishop Kennedy has admonished me, although even he is not certain of what we share. I prefer he never be sure of that."

"Why should you not be happy?" he demanded of her. "You are a widow, not a nun in a cloister."

"I am happy, but I am also the guardian of Scotland's king and the mother of his five siblings. Unlike a man, I may not flaunt my lover, my lord, and you well know it. Besides, there are those who, if they knew for certain, would be angry the king's mother had taken for her lover a mere Hepburn and not an earl. They would say your family's ambition was shameless. Are you ambitious, my lord?"

"All men are ambitious, madame, but not all men love you as I do," he answered.

Marie of Gueldres smiled at him again. "And that is why you are my lover, Adam Hepburn. I know when a man's heart is true."

Then together they entered the castle while below them on the beach the Laird of Dunglais walked with Alix. A light wind was coming off the water. Above them the skies were partly cloudy. One moment the sun shone brightly, and then it was gone beneath the lowering gray. The dark waters of the Firth of Forth lapped at the shale beach. They walked hand in hand for some minutes, but then Alix shivered.

"You are cold," he said.

"Aye, 'tis chilly along the water," Alix admitted.

"The beach is low here," he said. "We'll climb up and walk back through the fields, lambkin." He put his arm about her now, and together they mounted the hillock, easily gaining the field above it. They reached an open shed as it began to rain. "It's only a shower," he assured her as they ducked inside. And then he pulled her into his arms. "For the first time since we left Dunglais I have you alone and to myself," he growled.

"Nay," she said. "There was our first night at Ravenscraig when you accused me of flirting with other men and dragged me from the hall."

"I'm a fool," he said, and then he kissed her a slow, hot kiss, crushing her breasts against his leather-clad chest. The scent of her filled his nostrils, and his lust leaped.

"I miss you," she admitted. "I miss being in your bed, in your arms, Colm." Her fingers brushed lightly over the nape of his neck. Aye, she loved him.

The shed was filled with fresh hay. The laird pulled Alix down upon it. His hands pushed her skirts up, and he stroked the sensitive flesh on the insides of her thighs. The bodice of her gown felt as if it would burst open. He smiled down into her face, and she smiled back in agreement. No words were necessary. He wanted her, and she wanted him. The laird released his cock, which was already hard with his longing.

Alix pulled his head down to hers and began to kiss him hungrily. "Hurry, my lord," she whispered hotly against his mouth. "I have missed your hard length inside of me. I have missed the passion we share. Ahhh!" she cried as he thrust deep into her.

Having pushed within her, he lay quiet for several moments. He had been so desperate for her that he felt if he moved again even slightly he would lose control over himself. He had never needed a woman as much as he needed her. Aye! He loved her.

Alix sighed with pleasure, feeling his thick length within her velvet sheath. She undid the buttons of her jerkin and unlaced her shirt beneath so he might have access to her full round breasts. He groaned, and dipping his head, began to suckle upon one of her breasts. Her hands caressed him, silently encouraging him in his passion. Finally she whispered to him, "*Please, Colm! I burn for you. Fuck me! Please!*"

The laird lifted his head up and their eyes met. "You must keep your eyes open, lambkin, when I do. If you close them I will cease," he said wickedly. Then he began to move on her. She was like wet silk, like honeyed fire. He had thought himself near to release when he had first penetrated her, but now he had regained control of himself. He moved back and forth slowly at first, then with increasing speed. He looked deep into her eyes as he used her, enjoying the passion that burned within them until finally he saw her struggling to keep her eyes open as he had commanded. He increased his efforts, and Alix screamed his name. "Colm! Oh God, you are killing me!" Her eyes rolled back in her head as her body shook with fierce tremors, and he let his own passion pour into her with short, hard spurts until her sheath had milked him dry, and he collapsed atop her.

Finally they came to themselves, and he rolled off her body, laying on his back, his breathing slowly returning to normal. God help him! He would never get enough of her.

Alix sighed happily. "I'm glad we have found this little place where we may be together. I never again want to live without your passion, Colm."

"Nor I yours, lambkin," he told her. "Beg the queen to release us soon. She will give you what you desire, for your kinswoman's sake."

"I will, my lord," Alix promised him.

They reordered their garments, and as the shower had now stopped and the sun was peeping from behind a purple cloud bank, they returned to Ravenscraig Castle hand in hand. That night as they sat at the high board Alix spoke softly to the queen.

"Madame, my lord and his daughter are missing Dunglais, and so am I. May we not depart soon? The weather grows colder, and my lord's people will be worried if he does not return soon."

Marie of Gueldres sighed deeply. "I know it is not fair to retain your company any longer," she admitted. "You are free to leave on the morrow, Alix Givet. But before you go you will come and speak with me, for there is something you should know."

"Thank you, Your Highness," Alix replied. And she wondered what it was the queen could possibly have to say to her.

Chapter 8

ater that evening in the hall Alix managed to steal a moment with her lover. "We are free to leave on the morrow," she told the laird. "But the queen wishes to speak with me before we go, my lord."

"I will alert our men," he responded.

"Remember, she does not receive anyone before midmorning. We shall not get an early start, I fear," Alix reminded him.

"But we shall be gone from Ravenscraig, lambkin, and be making for the borders before the sunset. I'll send a rider ahead to the nunnery of St. Margaret begging accommodation for tomorrow night," Malcolm Scott replied. "On the following morning we will depart immediately at first light."

Alix smiled at him. "I cannot wait to get home," she said, "and have the winter set in so we may be safe from all visitors."

"If we are fortunate, my uncle will have come with his latest candidate while we have been away. He will be very disappointed, I fear," the laird chuckled.

Alix excused herself from the queen's presence and hurried to the little chamber she shared with Fiona. She packed up their belongings carefully, leaving out the clothing in which they would travel on the morrow. Then she went to find Fiona in the royal nursery, where the little girl was deeply involved in a chess game with the king. Fiona had learned the game quickly and proved a good player, to the young king's delight.

James Stewart looked up. "You wish to speak to us, Mistress Givet?" he asked.

"It is time for Fiona to go to bed, Your Highness," Alix answered him politely.

The king sighed. "But she is near to besting me for the very first time," he said.

Alix smiled a little smile. "And how long do you think it will take her to do such a thing, Your Highness?"

"Two moves, if she is clever," James Stewart said seriously. "But if she is not, I shall best her in three."

"Then with Your Highness's permission I shall wait," Alix replied.

"Granted," the boy king responded, and then he turned his attention back to the game table.

Alix did not sit, for she had not been invited to do so. She stood patiently as the end of the game was played out. She saw that the king might actually have easily won, but instead he allowed Fiona the small victory, grinning when she clapped her little hands in glee with her triumph.

"I have beaten you at last, Jamie!" she crowed.

"Indeed, Fi, you have," he agreed. "But tomorrow is another day."

"I regret to tell Your Highness that we shall be leaving Ravenscraig tomorrow," Alix said to the king. "Fiona, make your farewells to His Highness and thank him for his kindness and for teaching you to play chess."

"Do we have to leave tomorrow?" Fiona said. "Why can we not remain?"

"We must leave tomorrow," Alix told the girl. "You must remember your father has responsibilities at Dunglais. It would not do for the winter to set in and the laird be gone from his keep."

Fiona arose from her seat at the gaming table. She curtsied a perfect curtsy to the king. "I thank Your Highness for teaching me how to play the game of chess. I regret I cannot give Your Highness the opportunity of a rematch."

The king stood, and taking the girl's small hand in his, he bent and kissed it. "We have enjoyed your company most greatly, Mistress Fiona. Godspeed, and a safe journey home to your Dunglais. Perhaps if we travel to the borders one day we may have the pleasure of visiting you."

"Thank you, sir," Fiona responded. "I shall look forward to it, and Your Highness will be more than welcome." Then she took Alix's hand and they departed the royal nurseries.

"That was very nicely done, Fiona," Alix complimented her charge proudly. "I am going to tell your father how well you did."

"I'm sorry to have to leave Ravenscraig, and yet I will not be unhappy to go home," Fiona admitted to her companion.

"I have already packed our few possessions and laid out our travel garments," Alix said. "We'll wash tonight so as to be ready. I am commanded to see the queen before we leave, and you know she does not arise as early as the rest of us."

But to Alix's surprise she had no sooner finished breaking her fast in the great hall with the laird and Fiona than one of the queen's ladies came to fetch her. Alix followed the woman and was led to a charming small room with a view of the Firth of Forth. The sun was just risen and dappled the waters gold.

"Good morning, Mistress Alix," Marie of Gueldres greeted her. "Sit down, and I will tell you what it is I wish to tell you."

Alix took her seat upon a footstool that had been placed before the upholstered high-back chair where the queen sat. She looked expectantly up at her.

"Last summer a messenger came to me from my kinswoman Margaret of Anjou," the queen began. "Her letter was quite detailed, and inquired if her goddaughter, one Alix Margot Givet, had come to me seeking a place in my household. It went on to explain she had matched her godchild with the son and heir of an English baron. That the girl's husband had died under tragic circumstances. But as there was no issue from the marriage, and the young man's father was now heirless, the baron had sought a dispensation to wed the girl himself from the archbishop of York. The dispensation was granted early last summer, but the girl had run away from the gentleman's home in the meantime. It was assumed, as she had been a member of the former queen's household, that she would not flee south into England but north into Scotland."

"Then you knew who I was once you learned my identity," Alix said softly. "Even before I told you my tale."

"Aye, I knew," Marie of Gueldres replied. "And I was as appalled that my kinswoman would even countenance such a second marriage for you, as I said to you when you told me your tale. However, Sir Udolf came over the border and sought out your godmother. He prefaced his request that the queen approach me with a rather good-size purse. Your godmother is, as you can well imagine, in desperate straits, Mistress Alix. And so she wrote to me asking if you had come to me and if I knew of your whereabouts. Of course, at the time you had not come to me and I did not know where you were."

"Will you tell her now?" Alix asked fearfully.

Marie of Gueldres shook her head. "Nay, I will not. I do not, as I have said to you previously, approve of a marriage between you and your late husband's father. It is an unnatural thing. And besides, you are in love with Malcolm Scott, and he with you. True love is a rare and beautiful thing, *ma petite*. I will not destroy it for you."

"The laird is not in love with me," Alix said, disbelieving.

The queen laughed merrily. "He is very much in love with you, else he should not have dragged you from my hall several nights ago when he grew jealous that my captain and Adam Hepburn were paying you compliments and enjoying dancing with you. Believe me, *ma petite*. The Laird of Dunglais is besotted with you."

"He has not said it," Alix murmured.

"Men rarely declare their love unless they are certain they will not be rejected. I know the tale of your laird's marriage. A man betrayed is even more cautious," the queen told the young woman. "Be patient with him, *ma petite*. Love him, and all will be well."

Alix smiled shyly. "I will try, Your Highness," she said.

"Go home now, *ma petite*, but beware. Sir Udolf has been seeking among the border families for you. If he finds you, however, I will protect you if your laird cannot. You will not be forced into a marriage with this man."

"Thank you, Your Highness," Alix said, rising and curtsying to the queen. Then she backed from the room, and hurried to make her way back to her chamber where she had left her cape. She found their trunks gone, and picking up her cape, returned back to the hall where the laird and Fiona were waiting for her.

Adam Hepburn was in the courtyard waiting to bid them farewell. He lifted Fiona onto her mount and then put Alix into her saddle, stealing a kiss as he did so.

"My lord!" she scolded him. "You will make the laird jealous." But she was laughing, and so was he.

Still and all Malcolm Scott looked slightly annoyed, but when the Hepburn poked him with a wicked grin, he could not help but grin back.

"Now that I know what delights your Dunglais holds, my lord, I may come and visit you," Adam Hepburn teased the laird.

"You'll be welcome," Malcolm Scott said, laughing now.

They rode forth from the castle of Ravenscraig, turning south back towards the borders.

"The queen had matters to speak upon before we departed," Alix said to the laird once their journey was well underway.

"What had she to say, lambkin?" he asked her.

Alix told him of her conversation with Marie of Gueldres.

Malcolm Scott's face darkened. "If he comes, I'll not let him have you," the laird said. "And if the queen is on our side then we are certain to triumph."

Our side! He had said *our* side and not *your* side. Alix's heart soared happily. "I would die before I left you, Colm," she replied quietly.

Her sweet declaration left him briefly speechless. Could it be she loved him? Really loved him as he loved her? Would she be faithful to him and not betray him as Robena had done? Could she be trusted? So many women could not. He thought a moment of Eufemia Grant, the wife of the queen's captain who had so boldly tried to seduce him that first day at Ravenscraig. She was a whore by nature, Adam Hepburn had told him. Grant had only married her because James Stewart, the former king, had asked him to, and offered Grant the position of captain of the queen's guards if he would. An older man whose entire life had been in the king's service, Grant had agreed. His connections were not great and, while he deserved the promotion he received, he could have never gained it by being a most competent soldier. Another poor Stewart relation might have been content to be given a good husband. But Eufemia Grant was far more ambitious and a captain of the guard was not good enough for her.

Malcolm Scott shook his head. But most women were greedy for more than they had. His own mother had never been satisfied with what his father was or what he possessed. And after birthing her only child, she had gone on to have a series of stillbirths until finally she had refused his father her bed. Then she had spent the rest of her days an invalid, complaining about his father's many mistresses, each one of which had been more acquisitive than the previous one. He had not been overly sad when his parents had died within a year of each other. His mother of her own bitter choler. His father of the pox.

And then he had heeded his uncle of Drumcairn's advice, and married Robena Ramsay. But Robena had soon proved even worse than his mother, birthing Fiona, ignoring her because she was not a son, and making his life a misery until he took her to court. At the court of his friend King James II, his wife had blossomed as her extraordinary beauty, and the wardrobe that almost beggared him, brought her the attention and adulation of many powerful and wealthy men. He had never been certain that she hadn't begun her unfaithful behavior there. The Earl of Huntley had been most admiring of her. More so than most. And because he wasn't sure, and because he did not choose to be mocked as a cuckold, he had taken Robena back to Dunglais before any scandal might break.

She had, of course, been furious with him. He had admonished her that her duties were that of a chatelaine, a mother, and a wife. She had eschewed all of those duties, leaving the household to his kinswoman, Fenella, their child to him, and locked her bedchamber door. Malcolm Scott was too proud a man to make an issue over that. She would eventually come to her senses because she had no other choice than to accept what she had and not what she thought she wanted.

But he had been wrong in his assessment of the situation. Robena had taken to riding out day after day on a great white stallion she had brought with her to the marriage. Suddenly they had all noticed a change in her. She laughed at the most inappropriate times. A wild, high-pitched laugh. She was secretive, and more and more high-strung. He could ask nothing of her that she did not refuse with absolute defiance, almost daring him to stop her behavior. He had gone to his uncle of Drumcairn for advice, and Robert Ferguson had returned with him to Dunglais to see with his own eyes what it was his nephew had to complain about. Although Robena was at her most charming to him, she was still out of control and Robert Ferguson had no idea what to tell his nephew.

And then had come the day when he had learned his wife had just ridden out carrying a pouch with her jewelry. He had, of course, followed after her. When he finally caught up with Robena, she was in the arms of his bastard half brother, Black Ian Scott. His wife had been shocked to realize they had been caught. But Ian had laughed.

"First yer wench, Colm, and then the lairdship, which should have been mine," Ian had said, drawing his sword.

Malcolm Scott's eyes went to his wife. Her beautiful face was alight with her excitement. She looked from him to his half brother. "Is this what you want, Robena?" he asked her in a quiet and reasonable voice.

"Aye!" she said. "Fight for me, Colm. And I will laugh when Ian kills you, for I hate you. And when Ian is Laird of Dunglais I'll see your precious daughter put out on the moors to live or die. I care not!"

"Fiona is your own child, from your own womb," he replied, shocked.

"She matters not to me!" Robena said, and she laughed at the look on his face.

"When I have killed my brother, *Wife*," Malcolm Scott said in a cold, even voice, "I will see to your punishment. Do not doubt it for a moment, Robena." And then he drew his sword even as his half brother jumped forward to attack him.

Above them the sky was a dark gray with an approaching storm. Thunder was in the air. The two men battled back and forth for several long minutes. Each pricked the other, and then Ian Scott delivered his sibling a blow that opened a wound on the laird's left shoulder, blossoming scarlet onto his shirt.

Robena screamed with delight, her face avid with blood lust. "Kill him, Ian! Kill him!" she screamed, elated to see what she believed was the beginning of the end for her husband. She began to pace back and forth like a caged animal.

Hearing her cruel words, Malcolm Scott was suddenly free of any affection he might have held for his wife. He had no intention of being killed by his bastard half brother. He had no intention of allowing his darling child to be abused by her own mother. A black fury at the pair who had betrayed him rose within him, and he was suddenly filled with renewed energy.

The Laird of Dunglais pressed forward, attacking his opponent with a fierce vigor. Ian Scott was older and heavier than his brother. To his surprise, and then a budding fear, he began to tire. Malcolm Scott's blade did not flag, and his opponent, suddenly aware that he could lose, lost his concentration for but a moment, stumbled, and fell. His sword went flying a small distance across the moor. On his back he looked up at the laird.

"Mercy," he cried.

"Go to the hell where you belong!" the laird responded, and thrust his sword into his half brother's heart, killing him instantly.

Robena Scott shrieked and, looking about frantically for her lover's sword, she found it, picked it up, and charged her husband, flailing at him with the weapon. He knocked it from her hands with his own sword. Robena Scott turned and began to run.

"Now, *Wife*, the question is what am I to do with you?" he called after her. Then, realizing the answer, he had done what he knew must be done, and sometime afterwards taken his half brother's body back to Dunglais to be buried.

Now once again a woman was at the center of his decision. The solution had been easy with Robena. It was not as easy with Alix. He had not loved Robena. He loved Alix. But would she betray him? She said not, but could he trust her word? Women were prone to lie, especially to men. Had he not been witness to it? His own mother. His wife, and only a few days ago, Eufemia Grant, who would have bedded him, would have lied to him and to her husband. Could he trust Alix? Dare he trust her? But if you truly loved someone, didn't you trust them? And then Malcolm Scott realized to his surprise that he was afraid. He was afraid to make a decision for fear he would be wrong. He didn't want to be hurt, yet what kind of a man did that make him? Was he a coward?

"Are you all right, my lord?" Alix's sweet voice pierced his thoughts.

"My head hurts," he admitted to her.

"We will soon be at St. Margaret's," she said. "The past few days have been busy for us. You are not used to even an informal court such as Queen Marie's. We will be home in a few days, and you will be better."

"Aye, it will be good to get back to Dunglais," he agreed.

The weather was beginning to turn. Their first day of travel had been beneath a weak sun and a still wind. The second day was gray and the wind had begun to rise, but at least it was at their backs.

Halfway through the third day it began to snow lightly, but the winds had picked up. The tiny white flakes melted at first as they hit the ground, but as the snow grew heavier it began to stick, and by the time Dunglais Keep came into view it was barely visible. The laird had transferred Fiona from the small gelding she had been riding. He had set his daughter before him, wrapping his own heavy cape about her to keep her warmer. He looked to Alix, who rode by his side. She was hunched down, the hood of her cloak pulled well up, her head down.

"We're almost there, lambkin," he said to her.

She looked up briefly, giving him a smile. "I hope Fenella has a hot stew," Alix responded. "I am ravenous after this icy day and our cold ride. I thought the meal served this morning at St. Ninian's was paltry, and they gave us nothing for our bellies along the way. It was stingy," Alix grumbled.

He chuckled.

"Is Fiona all right?" she asked him in a concerned tone.

"She's fallen asleep, poor mite," he answered her. She loved his child. Was not that a point in her favor? Robena had disliked their child for no other reason than she had been a female, which meant his wife must attempt once again to get an heir. He had not been unhappy with a daughter.

"Is she warm enough, Colm?" Alix wanted to know.

"She's not freezing, and we'll be home shortly," he said. The keep was getting nearer and nearer.

"It was like this the day I sheltered among your cattle," Alix said.

"It's early yet for snow," the laird said. "It will not last."

"I was so fortunate to be found by your men before I died," Alix remembered.

"You may show me your gratitude for rescuing you this evening," the laird teased.

Alix laughed.

And then they were riding into the courtyard of Dunglais Keep.

Stable lads ran out to take their horses. Alix jumped down from her mare, and reaching out, took a sleepy Fiona from the laird. He dismounted, and together they hurried into the house. Both Iver and Fenella came forward wearing broad smiles.

"Welcome home, my lord!" they chorused.

In the great hall the two hearths were heaped high with logs and burning brightly.

Alix set the half-conscious Fiona gently on her feet, an arm about the child. "Wake up, sleepyhead," she said. "We are home at last."

Fiona's bright blue eyes snapped open. "Home?" She looked about her, and then she cried, "We are home! We are home!"

"You would never know she had a wonderful time at Ravenscraig," Alix told Fenella. "The king himself taught her to play chess."

"Gracious!" Fenella exclaimed. "Consorting with a king, were you, my bonnie?"

"He's ever so nice," Fiona said. "Not at all like his three rough younger brothers. I didn't like them at all, Fenella. Especially the Duke of Albany. He is very rude. The two earls are not so bad, but bad enough."

Fenella's face registered the proper amount of interest and awe. Then she said, "Fuzzytail had her kittens while you were away. Would you like to come and see them? They have just opened their eyes today."

"Oh yes!" Fiona replied excitedly.

"The meal will be on the table shortly," Fenella said. Then she took Fiona off to see the new kittens.

Iver took brought them goblets of mulled wine and took their capes away. Together the laird and Alix sat down upon a settle next to one of the hearths, the heated spiced wine in the goblets warming their hands. They remained silent for a few minutes, the crackling of the fire in the fireplace the only sound.

Then the laird said, "Are you glad to be home, lambkin?"

"Aye, I am," Alix said.

"Queen Marie would have gladly had you in her household," the laird noted.

"But I prefer the company and life at Dunglais," Alix responded.

"*Why?*" he asked her pointedly.

Alix considered a moment. Then she said, "Are you not happy to have me here, my lord of Dunglais?"

"Of course I want you here!" he said half-angrily. "Do you think otherwise?"

"Why do you want me here?" she inquired, neatly turning the tables on him.

"You are good to my daughter," he answered her quickly.

"Is that all, Colm?" she replied.

He was very quiet for what seemed a long time, and then he answered her with another question. "Do you love me, Alix?" His gray eyes searched her face anxiously.

"Aye," she answered him without hesitation. "Do you love me?"

"Aye," he responded as quickly, gazing into her hazel eyes, and his heart leaped with pure happiness at the look of joy upon her sweet face at his answer. He took her two hands in his and kissed them passionately. "You will marry me!" he said. He didn't ask. It had been a statement pure and simple.

"Aye, I will!" she told him, laughing. Then she grew serious. "But what of Sir Udolf of Wulfborn, Colm? He still seeks among the families on both sides of the border for me. Does the dispensation he carries require my obedience? Must I marry *him* unless he frees me of the obligation?"

Malcolm Scott looked puzzled. "I do not know," he admitted, "but if we have wed according to the laws of Holy Mother Church in Scotland, can the rite be denied by the church in England?"

"I am not a scholar," Alix said. "We must ask your priest. Until then say nothing, my lord. And after we have had the benefit of clerical counsel I would like us to tell Fiona first. She should be consulted also if you propose to make me her mother."

At that moment Fiona came running into the hall cradling in her hands a small white kitten with a tiny pine tree of a tail that was both black and white. "Look!" she said. "This is Fuzzytail's daughter. She has two brothers, but they are not nearly as pretty as she is. Can I have her, Da? Please!"

The laird looked to Fiona. Then he looked to Alix.

"I think Fiona is old enough to have her own cat," Alix said. Then she turned to the girl. "But the kitten is not ready to leave her mother, *ma petite*. She is still just a wee babe. You must take her back to Fuzzytail until her mama can wean her from her teat and teach her to hunt. But you can certainly visit her every day and play with her."

"What will you call her?" the laird wanted to know.

"Bannerette," Fiona replied.

"Bannerette?" The laird looked puzzled.

"It is very clever, Fiona," Alix told the child. "I think it a perfect name."

Fiona beamed proudly. "I will take her back to Fuzzytail now, Alix."

"Hurry, *ma petite*. I see they are about to serve the meal."

Fiona ran off with the kitten.

"*Bannerette?*" the laird repeated.

"The kitten's tail is like a little black and white banner. When she grows up, it will be more obvious. And since she is a female, she is Bannerette, not Banner," Alix explained to him.

"As Fiona grows, I understand her less and less despite the fact I adore her," Malcolm Scott said. "But you understand her completely."

Alix laughed. "She is a girl. Of course I understand her."

The laird pulled Alix into his arms and, caressing her face, he said, "You are the most perfect woman, lambkin."

"And you are the most perfect man," she responded, gazing up at him adoringly.

He kissed her tenderly, wondering why it had never been like this with his wife. But he had been given a second chance, and he was going to take it. He loved her, and she loved him.

"I will give you all the children you want, Colm," Alix told him. "A son, however, will displace Fiona as your heir. Will you mind?"

"You want more children?" Was he pleased? Of course he was pleased!

"Don't you?" She looked concerned by his question.

"Aye! I do! But if you did not want to have them . . ." His words trailed off.

"Of course I want children!" Alix exclaimed. "Why would I not? Son or daughter, my father did not care. But he and my mother had both agreed that they would only have one child. My mother did not want to give up her duties as one of the queen's ladies. Now I wonder if perhaps she had and we had gone back to Anjou, she would be alive today. But if that had happened, I should not have met you, Colm," Alix decided.

"You would have been wed to some wealthy merchant's son," he decided with a grin. "And you would get fat with his children and good cheese."

Alix laughed. "Now I will get fat with your babes. What is it you call them?"

"Bairns," he replied. "You will get fat with my bairns. And I intend plowing a deep furrow with you tonight, lambkin, and every night thereafter until you bloom with my bairn." The laird found her lips again and kissed her hungrily. "I did not like sleeping in a sleeping space at Ravenscraig while you lay alone in a tower chamber."

"I was not alone, my lord," Alix reminded him breathlessly. "I had Fiona with me, but for a wee lass she takes a great deal of space, and she kicks. I am quite bruised."

"I shall kiss those bruises away tonight," he promised her.

"Come to the board," Fenella said, and they realized that the hall was filling up with the men-at-arms and the servants.

And to Alix's delight the meal was a hearty venison stew filled with chunks of meat, carrots, and onions all swimming in an herbed brown gravy. There was crusty bread, butter, and cheese as well as baked apples with cinnamon that had burst their skins and oozed into the serving dish surrounded by thick yellow cream. The wine in their goblets was heady. Fiona fell asleep at the table. She was quite exhausted from her journey. Alix picked the little girl up and took her to her chamber, where she undressed her, tucking her into bed. Kissing Fiona's head Alix went to her own bedchamber.

To her surprise, Fenella was there overseeing some of the men as they brought hot water to fill a tall oak tub. "I thought you would like a bath," the housekeeper said.

"I could certainly use one," Alix admitted. "I have not had a proper wash since we left Dunglais almost a month ago. And I am surprised I do not have nits in my hair."

"While you bathe more than most," Fenella said, "I will admit a good bath tonight will not harm you. Downwind you do bring the flavor of the court."

"Where is the laird?" Alix asked her.

Fenella smiled. "Still in the hall," she said.

"I think he might use a bath too," Alix murmured.

The serving men had filled the tub and departed.

"Give me your clothing for the laundress," Fenella said.

"Where is Jeannie?" Alix wanted to know.

"Her mother is ill. She's been at her cottage caring for her and her brothers. I'll send for her on the morrow," Fenella replied.

Alix removed her traveling garments and left them for Fenella to sort through as she climbed into her tub. The water was blissfully hot. She washed her long honey-colored hair first, then took up a cloth and washed herself. She could almost feel the layers of dirt sloughing off as she scrubbed herself. Fenella had disappeared with her clothing. Briefly Alix enjoyed her solitude, and then the laird came into her bedchamber through the door that connected to his.

"Fenella says you think I need a bath," he said.

"You do!" Alix told him. "I'm through."

"Do not move from that tub, lambkin," he growled. "I expect you to wash me." He quickly pulled off his boots and his clothing. Then he climbed in with her. The water was dangerously near the top of the oak tub. He smiled a wicked smile. "Bathe me," he said.

And when she did so most efficiently, he was surprised. She washed his hair, and then she washed his face, his neck, his shoulders. "In olden days," Alix explained, "it was the castle chatelaine's duty to bathe her important guests. My mother told me that it was a custom still practiced in more rural areas of Anjou. She said bathing a man was like bathing a baby, except everything was bigger on a man."

"Much bigger," he agreed, taking her hand and drawing it beneath the water to where his long thick cock bobbed.

Alix's fingers closed about him. She fondled him, her hand moving up and down the turgid manhood. She leaned forward and kissed his mouth with her open mouth. Her tongue traced a path about his lips. "Is such a thing possible?" Alix asked him, and he knew exactly to what she referred. "We mustn't spill water on the floor."

"It is indeed quite possible," he told her. "And if we are careful we will not spill a drop of this water. And you have made the act a necessity with your wicked fingers, lambkin." Reaching down, he clasped the delightfully plump cheeks of her bottom as Alix wrapped her arms about him. He raised her up, carefully impaling her slowly on his eager cock. Her legs had clasped him about the torso with primitive instinct. Slowly he backed her against the tall sides of the wooden tub.

Alix had gasped with unadulterated pleasure as he filled her. She wanted it to be just like this for the rest of her life. The one small interlude they had enjoyed a few days ago had but whetted her appetite for him. "Fuck me, my lord!" she whispered in his ear, licking the flesh, nipping at the lobe. Then she gasped again as he began to comply. Alix could feel every inch of him as he delved into her depths. She sensed his high lust as his manhood grew even firmer within her wet heat. The beast throbbed, and it quivered with its desire. Alix could hardly breathe now, so great was her own excitement.

"Yes! Yes!" she hissed in his ear.

"Tell me when, my sweet lambkin!" he groaned back.

"Not yet! Not yet!" She trembled in his arms as he vigorously used her, and then she screamed softly, *"Now, my lord! Now!"*

He felt the tremors racking her as his manhood satisfied itself, and she collapsed, sighing, on his neck. "There will be more tonight, lambkin," he told her as her legs fell away and his hands released her buttocks. "I have a new delight to teach you soon."

They exited the tub and dried each other before climbing into bed. The servants would remove the tub in the morning. Malcolm Scott drew Alix into his arms and kissed her forehead. "Whatever happens," he told her, "you are mine, lambkin. I will not allow this Sir Udolf to have you. I will kill him first."

Alix snuggled happily against her lover. For the first time in months she felt really and truly safe. Whatever the church said, she would not marry the English baron. But perhaps it would never come to that if he did not find her. How likely was it that Sir Udolf Watteson would come to Dunglais? And certainly when he learned she was the laird's mistress, perhaps even when or if that time came, his wife, he would give up. Wulfborn was a fine estate. Now that Hayle was gone there had to be some good family with a daughter Sir Udolf could marry and get children upon. But she would not be that woman. "What is it that you would teach me?" she asked the laird.

"To suck my cock," he told her. "And when you have mastered that talent, I shall reward you in kind," he promised her. "But not tonight. We have traveled long and I will admit to needed sleep now, lambkin."

"I am content," Alix told him. Their water sport had been vigorous, and she was sleepy too. She was glad to rest. And then in the gray of very early morning she awoke to find him stroking her body with gentle hands. Alix sighed and stretched herself, almost purring. He said nothing as his hands fondled her breasts. Spoke not a word as his lips brushed the nape of her neck. She could feel him harden as he pressed against her. Alix turned, her round naked breasts pushing against his smooth warm chest. Their bellies and thighs meeting, flesh upon flesh.

Then he was kissing her, and their tongues were dancing between the cavern of his mouth and the warm cave of hers. Their mouths fused against each other. One kiss melted into another, and another, and another until Alix found herself dizzy. And still no word had been spoken between them even as he put her onto her back, mounted her, and thrust into the welcoming heat of her eager and ready sheath.

And then he groaned. "Ahhh, lambkin, God help me, but I love you!" He thrust deep and he thrust hard over and over and over again as if he could not obtain enough of her. There was almost a desperation in his action. His lips found hers again.

Alix melted with pleasure as he rode her. His words! His lips! How could she have been so fortunate as to have found such bliss? She had not believed it possible. "Colm! Colm!" she half sobbed his name. "I love you! *I love you!*" Her head spun. Her body burned with what seemed an unquenchable fire for his passion. She seemed to soar high and higher until she teetered upon the brink of . . . of . . . there was no name for it! And then she was overwhelmed with a wave of incredible pleasure that sent her hurtling into a warm darkness that seemed to leap up to enfold her. Alix cried aloud, and it was a sound both mournful and joyous at the same time.

He shuddered hard and shouted her name as his own passion crested and burst. *"Alix! My love!"* And then his love juices exploded, thundering into her secret garden, shattering him, leaving him weak but sated. The scent of her skin intoxicated him as he lay still half atop her, gasping, struggling to gain enough energy to roll away so he would not crush her.

She had surely died, Alix thought, and then she realized that she was still alive. She sighed deeply and, reaching out, stroked the dark head that now lay on her breasts. His hair was soft for a man's, she thought. Happiness overwhelmed her. She was loved, and she loved in return. This was the kind of passion her parents had felt for each other. That elusive something she had never believed she would be fortunate enough to attain, and especially after her brief marriage to Hayle Watteson. "I love you, Colm," she whispered to him, and then smiled when she heard the tiny snore. He had fallen asleep. Alix drew the coverlet back over them and let herself sleep again.

From that moment on it became apparent to all within the keep that the laird had fallen in love and that he was loved in return.

"You see!" Fenella crowed to Iver.

"There's no marriage yet," Iver replied, but he was actually as pleased as Fenella was. Still, he enjoyed teasing her. "I'll believe it for certain when he marries her."

"He will!" Fenella responded.

"Who will?" asked Fiona, who had wandered into the hall. "Who will what?"

" 'Tis not our place to say, small mistress," Iver told the little girl.

"What do you want more than anything else in the whole wide world?" Fenella asked Fiona.

"Fenella!" the steward cautioned.

"A mother," Fiona replied. Then her bright blue eyes grew wide. "Oh, Fenella!"

"I've said naught," Fenella spoke quickly. "Just wait, my bairn. Be patient and wait. Who knows what will happen. You might have a new mam soon."

"But I want Da to marry Alix!" Fiona told the housekeeper. "Did the queen call him to court to give him a new wife? I will hate her! I want Alix for my mother!"

"Hush, child," Fenella cautioned.

Fiona burst into tears. "I w-w-want Alix for my mother!" she wailed. "I don't want some stranger! I w-wa-want Alix!"

"Now you've done it," Iver scolded the housekeeper.

"*Alix! Alix!*" Fiona howled, her small face red and wet with her tears.

Both the laird and Alix came into the hall at the same time. They ran to the little girl, and Malcolm Scott picked his daughter up in his arms to comfort her.

"Fiona, what is it?" he wanted to know.

"I want Alix!" Fiona sobbed.

"I am here, *ma petite*," Alix assured her, reaching up to wipe away the tears streaming down the child's face.

"I don't want a strange mother!" Fiona wept. "I want Alix!"

"God's foot!" the laird swore. "What is the bairn talking about?"

"I'm sorry, my lord, I may have spoken out of turn," Fenella began.

"*ALIX!*" Fiona sobbed loudly as she held out her arms to her companion. "I want Alix!"

"Give her to me, my lord," Alix said, and took the weeping child from him.

"What the hell did you say to her?" Malcolm Scott demanded of Fenella.

Iver gave the housekeeper an *I told you so* look.

"Well, my lord, we were speaking on what Fiona desires more than anything else in the world," Fenella began, attempting to explain the situation.

"I want Alix for my mother!" Fiona sniffled, now comforted by the warm arms holding her. "I don't want some poxy woman from the queen's court. *I want Alix!*"

"Very well," the laird said in an agreeable tone. "You shall have her."

Suddenly Fiona's tears ceased. A smile broke out upon her face. "Really, Da? *Really?* I can have Alix for my mother?"

"If she will accept me for her husband," Malcolm Scott said, a small smile upon his lips. "It's actually all up to Alix, Fiona."

Iver's mouth fell open. Fenella grinned triumphantly.

"Will you be my mother, Alix?" Fiona asked. "Please!"

"If your father will ask me properly," Alix said, "I will give you both an answer." Her heart was soaring with her joy. She had lost her family only to gain another one. And she was loved! Loved by the laird and loved by this little girl in her arms.

"I thought I had asked you," the laird said, his gray eyes twinkling.

"Not properly," Alix replied mischievously.

The Laird of Dunglais knelt before her, and taking a hand in his, said, "Alix Margot Givet, will you do me the honor of becoming my wife?"

Alix tilted her head first to one side and then the other. "Hmmmm," she pondered as if seriously considering the matter.

"Say yes!" Fiona whispered excitedly in her ear. "Say yes!"

"Do you really think I should?" Alix teased the child.

Fiona nodded her head vigorously.

"Very well, my lord," Alix told him, and the smile she gave was for him alone. "I will gladly be your wife and mother to this wonderful little girl."

"Hoo Ray!" Fiona cheered. "I have gotten my birthday present early."

Alix set her down upon the floor. "Do you feel better now?" she asked.

"Aye!" Fiona responded. "Can I call you Mama now?"

Alix felt tears pricking at her eyelids. She nodded. "Aye, my Fiona. You may call me Mama if that is all right with your da." She looked to him.

He nodded, smiling.

"A Christmas wedding!" Fenella said. "We'll have to start planning right away, for tomorrow is the first of December. We must send to Drumcairn to your uncle. He will be so pleased. And my lady must have a new gown in which to be married."

Afterwards as they sat in the kitchens Iver said to Fenella, "Well, you escaped the wrath you deserved. I knew he was bedding her, but I didn't think he'd marry again."

"I told you he would," Fenella said. "It isn't natural for a man to live without a wife. Just because the Ramsay was the wrong woman didn't mean the right one wasn't out there, Iver. The lady is perfect for him. She'll never betray him like the other did."

The priest was called for, and he came from the laird's village of Dunglais, which was nearby. His name was Father Donald, and he was a man in his middle years. Learning that the laird wanted to wed Alix, the priest posed several questions. "You are both free to wed, my children?" he asked them.

"I am widowed," Alix responded. "My late husband is dead, God assoil him."

"And I am free, as my first wife's bones were found out on the moor," the laird said quietly.

"You both wish to have children?" Father Donald asked Alix, his mild brown eyes searching her lovely face. He had been at Dunglais for twelve years and had known the beauteous but high-strung Robena Ramsay.

"Aye!" Alix said without hesitation, causing the priest to smile.

"And you, my lord?"

"Aye," the laird said, looking at the object of his desire. "Son or daughter, it matters not to me. But our home should be filled with the laughter of children, and Fiona should have siblings. Family is most important to me."

"There is one thing, Good Father," Alix said. "My late husband's father wanted to wed me, and sent to York for a dispensation. I thought this desire unnatural and against church teachings. I fled his home. I am told he obtained that dispensation."

The priest looked troubled. Then he said, "That is England. This is Scotland. No dispensation can make clean that which is unclean, my daughter. I believe Bishop Kennedy at St. Andrew's would agree with me. I will marry you. You have but to name the day," the priest told them. "I am pleased, my lord, that you have decided to take this step. Your uncle at Drumcairn has been most worried. Have you sent to him yet?"

"We but awaited your blessing, Good Father," the laird said.

Father Donald chuckled. "No matter what I might have said,

my lord, you would have found a way to make your union with this young woman a legal one. I shall draw up the marriage contract for you in the next few days."

"I can bring my husband a dower," Alix said proudly. "My father gave me a small bit of gold and silver before he died. He said it was for me alone. I will not come to my husband in naught but a chemise, Father Donald."

The priest nodded. "Bring me your portion then, my daughter, and when the contracts are signed it will be turned over to your husband," he told her.

Robert Ferguson, upon receiving word that his nephew was to remarry, came with all haste from Drumcairn. Although he had wanted Malcolm Scott to wed again, he was a bit disappointed that his nephew had not chosen one of his candidates. But when he learned of Alix's dower, he decided the laird had not made a bad bargain. True, Alix was English, but her parents were French, and Scotland was allied with the French. True, she had no relations who might be of use to the Scotts, or who would fight beside them, but she had a queen, albeit an English queen, for a godmother, and Scotland's queen had become her friend. And she was certainly pretty. And biddable without being boring. And both his nephew and little Fiona obviously adored her. It would be a good marriage, and he wagered silently to himself that Dunglais would have a male heir within the year.

Chapter 9

The marriage contract between Alix and Malcolm Scott was drawn up. The bride brought her dower portion to the priest.

"Is this all of it, my daughter?" Father Donald asked as he took the small chamois bag. He would count it out when he was alone and add the amount to the contract.

"Nay," Alix told him honestly. "My father always said a woman should have a bit of her own money put aside." Then she drew two full-weight silver coins from her pocket and gave them to him. "A donation for the church, Good Priest."

"Your sire was a wise man," Father Donald said with a smile as he pocketed the coins she had given him.

"I have kept only a wee portion for myself," Alix said. "One day I will use it for whichever of my children needs it most."

"I can see you are nothing like the other," the priest said. "And you love him."

"Aye, I love him," Alix answered him simply.

"I understand you read," Father Donald said. "Since, having no family, you must act for yourself, you may read the contract I have drawn between you and the laird."

"There is no need," Alix told him. "I have faith in you, and know you have done what is right, Father."

The priest nodded. Her trust pleased him. She might be intelligent, which was not exactly an asset for a woman, but she had obviously been raised to respect the church. "When do you wish the contract to be signed and the blessing to be given, my daughter?"

"The laird and I have discussed it," Alix said. "Fiona's birthday is on the fifth day of this month. My lord and I will marry on the sixth, the feast of St. Nicholas. His uncle of Drumcairn and his uncle's wife have already been summoned."

It was but two days away, but the priest could see no reason for a delay. He knew that married or no the laird would spend the long winter night in his bed with Alix, getting a child on her. Better the child be born legitimate, especially if God granted the pair a son and heir. "So be it, my daughter," he answered her.

"The signing will be in the hall with the blessing in the keep's small chapel," Alix continued. "This will be no grand affair. In the summer, if there are no raids, we will invite our neighbors to come and celebrate with us."

"Perhaps at the baptism of your first child?" the priest suggested.

Alix laughed. "Aye! That would be a fine occasion for it," she agreed.

When she had gone, the priest emptied the chamois bag she had given him onto the wooden table in his cottage. He was surprised by what he saw. There were four gold coins and ten of silver. All were full weight. There was not even the hint of clipping. It was the dower worthy of a noble's daughter. He knew her father had been physician to royalty. He had obviously been well liked by his masters and careful in his personal spending. And the bride had been scrupulous in holding back something of her small wealth for herself. He was not certain he fully approved, yet his instincts told him Alix would be a good wife to Malcolm Scott and a good mother to his wee lass.

Alix had returned to the hall to find that Fenella had finished the gown they had been fashioning together for the wedding day. Of royal-blue silk brocade it had a high waist and long tight sleeves with light, almost-white fur cuffs. The hem was fur-trimmed as well, and the low-cut neckline had a fur collar edging it.

"It's beautiful," Alix told Fenella. "Thank you for finishing it for me."

Fenella smiled. "There wasn't a great deal left to do, and with Fiona's day tomorrow and the Drumcairns arriving I thought it should be done."

"I brought my dower to the priest," Alix told her.

Fenella nodded. "Then it's just about done. I am happy for you, my lady."

Alix immediately noticed the change in Fenella's attitude, and said, "We will remain friends, won't we, Fenella?"

"Aye, my lady!" Fenella smiled, broadly pleased by the question. "I'm happy to serve the laird's wife. At least *this* wife."

There was suddenly a great stir at the other end of the hall as the Fergusons of Drumcairn arrived. Big and bluff, Robert Ferguson greeted his nephew jovially. "Well, praise God and his Blessed Mother, Colm! And I like the lass, although I could have gotten you a virgin with a large dower. Dunglais could have used a lass with a big dower. Still in all, she's young and will hopefully prove a good breeder." He clapped the laird upon the back, grinning.

"Is a dower of four gold coins and ten of silver, all full weight, enough of a dower for Dunglais, Uncle?" the laird asked Robert Ferguson.

"God's foot, lad! That kind of a dower is more than respectable. Who would have guessed that pretty little Englander would have all that sewn in her skirts." And he chuckled. "A clever wench, Colm. A very clever wench indeed." He turned to his wife. "What think you, Maggie?"

Robert Ferguson's wife, a pretty woman with warm amber eyes and chestnut-colored hair, grinned up at her mate. "I think that Colm did not need you after all, Husband. It seems he was more than capable of finding a wife without you. And a young woman of wealth too. But where is she? I wish to meet her."

At this point Alix had managed to get down the hall and greeted the Ferguson of Drumcairn with a pretty curtsy. "Welcome back to

Dunglais, my lord," she said, and then she turned to Maggie Ferguson. "I am Alix Givet, madame, and as the laird's betrothed wife I welcome you too." She kissed the other woman upon both of her cheeks.

"Pretty and mannerly," Maggie Ferguson said with a smile. "Aye, Nephew, you have indeed done well in your choice of a wife."

The next day was the fifth day of December, and they celebrated Fiona's birthday. Alix gave her a little pearl ring her mother had given her as a child. It was too small for her now, but it fit Fiona perfectly. The little girl was delighted, waving the hand with the ring about so all could see it. "My first piece of real jewelry!" Fiona crowed. Then she greedily undid the cloth hiding her father's gift and squealed, delighted. Inside was a little gilded leather girdle and a filigreed pomander that could be hung from it. "Oh, Da! Thank you! It will be perfect with my new gown."

"A new gown?" The laird feigned surprise. "And when am I to see this new gown, Daughter? It would seem to me as you grow up you are becoming more of an expense," he teased her. "You will need a wealthy husband, I fear."

"Oh, Da! You knew I was to have a new gown for the wedding," Fiona said.

"The wedding?" He continued to beleaguer her. "Is it soon?"

"It's tomorrow, Da!" Fiona giggled. "Don't you remember?"

"I don't think I have anything to wear," the laird responded, pulling a long face. "It would seem everyone has been too busy sewing for my ladies."

"Stop your teasing, my lord," Fenella cautioned, shaking her head. "You'll upset the lass. You know how she can be sometimes."

An odd look came over Malcolm Scott's face. Then he said, "Aye."

"Cook has baked an apple tart to celebrate our daughter's birthday," Alix announced, breaking the brief tension.

"It's my favorite!" Fiona said excitedly, and she danced about the hall.

The laird reached out and took Alix's hand in his, his eyes meeting hers. "Thank you," he said. "You are a better mother to Fiona than the cursed wench who birthed her."

"I love her, and I can see she is high-strung, Colm. Most little girls her age are. I will teach her restraint, but she is just seven today. Little girls are quite often sensitive. She isn't Robena, my lord. I will lead her by example."

"She is right, you know," Maggie Ferguson said. "As the mother of daughters, I could tell you tales." She chuckled.

"You have been very good for her," the laird admitted, looking into Alix's eyes and smiling. Then, "How is it you understand me so well?" he wanted to know. "I sometimes think you know me better, lambkin, than I know myself."

Alix laughed. "Will you be offended if I tell you that you are not a very complex man? You are honest and straightforward. I quite like it, my dear lord. The world in which I was raised was filled with men intriguing and plotting. Each word they spoke had to be considered carefully. The truth was a rare commodity. I often wonder if King Henry had been sound of mind and a strong man what his rule would have been. I would certainly not be here at Dunglais had it been."

"Do you miss that world?" he asked her. He knew the answer, of course, but he needed to hear her say it again. Now that she was to be his wife, he found that he needed reassurance that she truly loved him. It had never been this way with Robena.

Alix stood before him and, reaching up, stroked his jaw as she gazed into his eyes. "I would rather be with you and here at Dunglais than anywhere else. I love you, Colm Scott, my dear, good lord." Then her voice dropped so only he might hear her. "You have become my life. I want no man but you. I will never leave you, my darling. Do not be afraid, Colm. Our marriage is meant to be, and it will be good." Standing on her tiptoes Alix kissed him sweetly and gently.

The laird's voice was equally low as he spoke to her. "When

Robena betrayed me, only my pride was hurt. As I saw her standing there in my half brother's arms I knew I had never had any real love for her. She had nothing of my heart. But you, my lambkin, you have captured my heart. You hold it captive and you always will." He kissed her back, and his kiss was one of deep longing.

"I belong to you, my lord," Alix told him softly.

"And I belong to you, my love," the laird replied.

When she had seen the way the situation was going, Fenella had eased away from the pair, Fiona in her care. The guests moved away too. But, seeing the servants bringing in the meal, Fenella called out, "My lords, my ladies. Come to table. Fiona's feast is now set, and it smells delicious. Look, child, prawns!"

The laird and Alix turned from each other. Hand in hand they came to the high board, Malcolm Scott picking up his daughter and bringing her to the place of honor, where she held court the rest of the evening until she was finally carried to bed by her father and tucked in by Alix. Then they returned to the hall to be with their guests. The laird's piper played for them, and the old bard who made his home at Dunglais entertained them with tales, some spoken, some half sung.

"You really do love him," Maggie Ferguson said. "I can see it in all you do. You are so very good with Fiona, Alix. And your servants already respect you. I could not have wished for a happier ending to Colm's woes than this."

"They say she was beautiful," Alix said. "I am pretty, but I am certainly not beautiful. Yet he loves me. I know he does, for I see it in his eyes. Why could he not love her if she was so beautiful?"

"She was beautiful," Maggie said. "Breathtakingly beautiful, yet it was all on the outside. But when he chose her he did not know it. None of us did. She was a beautiful virgin from a good family, there was no scandal about her, and she brought him a respectable dower. It was the kind of arrangement made among families every day. My Robbie tells me you were brought up in the court of the old English queen. You have certainly been witness to many matches, and did any of them involve love?"

"Nay," Alix admitted. "They involved wealth, prestige, power, land. Now and again a matched couple would know and like each other. The queen's ladies would sigh and remark on how fortunate they were, but most matches brought strangers together. My parents knew each other when the Count of Anjou ordered their marriage. They grew to love each other, and I always wanted what they had."

"And have you gained it with Colm?" Maggie Ferguson asked.

"I think I have gained far more," Alix replied softly.

"You want children? Robena really did not," Maggie told Alix.

"Oh, yes! I very much want children," Alix replied. She did not tell her companion that she had a means of preventing conception that she had gained from her father. And she had faithfully used it once she had become the laird's mistress. But she had taken her supply of wild carrot seeds and stored them away this very day. Tomorrow she would be the laird's wife, and the sooner she could give him a son the better.

The evening ended, and they went to their chambers. Malcolm Scott did not come to Alix's bed that night, and she was glad. In a way it put an end to the relationship that they had had, but tomorrow night when she lay in his arms it would be as his wife and not as his mistress. They would begin anew. When morning came, Fenella oversaw her bath. The steam from the perfumed water filled the air of her bedchamber.

"The laird is having his bath in the kitchens," Fenella told her. "He'll not linger long, for the kitchen maids cannot help themselves and are peeping at him from the larder." She chuckled wickedly. "The cook cannot keep order, I fear."

Alix laughed. "Let them look their fill, if they wish. The laird is mine!" She stepped from her own tub and wrapped herself in a large piece of toweling as she sat down by the fire to dry her hair. "I set Jeannie to look over Fiona while I dressed." She began brushing her hair, leaning forward so that the heat touched it. Finally she began to dress herself, Fenella helping her first into her chemise and then into the royal-blue gown. The high waist on the garment flattered her breasts, pushing them up so that they appeared even rounder. She fitted a gold and silver gilt leather girdle about her torso. It had belonged to her mother. To it she attached her mother's jeweled rosary. The very long strand of pearls that she possessed was a trifle shorter, for Alix had taken some of the pearls to make a little rope of pearls for Fiona. She smiled, looking at the miniature strand and thinking how pleased the child would be, then slipped the pearls and her two gold chains over her head. They settled upon her chest and the beautiful blue brocade beneath it.

Fenella now brushed Alix's long hair out. She had taken it upon herself as the keep's housekeeper to help prepare the bride. She fitted a beautiful gold caul dotted with tiny freshwater pearls on Alix's head, carefully stuffing the long hair into the delicate netting. "I took the liberty of having the cobbler in the village make these for you," she said, fitting a pair of sollerets on Alix's feet.

"Oh, Fenella, thank you!" Alix exclaimed. "I had to leave my sollerets at Wulfborn, for I felt they would be too heavy to carry when I fled there."

"A lady shouldn't have to wear boots beneath her brocade gown," Fenella said. Then she said, "Well, my lady, I believe you are ready to go into the hall."

Alix stood up, and her gown settled itself, molding her torso and her hips, the pale fur on her hem brushing the floor. Together the two women descended the stairs. At the entrance to the great hall the Laird of Dunglais awaited his bride with his daughter. His garb was simple. He wore a length of his red Scott plaid wrapped about his loins, and a white shirt. Alix thought he looked very handsome as she slipped the small strand of pearls from her pocket and put them over Fiona's head. The child's mouth opened with surprise as she gazed at the pearls now gleaming against the deep rose velvet of her gown.

"They are now yours," Alix said softly. "Take good care of them, Fiona."

"Oh, thank you, Alix!"

"*Mama*," Alix gently corrected her. "From this day on I am your mother." And she felt the laird squeeze her hand. Looking up at him, she smiled.

Then together the trio entered the hall, walking to the high board where Father Donald was waiting for them with the marriage contract to be signed.

"Good morrow, my children," he greeted them. The priest then handed the laird an inked quill. "You will sign there, my lord," he told Malcolm Scott. "There are two documents. One for you and one for the church."

The Laird of Dunglais took the quill and scrawled his name twice where the priest had indicated. Then he handed the quill back to him.

Father Donald inked the quill again and handed it to Alix, pointing to where she was to sign.

She took the quill up and added her name, *Alix Margot Givet*, in an elegant hand to both copies of the marriage contract.

Next to sign were the Fergusons as witnesses to the deed. Robert Ferguson, like his nephew, scrawled his name. His wife made her mark where the priest had written her name and handed him back the quill.

Father Donald carefully sanded the signatures on both copies and then rolled each one neatly up, closing it with sealing wax into which the laird pressed his seal ring. He then handed the laird his copy and tucked his own into the pocket of his long brown robe. "And now we will adjourn to the chapel, where I will bless this union," Father Donald said with a broad smile.

Malcolm Scott handed the rolled document to his steward, Iver, who would put it away with the other papers that were of importance to Dunglais.

The keep's chapel was located just off of the great hall. It was a small room with a single arched glass window on one side. Within a leaded circle there was a cross of red and blue glass at the center of the window, indicating to any outside that the chamber within was a holy one. The altar was oak. It was set with a linen cloth. There were two fine polished brass candlesticks upon it and a simple silver crucifix set in a base of black wood. Together Malcolm and Alix knelt on the step below the altar while the priest blessed their union. Then they stepped back to join the Fergusons and Fiona as Father Donald said a brief Mass so they might take communion, which was considered to be good fortune when beginning a new marriage.

And when the Mass was over they returned to the great hall, where they broke their fast. There were eggs that had been poached and were now served with a cream sauce made from white wine and dusted with nutmeg. There was oat stirabout with bits of dried apple and pear in it. It was served with honey and heavy yellow cream. There was ham and bacon, fresh-baked cottage loaves, sweet butter, hard yellow cheese, and plum jam. There were both watered red wine and sweet cider to drink.

But when the meal was over the Fergusons made ready to depart. It was not even midmorning yet, but the weather was fair this day. If they left now they would be back at Drumcairn by the early nightfall. Their stone house was not fortified, and while winter raids were unusual they did not like leaving their young daughters to their servants for more than a night or two. And there was the weather that could turn at any moment at this time of the year. Alix was sorry to see them go, for she had enjoyed Maggie's company, but she understood.

"The next time I see you, and I will come in the spring," Maggie Ferguson said, "I hope your belly is rounding with new life."

"I will do my best," Alix told her.

"And so will I, dear aunt," the laird said, having overheard them.

They all laughed, and then the Scotts of Dunglais watched as the Fergusons of Drumcairn made their way from the keep's small courtyard and out onto the frosty moor.

As they returned to the great hall Alix said, "I'll go and put my gown away now. I can hardly take up my duties dressed in such finery."

"An excellent idea," he agreed. "I will come with you, *Wife*."

The very word sent a thrill of delight through Alix. She was married! And she was married to a man she loved. It was the kind of marriage she had always dreamed about. The kind of marriage she had not had with Hayle Watteson, nor would she have had this kind of marriage with his father. She shuddered slightly thinking of it.

Her bedchamber was empty. "Where is Jeannie?" she said aloud.

"I'll help you," the laird purred in her ear, as coming up behind her, he slipped an arm about her. A hand cupped her breast, squeezing gently as he kissed her neck.

"It's the nicest gown I've ever had," Alix said softly. "I used the best fabric in the storeroom, my lord. We have no other."

"Then we must take particular care with your gown," he murmured, reaching for the lacing and undoing it carefully. When he had the gown unfastened, he slid it off of her, lifting her from it, setting her down, and then carefully laying the gown upon a small chair. Then he drew her chemise off and set it aside. Alix was quite naked but for her stockings, shoes, and jewelry.

He stepped back and smiled a slow, wicked smile. "I quite like you like this," he told her. Her round breasts with their pert nipples, her graceful torso, her fair skin gleaming in the firelight. There was something deliciously sensuous about a naked woman in her stockings and shoes. He lifted her pearls and her gold chains from around her neck and laid them down on the bedside table.

"My lord, we have our daily duties to perform," she said.

"This is our wedding day, madame. They will manage quite well in the hall without us," he told her.

"But Fiona's lessons will be neglected," Alix protested faintly.

"It is a holiday," he said. "Fiona is being well cared for, madame. I think it is your husband who needs caring for right now. Will you be negligent in your duties to him?" He stood behind her, his hands now cradling her two naked breasts. "I am afire with my lust for you, lambkin." His lips pressed a hot kiss on her bare shoulder. His hands gently fondled the twin orbs in his possession. Then, retaining possession of one breast, he let his other hand wander freely over her body.

Alix sighed as he touched her belly and then moved down to stroke her smooth mons, which he very much enjoyed, for it allowed him a freer access to her most intimate parts. He had recently taught her the pleasures of sucking upon such parts. She had been a most eager and capable student. He remembered how Robena had protested such actions on his part, complaining it was unnatural and wrong. Yet when he had first watched her with his brother, she had been on her knees before him quite obviously enjoying herself.

Alix broke into his thoughts, turning about in his arms and unfastening his plaid. It fell to the ground as she unlaced his shirt and drew it off over his dark head. Then she fell to her knees before him and began to caress his length with gentle fingers. His hand went to her tawny head, kneading the scalp as he encouraged her further. Alix began to slowly lick him up and down. And after a time she pushed his foreskin back and the pointed tip of her little tongue encircled the flesh beneath the rim of the head of his cock.

The laird drew a sharp breath. She continued to tease him in this fashion until finally she took him into her mouth and began to suck upon him. At the first tug of her mouth on his manhood, Malcolm Scott almost screamed like a girl, so unbearably sweet was the sensation her mouth produced. As she continued to draw rhythmically upon his sensitive flesh, he groaned with acknowledgment of the pleasure she was giving him. And when he was thick and hard and could bear no more of her torture he growled, "Cease, lambkin! I would put my seed tonight where it should go."

He pulled her up, and she pushed his shirt from his frame. Their naked bodies met. Breast to chest. Belly to belly. Thigh to thigh. Their mouths fused into one as kiss melted into kiss and tongues jousted within the warm cavern of mouths. He backed her over to and pushed her down upon the edge of the bed. Kneeling quickly, he pushed her legs apart and began to lick first at the soft insides of her thighs. His tongue then licked the length of her moist, shadowed slit. His thumbs opened her to him and his tongue found her sweet core with perfect aim. He licked it for several long and heated strokes. Then, pressing his dark head between her open thighs, he fastened his lips about that little nub of sensitive flesh and began to suck hard upon it.

Alix screamed softly. Ever since he had introduced her to this particular pleasure she found she could not get enough of it. He would suck and suck upon the sentient nub, and it would swell and tingle, and the tingling would increase until it was unbearable and it finally burst. And when it did she would feel a small release, but then she would yearn to be fucked until the larger delight became totally insupportable and finally crested, leaving her utterly replete and weak with pleasure.

The first release came, and she sighed with utter contentment, but then the longing began to evince itself once more. "Hurry!" she begged him.

"Greedy wench," he teased as he rubbed the tip of his cock against the opening of her sheath. "Do you want this, my love?"

"Damn you, Colm, aye!" she cried.

"Beg me for it," he taunted her.

"Never!" she swore as he rubbed himself tantalizingly against her. He laughed. "Beg!" he repeated.

In reply she pushed him from her and rolled away from him. He followed her onto the bed, reaching for her, but Alix eluded him, laughing. "Now 'tis your turn to beg, my lord," she teased him wickedly.

They rolled back and forth across the large bed until finally the laird caught his bride. He forced her beneath him. "Now beg!" he told her fiercely.

"You beg!" she insisted. "Do you not want to sheathe yourself deep inside my warmth, *Husband*? Do you not yearn to take your pleasure?"

"Aye!" he told her, and pushed just the head of his cock inside her. "And you, *Wife*, do you not long to feel this thick and lengthy peg throbbing within you?"

"Aye!" Alix agreed.

"Then as we are of the same mind," he said, and he thrust hard.

The breath went out of her as she felt the denseness sliding into her. He loomed over her, taking her legs and pressing them as far back as he could without harming her. Then he thrust hard a second time, and plunged deep over and over again until Alix was indeed begging him not to stop. She squeezed thick flesh probing her hard. He groaned and she smiled, for she realized that they were gaining equal pleasure. And then her head began to spin, and she saw stars behind her closed eyes. She heard herself calling to him, "Please! Please! Oh, Colm, please!" And then she was spinning and falling even as she felt his juices exploding to flood her with his essence.

When she finally came to herself again Alix found herself in her husband's arms. "And it isn't even noon," she half whispered to him.

He laughed softly. "Understand, madame, I don't intend letting you out of this chamber until the morrow. And if it rains on the morrow we will remain here."

"But I'm hungry," Alix said.

"Food will be brought to us," he promised her.

"You have schemed all this out beforehand," she accused him.

"I have," he admitted freely. "I love you, lambkin, and now that you are my wife I do not have to pretend. All in the keep knew it. But we are newly wed and shall have this day, and perhaps another, just the two of us."

They had three days, for on the seventh of December it rained an icy rain, and on the eighth it snowed. And while on the morning of the ninth it was still snowing Alix insisted on leaving her bed-chamber for Fiona's sake. The laird, while grumbling, knew she was right. His daughter was bright and lively, but she was also fragile. She had become very used to both Alix and her father being there for her. She greeted them almost with relief when they entered the great hall.

"Where have you been?" she demanded to know. "I was afraid, but Fenella said it is the custom for a bride and groom to be alone for some few days. She said you would be back when that time was over. What were you doing?"

"We were doing what a bride and groom do when they are alone, and one day you shall learn that for yourself," her father said.

"Have you enjoyed your holiday from your lessons?" Alix asked the child.

"Father Donald came when you were not here, except on the wedding day," Fiona grumbled. "He is not as much fun as you are, Al—Mama. All he wanted me to do was read my Latin with him. He said I didn't need to know how to do mathematics. That my husband would do all that was important one day. But I like mathematics."

"And we shall do some this morning," Alix promised her. "Iver, send to Father Donald and tell him I have returned and will take up my daughter's schooling now."

"At once, my lady," the steward said.

"I'm so glad you're back," Fiona told them. "I missed you. I was afraid you had left me, Da. Alix is now your best girl."

"Nay, Fi," her father assured her. "Alix is my lady, but you will always be my best girl, even when you have brothers and sisters to play with, my bairn."

"When will I have brothers and sisters?" Fiona wanted to know.

"Alix and I are working very hard to make them for you," the laird told his daughter, who clapped her hands with delight. "That is why we were away."

"But we need not go away again, *ma petite*," Alix assured her. "We shall make your brothers and sisters right here at Dunglais, won't we, my lord?"

"Aye, madame," he told her with a grin. "We most assuredly will."

And Fiona was satisfied. The days grew very short as December progressed. As Alix had told Fiona the year before, she would be in charge of Christmas decorating this year. The two, in Fenella's company, ventured out from the keep one morning to cut pine and other greenery. Over the next few days the hall was festooned with all manner of greenery and holly, along with many beeswax candles.

The Twelve Days of Christmas began on the twenty-fifth and ended on the sixth day of January. They had had a wonderful time just the three of them. Malcolm Scott couldn't ever recall having had such a glorious celebration as he did that year. And he realized he was unbearably happy. Really and truly happy for the first time in all of his life. He wondered if Dunglais had ever seen a happier time.

His father had been a hard man, but then it was a hard world in which they lived. His mother had been loving and patient. He was his parents' second child. His older brother had died at birth. And when he had been Fiona's age, his mother had given birth to a daughter who lived but several months. His father loved his mother and, oddly, had been satisfied with a single son even after Colm's mother died and he might have taken a young wife to assure his line.

Times were particularly difficult when he was growing up. The king, James I, had been an honored captive in England since he was a boy of eleven. The last heir of Robert III, his father had sent him into the custody of the French king to keep him safe. But the boy's ship was captured by pirates and the young Scots heir taken to the English king. Although his elderly father had died upon learning of his heir's fate, James I was not able to regain his throne until he was twenty-nine. He returned with an English queen, Joan Beaufort, the great-great-granddaughter of King Edward III of England.

Queen Joan bore her husband eight children, but unfortunately six of them were daughters. And then twin sons, Alexander and James, were born at Holyrood Abbey in the midautumn of 1430, but only James survived as his father's heir. When James I was murdered at Perth during the Christmas season seven years later, his son, James II, took the throne. The queen had been injured attempting to save her husband. She saw to the executions of his killers quickly and without mercy. Two years later she remarried to one of her husband's cousins, James Stewart, known as the Black Knight of Lorne. They had three sons, but though others were now responsible for her first son, the young king, Joan Beaufort at least was able to give him a few companions who were not part of the squabbling factions running the boy king's life.

Malcolm Scott smiled to himself, remembering. He had been called to become the king's companion at the age of nine. The king was two years his senior. Oddly, the lad from a not particularly distinguished border family and the young king had become fast friends. While the other boys had either dropped away, or at their family's urgings allied themselves with those controlling the king's life, Malcolm Scott had remained loyal to James II. It had not brought him wealth or prestige once the grown king took charge of his life and his kingdom, but the two men had remained good friends. He had been happy then, but not like he was now with Alix.

January passed, and on the second day of February Alix brought Father Donald a supply of fine beeswax candles that would last the Dunglais church for the year. The day was called Candlemas. The ewes were once again lambing, and the days were growing longer again. Their lives had taken on a comfortable familiarity. Fiona was suddenly growing taller, and the nights were long and sweet as the laird and his bride worked to make a child. March came and went.

And then one late April day, the snows finally gone from the moors and the hillsides, the watch on the tower called out that a party of armed men was approaching the keep. At once the drawbridge was pulled up and the gates closed behind it. They did not appear hostile, and there were but six of them who rode with a gentleman. It was the gentleman who came forward and waited to be challenged.

"Who goes there?" came the expected query.

"I am Sir Udolf Watteson of Wulfborn Hall. I seek to speak with your master, and I request shelter for my men and me this night."

"You must wait," the man-at-arms called down, and the visitor nodded.

"Send to the hall," the man-at-arms said to one of his fellows. "Tell the laird Sir Udolf Watteson asks to speak with him and begs shelter for the night. He's an Englishman, but he seems peaceable enough."

The soldier nodded and ran off to the great hall, where the laird and his wife were seated. The man bowed to the laird. "There is an Englishman at the gates, six men-at-arms riding with him. He asked to speak with you, and he begs shelter for his party this night, my lord."

"Does this Englishman have a name?" the laird asked.

"Sir Udolf Watteson of Wulfborn Hall," the man replied.

Beside him the laird heard the sharp intake of Alix's breath. He turned to see she had gone pale. Very quietly he said, "Go to our chamber and do not come out unless I send for you. I will send Fiona to be with you."

She did not argue, but arose and almost ran from the hall.

"Fenella," the laird called, and the housekeeper came from another part of the hall. "Find Fiona and take her to my wife. They are to remain abovestairs until our guest has departed. It's the Englishman she fled."

"Right away, my lord," Fenella replied, and hurried to fetch Fiona.

"Go back to the watch," the laird said. "Sir Udolf is welcome at Dunglais. Put his men in the stable to sleep. They can be fed here in the hall, but make certain we outnumber them. Do you understand?"

"Aye, my lord," the man said, and hurried out.

"Iver, go and bring our guest into the hall," the laird instructed his steward.

Iver bowed to his master and went from the hall. He knew who their guest was, for Fenella had told him of Alix's history as she had told the housekeeper. The laird was right to keep his wife from the hall. There was less apt to be difficulty if Sir Udolf was unaware of her presence at Dunglais. Iver entered the courtyard as the Englishman was slowly dismounting his horse. "My lord, I am Iver, the laird's steward. Welcome to Dunglais. If you will follow me, I will take you to my master."

"Aye, thank you," Sir Udolf said. He had almost bypassed this keep, for it was small and certainly undistinguished, but he could not be satisfied that he had lost Alix until every nook and cranny had been investigated. But he was weary and sore from his days of riding. He had to admit to himself that he was not the young man he once was. He was surprised to find the great hall of the house warm, clean, and quite pleasant. A woman lived here, he was quite certain.

The laird came forward, his big hand stretched out in welcome. "Sir Udolf, I am Malcolm Scott, the Laird of Dunglais. Since our two countries seem to be at peace with each other I welcome you. What brings you to my keep?" The laird cast a quick glance at Iver, who, snapping his fingers at a serving wench, brought her quickly forward with a tray containing two goblets of wine that she offered with a curtsy to her master and his guest. "Come and sit by the fire," the laird invited. And when the two men had settled themselves and taken their first sip of wine, Malcolm Scott looked expectantly to Sir Udolf Watteson. "You have ridden far?" he asked.

The older man nodded. "I have been back and forth across the border for some months now, my lord," Sir Udolf said. "I seek a young woman who is my betrothed wife." He sighed. "She was wed to a blood relation of mine. When he died tragically, I decided to take her for my own, as my wife was long dead. The lady in question is of good family and sweet nature. What better woman with whom to spend my later years? While I waited for the dispensation from York so that we might wed, she grew discouraged and departed my house without my knowledge. I have sought for her ever since."

"A sad tale indeed," the laird said. "But why do you think her in Scotland?"

"Her godmother is here," Sir Udolf replied. "I have already visited her and gained her permission to wed her godchild, as she has no other living family."

"How fortuitous," the laird murmured.

"I have visited many keeps these past months, but no one has seen or heard of my betrothed. I am almost ready to give up," Sir Udolf said.

"If the lady was traveling alone," the laird began. "You are certain she was traveling alone, aren't you?"

"Most assuredly!" Sir Udolf replied, his tone slightly offended. "She was a lady of the highest moral character."

"A woman traveling alone could easily have been attacked and killed for her horse and any valuables she carried," the laird said.

"She was a-foot," Sir Udolf answered him. "She had her own mount in my stables, but such was her good character that she would not take the beast."

"A-foot!" the laird exclaimed. "Why, then, it is certain, my lord, the lady is long dead. A woman alone and out upon the moor would be vulnerable not only to wicked men, but vicious beasts as well. Only five years ago the bones of a woman were found out on the hillside."

"But how did you know it was a woman if there were only bones?" Sir Udolf wanted to know.

"There were scraps of her clothing amid the bones," the laird replied. "If your lady did not go to her godmother, which was undoubtedly her destination, and no one has seen her, it is likely the poor soul is dead."

"So I fear," Sir Udolf said, "but as soon as the snows left the hills I thought I must look one more time." He sighed, and then said, "Your hall is a fine one, my lord. Your wife and her servants keep it well."

"They do," the laird agreed. "I must apologize that my wife cannot join us. She has been ill these past few days, and our daughter too. Margaret is a good mother to our little Fiona, and it is possible she is breeding once again. We are eager for a son."

"Aye, a man needs an heir for his house and his lands," Sir Udolf said.

"Your men will sleep in the stables, for my house is small as you can see, but there is a comfortable bedspace for you here in the hall," the laird told his guest.

Iver came to say that the meal was about to be served, and so the two men took their goblets and moved to the high board. Sir Udolf was frankly surprised by the quality of the meal he was offered. It was simple but tasty and well prepared. First came a platter of fish that had been poached in white wine. Trout from his own streams, the laird told him. He had royal permission to take both trout and salmon from the waters running across his lands.

Again Sir Udolf was surprised. "How did you gain such permission?" he asked.

"The late king, James II, and I were friends," the laird answered truthfully. "Our kings in Scotland are more apt to make friends of humble border lords like myself than your English kings with their fine courts."

Sir Udolf nodded. It was a known truth, but he was still impressed. Nonetheless his attentions were quickly turned to a fat capon that had been roasted crisp and golden along with a tasty venison stew. "You keep a fine table," he complimented the laird as he filled his trencher with the stew and a quarter of the capon.

"I shall tell my Margaret of your praise. It will give her pleasure," Malcolm Scott said. He could not under the circumstances call his wife by her first name, but he knew it would seem odd to Sir Udolf if his wife was not referred to by name. So he had taken her saint's name instead. Margot was a French diminutive of Margaret, and Margaret was not only Scotland's saint, but it was also a popular name.

Sir Udolf reached for the cottage loaf and tore off a piece. He cut himself a chunk of the half wheel of cheese upon the board. "You have a good wife," he noted as he filled his belly. He was hungry, and it had been a long time since he had enjoyed such a fine meal. A man with a good cook and a wife who knew how to direct that cook was a fortunate man indeed.

The meal finished, the laird invited Sir Udolf to play a game of chess with him. The two men played for two hours, and then Malcolm Scott arose from the game table.

"I will leave you, my lord," he said. "My housekeeper, Fenella, will show you to your sleeping space. I shall see you on the morrow. Good night." He bowed to his guest.

"Good night, my lord, and thank you," Sir Udolf replied, returning the bow.

The laird hurried from the hall and upstairs to the bedchamber he now shared with his wife. She was standing by the hearth warming her hands as he entered.

"Is he gone?" Alix asked, turning to face him.

"He's sleeping in the hall and will be gone on the morrow," her husband answered her. Then he took her into his arms. "Dinna fear, lassie. He's just about ready to give up his search for you. But you know he went to your queen, dispensation in hand, to gain her permission to wed you."

"And brought her a bag of coins to ease her conscience," Alix said bitterly. Then she sighed. "Poor queen. She is desperate by now, I imagine. It has been over two years since they departed England. The new king must be well established by now. I wonder that my queen, the prince, and the poor king do not go to France. It would seem they have few if any adherents left in England, and while Scotland lets them shelter here they will offer no aid. Queen Marie must consider her son's position in all of this. She has offered Scotland's friendship to the English."

"Which has given us a respite here in the borders," Malcolm Scott said. "I have never known it to be so peaceful."

"You are certain he suspects naught?" Alix asked nervously.

"I apologized that my wife, *Margaret*, was unable to entertain him, but alas she was ill, and our daughter too, and my wife might even be breeding again."

"Might I?" Alix said with a smile.

"Well, if you are certain you are not, madame, then we must immediately get to work to remedy that and ensure I am not a liar," the laird teased Alix.

She laughed happily. "I do love you so very much, Colm," she told him. "I could have never wed Sir Udolf even if I wasn't repelled by what he proposed. How does he look? Is he well? I wish him no ill."

"He looks tired," the laird said. "And sad. He is, as you have always said, a decent man. I enjoyed his company, but I hope I have discouraged him from seeking you further, lambkin. He certainly is not young, but he is not too old to sire a child. There must be some woman of respectable blood who would have him."

"Now that Hayle is gone, aye, there should be," Alix agreed. "I wish him luck, but I must admit I will be relieved to see him go on the morrow."

And in the morning after he had eaten a most delicious breakfast, Sir Udolf Watteson bid his host farewell and departed Dunglais. As he rode away from the keep, his captain, who rode at his side, said, "She is there, my lord."

"You are certain?" Sir Udolf said quietly.

"Aye, I am. I made an assignation with one of the maidservants who served below the board. After we had enjoyed a lusty bout in the hayloft of the stables we talked. I asked about the laird's wife. Was she a Scot? Nay, the girl told me. She was English, but everyone loved her, particularly the laird's little daughter. She said the laird's people found her almost frozen to death upon the moor two years ago. He had taken her in as his daughter's companion but then made her his mistress. Several months ago they wed, the wench said. Her lady's name is Alix, my lord."

"Their marriage cannot be legal," Sir Udolf said angrily. "She was already my betrothed wife, and I will have her back!"

"Will we return to Dunglais now?" the captain asked his master.

"Nay. We will go home while I decide what it is I will do. If I am clever as this laird has been, I can regain my Alix and he will never know it," Sir Udolf chuckled. And when they reached Wulfborn Hall its master sat in his hall and considered what he should do. He spoke with his priest.

"Your claim is the legitimate one, my lord," Father Peter said. "And you have the permission of the lady's former guardian, Queen Margaret."

"Then I shall take her back!" Sir Udolf said determinedly.

"Yet, my lord, you must consider if you would have her back. Did she not betray you by fleeing Wulfborn? And did she not spread herself for another man? Is this truly the kind of woman you wish to wed? There are at least two women of good birth nearby who would be happy to be your wife, my lord. Women of good character and strong moral fiber."

"But are they young enough yet to give me a son?" Sir Udolf demanded of his priest. "Nay, they are not, and I know it, Father. I must have a son!"

"Your sister's second son would make you a fine heir, my lord," the priest said.

"Nay! I want my own son, and Alix can give me that son. You say my claim takes precedence over any other. Then I will have her back!"

"But how, my lord? *How?*" the priest wanted to know. "I do not believe the laird will give her up to you. Certainly he loves her or he would not have married her."

"He has forced her into this marriage, I am certain of it!" Sir Udolf said. "He needed a mother for his daughter. He wants a son of his own. He cannot love her."

"Do you, my lord?" the priest asked candidly.

"She belongs to me," Sir Udolf said. "She is mine, and as she lives, I shall have her! The church will uphold my claim. Queen Margaret will uphold my rights."

The priest sighed. It was not that he disagreed with Sir Udolf, but the woman he so desperately desired had run away from him and then given herself to another man. "How, my lord," he repeated, "will you regain the lady? The Laird of Dunglais will not give her up without a fight."

"My captain has found me a group of renegade Scots. They will take the lady when she is out riding one day. It will appear to be a border raid, and I shall not be involved in the matter at all. The naked and disfigured body of a young woman will be found and assumed to be the laird's woman. He will never look for her after that body is found, and Alix will be mine as the archbishopric at York has said."

"My lord, you propose the murder of an innocent!" the priest cried, shocked.

"I will have my betrothed wife returned, Priest, and it matters not to me how it is done. I shall not be involved," Sir Udolf said coldly.

"My lord, I believe you have gone mad with your lust for this woman. I shall pray you see the wrong before you allow it to be committed," Father Peter declared.

"If he does not believe her dead," Sir Udolf replied stubbornly, "he will seek her out and eventually he will come to Wulfborn. What I propose to have done is for both of their sakes. If he believes her dead, he will mourn her and move on with his life. If she knows he thinks her dead, she will reconcile herself to her fate as my wife. She will give me another son to replace the one who died."

"Your son visited her almost every night of their marriage, yet she did not conceive," the priest pointed out to his master. "Perhaps she is unable to conceive, my lord. Have you considered that her womb is a barren one? Her own mother bore but one child, and a female at that. Will you risk your immortal soul in this matter, knowing the murder of an innocent is to be committed so you may take this woman back? And do you think God will reward you with a son for it?" the priest wanted to know.

"Alix Givet is mine by all rights," Sir Udolf responded. "It was God who brought her to us. It was God who gave me the idea to make her my wife after my son died. It is God who got me the dispensation from the archbishop at York. God will return Alix to me, and he will see I have another son on her body."

The priest shook his head. Sir Udolf was mad. It was a madness that came from believing he was right and that God was on his side. But he was not right, and God would certainly punish the baron for what he was about to allow done so that he might regain Alix Givet. The wench was not worth it. *But what can I do to stop my master?* the priest asked himself. When an answer was not immediately forthcoming, he decided to pray. God would certainly give him a resolution to this problem if he prayed hard enough. He might have sent to the Laird of Dunglais warning him, but Father Peter did not. He might not approve of his master's actions, but he would never betray him.

Chapter 10

The summer came, and at Lamastide Alix knew she was with child. Fenella confirmed it, smiling. The two women hugged each other and, seeing it, Iver asked Fenella afterwards, "Why were you embracing our mistress?"

"You will know soon enough," Fenella chortled, "but first the laird must know."

"Woman, you have as good told me our mistress is with child," Iver said.

Fenella clapped her hands over her mouth, but then, removing them, said, "I have told you naught! And do not dare to say I did."

The steward grinned at her. "I know how to keep a secret," he replied. "You need not worry about me. It is the laird who will announce this happy news to all of Dunglais after she has told him. I will say nothing, and you had best stop being so smug because you have the confidence of our mistress."

Alix sought for her husband and found him at the keep's smithy talking with the blacksmith. He had recently found his cattle herd increased by several beasts, and they had no markings on them. He wanted them marked with the Dunglais D so if they wandered again he could find them. He had waited the summer long for someone to come and claim them, but no one had. She waited while he discussed the matter, and when he had finished he turned to her, smiling.

"Why have you sought me, lambkin?" he asked her, taking her

hand and walking from the smithy. "Have you missed me this day?" He raised her hand to his lips and kissed the palm tenderly.

"I have news I believe you would want to hear," Alix told him almost shyly. "I am with child, Colm. Come late winter, with God's blessing, I shall give you a child."

The laird gave a joyous whoop, and picking Alix up, he swung her about. "A child!" he exclaimed happily. "We are to have a child!" Then he kissed her hard. "Thank you, my darling lambkin! Thank you!"

"You want a son," Alix said as he set her down upon her feet again. "I hope it is, but it could also be a darling little girl like our Fiona."

He sighed. "Aye, I find I am like other men after all," he admitted. "I do want a son, but should it be another daughter I will be content, Wife."

Alix glanced about the courtyard at the curious faces of the men-at-arms. "We must tell Fiona before you announce it to the hall," she said.

"You are certain?" he asked her anxiously.

Alix nodded. "Aye, and Fenella concurs. I have had no show of blood since the end of May, my lord. And my breasts are growing fuller and I am suddenly always craving cheese."

"You always loved cheese," he noted.

"But not like this, my lord. I sat at the high board after you had left it this morning and ate cheese until Fenella finally took it away from me," Alix told him. "She says there is no doubt I am with child."

"Do you know when?"

"We think sometime in late February or early March," Alix said.

They entered the house to seek out Fiona. They found her playing with her cat in the hall. Both the little girl and the creature were enjoying themselves as Fiona pulled a piece of yarn to which was tied a rag and the cat pounced and wrestled with the toy. She looked up as her father and stepmother came into her view. "Bannerette likes to play with me," she announced to them. "She is more fun than her mother ever was."

"Her mother is older, and older cats do not play as much," Alix said. "Come, Fi, and sit with us. Your father and I have something to tell you."

Fiona arose from the floor where she had been sitting and came to join them by the hearth. "Am I to be betrothed?" she asked. "Have you found a husband for me? Is he handsome? Is he rich? How old is he?"

The laird laughed. "Ever since you visited the king you have been fixated upon a match for yourself. Nay, lass, I am not of a mind to let you go yet. Perhaps when you are thirty or forty I may consider it."

"Da! You know I should be wed by the time I am fifteen or sixteen else I be too old," Fiona scolded. "Well, if it is not a marriage, then what is it?"

"Your mam is with child," the laird told his daughter. "You will have a brother or a sister come the spring."

"I hope it's a brother," Fiona surprised them by saying. "I don't want to be the heiress of Dunglais. That would mean I would have to stay here and have a second son for a husband. I want only a first son and an even bigger keep of my own."

"Gracious!" Alix exclaimed. "You have been thinking about this, haven't you?"

"I will be eight this year," Fiona said. "The young king explained to me the importance of making a good match and making it early. Why, surely you remember that before the old king died he made a match for our king with the king of Denmark's daughter, and James is but two years my senior. But his bride is younger."

"The old king began the marriage negotiations, but they are not yet confirmed," Alix told Fiona, "although Queen Marie says they will be. It takes time to negotiate a proper marriage contract between kings." She reached out and smoothed her daughter's dark hair. "Are you content you are to have a sibling, my daughter?"

"Aye," Fiona said with a smile. "But, Mama, please have a lad."

The laird laughed. "I am pleased to see you will not be jealous," he told his child.

"Da!" Fiona gave an exasperated sigh. "Why would I be jealous of a bairn? I shall be married and gone long before he is grown. I have seen bairns in the village. They suck, shit, and sleep, and then suck some more for at least a year. They are really not very interesting at all." Then she put her arms about Alix. "I am glad for you, Mama." And she kissed Alix's cheek sweetly. Then she ran off to find her cat, who had disappeared from the hall.

"I suppose you must begin considering a match for her," Alix told her husband.

"Not until she is twelve and her beauty can be seen. Her dower won't be a great one, and so it is her beauty that must help us to make Fiona the best match we can."

"You know I saved some of what my father gave me for myself after I gave you a dower portion," Alix said, and he nodded. "I will have a gold piece for Fiona's dower."

"How fortunate I was that you were found on my lands, lambkin," he said. Then he reached out and gently touched her belly.

"How fortunate I was that it was your men who found me and not some hungry beast," she answered him, holding her hand against her still-flat belly.

In the hall that night Malcolm Scott announced to all there that his wife was with child. A child to be born at the very end of the winter. A health was drunk to the laird's wife by all there. By the following day all of the Dunglais folk knew that Alix was expecting a bairn. Walking or riding through the village she was smiled at and blessings called out to her. Dunglais would have an heir, for it was certain that the laird's wife would have a son, all the women of the village decided.

The autumn arrived and one bright blue and gold late October day Alix decided that she would ride out one final time, for now that her belly was beginning to grow round she thought perhaps it would be wiser to forego her daily ride. And the winter would set in before long, making it impossible to ride anyway. She was accompanied by two of the castle's men-at-arms and little Fiona. The sun was warm upon their backs as they rode.

But as they topped a hill they unexpectedly came face-to-face with a large band of men coming up the other side. Immediately one of the Dunglais men-at-arms reached for the bridle of little Fiona's mount, and turning, began to dash back towards the keep. The other soldier with Alix called to her to do the same while he remained behind to give her a head start and defend her flight. A band of armed men in daylight upon the moor could only presage a raid or some other mischief. Alix took flight, as she had been bid.

She turned back once to see the Dunglais man battling valiantly, but he soon fell to the ground mortally wounded. There was also a group of men galloping after her. Alix urged her mare to greater speed, but to no avail. The creature could only go so fast. She was shortly surrounded. A man reached for the mare's bridle. Alix slashed out at him with her reins. "Take your hands from my horse!" she shouted at him. "How dare you attack a woman out riding upon her own lands?"

"You have a choice, madame," the obvious leader of the group said. "You will come quietly with us upon your own mount, or I will take you by force upon mine."

"Do you know who I am?" Alix said. She was terrified, but would not show it.

"You are the Laird of Dunglais's mistress," the man replied.

"I am the laird's lawful wife, you fool!" Alix snapped back.

"Not according to the church in England," the man said.

"We are not in England," Alix answered, but an icy chill ran down her spine.

"We will be by tomorrow" came the reply.

"Sir, I am with child," Alix told him. "My husband will pay the ransom you ask, if you will but approach him. Even now my daughter has regained the keep and given the alarm. You will quickly be caught. Do not be foolish, and endanger your life or that of your men. My husband is a fierce fighter." Alix attempted to bargain with the man.

"Madame, I have been sent by your betrothed husband, Sir Udolf Watteson, to retrieve you from the shameful captivity in which you have found yourself," the man told her. "I have come to bring you home to Wulfborn. What Sir Udolf does with the bastard you now carry is not my affair. I have but one mission. To bring you back to Sir Udolf. Only then will my men and I be paid."

"Sir Udolf is *not* my betrothed husband," Alix said, struggling to keep calm. "I am wed under Scotland's laws and in Scotland's Holy Catholic Church to Malcolm Scott, the Laird of Dunglais. It is his heir I carry. Please, sir, I beg of you, allow me to pass and return to my home."

"For the sake of your unborn bairn, lady, I advise you to come quietly," her captor said. "I am a man of my word, and I gave it to Sir Udolf." He reached out again for her bridle, and Alix again lashed out at him, but this time he grabbed the small riding whip from her, yanking it roughly from her gloved hand and flinging it to the earth. Then, grasping her horse's bridle, he leaned over and clipped a leading rein to it.

Alix opened up her mouth and screamed at the top of her lungs. Her cries were of no use, for her captors led her away nonetheless. She continued to shriek until she could cry out no longer and her throat was raw with her efforts. Then they rode in silence, and they rode swiftly, putting as much ground between the laird who would be pursuing them shortly and themselves. They did not stop the day long, only slowing now and again to give their horses a chance to catch their breaths. Alix was hungry and very thirsty by the time they finally came to a halt.

They stopped in a deep hollow even as the sun set. She was lifted from her horse, and to her embarrassment her legs gave way beneath her. The captain of the raiders caught her and set her down carefully in the grass. He gave her a drink from his own water bottle and handed her an oatcake to eat. Alix was exhausted and fell asleep shortly after she had managed to swallow down her small nourishment. She was astounded to be awakened while it was yet dark, and protested.

"There's a good bright border moon rising tonight, lady," the captain told her. "The horses are rested enough to go on, and so must we." He pulled her to her feet. "Your mare has been watered and grazed for the past few hours. We must be on our way." He helped her to her horse and boosted her into her saddle before she might protest further. "We'll get to Wulfborn by midmorning if we leave here now," he said.

Alix had always preferred riding astride when she could. As part of the queen's household she had been forced to ride sidesaddle when she was with her godmother, but when she was not she rode astride. She was relieved she knew how, for it made the pace they were keeping easier for her. A full moon was just rising as they began their journey again. Soon the bright moon made it almost as bright as daylight. But it was cold and slightly damp. Alix was glad she had her cloak with her. It helped some, but she was still chilled to the bone. Where were Colm and his men? Why hadn't they caught up to the raiders by now?

The Laird of Dunglais had already heard the shouting in the courtyard of his keep when his little daughter burst into the hall screaming his name.

"*Da! Da!* Some men have taken Alix!"

The man-at-arms who had accompanied Fiona back to the keep ran into the hall. "My lord! My lord! The lady has been stolen by raiders. Tam remained to defend her and allow her retreat, but when I looked back I saw them reach her and lead her away. Tam can only have been killed, for he would fight to the death to defend the lady."

"Fenella!" the laird called out. "Take care of Fiona!" And Malcolm Scott, hurrying from his own hall, called out to his men and for his stallion. "Bar the gates and lower the portcullis," he instructed the few men who would remain behind. "Open to no one but me no matter what they say to you. Do you understand me?" And when he was assured that they did, he mounted his horse and rode from Dunglais Keep, a large party of men accompanying him.

Led by the man-at-arms who had been with Alix and Fiona, they reached the spot where Alix had last been seen. Noting the trampled grass, the laird could determine that it had indeed been a large party of raiders. Now they had to discover in which direction these strangers had gone. At first the riders had gone in one direction. East. But then after several miles it appeared as if they had broken into two groups. The laird stopped to consider. One group had turned northeast while the other had gone south. Malcolm Scott considered carefully before turning northeast, but night set in quickly as it was late October. They were forced to stop.

"We'll rest here until moonrise," the laird said, "and then continue onward."

And when the moon arose they moved out again, until suddenly, to their surprise, they came upon an encampment of men, all sleeping but for the watch, who had little time to cry out before the laird's men were upon them.

"Which one of you is in charge?" the laird demanded when all the sleepers had been roused and stood before him. No one spoke. With a sigh the laird stepped forward and yanked one of his prisoners to him, pressing his dirk to the man's throat. "Who is in charge?" he asked again. The man in his grip shook his head, and so Malcolm Scott pressed the sharp tip of the dirk into the flesh beneath it, drawing a small bubble of blood. "You have taken my wife," he said in a cold, hard voice. The dirk pressed deeper, and the flow of blood grew just slightly. "Now, who is in charge? Fail to answer me this time, and I'll slit your throat and move on to someone else until I have gotten my answer. Or killed you all. You understand me?"

The man's eyes bulged with fright as he looked into the laird's merciless face, and with a small whimper he pointed to another man among the prisoners, gasping out one word. "*Him!*" Then, as the laird released him, the man fell to the ground, soiling himself in relief, although he still wasn't certain they wouldn't all be killed.

The Dunglais men grabbed the man pointed out to them, dragging him to where the laird stood and forcing him to his knees.

"Where is my wife?" Malcolm Scott asked in a soft but deadly voice.

"I don't know," the leader of the raiders said, yelping as one of the laird's men hit him a fierce blow. "My lord, I swear I do not!"

"Do you deny taking her?" the laird asked. "Lie to me, and I will personally see you suffer a most painful and drawn-out death."

"Nay, my lord, we were part of the band that took her, but we do not know where she has been taken," the man said. "We are Douglases from near Jedburgh. We were contacted by some of our English kin a few months back. They told us the wife of an English lord had been taken and he wanted her back. When the time was right they would send for us. We joined with our kinfolk yesterday and took the woman. We were then paid for our trouble and told to go home. But we don't know who this English lord is. I swear to you, we don't!"

"But I think I may," Malcolm Scott said. "I am the Laird of Dunglais, and rest assured I will inform the king of this treachery. Do you Douglases have no loyalty except to yourselves? Do you always betray your fellow countrymen?"

The Douglas captain flushed angrily, but he held his peace except to say, "You are free, my lord, to inform that puling brat who is our king. We Douglases care not!"

"Take their horses and the coins they were paid for their perfidy," the laird said coldly. "I will have something for my trouble before we ride after my wife."

"But we're miles from home!" the Douglas captain protested. "And we earned that coin fairly, my lord. How are we to feed our families if you steal from us?"

"You purloined from me something far more precious than a handful of coins. You took my wife who is with child. While you are walking, consider the sin of disloyalty," the laird snapped. "And the coin you earned was hardly acquired honestly, stealing my wife to deliver to some English lordling!" Reaching out, he cut the purse from the Douglas captain's belt, hefted it in his hand, and smiled at the weight of it. "Aye, this will compensate me somewhat for my trouble."

While the laird had berated the Douglas captain, his men gathered up their horses and were ready to depart. Malcolm Scott mounted his stallion, and without a further glimpse at the Douglas clansmen, rode off with his own men and their newly acquired beasts. As they rode towards Dunglais, the captain of his men-at-arms spoke up.

"Why do we return home, my lord? Should we not go over the border after our good lady?" The captain's name was Dugald, but he was called Beinn, which meant mountain, by all who knew him, for he was a giant of a man standing six feet six inches tall with a massive head covered in russet hair, and limbs like tree trunks.

"I am certain I know who has absconded with my wife," the laird explained. "She will be safe once she has reached her destination. He will not harm her. We will get these scrawny beasts safely back to Dunglais, and then tomorrow we will cross over the border to retrieve my wife. We can hardly go raiding with a herd of horses now, can we?" He grinned at Beinn, who grinned back.

"Aye, my lord. But can you tell me, do you know, why this Englishman took our lady?" For all his size Beinn was a gentleman except when provoked. All the village children and every dog for miles around loved and gravitated to him.

"This lord believes my wife was betrothed to him. She was not," the laird told the faithful Beinn. "You recall how my lady was found?"

And Beinn nodded. "Aye, I do."

"She had been fleeing this man," the laird explained. "Do you remember the Englishman who came to the keep some months back? It is the same man. My wife and daughter kept to their chambers while he was at Dunglais overnight, and I told him I had no knowledge of the woman he sought. He is half-mad, I believe, but he will not harm Alix. Of that I am certain."

Alix, however, was not certain at all that Sir Udolf was harmless. She was utterly exhausted when they finally arrived at Wulfborn. Had it always looked so bleak and lonely out upon the moors? Aye, it had, she thought with a shiver. It had been almost two years since she had escaped from here, and she was not pleased at all to be back when she first saw the house from a distance. The captain of the raiding party came to help her down from her mare. As shaky as she felt, Alix pushed him away, glaring.

"I don't envy your lord, lady," he said quietly.

"The old fool who lives here is *not* my lord. I expect my husband is not far behind, and there will be blood before this is all over," Alix snapped. It was all she could do to keep standing.

And then Sir Udolf hurried from the house, smiling broadly. "My darling Alix, welcome home!" he gushed and made to put his arms about her so he might kiss her.

"This most certainly is *not* my home, Sir Udolf!" Alix said, shoving him away and wondering where she had gotten the strength to do it when she could hardly remain on her own two feet. She was surely going to collapse if she didn't sit down soon. Pray God the bairn was all right. *The bairn!* She had called it the bairn. *I am becoming a Scot*, she thought, and almost smiled, but caught herself in time lest Sir Udolf think she was smiling at him. She gazed hard at the man in front of her. He had aged. How old was he? she attempted to recall. In his late fifties, for he had been close in years to her own father. "I am weary beyond telling," Alix said coldly. "Let us go into the hall." And she pushed past him as she moved into the house.

God's wounds! The hall had become a pigsty. There were rushes upon the stone floor, and those rushes were filled with animal bones and other bits of garbage. The whole place stank of sour wine and beer, rotting food, and chimneys that were not drawing properly. It had certainly not been this way when she had first come to Wulf-born, nor while she lived here.

"He beat me black-and-blue when it was discovered you had escaped him," a voice whined by her elbow.

"Why is the hall so filthy, Bab?" Alix demanded to know, recognizing the woman's voice. "Where are the servants?"

"He kept saying you would take care of it all when you came back," Bab told her, coming around to face Alix now. She hadn't changed either, Alix thought. She was still a bawdy old slattern.

"I did not come back," Alix told the serving woman. "He had me kidnapped from my own lands, from my husband, Bab. The laird will be here soon, and I will return home to Dunglais with him."

"He were very excited when he found you," Bab nattered on.

"I am not remaining," Alix told her.

"He won't let anyone else have you, lady, and under the law you are his wife."

"As his son's widow it was my right to choose a new husband if I wanted one. Your master is a lustful fool, but no decent woman would wed her father-in-law," Alix told Bab. "It is ungodly. It is incest certainly."

"But he got his dispensation from York," Bab protested.

"A dispensation he told me he would buy," Alix said. "When I could not dissuade him from his folly, I fled Wulfborn as any respectable woman would have done! I am not betrothed to your master, nor am I his wife. I am the wife of the Laird of Dunglais, as all at Wulfborn will learn to their misfortune when my husband arrives. Our marriage was sanctioned by the bishop of St. Andrew's. Now, Bab, I am exhausted. I must rest. Tell your master I will see him on the morrow." And without another word Alix went upstairs to her old bedroom.

She was shocked to find everything exactly as she had left it two years ago. Although dusty, it was still obviously the cleanest room in the house. Her trunk was yet at the foot of her bed and filled with her own clothing. The scent of roses assailed her nostrils as she opened it. It would appear it had not been opened since she had left Wulfborn. Alix whirled at a scratching on the door. "Who is it?" she asked.

"Only me," Bab said, coming into the chamber with a pitcher of water. "I remember how you liked to bathe yourself, and you have been traveling for several days." She set the pitcher down on a table. "I told the master what you said, and he has agreed to see you on the morrow. Are you hungry? If you are I'll fetch you something to eat."

"Aye," Alix answered her. "I would like that. Thank you, Bab."

The serving woman left the chamber. Alix stripped off her cape. It was dusty. She would have Bab brush it. Pulling the chamber pot from beneath the bed, she peed, tossing the water from the window. Then she bathed her face and her hands in the water Bab had brought. The woman had remembered she preferred warm water to wash in, and not cold. Where was Colm? Alix wondered. Certainly he had been only a few hours behind her captors. She had been surprised when he hadn't caught up to her before they arrived at Wulfborn. Sir Udolf would not be easy to deal with, but her husband would quickly settle the matter to his own satisfaction, but not to Sir Udolf's.

Bab returned carrying a small bowl of soup, half a loaf, and some cheese. She set it down upon a small table near the hearth. "You'd best eat it while it's hot, lady," she advised. Then she sighed. "The soup I fear will taste of nothing. The bread is stale, and the cheese hard with age. Nothing has been right since you left us."

"Do you understand why I left, Bab?" Alix asked the serving woman.

"Aye," Bab said. "So you have told me. But he's mad. The dispensation he gained cost him dearly. The priest had to make two additional visits to Yorkminster before it was granted."

"God and his Blessed Mother!" Alix swore lightly. Then she shook her head. "Are there no suitable women of childbearing age hereabouts he might take as a wife? Why has he fixed all his hopes upon me?" She broke off a piece of the stale loaf and dipped it in the soup to soften it before popping it into her mouth. Bab was correct. The soup had no flavor at all, and she would swear that the piece of cheese brought to her had the marks of mouse teeth in it. She pushed it away.

"I think most of the gentlefolk in the region kept their daughters from the Wattesons because of Master Hayle. He were an odd boy, as you would surely know, lady. Sir Udolf has not spoken with his neighbors in many years now. I think he took offense towards them because of their attitude against Master Hayle," Bab said. "But I know there are at least two ladies still young enough to give him what he wants that he might take to wife. Their families are good and equal to his. He just doesn't know how to approach these families after all the time that has passed and the animosity between them. And you were here. Young and fecund, lady."

"But after I was not here why did he pursue the matter?" Alix wondered aloud.

"Sir Udolf is like a flock of sheep. Once he gets going in a certain direction, 'tis nigh impossible to turn him onto another path, lady, without much effort."

Alix shook her head. "I wish your master no ill, Bab, but my husband will come for me, and when he does I will go with him. If Sir Udolf attempts to stop us, Colm will surely kill him. As it is, I shall have to dissuade him from slaying Sir Udolf when he first arrives. My husband is by nature a peaceable man, but he loves me and will be very angry that I, or the bairn I carry, might have been harmed."

"You're with child?" Bab exclaimed, and then she looked closely at Alix. "Aye, I can see it now. When is your child due to come into this world?"

"Late winter," Alix told the woman.

"Will you tell the master?" Bab wondered fearfully. Sir Udolf was not going to be pleased at all to find that his heart's desire was carrying another man's child.

"I most certainly will tell Sir Udolf, Bab. Do you think I want to endanger my bairn, having to fend off his unwanted advances?" Alix pushed the tray away. "And you say naught to any until I have."

Bab nodded her grizzled head. "Aye, lady, you may be certain I will say nothing, for I do not wish to be the victim of Sir Udolf's disappointment and outrage when he learns your secret. I still ache two years after the fact from the beating he gave me when you ran away," the older woman said.

"He should not have punished you at all," Alix said angrily. "Everyone had been told I was praying and fasting and had no wish to be disturbed. You were simply obeying the orders that he himself had approved."

Bab picked up the tray. "I'll leave you, then, but a word of warning, lady. Bar your door this night against any surprise incursions." Then she left the chamber.

Taking her advice, Alix went and turned the key in the lock of her door. She then took the heavy wooden rod that was used to barricade the door to ensure her privacy, and lifting it not without some difficulty, Alix set it in its place. The master of Wulfborn would not be disturbing her this night. But where was Colm? Should he not have come to retrieve her by now? But as he had not, Alix lay down on the bed to rest. She would just have to wait. Today was over, but Colm would come tomorrow, she was certain.

"It isn't her," the Laird of Dunglais said, looking down at the ravaged body of the almost naked woman who had been found out on the moor and brought back to the hall by the men who had made the gruesome discovery. He looked down with pity on the bruised and battered body. The woman had been very ill used, raped and beaten. Her face was a swollen mass of bloody pulp. It wasn't Alix. *It couldn't be!*

"Can you be sure, my lord?" one of his men asked nervously.

"It is not my mam," Fiona Scott said with great certainty as she came around her father's tall frame and peered down at the body curiously.

"Fiona! What are you doing here? Fenella, take her away," the laird cried, disturbed that his almost-eight-year-old daughter should have seen such a terrible sight.

"Da, it is not Alix," Fiona insisted. "Alix was wearing breeks. Those shreds of clothing still left on that poor lass are not from her breeks. And look closely at her hands, Da. The nails are cracked, broken, and dirty. And they are large hands. Alix has dainty hands, and her nails are never broken nor her cuticles cracked. And this lass has no belly. My mam's belly was beginning to grow round with my brother."

"The lass is right," Fenella said quietly, quite startled by the child's sharp perception as she too stared down at the body. The woman was too big-boned to be Dunglais's lady. "This isn't your wife, my lord."

"The Englishman is clever in attempting to make me believe it is. Yet he was careless in his choice of henchmen to carry out his nefarious plot," Malcolm Scott noted. "They did not bother to consider the differences between my wife and the victim they chose to masquerade as her. Poor woman. Can anyone identify her?"

"It may be Vika from over the hill," Beinn said thoughtfully. "She's a local whore, my lord." He looked the body over very carefully and then nodded. "Aye, that's just who it is, my lord. See that round pinkish brown mole there on the side of her ankle? Vika had just such a mole."

Another man-at-arms sidled forward and peered down. "Aye, 'tis Vika, poor lass. She were a good whore, and never stole from a man when he slept," he remarked.

"Fenella, find some respectable garments for the woman, and we'll bury her decently. Someone go and fetch the priest. Father Donald can say a word over her. Did she have any bairns?" the laird wanted to know.

"Two," Beinn answered him. "Lads both. Maybe three and five."

"Is their sire or sires known?" the laird asked.

"If Vika knew, she never said, my lord," Beinn told him.

"Find those lads," the laird instructed, "and bring them to the keep. In an odd sense their mam died for my wife. I'll see her lads aren't left to starve or be mistreated."

It had been a day now since Alix had been kidnapped, but with the discovery of the dead whore Malcolm Scott was once more delayed from leaving Dunglais to seek out his wife at Wulfborn and bring her home. The Englishman had to be mad to concoct such a wicked scheme. And what in the name of all that was holy had convinced him he could get away with it? While Malcolm knew Alix was safe, he was still concerned for his lambkin and the bairn she carried. An almost-two-day ride across the hills and over the border could not have been easy. If anything had happened to either his wife or his son the Englishman would regret his folly with his last dying breath, which the Laird of Dunglais promised himself would be a long, painful time coming. And not a stone of his house or village would be left standing.

Malcolm Scott decided he needed more men to ride with him. He sent to his uncle at Drumcairn, requesting that he come with all haste, bringing his clansmen with him. Then, despite his impatience, he waited another day, for to meet up with his uncle in the roadless borders would be more difficult. Early the next day Robert Ferguson arrived at Dunglais with twenty of his clansmen.

"What has happened, Nephew?" he asked as he dismounted his horse.

"Come into the hall," the laird invited him, "and the rest of you. You'll eat and then we ride for England!" He led the way, his uncle hurrying to keep up with him. Once at the high board Malcolm Scott explained the situation to his uncle. "I don't know how he learned she was here, but he did. Now I must go and retrieve my wife. She is with child, Uncle. She carries my son."

"Or a daughter," Robert Ferguson said.

"Lad or lass, I care not," Malcolm Scott said. "I want my lambkin back, and my bairn safe. The Englishman's a fool to believe I won't come for her."

Robert Ferguson speared himself a slice of ham with his dirk and began to eat it. "How far?" he wanted to know.

"I only know the direction in which they went and the area where this Wulfborn Hall is supposed to be located. I sent scouts out yesterday to find exactly where this Englishman makes his home, but Alix always said it was very isolated, and she never met any neighboring families. But I also know it cannot be more than a day and a half's ride over the border from Dunglais."

The Ferguson of Drumcairn chewed his breakfast with thoughtful care. "What exactly do you intend doing when we reach this Wulfborn Hall, Nephew?"

"I shall demand my wife be returned to me immediately!" the laird told him.

"And if this English lordling refuses?" was the question.

"I'll pull his house down around his ears until I have my wife back!" Malcolm Scott said.

"Hmmmm," Robert Ferguson said. "How is the house defended?"

"I don't know," the laird said irritably.

"How many men does he have?"

"I don't know," the laird said again. "But I do recall Alix saying there were not many tenants, for the land was poor and not particularly arable."

"Hmmmm," Robert Ferguson considered further, but he could think of no other questions to ask his nephew. "Well, then," he said, "I suppose the first thing is to find Wulfborn. Unless the house is well defended we should be able to take it without sustaining serious losses, laddie. Will you kill the Englishman?"

"Only if I have to," the laird said grimly.

Robert Ferguson removed the last hard-boiled egg from the bowl before him, and after peeling it, neatly popped it into his mouth. "Well, then," he said as he chewed it, "I suppose we must ride. We've still got several hours of daylight before us."

After giving his housekeeper explicit instructions, and promising his daughter to return with Alix, the Laird of Dunglais, in the company of his uncle of Drumcairn, left his hall. Going into the courtyard of his keep, he mounted the large stallion he favored. Next to him Robert Ferguson had climbed atop his own horse. Raising his hand, the laird signaled his men to move forward, and they rode forth from the keep in a double line. Fiona and Fenella watched them from one of the keep's two towers.

"He will bring Alix home, won't he?" the little girl asked the woman by her side.

"Aye, he'll bring her home, lass," Fenella assured the child.

"I've lost one mother," Fiona said. "I do not want to lose another. This one loves me while the other did not."

"Whoever told you such a thing?" Fenella wanted to know. It might be the truth, but it wasn't a truth a child should be aware of, she thought angrily.

"I hear things," Fiona said, noting that the housekeeper did not try to tell her it wasn't so. "People do not pay a great deal of attention to me when they are involved in their own purposes, Fenella. She who birthed me did not love me. I tell everyone she loved my father, but if she did not love me how could she love him?"

Fenella pressed her lips together. How could she admit to the truth of what little Fiona was saying? She would not hurt this child, though it would appear Fiona Scott was wise beyond her years. "Let the past lie, my bairn," she told the girl. "Your father loves your stepmother, and your stepmother loves you both. It is far more than most people get in this life."

"I will only marry for love," Fiona responded.

"Neither your da nor Alix would ever force you into a marriage that did not please you," Fenella assured her young companion. "But you are just going to be eight in a few weeks, my bairn. There is more than enough time for marriage."

The day was gray and the air about them still as they stood watching the laird, his uncle, and the fifty men with them ride over the hill and out of sight.

"Will they be gone long?" Fiona wondered.

"A few days, certainly no more," Fenella said, and hoped it would be so. "Your da will send to us if 'tis to be longer. Now, is it not time for you to go to Father Donald for your Latin lesson, Fiona Scott? Just because your mam isn't here does not mean you can shirk your duties. With Martinmas near, I am going to teach you how to salt meat today. Bacon does not appear magically upon the high board." And Fenella led her charge from the tower top back down into the hall of Dunglais Keep.

Chapter 11

The clansmen followed the track they had followed several days previously, turning south this time where the raiding party had split in two. They moved along at a steady pace, stopping to rest their horses briefly and take a few moments of ease. They carried with them oatcakes, which they ate a-saddle when hungry. Each man's flask held his own personal preference for liquid refreshment. When the short autumn day began to wane they found shelter by an ancient cairn of stones. Gathering wood for a fire, they soon had one going. Others among them went on foot onto the moor and trapped several rabbits and two game birds, which were dispatched quickly to be brought back for supper. The creatures were swiftly skinned, the birds plucked. Then they were put on spits to be roasted over the open fire.

When the game was nicely cooked it was portioned out among the men to eat with their oatcakes. Afterwards a watch was set for the night, and those who could, slept. The skies had cleared near sunset. As he lay upon his back staring up at the night sky admiring the bright stars, Malcolm Scott considered that it had been a very long time since he had gone raiding. The borders were not always as quiet as they had been of recent years, but then the English had had—still had—problems with their monarchs. Everyone chose sides, and they had been so busy fighting amongst themselves that there had been no time to fight with the Scots.

He wasn't certain as he lay there that he didn't miss the

excitement of the raiding that had gone back and forth during the previous years. It wasn't over yet, of course. It would never be over. He expected that once England settled down with this new king of theirs and the matter of poor mad Henry VI was concluded, the raiding would begin anew. He smiled in the darkness thinking of how he would take his sons with him and teach them how a border lord went raiding. He would show them there was a time for harshness and a time for mercy. That cattle, horses, and sheep, not women, were the best part of a raid, for they added to a man's wealth. But, of course, first he had to regain his wife from that stubborn fool of an Englishman who thought that Alix was his.

He awoke when his uncle shook his shoulder. It was still dark, but the darkness was lightening, and the distant horizon was beginning to hint at morning. Around him the men were gathering up the horses that had been grazing and resting during the night. After watering the horses at a nearby stream, the men were now preparing to ride.

"Mount up!" the laird called to them as he sprang into his saddle.

The borderers moved slowly off from their encampment. The air was distinctly colder this morning, but as the sun slowly began to rise, the dampness eased. With more light the horses picked up the pace as they rode south. In late morning, close to the noon hour, they had the good fortune to come upon a small three-wagon caravan of tinkers who were also traveling south to find a milder winter. The wagons stopped as the laird and his troop came upon them.

"Good morrow, my lords," the obvious leader said, bowing nervously as he waited to learn the fate God had decided for him and his family. He was a swarthy man, but roughly dressed. From the wagons about him children peeped out curiously. There was no sign of women, only other men with faces that said nothing.

"Do you know of a place called Wulfborn Hall?" the laird asked pleasantly.

"Wulfborn Hall?" The tinker considered carefully, and then he saw the gleam of silver in the laird's fingers. "You are quite near it, my lord," he said quickly.

"How near?" the laird asked casually, tossing the silver piece into the air.

The tinker watched the coin with dark eyes as it fell back into the laird's big palm. He could tell it was full weight by its size and the faint sound it made as it hit the skin. "Perhaps ten miles just south and slightly to the east, my lord," he replied, deftly catching the coin as it was sent through the air in his direction. He bobbed his appreciation.

"My thanks," Malcolm Scott said, and he signaled his men forward again.

The tinker watched them go, thinking that so large an armed group did not bode well for Wulfborn Hall. He beckoned his caravan onward.

"Do you think he told the truth?" Robert Ferguson asked his nephew.

"He had no reason to lie," the laird said, and then he called to Beinn. "Send two men ahead to ascertain the exact location of this place we seek."

"You want to find the right place, Nephew. It would not do for us to attack someone innocent in this matter," the Ferguson of Drumcairn remarked.

"Alix said there were no neighbors for miles around," Malcolm Scott replied.

Two scouts broke off from the main party and rode ahead seeking out Wulfborn Hall. They were not long in finding it, for the tinker had not lied. One of them rode back to the laird while the other waited and watched. The house that stood on a small rise at one end of the village was constructed of stone. It had a slate roof, and its windows were long and narrow. It was a house that could be properly defended. The village was small and poor looking, but it did have a little church at the opposite end from the house. There were few signs of life on this autumn day, for the harvest was long in. Most of the cotters would be keeping to their hearths until spring came. There was a respectable flock of sheep grazing on a hillside in the weak sunshine, and maybe half a dozen cattle in the nearby meadow. The place was hardly worth pillaging, the clansman observing in the shadows thought to himself as his horse shifted beneath him. Sensing the arrival of his clansmen, the watcher turned as the laird rode up by his side.

Malcolm Scott gazed down on the scene. "It seems a peaceful enough place," he said. "Is it not guarded?"

The clansman shook his head in the negative. "Shepherd and his dog over in yon meadow, my lord, but other than a goodwife scurrying to the well in the village I've seen no sign of men-at-arms. 'Tis obvious this Englishman believes he is safe from attack."

"Umm," the laird grunted, and then he said, "The house looks as if it is fortifiable. Stone walls as thick as any keep. And the door will be oak bound in iron, I'll wager. Not easy to hack through, but it can be done. No walls though about the place." He thought silently for a long minute. How to proceed? Would the Englishman, faced with fifty armed Scots, turn Alix over to him and admit his defeat? Or would he persist in the fantasy that Alix belonged to him, thereby forcing the Laird of Dunglais to strong action? There was no way to know the answer to his questions, of course, until he himself proceeded one way or another.

" 'Tis never wise to show one's full intent," the Ferguson of Drumcairn said to his nephew quietly.

Malcolm Scott nodded thoughtfully. Then he spoke. "You and your clansmen remain here, Uncle. I shall take mine down the hill and up to the door of Wulfborn Hall to see what I can accomplish with this lordling."

"He's not likely to give her up," Robert Ferguson noted.

"Probably not, but before I destroy his village, drive off his livestock, and take his people to sell in the Jedburgh market, I should like to offer him the opportunity to be reasonable and save most of what he has from my ire," the laird said.

" 'Tis fair," his uncle agreed, "and most generous of you, Colm, considering the scurvy fellow stole your wife." He turned to his own clansmen. "We'll be remaining here for the interim, lads," the Ferguson of Drumcairn told them.

The laird turned to his captain. "We'll go quietly," he said, "but ride slowly through the village to instill the proper amount of fear in these English. In the end I have no doubt we'll have to fight to regain possession of my wife, but perhaps a show of force will frighten this Englishman into being reasonable. Tell the men."

Beinn nodded, and then moved among the Scot clansmen speaking quickly and quietly. Then he returned to his lord's side. " 'Tis done, and they understand," he said.

The Laird of Dunglais raised his arm and signaled his men forward. They came from the wooded hillside into the open, riding slowly and silently down the hillside. The shepherd in the meadow saw them first, and a shiver of dread ran down his spine, but he remained with his sheep, for the clansmen made no threat to him. Indeed they didn't even look at him as they rode by.

A woman coming from the communal well saw them as they passed the little church and came down the street of the village. Dropping her full pail she ran shrieking at the top of her lungs towards her cottage. Several cotters, hearing her distressed cries, came to their doors, leaping back with fright and slamming them shut as the troupe of clansmen rode mutely by them. They continued on up a small rise until they reached the house, and it was there that they stopped. The Laird of Dunglais climbed down from his big stallion, and walking up to the iron-bound oak door, pounded furiously upon it. Then he stood and waited, but there was no answer. He beat upon the door a second time.

"Open the door to me, Sir Udolf Watteson! I have come for my wife, and as God is my witness, I shall have her!" Malcolm Scott called out. He banged the door again.

Finally a tiny window high up in the door opened. It had an iron grating and all but obscured the face of the man who spoke from it. "What is it you want, Scotsman?"

"Are you Sir Udolf? For I shall speak only with him," the laird told the speaker.

"I am he" was his answer.

"You have my wife, my lord, and I have come to take her back," the laird said.

"You are mistaken," Sir Udolf replied. "Go away!"

"Alix Givet was married to me in the rite of our Holy Catholic Church," the laird answered quietly.

"Alix Givet is my betrothed wife," Sir Udolf responded. "I have the dispensation from Yorkminster that permitted me to take her as my wife. My claim is prior, and it is just. You cannot have her."

"You had no authority over the lady, my lord. Therefore your dispensation is not valid, for it was obtained under false circumstances," Malcolm Scott said. "Alix is my wife, and she is carrying my bairn. I want them back."

"You lie!" Sir Udolf told the laird in a tight voice. Alix with child? She had not told him that. But in the week he had had her back she had spoken but few words to him. She could not be carrying this Scot's bastard! He would not allow it! She was meant to bear him a child. Another son to take Hayle's place. A son to inherit Wulfborn one day. "My wife is not with child," he finally said to the laird.

"That could possibly be truth if you had a wife, Sir Udolf, but you do not. I do, and she is with child. You are holding her captive in your house. Release her, and I shall go my way peaceably. Deny my request, and you will feel my wrath," the Laird of Dunglais said in a hard voice.

"Get you gone from my lands," Sir Udolf responded. "Alix Givet is mine. If she is indeed with child, I will gladly return your bastard to you when it is born, but its mother remains with me, you rough savage. You have raped and abused her! You have forced her into an unholy and illegal union! But I shall protect her from you! Go!"

Malcolm Scott shook his head in disbelief. "If you truly believe what you say, my lord, then you are a bigger fool than I took you for," he told Sir Udolf. "Release my wife to me, or suffer the consequences of your folly."

The little window with its grating slammed shut above him, but not before Sir Udolf had shouted, "I will see you in hell first, you filthy Scot!"

"God's wounds!" the laird swore angrily, and his stallion danced nervously as its master swung it around and galloped back through the village and up the hill with his men to where his uncle waited with his own clansmen. "The stubborn fool wants a fight, for which he is neither prepared nor able to win," he said to Robert Ferguson.

"The house is strongly made," Beinn said to his lord. "While you spoke with the Englishman I sent several of our men to ride about it, looking for weaknesses in the structure. There are none we could see. The windows are all shuttered for winter, and there are but two doors. The one before which you stood, and a tiny door that probably leads to the kitchens. Like its larger mate, it is iron-bound and oak. The walls are all stone and of a deep thickness. It needs no wall or moat about it, for it is as strong as any keep, my lord. We are not equipped to batter it down as we are now."

The laird said nothing for what seemed a long few moments, but then he spoke. "This Englishman sits behind his house walls smugly holding my wife and our unborn bairn as his captives and thinking she is his for the taking. We will fire the village and take his livestock first. But when I return it will be for my wife, and once she is safe I will kill Sir Udolf Watteson myself for his temerity. Which will you have, Uncle? The four-legged sheep or the two-legged ones?"

"I'll take the four-legged," the Ferguson of Drumcairn replied. "Easier to manage, and I won't have the bother of selling them off. What about his cattle?"

"Next time," the laird said grimly. Then, before they realized what he was doing, Malcolm Scott rode back down the hill, through the village, and up to the front door of Wulfborn Hall. *"Alix,"* he shouted in as loud a voice as he could. *"I will be back for you, lamb-kin! Do not dispair! I will be back!"*

Seated in the hall of the house Alix heard him calling to her through the closed shutters of the windows. She smiled, and her hands encircled her belly in a soothing motion. "There, my bairn," she whispered. "Do you hear your da?" And she smiled to herself even as Sir Udolf stormed into the hall, coming over to the hearth where Alix sat.

"Is it true?" he demanded to know.

"Is what true?" she responded in a cool voice.

"He's put a bastard in your belly," the master of Wulfborn said.

"My husband and I are expecting a child, aye," Alix answered him.

"He is not your husband! I am your husband!" Sir Udolf almost screamed. "I have the papers declaring a betrothal between us. You are mine!"

"You had no right to seek a betrothal between us," Alix told him quietly. "You are not, were not, my legal guardian. I was a widow, and free to choose my own husband if I wanted another. You were my father-in-law, and I told you when you suggested it that I wanted no marriage between us. How could I when I thought of you as I thought of my own dear father, God assoil his soul? I should have felt as if I were committing incest. And certainly the church would not allow such a union."

"And yet it did," Sir Udolf said almost triumphantly.

"You as good told me that you would buy this dispensation, and I have been given to understand it took Father Peter three trips to York before your wishes were granted. And how much gold did it cost you, my lord? And it has all come to naught. Let me go home to my husband. He's still out there, isn't he? I could hear him through the shutters in the hall when he cried out to me."

"He has bewitched you!" Sir Udolf insisted. "And seduced you not only in body but in soul. When your bastard is born it shall be taken from you. Then we may count this unfortunate incident closed. Father Peter will bless us and our union, and you will give me a son to replace the one you took from me."

Alix looked at him, astounded. "Are you mad, my lord?" she wanted to know. "I took nothing from you, but that son who grows more saintly in your eyes daily took much from me. He took the most precious gift I had to offer any man, my virginity. On our wedding night he took it cruelly, brutally, and then left me to return to his mistress. I lay in a cold dark chamber frightened and in pain. Hayle hated me for being his wife. He called me a whore because I agreed to our union so that my father would be safe in his last days, so that I might have a home. I know that most marriages do not begin with love, and knowing your son's devotion to his Maida, I did not expect his love. But I was entitled to his respect, for I was willing to give him mine. And a little kindness would not have gone awry with me. Instead I was mounted in the dark almost every night like a mare in heat. He did not want to see my face or even have me looking at his shadow, for the guilt that overwhelmed him at the taking of a woman other than Maida was too much for him. Hayle was like a boy with his first and only love. Sometimes I felt as if I were years older than he was, and yet it was he who was the elder."

"But I would not—could not—treat you like my son did," Sir Udolf told her.

"I know you would not, and I do not disagree that you need another wife, my lord," Alix said. "But you cannot have me. I am already a wife to the Laird of Dunglais, and soon to be a mother to my husband's son. Let me go, and find yourself another. I am certain there is a family hereabouts who has an eligible daughter. I know you have not spoken to your neighbors in years, but now would be a good time to renew your acquaintance with them. We are all at peace with one another."

Before he might answer her, a serving man ran into the hall. "My lord! My lord! The Scots are burning the village! They are driving off the people and your sheep!"

For a moment Sir Udolf looked befuddled and bemused. Then he cried, "This savage whose bastard you carry has done this! He will never have you back! *Never!* And when the brat springs forth from your womb, madame, I will slay it myself and send its body back to him at your Dunglais."

"You have brought this upon yourself!" Alix told him angrily, coming quickly to her feet. "If you had returned me to him when the laird asked you, we could have gone home. My husband would have left you in peace. This is his answer to your intractability, my lord. You wish to blame someone for this misfortune? Blame yourself!" Then she pierced him with a hard look. "And if I have the misfortune to still be at Wulfborn when my son is born, I give you fair warning. Make one move towards him, and I will kill you myself! You are mad to believe I would allow you to harm my child." And turning on her heel, she left the hall while behind her the few servants stared open-mouthed at Alix's outburst.

Sir Udolf Watteson sat down heavily, remaining silent and still for several long minutes. Finally he stood up, and climbing to the top of his house, opened the shutters on the very window from which his son had hurled himself. Looking out he saw his village burning merrily and heard the faint cries of the wounded. His flock of sheep was gone from the hillside, as was the shepherd and his dog. His few cattle, however, remained. Of the Scots there was no trace now but for the destruction they left in their wake. He sighed as he drew the shutter closed and returned to his hall.

None of it mattered. Some of his villagers would have escaped the borderers. They would return to rebuild the village, and it would be the same as it had ever been. He would take the cattle to the final cattle fair of the year while they were still healthy with their summer grazing. In the spring he would purchase another flock of sheep with the monies he had gained from the cattle sale. He would have no livestock to feed over the winter months, he thought, pleased with his own cleverness.

And best of all Alix Givet was still his. While her strong will was pleasing on one hand, for it indicated the kind of sons she would give him, on the other hand it was not at all agreeable. He would have to beat her regularly in order to keep her in line. It was imperative a wife maintain her place in the order of things. A man could not be overruled in his own house, but then, and he smiled to himself, she was young. Once she understood what was expected of her he was certain she would become a model spouse. Alix was intelligent, and no one could call her a fool despite her stubborn insistence that she loved the Scot whose child she carried.

Alix did not come out of her chamber after that, much to Sir Udolf's dismay. She did give orders from her self-imposed isolation that the hall was to be cleaned. She instructed the cook and his staff what to serve so that Wulfborn Hall once more became a pleasant habitation. But he did not see her, and she kept her chamber door barred to him. Only Bab was permitted admittance, and to Sir Udolf's surprise Bab became devoted to Alix. He considered denying her food and drink. Perhaps she would miscarry her bastard, and the connection she seemed to have with the laird would be severed. But Sir Udolf suspected if he did that his servants would see she wasn't fed and brought liquid refreshment.

Father Peter had escaped the conflagration that had engulfed the village along with some elderly villagers who had fled to the church for sanctuary. Sir Udolf knew they had been left in peace because the elderly were of little value. The priest made plain his disapproval of the master of Wulfborn's actions. "No woman," he told Sir Udolf sternly, "is worth the misery and destruction you have allowed."

"She is mine by right," the baron muttered.

"You are ensorcelled," the priest responded.

"Yet you went to York for me," Sir Udolf snapped. "Thrice!"

"Because you would not listen to reason," the priest said. "When I returned that first time and learned Mistress Alix was gone, I told you to look elsewhere, but nay, you would not. When my contact in York wrote that more coins were needed for God's work in order to make your dispensation a reality, I warned you to cease your foolishness and seek elsewhere for another wife."

"Were those at Yorkminster going to return my offering?" the baron demanded.

"Of course not!" the priest said irritably. "You gave it for God's work."

"I gave it to get my dispensation to marry Alix Givet. God's work indeed! We both know my coins went into the pocket of he to whom you gave it," Sir Udolf said.

"You might have had another to wife by now. I would have sought for another good woman of childbearing age for you among our neighbors' families if you had but asked me. And with God's blessing that wife might have proved fecund, ripening now with a son for you as Mistress Alix ripens with her husband's child, my lord."

"He is not her husband! Do not call that Scots savage her husband, Priest!"

"I will know if he is her lawful husband, as she claims, once I have spoken to her again," the priest told his master. "Where is the lady?"

"In her chamber," Sir Udolf said irritably. "She has been there since the Scots burned the village. She will not come out, and only Bab is permitted her company."

"I can see, however, that her influence has extended into your hall, for it is clean again as it has not been in months. And your table has been most tasty these past few days," Father Peter remarked dryly.

"Go and seek her out, then," the baron said. "And remind her of her proper duties as my wife and lady of Wulfborn." Then Sir Udolf held out the large goblet in his hand to be refilled, and a servant jumped swiftly to do his master's bidding.

The priest arose from the high board, where they had both been sitting. Familiar with the house, he found his way quickly to Alix's bedchamber and knocked upon the door. A voice within inquired as to his identity, and he answered, "Father Peter. I wish to speak with Mistress Alix."

"Are you alone?" He now recognized Bab's voice.

"I am, God's word upon it," Father Peter replied. He heard the heavy wooden bar being lifted from its brackets and then the iron key being turned in the lock. The door opened and he stepped quickly inside. At once he noticed the door was relocked and the bar replaced into its supports.

Alix sat by the small hearth in the room. It was burning merrily, and there was a large stack of wood on the wall next to it. A small iron pot hung from an iron arm that could be swung over the flame or not. The bed with its hanging curtains was neatly made, and the shutters at the window were closed, a drapery pulled across to shield it and keep out any draft that got through the shutters.

"Come, and sit down, Father Peter," Alix invited him.

There was a chair on the opposite side of the hearth from the settle where Alix now resided. Bab sat next to her, sewing a tiny garment. The priest found the situation most pleasant and normal. He sat down and then leaned forward to speak to her.

"Will you swear upon the good and faithful souls of your deceased parents now in purgatory to answer my questions honestly, Mistress Alix?" Father Peter asked quietly.

"I will," Alix replied, and she kissed the crucifix he held out to her.

"Were you married in God's church and under God's law?" the priest asked.

"The marriage contract between myself and the Laird of Dunglais was drawn up by Father Donald, the keep's priest. It was signed in the great hall beneath his eye and witnessed by the laird's uncle, Robert Ferguson of Drumcairn, and his wife, Margaret. We then went to the keep's chapel, where our marriage was blessed and a Mass held to celebrate the event."

"But was the marriage you entered into an honest and valid one, my daughter?" Father Peter inquired. "Was he fully apprised of your past?"

"He was. I held nothing back, Good Priest," Alix said candidly. "That is why when Sir Udolf came to Dunglais Keep several months back my husband kept me hidden. He wanted no difficulties with Sir Udolf."

"But you know, and if you are being honest with me, your husband knew Sir Udolf had sought a dispensation. And when he came to your home he said he had obtained that dispensation. Is that not so, my daughter?"

"It is," Alix replied. "But Father Donald had told us the bishop of St. Andrew's would have never upheld such a document. That it was undoubtedly obtained by means of fraud. Now you answer me honestly, Priest. *Was it?*"

The priest shifted uncomfortably in his chair, and Bab cackled knowingly. "There was a donation made at Yorkminster for the archbishop's Christian work," he admitted to Alix.

"There was a bribe made," Alix responded dryly. "And not once, nor twice, but three times. Shame, priest! Shame! Now to salve your own conscience you must tell Sir Udolf I am indeed wed to another. That he must release me back to my husband."

"Lady, I have already given him such advice, but he will not listen, I fear," the priest said, sighing nervously, his cheeks flushing with her rebuke.

"Colm has burned Wulfborn Village, taken its people into bondage, and made off with the sheep. He has sworn to return for me, and he will. When he comes, he'll batter down the door to this house and kill Sir Udolf Watteson. I do not want my former father-in-law's death on my conscience, and it will certainly be if he persists in his foolishness. Has he lost his wits entirely? Why has he not sought out a local woman of good family to wed and give children to instead of insisting I must be his wife?"

"Lady, I do believe the death of his only son, his only child, has indeed rendered him somewhat mad. When I returned from York two years ago and you had fled in my absence, he alternated between rage and great sorrow. There was nothing we could do to calm him at first. He was surely as one who had lost his wits, but then he grew calm once more and spoke most reasonably. I suggested your flight freed him from any further obligation towards you, and at first he agreed. But then he began to worry because you had gone on foot, leaving your own horse behind. I said such action proved to me you were an honorable woman and wanted to begin your life afresh. He countered that as the beast had been yours when you came to Wulfborn it said to him that you were distressed. He said that you were obviously overwhelmed by his plans for you and had run off in your confusion," the priest told Alix.

Alix snorted. "I left because the thought of my father-in-law bedding me was utterly repugnant," she said.

"He searched the region for several days after you left," Father Peter continued, "but he could not find any trace of you. When it snowed he was frantic with worry, but I almost had him convinced that it was God's will you were not found. I said he must let me seek among his neighbors for a suitable woman of childbearing age to marry. I told him it was his duty to marry again."

"Why, then, did he not?" Alix asked the priest.

"A messenger came from Yorkminster from my contact asking for more coin to facilitate Sir Udolf's quest for a dispensation."

"Why did you not keep it from him?" Alix inquired.

"The message was most cleverly directed to Sir Udolf. He gave the messenger what was asked and sent him back to York even before he spoke with me," Father Peter said. "When I asked him why he had acceded to the request when he had decided to accept you were gone from him, he replied he had been foolish to even consider letting you go because he knew he would find you, that the two of you were meant to be together."

"God's foot!" Alix swore, irritated. What was she going to do about this stubborn man who held her captive? The fire in the hearth crackled noisily, and sparks flew as a gust of wind blew down the chimney.

"In midspring a third and final request came for more coin along with the promise that when it was received the dispensation would be immediately sent. Sir Udolf paid a third time and the bishopric was true to its word. The dispensation came."

"He has threatened to murder my child when it is born," Alix told Father Peter.

The priest grew pale, but then he quickly said, "I will not permit it, lady!"

"You must get him to listen to reason," Alix insisted. "My child should be born in his own home. And my little stepdaughter will be frantic with my absence. She does not remember her own mam, as she died years ago. I have been with her two years, and am the only mother she has ever known. Fiona will be eight next month. She is a dear little lass, Good Priest. I miss her."

"I will do my best to help you, my lady," the priest said. "Perhaps if you came into the hall Sir Udolf might be made to see reason more easily."

"Nay. If I come into the hall he will press his suit more forcibly, I fear. My presence will give him the illusion of normalcy. He must not have that from me. You must press him to find a suitable wife."

"I will do what I can, lady, but Sir Udolf has never easily been brought to reason when he set his mind upon something he wanted."

"I must go home to Dunglais," Alix said, and her voice trembled slightly.

The priest left her and, heedless of Bab, Alix began to cry softly.

"Take me with you," Bab said suddenly.

"*What?* What did you say?" Alix asked the woman sewing by her side, sniffling.

"Take me with you, lady. I know you have your own servants, but I will care for your bairn," Bab told her.

"Are you certain you want to leave Wulfborn? You were born here, Bab."

"After you ran away that first time he took a terrible dislike to me, as if he blamed me for what happened. Then, as I have told you, he beat me, blaming me for your flight. And not just once, lady. I took to keeping out of his way because if I did not he would as likely beat me as not. I peeped through the shutters at your man. He is strong and he is determined. He will come for you. Of that I have no doubt. When you go again, which you will, despite the master's wishes and the priest's hedging, Sir Udolf will look again to me to take his ire out upon. And if Father Peter can convince him to wed another she will not want me, for if Sir Udolf dislikes me she will as well in an effort to please him. I am not as young as I once was, lady. But I can work hard and earn my keep, and I do not eat much. You'll need a servant for your nursling, won't you? I tell you I would rather be the lowest slavey in your kitchens than remain at Wulfborn when you are gone."

Alix considered the woman's words. She was a bawdy slattern, and she had not in the past been kind. But once Alix had earned Bab's respect, the woman had become devoted to her. And if Bab was telling the truth, then she had suffered because of Alix. "I must think on it," she told Bab. *Let the woman gain a bit more of my trust*, Alix thought.

" 'Tis fair, my lady," Bab responded with a nod.

November ended. Sir Udolf took to coming to Alix's chamber door and speaking to her. For the most part she ignored him, but one day he came and called to her, "We must set a date for the wedding day, my dearling."

Alix could not resist responding. "Have you found a suitable lady of good family and still young enough to give you children, then?" she asked him. There was a startled silence that caused Alix to smile.

But then he said, "You know 'tis you who is to be my bride."

"I have a husband," Alix told him. "The priest has spoken to you, I know, and yet you persist in this fantasy, my lord. I cannot wed you because I am already wed. I am with child by my darling husband. But if these things were not so, I would still not wed you, my lord. You are father to he who was once my husband. What you propose is unclean, and it sickens me you would think of she who was at one time a daughter to you as a wife with whom you would couple in an effort to gain children. 'Tis incestuous. For shame, my lord Udolf. For shame!"

"Were you his mistress?" came the question.

"Before I became his wife? Aye, I was! And I should have been happy to remain his mistress the rest of my life, for I love him! But he loved me enough to make me his wife." Alix wondered why he had not asked her that question before.

"I forgive you," he said.

Then Alix laughed. She could not help it. She laughed, turning away from the closed and barred door. If Sir Udolf wasn't mad, then he had to be the biggest fool to ever be born. And the infant in her womb took that moment to kick, for her laughter had disturbed its slumber.

"Alix," he called to her through the heavy door. "*Alix!*"

She ignored him.

He pounded upon the door to her chamber, but his blows did not even shake the portal on its hinges. Finally Alix heard his footsteps as they retreated down the hall.

"He is becoming dangerous," Bab warned her.

"How do you know?" Alix asked.

"He liked to tell everyone it was the result of nearly drowning that made his son like he was, but 'tis not the whole truth. The men in this family are usually well mannered and well behaved unless they are denied something they desperately want. But poor Hayle, like the child he was, he wanted everything he saw, and denied most of the time, he could not cope with living especially when his Maida died. Hayle seemed to have no control over his emotions or his desires, just like a child. But Sir Udolf's father killed a woman he desired who kept refusing him. He slew a horse that refused to be obedient. Sir Udolf has spent all of his life struggling to not be like his father, ignoring the same traits in his only son. But now there is something that he very much wants and cannot have," Bab concluded. "I can see his frustration is beginning to cause him to lose control over himself, which means he will become dangerous. Pray God your husband returns soon to storm this house and make you free again."

It began to snow that night and Alix was suddenly overwhelmed by a sense of hopelessness as she stared from her window the next morning and saw the hillsides covered in white. Two menservants worked shoveling snow to open a path to the barns. Alix sighed. If the winter set into the borders, a time when raiders on both sides kept to their hearths, how was Colm supposed to come and fetch her? She had confined herself to this chamber for several weeks now, and she was becoming restless. She didn't want to stay at Wulfborn a minute more. And she certainly didn't want her bairn born here!

And then, as she stared out, something appeared upon the horizon of the hills about Wulfborn. She could not make it out at first, but as she remained watching, the something began to take shape. Slowly, slowly the dark form began to reveal itself until Alix could see it was an enormous party of men. As they drew closer she immediately recognized the red plaid of her husband's family. And there were two different green plaids, one with narrow red and white stripes and deep blue squares she identified as Ferguson. But the other green tartan was not familiar to her.

"Bab! Bab! Come quickly," Alix called.

The older woman hurried to the window and looked out. "Well," she said dryly, "it would appear your husband and a few of his friends have come calling, my lady." Then she chuckled. "I can but imagine

Sir Udolf's face when they break down his fine front door. I would say you're going home today."

"*We're* going home, Bab," Alix said. "If you will come with me."

And Bab smiled the first smile Alix had ever seen her smile. "Aye, my lady! I'll come, and gladly."

Chapter 12

s the great party of horsemen drew nearer, Alix could
see they had brought some kind of weapon with them.
It rolled along on its own wheels and appeared to be
a long log with an animal's head fashioned from iron at one end. She
had heard of battering rams, but she had never before seen one. The
front door to Wulfborn Hall was strong, but it would certainly not
withstand the assault it was about to receive. Suddenly the two men
shoveling noticed the approaching party. They fled back towards the
house, shouting a warning. Alix considered what to do. Should they
remain safe in her chamber, or go below into the hall?

Bab decided for them. "We should remain here, my lady," she
said. " 'Twill be better. Once the door is broken through, the hall
will be the center of the fighting. Sir Udolf is no coward, and he will
defend his home and all he believes is his."

Alix nodded. Bab was right in everything she said, but the Laird
of Dunglais's wife knew her captor did not have the men to overcome the great group of Scots borderers. "Add more wood to the
fire, Bab," she said. "The morning is yet chill." Then she went to her
window to watch as her rescuers arrived, milling about before the
front of the house. Pushing the narrow casement window open, she
called down, "My lords, I bid you welcome. I am more than ready to
come home."

The borderers, seeing her, hearing her words, cheered lustily,
their horses stamping and snorting in the icy morning.

267

"I am relieved to see you, lambkin," the Laird of Dunglais called up to his wife. "Is your chamber secure?"

"It is, my lord," Alix assured him. She could see his breath in the cold air.

"Then remain where you are until this is over," he advised her.

"Do not kill him, Colm," Alix warned. "I do not want the death of a madman on my soul, or yours. Do what you must, but leave Sir Udolf alive to face his own demons."

" 'Tis poor advice, lady," and to her surprise Alix recognized Adam Hepburn. "A madman cannot be swayed in his thought or else he would not be mad. If you do not kill him, he will return again and again to trouble you until he is dead."

"I believe today's lesson coupled with that of my husband's last visit will convince Sir Udolf of his folly," Alix replied.

"I think you wrong, lambkin," Malcolm Scott said, "but I will attempt to follow your wishes, for the sake of our child you carry."

"*Grand merci*, my lord," she answered him with a smile, and drew the casement closed. Turning to Bab she said, "You had best pack our belongings." Then she began to dress herself for travel, pulling on a gown of dark blue jersey she had left behind when she had originally fled Wulfborn over two years ago. She could not wear the breeks she favored for riding any longer, and would, she knew, have to ride sidesaddle. It would be an uncomfortable journey, but she would make it if it meant getting safely home to Dunglais and her own hall. Suddenly they heard a great booming sound. The house shuddered and shook.

"They're storming the house," Bab said, and she chortled. "Ohh, I should like to see Sir Udolf's face right now."

The noise and the effect it caused came again and again and again. A great shout arose. There was a final boom, and the two women actually heard the door give way as the battering ram shattered the ancient iron-bound oak. A mighty howl was emitted from the borderers, and then they pushed into Wulfborn Hall, meeting absolutely no resistance from the servants, who had all hidden themselves away for fear of being carried off into bondage. Half charging into the great hall of the house, they faced Father Peter and Sir Udolf Watteson.

"I've come for my wife," the Laird of Dunglais said quietly.

"You will have to fight me for her," Sir Udolf cried, and he charged at Malcolm Scott, waving his sword.

The laird disarmed him easily, skillfully knocking his attacker's weapon from his hand with his own sword. "I will not fight you, my lord. My wife has asked that your life be spared in spite of the misery you have caused us. While I disagree with her, I will grant her this boon for the sake of the son she carries."

"Coward!" Sir Udolf shouted. "Will you hide behind her skirts? Alix is mine! I have a dispensation from York to make her my wife. I will give you the child she bears for you, but she is mine! I will not give her up! I will not!"

Suddenly Adam Hepburn stepped forward. Reaching out, he grasped Sir Udolf by the neck of his dark robe, pulling him forward so that they were face-to-face. "Old man," he growled, "I did not promise to leave you unharmed. One more word out of you, and I will slit your throat with the greatest of pleasure." He then shoved the Englishman to the floor, saying as he did, "Priest! See to your master. We are through here, and enough time has been wasted on this matter."

While he had spoken, the Ferguson of Drumcairn had gone with several of his own men upstairs, and was calling for Alix to come out, which she did, Bab behind her.

"Uncle, I am happy to see you," Alix said.

He stared at her big belly for a moment and then, grinning, said, " 'Tis a lad. My Maggie never carried as big. Well, come along now, lass. 'Tis past time we got you home. Your man is in the hall finishing up that bit of business."

"He has not harmed poor Sir Udolf, has he?" Alix asked.

"Nay, he's given in to you, but from what I see of the man he would be better off dead and gone. Now, have you anything you would take with you here?"

"The small trunk at the foot of the bed was mine when I first came with Queen Margaret. I should like to have it back," Alix told him.

"Bring it, lads," Robert Ferguson said. Then he eyed Bab. "And her?"

"Bab comes with me," Alix told him.

He nodded. "Well, then, let us be off. I think it best you not bid the Englishman farewell. Hepburn felt it necessary to speak rather firmly with him. No need to set the man off again in his madness." He led the two women downstairs, moving quickly past the wide entry to the great hall of the house.

Outside, to her surprise, Alix saw a small padded cart had been brought. Her escort led her to it. "This is for me?" she said.

"You can hardly ride with that belly," Robert Ferguson said.

"There are two horses in the stables that are mine. I won't leave without them," Alix told her husband's uncle.

"Two horses?" he said.

"When I originally fled Wulfborn I went on foot. I thought if my horse was found missing they would know I was gone. But the beast is mine, and I would have it back. My father, God assoil him, gave it to me. Bab knows which of the horses are mine," Alix explained. "Send one of your men with her to get them, I beg you."

The Ferguson of Drumcairn nodded, and dispatched a man to go with Bab. Then he helped Alix into the padded cart, laying a heavy fur blanket over her lap. "I'll go tell Colm you're safe and ready to leave," he said. Then he hurried back into the house, going directly to the great hall.

Sir Udolf and the priest were both being carefully bound and then tied into chairs by the hearth. Several of the laird's men had found the frightened servants. They secured them also and locked them in the pantry, a small windowless room with but one entrance, barring that entry. Eventually someone would manage to get free and would free the rest of the house's inhabitants. And it was very unlikely that anyone would come after the Scots borderers. Sir Udolf had few retainers left.

"Alix is in her conveyance, Nephew," Robert Ferguson said. "Come along now. I believe our business here is finished and the weather is lowering. We have a fair ways to travel, and the cart will slow us down, I fear, but the lady cannot ride. Her belly is large."

Without a further glance back at Sir Udolf Watteson, who was muttering in his chair, Malcolm Scott dashed outside to greet his wife. She was seated on the cart's padded bench wrapped in furs. Climbing up, he kissed her a hard kiss.

Alix melted in his embrace, her lips softening beneath his, sighing as he released her. "Good morrow, my lord husband," she said, smiling. "Thank you for coming for me. Your son and I are anxious to go home."

His big hand caressed her small face. "I can hardly believe you are here with me," he said, his voice thick with emotion. "I will never allow you to be put in such danger again, lambkin. Forgive me!"

"Oh, Colm, how could you—how could we—know that in his madness Sir Udolf would have me kidnapped? 'Twas not your fault. We are together again, and I will not be parted from you evermore." She kissed his lips softly.

The Laird of Dunglais smiled down at his wife and then he saw the other woman seated in the rear of the cart, along with a small trunk. "Who is this?" he asked Alix.

"Bab was my servant when I lived at Wulfborn before. After I fled, Sir Udolf treated her cruelly, beating her without just cause and blaming her for my flight. She was not, of course, responsible, for she did not know of my plans. I will not leave her again, Colm. She will care for the bairn when he is born."

"If she has served you well and suffered for your sake, then she will be welcome to Dunglais," the laird said, nodding at Bab. Then he saw the two horses tied to the back of the little cart. "I recognize the mare, but the gelding?"

Alix explained, and he chuckled.

"I am pleased to see you are becoming more Scots with each

passing day, lambkin. If the beast is yours, then to leave it a second time would be foolish. Your frugality delights me."

"The creature is used to carrying a female upon its back," Alix said. "I think it will prove a safe and reliable mount for Fiona. She is really becoming too big for her pony. One thing before we go, my lord. I would visit my father's grave a final time."

He nodded. "We will stop, lambkin," he promised her.

The great group of borderers had finally exited the house and were mounting up. An older Scott clansman climbed up next to Alix, nodding briefly to her and taking the reins of the horses that would pull the cart. She was surprised to see that there were four animals for the vehicle and not two. Then Alix realized that with four, the cart could move a bit quicker without jostling its occupants too roughly.

They moved off, stopping briefly at the burial ground on the hill where Alix bid a final farewell to her father and then left Wulfborn Hall behind them. The attack had come at dawn, and as there had been no defense made against their incursion it was still early morning. They traveled without stopping until the sun was at mid-heaven. Alix was ravenous, for there had been no time for Bab to find her breakfast. She eagerly gobbled the oatcakes and hard cheese her husband brought her. Then she swallowed down the cold water in his flask.

"Is there any place we can shelter tonight?" she asked the laird.

He shook his head. "Nay, but you and your woman can sleep comfortably in the cart. We can put an awning over you to protect you more."

"I need hot food," she told him.

"We set traps as we came. We'll have roasted rabbit for certain tonight, my lambkin. I know this is difficult for you, but we will be home soon," he murmured to her encouragingly, and kissed her forehead.

She smiled at him, but Alix knew better. The cart was slowing them down. It would be another full day of traveling, and then perhaps another half. But there was no help for it. She simply could not ride. But if she had one consolation it was that she would be home just in time for Christmas. That night, and the night after, she and Bab shared the large fur robe, huddling together to keep warm. Light snow came in short bursts as they traveled, but then it was winter and snow was to be expected. Midmorning of their second day of traveling the laird announced to them that they were once more in Scotland. Alix was relieved to learn it. It wasn't that she expected Sir Udolf to have escaped his bonds, gather a party of soldiers, and come after her. Nay, it wasn't that. It was just she had come to think of Scotland as her home.

Their second night on the road the snow was a little heavier and more sustained. It was so bitterly cold, although the wind was calm. Wrapping her cloak about her, Alix shivered nonetheless. She caressed her belly with her gloved hands more to reassure herself than anything else. Her child was most active and seemed to be dancing a jig within her womb. She slept sporadically, although Bab snored contentedly by her side.

Alix was not unhappy when the morning finally came. Colm had reassured her that they would get home by midday. The great party of Ferguson and Hepburn clansmen were still riding with them. Now Alix began to worry about how they were to be fed and housed before traveling on the morrow to their own homes. But certainly Fenella would be prepared for them, she finally decided.

And then through the gray she finally saw the shadowed outline of Dunglais Keep. She pointed it out to Bab excitedly. "We're almost home!" Alix declared, smiling.

"It looks a rough place," Bab said softly, nervously.

"The keep is older than Wulfborn, 'tis true, but inside it is warm and cozy," Alix told her serving woman. "But should you be unhappy, I will send you back to England in the spring."

"Nay," Bab said in a resigned voice. "There is no place for me there now."

Alix reached out and patted the older woman's hand comfortingly.

She had never known the quick-tongued Bab to be so subdued. She almost felt sorry for her, but then, she decided, as soon as Bab recovered from the shock of what had happened and regained her footing she would be as sharp as ever. "Fenella is the housekeeper, and I will put you in her charge," Alix said. "Respect her and the position she holds within the house and she will help you. I know it cannot be easy starting all over again, Bab, but you are a strong woman. This is not Wulfborn. It is a better, happier place."

The cart trundled up the hill to the keep. The laird had ridden on ahead to identify himself and their party. The little drawbridge was already lowered by the time they reached it. The cart rolled over it and into the courtyard. The laird was there at once to help his wife out of her vehicle. Beinn hoisted Bab from her place, setting her upon her feet, which were numb with the cold. Bab thanked him, and he nodded politely in response. Then she followed Alix into the keep.

When they reached the hall, a little girl dashed forward, half laughing, half crying. She flung herself at Alix, who caught the child in her arms and hugged her hard. "Oh, Mam, I was so afraid I had lost you like I lost the other one," Fiona cried. "I am so glad you are home." Then she stepped back from Alix and her eyes widened. "Oh, you are so fat with my brother, Alix! Will he come soon?" Her gaze swung to Bab. "Who is this?" she asked, curiously eying the older woman.

"This is Bab, who took care of me at Wulfborn when I lived there. When I left the first time I had to leave her behind. I would not leave her this time," Alix explained.

"But Jeannie takes care of you!" Fiona said.

"And she will continue to take care of me. Bab will be nurse to the new baby," Alix told her stepdaughter.

"Oh, then that is all right," Fiona replied. "Has Fenella met her?"

"As we have just this moment arrived, nay, but she will," Alix said.

And at that same moment Fenella hurried into the hall, her face wreathed in smiles as she embraced Alix. "My lady, welcome home! Oh my, the bairn grows, doesn't he?" She looked to the unfamiliar woman with her mistress.

"This is Bab." Alix explained briefly the relationship between them. "She will be nurse to my child."

"Very good, my lady," Fenella said in a neutral voice. "And I will see she has someone to help her. Taking care of an infant is not an easy task at any age." But then Fenella's good nature got the better of her. "You look fair frozen, Bab. Come with me to the kitchens, and I will see you are fed and warmed." And she led Bab off.

Fiona had not left Alix's side. Now she slipped her hand into her stepmother's and walked with her to the hearth so Alix might be seated and get warm. "You missed my birthday," Fiona told Alix. "I am eight now."

"The hall looks beautiful," Alix said. "Did you oversee the decorations, my lass?"

Fiona grinned proudly. "I did!" she crowed. "I wanted it to be perfect when you arrived." She snuggled against Alix. "It's almost Christmas. I know what Da is giving you on the first day of Christmas! Do you want me to tell you?"

"Nay!" Alix said, laughing. "Then it would not be a surprise."

The laird came and knelt before her to draw her boots and wet stockings off. He saw Alix's feet were red with the cold and swollen. "Have Jeannie fetch your mam's slippers," he told his daughter as he began to rub Alix's feet gently to restore the circulation to them. "You should be in bed," he told her.

"Nay, not yet," Alix said. "I want to sit by my own hearth and just revel in my happiness at being home, Colm. Let me remain, and let me eat at my own board. I will go to bed afterward, I promise. Oh, that feels so good!"

"You are a sensuous creature. I have missed you greatly," he told her, as he had at least a dozen times a day since they had been reunited.

Alix reached out to caress his face gently with her soft hand. He caught the hand up and kissed it tenderly. She sighed, and the sound was one of pure happiness. His hand then reached out to touch her belly. He lay his palm flat, and Alix placed her hand over his, pressing down slightly to see if the child would stir. It did, turning itself about, and a look of pure wonder filled the laird's face. "That is our bairn," she told him, and smiled. "He is strong, isn't he? And already determined to have his own way."

"I can feel him stirring strongly within you," Malcolm Scott said, amazed.

Alix laughed again. "Sometimes I cannot sleep for all his dancing."

Jeannie hurried into the hall carrying a pair of Alix's house slippers, which were lined with lamb's wool. "Welcome home, my lady," she said, and then as the laird arose, she knelt and slipped the slippers on Alix's feet, which were now a little warmer due to the fire and her husband's ministrations.

After a short time had passed the meal was served. Alix was helped to the table. Now that her feet were tingling with warmth again it was difficult to walk at first. But her appetite was excellent, especially as the food had come from her own kitchen. There was sliced trout with lemon, a large bowl of lamb stew with chunks of carrot and leek in a rich gravy, a fat roasted duck, bread, butter, and cheese. Alix ate greedily, her hazel eyes widening with delight when Fenella brought a dish of baked apples to table.

"It is all so good," she told the housekeeper. "And I have been starving for baked apples, Fenella. And they've been baked with sugar and cinnamon!" She splashed on some thick yellow cream from the pitcher Fenella handed her. "Ummm!" she approved, spooning some of the apple into her mouth.

"We never had baked apples at all while you were gone," Fiona said. "And they are my favorites too!" She sat as near as she could to her stepmother. "Promise me you will never leave me again, Alix," she begged. "And not just because I love baked apples."

"As long as the choice is mine to make, *ma petite*, I will not leave you again," Alix told her, putting an arm about the child's thin shoulders and giving her a small hug. "But one day you will leave your da and me to marry."

"Nay," Fiona said. "I love only you and Da. And my new brother."

Alix kissed the top of Fiona's dark head. *Poor child*, she thought. *She has really suffered the lack of her mother, but I am her mother now. I will take care of her.*

When the meal was over the laird wanted his wife to retire immediately, but now that her feet were warm she felt better. "Let me sit by the hearth and listen to the piper," she said with a smile, and unable to deny her anything, Malcolm Scott acquiesced. His heart contracted with pleasure to watch Alix seated happily by the fire, Fiona sitting upon a stool, her head in her stepmother's lap while Alix stroked the little girl's long hair soothingly. He had never imagined such contentment existed until now.

The piper played sweetly that night, and soon Fiona's eyes fell shut. At a nod from Alix, the laird came and carried his daughter upstairs, where Fenella waited to tuck the child into her bed. Returning to the hall, he came to sit by Alix's side. "It is good to have you home again, lambkin," he told her. "We have all missed you."

"I never realized before how the lack of her mother has hurt Fiona," Alix said.

"I do not think she has ever missed Robena," Malcolm Scott said candidly. "It is you she missed, for you are the mother she knows and loves." He took her hand and kissed it. "And I missed the wife I know and love. I am so sorry you had to suffer the difficulties of being kidnapped. How on earth did Sir Udolf discover you were here?"

"Bab told me one of his men took one of our maidservants to the stable loft that night they stayed at Dunglais. He obviously learned I was here then and reported to his master, who made plans to regain my person. I spoke with the Wulfborn priest, Father Peter. When I told him how we had come to wed and that Father Donald had said we were free to do so, he as good as admitted that Sir Udolf paid a large bribe to get that dispensation. The priest has been attempting to get his master to let him find another wife of childbearing years and of good family. Sir Udolf briefly agreed, but then decided he must have me back. Father Peter said there was no reasoning with him."

"You should have let me kill him," the laird said. "The man is touched by madness and will not give up."

"Oh, surely not, Colm!" Alix exclaimed. "Certainly now after what happened he will understand I am your wife and that is the end of it. His village is destroyed, his livestock gone, and his people disbursed. It must be obvious to him I am more trouble to him than worth." She looked up at him. "I think I am ready to go to bed now, my lord. Will you take me up?"

He smiled a slow smile and, standing, drew her to her feet. "Gladly, madame," he told her, and together they left the hall and mounted the stairs hand in hand.

In their bedchamber he helped her to disrobe, drawing off her gown and her chemise. He admired her ripening body, standing behind her to cup her full breasts in his hands. The rough balls of his thumbs stroked her nipples, and throwing her head back against his shoulder, Alix sighed with pure pleasure. His hands now moved to caress her swollen belly, and she quivered beneath his touch. "Ah, lambkin," he groaned in her ear, "I lust for you, but would not harm the bairn. Can we? Dare we?" His lips trailed down her slender throat and across her rounded shoulder.

"Aye, we can," she murmured, "but we must be careful."

"Get into bed while I shed my clothing," he said, helping her beneath the coverlet. Then he quickly pulled his garments and his boots off.

Alix lay there watching him. His physique was strong and well muscled. She had missed the feel of his body against hers. And his eagerness for her was evident. His cock was swollen and bobbed about. Alix rolled onto to her side as her husband entered the bed. His hand fastened itself about a breast, playing with the nipple. She felt his warm kiss on the nape of her neck. His tongue traced the shape of her ear, and he nipped upon the earlobe.

"I love you, lambkin," he told her. "And the thought of that man putting his hands upon you, kissing you, almost drove me to madness," the laird breathed in her ear.

"He never touched me or kissed me," Alix told him. "He was too intent upon being courtly when I arrived, and after scolding him I locked myself in my bedchamber with Bab. I did not come out until you came for me."

"And he permitted you that behavior?" Malcolm Scott was surprised, although he believed his wife's tale. "I would have broken the door down to reach you."

"I think the fact I flaunted my belly surprised him," Alix said. "Ummm, that is nice," she purred as his hand now stroked her belly and his fingers found their way between her plump nether lips to tease her. She squirmed with her rising excitement, grinding her bottom into him. "I have so longed for your passion these past weeks, Colm, my dear lord, and I so desperately desire to be fucked," Alix admitted to him.

"And I so need to fuck you, lambkin," he told her fiercely. She was wet with her arousal, and he tenderly entered her as they lay together on their sides. His hands stroked her full breasts, alternately kissing and nipping the nape of her neck.

He filled her, and Alix sighed with the pleasure she was gaining just by having him inside of her. And when he began to thrust gently she gasped, surprised by the intensity of the desire that overwhelmed her. Her belly was filled up with his child, and yet her lust seemed to know no bounds. "Don't stop," she whispered.

He smiled in the dimness of the room, lit only by the low fire that burned in the hearth. "You're a shameless wench, lambkin," he told her, and he thrust just a little faster. "Since the day we met, I have had no other woman." He grinned as he heard her sharp gasp. He had obviously found that wicked little spot that always set her body quivering with delight.

Alix was actually surprised. She had not expected to feel quite as she was now feeling. "Oh, Colm!" she cried softly. "It is so good, my lord! So good!" She shuddered as she was racked by the waves of pleasure that flowed over her, leaving her sated for now and weakened. The babe within her lay quiet.

He took his own release now, and when his cock had finished expelling his hot juices he sighed. "Aye, I've missed you," he said.

Alix rolled over onto her back, and turning her head towards him, replied, "So you have said several times in the past few days, my lord. I think I am beginning to believe you."

Grinning, he drew the disarranged coverlet over them and pulled her close again. They slept then until the gray light of dawn the following day. And the gray light was followed by a magnificent sunrise that everyone at Dunglais said portended a happy future for them all. The month progressed, and on the first day of Christmas the laird gave his wife a beautiful blue wool cape. Both the garment and its hood were lined in warm rabbit's fur. Alix had managed to finish the small tapestry she had been working on when Sir Udolf had kidnapped her. It depicted Dunglais Keep upon its small hill and, delighted, the laird ordered it hung behind the high board. Fiona was content again with Alix home. She practiced her French daily. Twelfth Night came and went. Winter set in with a vengeance with snow almost every day. Alix wondered if they would ever see the sun again. But at least it was quiet and peaceful. Nothing stirred to disturb the pristine landscape.

The snows continued on into February. Alix's belly was enormous to her eyes, and the child within her grew more active with each passing day. Preparations began for the anticipated birth. A birthing chair was found in the cellar of the keep and brought upstairs to be repaired and scrubbed. The family cradle was brought from the attic of the keep to be cleaned free of cobwebs and polished until the ancient oak, deep gold with age, glowed. Alix sewed and stuffed a new mattress for the cradle with a mixture of duck feathers and goose down. Fiona worked with Fenella to stitch a blanket for the baby. Fresh swaddling clothes were prepared for the infant, who already had a wardrobe of garments made by all the women in the household. They but waited for Alix to give birth to the child.

And then on February twenty-seventh, in the evening, Alix finally went into labor shortly after her water broke, surprising her. She had been sleeping, and awakened as a pain akin to a knife slicing her belly awoke her. Discovering herself in a wet bed, Alix called out to her husband, who had gone to sleep in his own bedchamber that night. The laird came at once, and remembering when Fiona had been born, he called for Fenella. Alix's main concern at the moment was for the feather bed atop the mattress, but Fenella assured her that it would dry. In the meantime it was replaced so that after the child came its mother could be comfortable in her own bed. The birthing chair was brought into the chamber. The laird was sent forth.

"This is women's work, my lord," Fenella told her master firmly.

He went half-reluctantly, half-relieved.

"Fiona?" Alix asked.

"Bab has put her to bed, but not before telling her a lot of pretty stories," Fenella replied. "I was not pleased when you brought that old Englisher here to Dunglais, but she is actually a good sort, my lady. And she certainly isn't afraid of hard work. With your permission I'll have my cousin Mary help her with the bairn."

"I couldn't leave her behind this time, Fenella," Alix said, and winced as a small pain touched her. "Her master beat her after I fled Wulfborn the first time, and took every opportunity to assault her after that. After what happened I am sure Father Peter convinced him to find another woman to wife, but Bab unfortunately would have always been a reminder of me. If he did not like her, then his new wife would not. As you have noted, she is not a young woman. With Mary to help her she will take good care of the bairn and end her days here."

Several hours passed, and the midnight hour came and went. Alix's labor, which had begun with a sharp pain and then subsided into bearable ones, now began to increase in ferocity as Fenella had made her walk back and forth. The young woman bit her lip until it bled. When Fenella asked her why she would not cry out Alix told her she didn't want to awaken Fiona and frighten her.

"Jeannie is sleeping with your daughter," Fenella said in practical tones. "If she awakens to your screams the lass will calm Fiona."

The door opened to admit Bab. "Is the child not born yet? The laird has worn a groove in the floor of the hall with all his pacing."

"She does not want to scream," Fenella said.

"My lady! Screaming is part of the birthing," Bab told her. "If you do not scream the child will think you do not want him."

Alix screamed as a pain tore through her. "Oh God, it hurts!" she cried.

"Good! Good!" Bab approved.

"Help me get her onto the chair," Fenella said, and together the two women lifted Alix into the large high-backed chair. It had a hole in its seat, and the arms of the chair were strong and wide. Bab spread cloths beneath the opening. Fenella peered beneath it. "You are almost ready, my lady," she promised.

Alix screamed again and then again.

In the hall below Malcolm Scott heard his wife's cries. He had gone through this process once before when Fiona had been born, but he had forgotten how heart-wrenching the cries of a woman giving birth could be. He remembered Robena's screams as she birthed Fiona, and her screams afterwards learning her child was a daughter, for she had wanted a son, had wanted to never be with child again. What if Alix had another daughter? Would she be angry? At first they had referred to the child she carried as *it* but of late it had been *he, him,* or *the lad.* Alix had even asked if they might baptize a first son James for the late king and Alexander for her deceased father. They had no name for a daughter, but it could indeed be a daughter. And if it was, would Alix, like Robena, refuse to bear him another child? Would she take the chance that she might bear another daughter? He paced back and forth until finally Iver put a goblet of wine in his hand.

"Sit down, my lord. Sit down. You know these things evolve in their own time and not a moment before," his steward said soothingly.

"What if it is a lass, Iver?" the laird asked. "What if it is like the last time?"

"My lord, all are certain it is a son, but should it be a daughter you and the lady will pray once more for a son," Iver replied. "This wife is nothing like the other wife."

The keep slept but for its laird, his wife, and her attendants. Malcolm Scott sat by his hearth with his steward. When the fire would burn low Iver would add more wood to it. The night deepened and began to move slowly toward a new day. And then as the skies outside of the great hall's windows began to show gray both men sat up, startled, as a great shriek echoed throughout the keep. They looked at each other, and then the laird jumped to his feet and, taking the stairs two at a time, burst into his wife's bedchamber.

Alix lay abed, soaking wet from her exertions, her honey-blond hair sticking to her face, but she had a smile upon her face. Fenella turned, and in her hands was a naked, red-faced infant who was howling at the top of its lungs. The child flailed its little arms and legs about as it roared. The housekeeper had all she could do to hold on to the baby, but she was smiling too.

Malcolm Scott stared at the newborn. Two arms. Two legs. A penis, and a sac beneath it containing two balls. "A *son!*" he breathed ecstatically.

"Aye, my lord, a son!" Fenella said. "Dunglais has an heir of your loins!"

The laird took the baby from her, holding him gently against his chest. The child was moist with his birthing and a slick of blood. Malcolm Scott looked down at him. "James Alexander Scott, welcome home!" he said quietly and, bending, he kissed the boy's wet dark head.

"Give me the laddie," Bab said, and she took the infant from its father, rolling her eyes towards Alix. "He must be cleaned and swaddled. Help me, Fenella."

The laird turned to Alix and, going to her, helped her from the birthing chair. She was naked and obviously very tired. "Thank you," he said softly to her. And, enfolding her in his arms, he kissed her tenderly.

Alix sagged against him, exhausted. "He's beautiful, isn't he?" she whispered, and then she collapsed against him, her eyes closing.

Malcolm Scott walked to the bed and tucked her into it. She was already sound asleep, and he smiled down at her. There was so much he wanted to say to her, but there would be time later. "I love you, lambkin," he murmured as he bent to kiss her again.

"We'll take care of her, my lord," Fenella said as he turned back to see his son. "Sit down here in this chair while we get the laddie ready for you."

He sat silently as they cleaned the infant free of all evidence of his birth and wrapped him in swaddling clothes. Then, smiling, they tucked him in the crook of the laird's arm. He sat contentedly as they then set to work bathing his wife with a sponge and putting her into a night garment. Alix never woke up. The laird gazed down on his newborn son, who was now quiet and staring back at his father. The child had large round blue eyes and was very fair. Startled, Malcolm Scott realized it was like looking into a mirror of himself. There was no doubt who this child's sire was, he chuckled.

"You've an older sister," he said. "Her name is Fiona, and you'll meet her tomorrow. And you'll respect me, for I'm your father, and respect and be good to your mother who just birthed you. She's the love of my life, lad. I hope you'll find a love like ours one day. And about your name. You bear the name of two fine gentlemen. My friend, James Stewart, who was king of this land. And your mother's father, a physician. You must never bring shame on your names, lad.

Any of them. You're of Clan Scott, a respected name here in the borders. We are honest men, and faithful to Scotland and to our king. I want you to remember that."

James Alexander Scott yawned a mighty yawn and then, closing his eyes, fell asleep in his father's arms.

The laird chuckled. "Bab," he called. "Take the bairn and set him in his cradle. He'll stay with his mam and me for now."

Bab grinned, showing several missing teeth. "I'll watch over him, my lord," she said. She cradled the infant looking down at him. "And protect him with my life."

"You're a good woman for an Englisher," Malcolm Scott said.

"And you're a good man for a Scot," Bab shot back.

Chuckling, the Laird of Dunglais left his wife and child and, going down to the hall where the sleepy servants were now arriving to begin a new day, he said, "Rejoice with me and praise God and his Blessed Mother! Dunglais has a healthy son and heir!"

And the servants, now awake with their delight, cheered lustily at the laird's announcement.

Chapter 13

*I*t had taken Sir Udolf Watteson three days to be freed from his bonds. Finally one of his serving men, the only one who seemed left in his house, came into the hall and released his master. He was dying of thirst, and had pissed himself a dozen times over during his captivity. "Where the hell were you?" he demanded of his servant as the man untied the priest, who was in an equally unfortunate condition.

"My lord, we were all bound and then imprisoned in the pantry," the man said. "When one of us finally managed to get free, the others were released."

"And where are the others?" Sir Udolf wanted to know.

"Gone, my lord," the serving man replied in a low voice.

"But you remained because of your loyalty to me," Sir Udolf said.

"Aye, my lord!" the servant responded.

The master of Wulfborn Hall knocked the man before him to the floor. "Liar!" he shouted. "You returned to see if I was dead, and had I been you would have stolen what you could from my house!" He kicked the cringing servant, who was trying to inch away from the angry man.

The serving man scrambled to his feet. "Nay, my lord! Nay! I am loyal. Were I not I should not have freed you and the priest from your bonds."

"He is being truthful, my lord," Father Peter said in a raspy voice.

"Go and tell the others they had best return to the hall or I shall set the sheriff upon them. When they are caught they will be branded as runaways so they cannot run ever again," Sir Udolf snarled. "Jesu! I stink of my own piss!" And his nose wrinkled in disgust. "I need to bathe. See the tub is set up in the kitchens and filled with hot water," he directed the servant. "When that is done, you will go and fetch the others back."

The serving man scuttled off to do his lord's bidding.

"My lord," the priest began, "I hope you realize how fortunate we are to be alive. The lady saved your life, although her husband would have been justified in taking it to serve honor. The other lords with him advised him not to heed her advice, but he did. We must thank God we were spared."

Sir Udolf Watteson glared at Father Peter. Had he not been a priest, the lord of Wulfborn would have struck him to the floor in his fury. "If God indeed spared us, Priest, it was so I might have my revenge upon that bold Scot and that whore he calls his wife. I will kill him! And then I will make that little bitch take her place by my side as she should. I will fuck her until she gives me a son. And then I will keep fucking her so she bears me more sons until she is worn with birthing and her tits are no longer firm and round, but slack from all the sucking my sons will do upon her. She is mine! I have a dispensation to wed her that says so. She will not continue to defy me or the church!"

The priest drew in a long breath. "My lord," he said softly, "let this anger and lust that is so consuming you go. The lady is another's wife."

"Priest, do not try my patience," Sir Udolf said grimly. "I will go to the king about this matter. I will have my justice!"

"My lord, what influence have you with this new king? Be reasonable," Father Peter advised. "You sheltered a fleeing king while another was crowned in his place. If that were to get out, you could lose all you have. And you seek to marry the goddaughter of that disposed king's queen. Think, my lord, think! Why would King

Edward give you aid and comfort? He won't, and you may endanger
yourself in the process. Alix Givet does not want you as a husband.
She made that patently clear when she ran away. She has wed another man. Is having his child. Why do you persist in embarrassing
yourself over this woman? I can find you a good wife, my lord. A
woman of childbearing years. A widow who has already proved fecund. A virgin if you prefer. Do not shame yourself over what has
happened."

"I will have my justice, and I will have my revenge," Sir Udolf
answered the priest. "She is responsible for my son's death. If she
had been a better wife to him he would have left the miller's daughter and cared not if she died in childbed. His heart would have not
been broken when Maida died. He would not have died. I offered
Alix Givet a home, a place of honor within my house and my family. I sheltered her father in his last days and buried him honorably.
And then she repays my kindness when I wish to make her my wife
by whoring with another man, carrying his bastard!" The lord of
Wulfborn Hall had begun to foam slightly at the mouth with his
fury. "I will have my justice and my revenge, Priest!" he repeated.
"I will!"

The priest sighed unhappily. The madness that had afflicted his
master over the matter of Alix Givet was not abating. Only the
return of the servant announcing that Sir Udolf's bath was ready
caused him to cease his pleas. And he too needed to bathe himself,
for he stank from their three-day captivity. "I will leave you, my
lord, to refresh yourself," Father Peter said. And he bowed himself
from Sir Udolf's presence to return to his own little cottage near his
church. The fire was almost out, but the wood box was full. He soon
had the flames in his hearth dancing merrily.

Heating some water, he stripped off his garments and scrubbed
his scrawny frame free of odor. He did not allow himself the luxury
of bathing too often, for it was a vanity he could ill afford, but the
circumstances today warranted a thorough cleansing of his person.
He hurried, however, through his ablutions for the air was icy. Then

he redressed himself in a clean chemise and his only other robe. Clean and dry, he knelt down on the stone floor of his cottage and began to pray. Father Peter hoped his pride was not deceiving him, but he believed if he just had some more time he might convince Sir Udolf to let go of his anger and his disappointment so that he might find another to wed.

And it seemed as if God was answering Father Peter's prayers. Sir Udolf grew ill with an ague the following day, taking to his bed for the next several weeks. Some of the servants, although not all of them, had returned. While Sir Udolf lay abed he knew little about the state of his household except there was a woman who came to care for him during the day and a young man who sat by his bedside at night. He was spoon fed soup and a gruel of porridge and heated wine into which an egg and some spices were beaten. By the time he had recovered enough to get out of his bed the hard winter had set into Northumbria, and travel of any kind was next to impossible. But with the coming of winter the remaining servants had returned to Wulfborn Hall, slipping quietly back into the roles they had previously held.

Father Peter pursued his campaign to get Sir Udolf to consider other candidates for his hand. "Sir David Sheffield has a much younger half sister from his father's second marriage. She is no more than twenty, and has not yet had a husband," he said to Sir Udolf. "Her dower is small, 'tis true, but her reputation is excellent, my lord."

"I have seen her" came the answer. "She is a plain creature with mouse-brown hair and a long nose. And how could I be certain she was fertile?"

"Her mother had two sons as well as the daughter, my lord. And then her husband died. Who knows how many more children she would have born her lord had he not?"

"She is still plain," Sir Udolf complained. "She is nothing at all like Alix, who was so fair with her honey-colored curls and laughing hazel eyes."

"Is it said, my lord, that all cats are black in the dark," the priest murmured.

"Priest! You shock me," Sir Udolf said half-angrily.

"I was a man before I was a priest, my lord," Father Peter replied softly. "There is also Sir John Graham's widow. She is yet young."

"She bore him no children," Sir Udolf said.

"She was a third wife, and he an old man," the priest responded. "Her position is a difficult one as her stepson's wife resents her presence." Father Peter was surprised that Sir Udolf knew as much as he did about his neighbors, as he hadn't associated with many of them in years. But then the servants were great gossips and not averse to sharing what they heard. Of course, that went both ways, and he wondered if Sir Udolf's neighbors knew of his insane obsession for Alix Givet. And if they did, would they be willing to put one of their women into his charge? When it was possible to travel again, he would put out feelers, Father Peter decided.

Finally the spring came, and Sir Udolf Watteson announced his plans to travel south to seek out King Edward IV. There was no reasoning with him, although Father Peter did his best to dissuade his master from this folly. "I will come with you," the priest finally said.

"Nay," Sir Udolf replied. "I will go alone. I will show the king my dispensation from York, and he will uphold my rights. By summer's end Alix Givet will be my wife."

"I will pray for you, my lord," the priest said, and he watched as Sir Udolf rode away on an April morning from Wulfborn Hall.

The Northumbrian baron rode south for several weeks until he finally found the new king briefly in residence at Windsor Castle. Finding the king, however, and getting an audience with him were two different things. Bribes were taken by servants with no real access to the king, but Sir Udolf did not know it. Finally he found a priest who knew the king's confessor. He poured out his tale to the priest, who was touched by what he had heard, and not just a little offended by the attitude of the Scots bishop of St. Andrew's. The priest went to the king's confessor, and finally Sir Udolf had his chance to speak with the king on the night before he was to move from Windsor and on to another castle. Clutching his papers, he was ushered into the king's presence.

Edward IV was a tall, handsome young man with inquisitive blue eyes and golden-red hair. He had been nineteen when crowned two years earlier. A skilled warrior, he was also a man who loved women and was never without one. To date he had not wed, although there was talk of a foreign princess. Unlike his predecessor, Henry VI, whose descent from Edward III, his great-great grandfather, was a direct one—through his father, Henry V; his grandfather, Henry IV; and his great-grandfather, John of Gaunt, who had been the fourth son of Edward III's twelve children—Edward IV, while descended directly from Edward III's fifth son, Edmund of Langley, claimed the throne based on the convoluted connection he had with his great-great-grandfather's second son, Lionel of Antwerp, through his only child, Philippa. Given the state of Henry VI's fragile health and the strength of Edward of York's adherents, he was now England's king.

Sir Udolf was ushered into a small chamber with a fireplace and a single chair where the young king now sat. This would not be the public audience he had hoped for, but at least he had managed to gain the king's ear. He bowed.

The king's eyes caught him in a hard gaze. "You are from the north," he said. It was not a question, but a statement. "Were you at Towton?"

Sir Udolf hesitated, but then he answered, "Aye, I was." He somehow felt that this young man knew the answer to the question before he spoke, and to lie would not help his cause at all.

"You fought for my predecessor, Lancaster." Again a statement.

"Aye, my lord."

"When did you last see him?" the king wanted to know.

"I have not seen King Henry since he went into Scotland," Sir Udolf replied.

"Hmmm," the king said. Then, "What is it you want of me, Sir Udolf Watteson?"

"Justice, my lord," the baron said.

"What sort of justice?" King Edward asked.

"My son was wed to a young woman." He hesitated, but then decided he could not prevaricate too greatly. "She was Queen Margaret's goddaughter, the child of her personal physician. Her mother had been one of the queen's ladies, and come with her from Anjou. Queen Margaret could no longer afford to keep her physician or his daughter with her. I needed a wife for my only son. The bargain was struck. My son died some months later. His wife's father as well. Because I now needed another heir, I sent to Yorkminster for a dispensation to marry the lady. There had been no children of the marriage, and so we shared no blood bond."

The king nodded. "Go on, Sir Udolf." He was fascinated by this tale, and wondered where it would lead. He also wondered if the physician's daughter had been a pretty girl. Probably she was, that Sir Udolf coveted her.

"My bride-to-be was overwhelmed by all that was happening, had happened. In confusion she fled my home. When I found her, she was mistress to a Scots border lord. She would not leave him despite the fact I had the dispensation to wed her. I sent an armed party to take her one day as she rode out."

Edward of York sat up in the chair where he had been so casually sprawled. The tale grew more intriguing and he was frankly fascinated.

"She locked herself with a servant in her chamber," Sir Udolf continued. "She claimed she was already wed to the border lord. That my dispensation was no longer valid. But, my lord, I had the prior claim on her. She was already with child when I brought her home. I told her I would see her bastard returned to its sire, but she would not listen to reason. And then this border lord attacked my home, stealing my livestock, carrying off my people, and demanding I return *his wife*. I naturally refused, but then he returned with a larger party of men and took her back, almost killing me and my priest. I have not seen her since."

"If the woman is wed and with child, Sir Udolf, it would appear to me the matter is settled. What is it you seek of me, my lord?"

"I want you to uphold the dispensation I gained from York," the baron said. "I want you to communicate with Queen Marie of Scotland and demand she see that Alix Givet, for that is her name, is returned to me with all possible haste. The woman is mine by right. I have my dispensation! We are at peace with Scotland, yet my village has been burned by these barbaric, thieving Scots, my sheep stolen, my people carried off, and my bride taken. I seek justice pure and simple, my lord."

Edward of York didn't know whether to laugh or have this obviously mad northern baron removed from his presence. The thought of this old man marrying his daughter-in-law was repellent, and he suspected the dispensation had been obtained by fraudulent means. He also suspected the girl hadn't been *confused* at all. She had wisely fled her lecherous father-in-law, and had the good fortune to marry some rough border lord. Still, the north was always troublesome, and until he knew just how important this baron was he would tread carefully. "Return home, my lord," he told Sir Udolf. "I will set my people to look into this matter. If justice is due you, you will receive it."

"Thank you, my lord!" Sir Udolf said, bowing several times. "Thank you!" He was then ushered from the king's presence by the same page who had escorted him there.

The lord of Wulfborn Hall arrived home by the end of June. Most of his fields were overgrown because he had no one to work them anymore. But he saw two small fields planted and cared for by the few servants he had left. He was pleased to find Father Peter awaiting him, and told him King Edward had promised him justice.

"It is just a matter of time, Priest, before Alix is home, and we shall begin our life together," Sir Udolf said, smiling smugly.

The priest nodded, but he wondered what had actually taken

place. Had his master really seen the king, or had he just spoken to some secretary or other flunky? And as the next few weeks passed he continued to wonder, for it appeared that nothing had changed. Sir Udolf spent his days planning for the return of Alix Givet, something the priest accepted was unlikely to happen. Each time he would broach the possibility of his master taking another woman to wife the baron would wave him away.

Finally Father Peter pointed out to Sir Udolf that he could hardly maintain a wife with his lands in the condition they now were, and his village still basically a ruin. "You must find new villagers, my lord, and there are those who barely subsist living all around us in the hills. Send me out with your steward to find the best of these people and bring them to Wulfborn so they may rebuild the village and till your fields. If we go now, by winter the cottages will be livable again, and your fields prepared for planting next spring. You cannot bring a wife to Wulfborn as it now is, my lord."

And to his relief Sir Udolf agreed, saying, "It will take time for King Edward to negotiate with Queen Marie for the return of my bride. And of course York must make St. Andrew's understand it has precedence. Aye! Everything must be perfect for Alix's return, Father Peter. I have been negligent. I will not send my steward with you. I will go myself. I have a good sense of honest men and strong backs."

The priest was pleased to see his master finally interested in something other than attempting to regain a woman who was wed to another and obviously content. His master's mood would improve immeasurably once he saw his estates reviving. And then Father Peter was certain he could be reasoned with to take another woman for his wife. It was unlikely that King Edward had done anything in that direction no matter what Sir Udolf thought. The king had nothing to gain by aiding an unimportant northern baron who could offer him nothing in return. If there was one thing the priest understood it was power. Sir Udolf had been naive to think the king would help, but he was not quite ready to face that fact. Hard work would alter

Sir Udolf's attitude and make him more reasonable, the priest was certain.

But the hard work to restore Wulfborn to itself did not change Sir Udolf's position. If anything, it made him more determined to regain Alix for his wife. Everything he did over the next few months was for *her*. He sought out hard workers and their families, choosing his new folk with an eye to pleasing her. The cottages were rebuilt as the priest had predicted before the first snows fell. Looking down upon them from his own house one early evening, lights again in the windows, smoke rising from the chimneys, the master of Wulfborn remarked that Alix would be approving.

"She is a woman who likes order about her," he said with a smile.

"You need stock," Father Peter said, attempting to distract his lord once again.

"I will purchase them in the spring," Sir Udolf replied. "No need to get them now, for I should have to purchase grain to feed them as we grew little this year. What grain we have grown is for our people. The new miller is an excellent man. Did you know, Good Priest, that some of these folk we gathered in had grandparents who were ours? But there wasn't enough land for all the children born then, and some had to strike out on their own. Now, because of our tragedy, they are returned home again. God works in mysterious ways, Father Peter."

"Have you heard from King Edward?" the priest ventured slyly.

"Nay, I have not. Were it not so late in the year I should send you to Yorkminster to learn what is happening. But there is time for that in the spring," Sir Udolf decided. "The king will not fail me, Father Peter."

But Edward of York had forgotten entirely about the obscure Northumbrian baron who had pleaded for justice a year ago. The winter had passed, and he was in love. Not with a foreign princess, however, but with the widowed Lady Elizabeth Grey, née Woodville, who was not at all a suitable match for a king of England. Her father had been an unimportant knight. Her mother, however, had been Jacquette of Luxembourg, the widow of Henry IV's son, John, Duke of Bedford. Still, the connection was not fine enough to suit the king's mother, Cecily Neville, known as Proud Ciss. The king's interests nonetheless were engaged elsewhere now. Yet he had sent an inquiry to York in the matter shortly after he had spoken to Sir Udolf.

Unfortunately the inquiry from the king regarding the situation had ended up in the hands of the same secretary who had taken the bribes needed to gain Sir Udolf his dispensation. This priest had tossed the royal parchment in his hearth and then sent a note to the king declaring the matter had been properly settled. He knew it was very unlikely to be pursued further, and he would see it wasn't. The secretary then sent off a dispatch to Sir Udolf assuring him his dispensation was valid and that St. Andrew's was now ready to acknowledge it. Then the priest put the problem from his mind. And Sir Udolf, receiving the assurances from Yorkminster as spring arrived, rejoiced.

"You see!" he crowed to Father Peter. "The king has indeed given me my justice. As soon as the fields are planted, we shall travel into Scotland to this Dunglais and fetch my bride home. I will make no attempt to steal her this time. I shall go openly."

Father Peter was surprised King Edward had actually aided Sir Udolf. He had not believed his master, who had nothing to offer in return, would have mattered to a king. But there was the parchment from York with the archbishop's seal upon it. Still, he made a final attempt to change Sir Udolf's mind. "My lord, the lady in question has been gone from you for several years now. I do not believe she will leave her man and her family because of a piece of parchment. I do not believe the lord of Dunglais will allow you to take his wife. Wulfborn is beginning to look as of old. Your fields are tilled and being planted. There are sheep and lambs in your meadow. Either Sir David's sister or the widow Alyce Graham would suit you, my lord. Choose one of them for a wife. Do not persist in this folly."

"You call a church document folly, Priest?" Sir Udolf said icily.

"Nay, my lord, I do not. What I tell you is that that document will not matter to the Laird of Dunglais or his wife. They will not be parted."

"Do not call her his wife. She is not his wife! She belongs to me!"

The priest threw up his hands in defeat. This would end badly, but he had done his very best to turn the lord of Wulfborn away from his madness. He could do nothing more but pray for Sir Udolf. Alix Givet was not going to come back, and nothing Holy Mother Church said or did was going to change that. But he would travel with his master and be there for him when he was finally forced to face the truth of the matter.

They departed Wulfborn several days later, taking with them six men-at-arms whom Sir Udolf had trained from among his new villagers. Six were enough for protection, but not enough to appear hostile. Reaching Dunglais two days later, they found the small drawbridge that stretched across its moat raised. Father Peter noted that the moat was kept filled by a natural stream that traversed the hill upon which the stone keep known as Dunglais stood.

"Identify yourselves!" the guard on watch called down to the party before the keep's gates.

"Sir Udolf Watteson, and Father Peter to see the laird," the lord of Wulfborn called up to the man-at-arms.

"You'll have to wait" was the reply, and the guard turned away to speak briefly with another man on the walls. Then he climbed down the stone steps from the wall and into the courtyard. Entering the keep proper, he hurried to the great hall, where the laird was sitting with his wife and their children. "There's a Sir Udolf Watteson and his priest at the gates, my lord, requesting entry. English by the sound of him."

Alix grew pale and looked wordlessly at her husband.

"I told you I should have killed him," Malcolm Scott said. "Refuse him entry, and tell him if he returns to Dunglais again I will slay him."

"*No!* Wait!" Alix called out to the man-at-arms. Then she said to her husband, "If you refuse him entry, I shall never be able to go outside the keep again as long as he is alive. He'll send men to take me again. Let him in, I beg you. Let him see Fiona and little James. Let me tell him I am again with child to be born at year's end. Together we can convince him, we *must* convince him, that his desire for me needs to be put to rest. The priest comes with him, and while old-fashioned in his thought, Father Peter is a reasonable man, Colm. And send for Father Donald to join us."

"I want the children gone from the hall," the laird said.

"Nay, let them remain. Sir Udolf needs to understand this isn't just about a man and a woman. This is about a family," Alix said.

"I don't want them frightened, and this will eventually become unpleasant," the laird said.

"If we see it degenerating, we will send them away," Alix promised.

"Go and tell Sir Udolf he and his priest may enter. His escort will remain outside. He has my word no harm will come to either of them while they are in my house," Malcolm Scott said.

With a brief nod the man-at-arms hurried off to deliver the message. Iver, who had heard everything, went to seek out Father Donald. By the time Sir Udolf and Father Peter had reached the hall of Dunglais, Father Donald was there as well. The Englishman's eyes went immediately to Alix. He smiled. She did not smile back.

"My dear wife, I am happy to see you looking so well," Sir Udolf said.

"I am not your wife," Alix responded.

"Why are you here?" Malcolm Scott demanded.

"A year ago I went to King Edward and asked him for justice. He interceded for me at York, and York interceded with St. Andrew's. This marriage union you claim with my wife is illegal. Holy Mother Church orders you to return Alix Givet to me immediately. I have come to you openly and honestly, my lord. I travel with no great army of men, but only with a small party to guard me while I journey." He reached into the leather packet he carried and withdrew several sheets of parchment. "Here, my lord, are the documents from York, including a recent letter upholding my claim upon Alix Givet. If you can read, read them. If you cannot read them, have your priest do so."

To his credit Malcolm Scott did not leap up and throttle the Englishman, although he was tempted to do so. He was a man of honor, and he had given his word that Sir Udolf would not be harmed in his house. But he did wave away the parchments. Instead he said, "My lord, do you see this girl who sits by Alix's side? It is my daughter from a previous union. The only mother she has ever known is Alix. Do you see the bairn in Alix's lap? That is our son, James Alexander, named for the late king, who was my friend, and for Alix's father. And there is another bairn in Alix's belly who will be born at year's end. Now do you really believe, my lord, that anything written upon those parchments will induce me to give my wife, the woman I love and prize, to you?"

"The church and the law are on my side," Sir Udolf said stiffly.

"To hell with both the church and the law!" the Laird of Dunglais said vehemently. "Whatever your documents may declare, Sir Udolf, Alix is *my* wife."

"My lord," Father Peter said quietly, "you cannot take a mother from her children."

"Priest! You overstep your authority," Sir Udolf snarled.

Suddenly Fiona jumped to her feet. "You will not take my mam from me again," she cried, launching herself at Sir Udolf to attack him with her small fists. *"You will not! You will not!"*

The laird quickly rose and pulled his daughter from the startled Englishman.

The little girl yanked away from her father and tried to squeeze herself into Alix's lap with her brother, who was now beginning to whimper nervously.

"Fenella, take the bairns from the hall," Alix called out. She brushed a lock of black hair from Fiona's small face. "I am not going anywhere with this man, Fi. I told you when I returned I would not leave you again. Now go with Fenella and play with James so he will not be frightened." She kissed the girl's tear-stained cheek.

"Aye, Mam," Fiona said with a sniff, reluctantly taking her baby brother's hand and helping him as he toddled from the hall. But before she left she gave Sir Udolf a fierce look that actually made him quail.

"The brat has the evil eye," the Englishman declared, crossing himself piously.

"Let me see these documents you carry," Father Donald said, quietly reaching out to receive them from his fellow cleric. Carefully he perused them, and then he said, "This letter purported to come from the bishop of St. Andrew's does not. I know the handwriting of both of His Grace's two secretaries and the four undersecretaries. The hand that composed this letter does not belong to any in St. Andrew's precincts. Nor is the seal of the bishop attached, which it would have to be to be authentic. From where did this letter come?"

"It came from York, along with a document from the archbishop there declaring the dispensation valid and true," Father Peter replied hesitantly.

"Do you believe the dispensation valid?" the Scots priest asked the English one.

"I am suspicious, for coin was exchanged several times," Father Peter answered truthfully, "but I cannot be certain. The donations were said to be for the archbishop's charitable works. I am no fool, and I know they could have as easily gone into someone's pocket. But is not that how the business of the church is conducted? On a large scale for men of importance, and a smaller scale for those of lesser importance like my master?"

"Of course the dispensation is valid!" Sir Udolf shouted. "The archbishop's seal is on it! It is true, and Alix Givet is mine by right! Are you suggesting bribes were exchanged? Are you offending my honor? For I am a man of honor!"

"If you call my wife yours one more time, my lord," the laird said through gritted teeth, "I will throw you out of my house, for I have given my word not to harm you while you are in it. But once you have crossed my drawbridge my promise no longer holds."

"The dispensation from York is valid," Sir Udolf repeated stiffly.

"But the letter from St. Andrew's is not," the laird replied, "and so we are at an impasse. English law does not hold in Scotland, and Alix is my wife under Scots law."

"And she is mine under English law," the lord of Wulfborn said stubbornly.

"My lord," Father Donald addressed their visitor, "is not possession nine-tenths of the law? And does not the fact my lady is the mother of my lord's bairns overrule your right? Ask the lady what it is she desires in this matter."

"What she wants does not matter," Sir Udolf said. "The law is the law."

"Since we speak of English law and Scots law then this matter must be settled in the courts, but of course then the question arises whose court? England's or Scotland's? And a civil court or an ecclesiastical court?" Father Donald said. "Would it not be simpler to relinquish your claim on the lady? I am certain my lord would pay you an indemnity for any damages you feel you have suffered in this matter."

Alix spoke suddenly. "I do not love you, Udolf. The thought of being your wife is repellent to me. You were the father of my first husband. I think of you as a father. I could never consider you a lover. Indeed, the very idea is repugnant. But I do love Malcolm Scott and our children. Dunglais is my home and I will not leave it."

He looked her, and as if he had heard nothing she had said to him, told her, "We have repaired the damage the Scots inflicted upon Wulfborn, my dear. The village is rebuilt and repopulated once again. There are sheep in the meadow, and the crop promises to be good by harvestide. When you come home, you will see."

Alix stood up, smoothing her pale blue skirts. "I shall go to the bairns," she said. "With your permission, my lord, I shall not return to the hall until this man is gone."

He nodded. "Go, lambkin." Then he spoke to his guest. "It is several hours until dark. I will not shelter you in my house this night, Sir Udolf. Get you gone from Dunglais, and never return. If you do, I will, despite my wife's gentle heart, kill you."

"I want what is mine!" the Englishman shouted.

The laird nodded to Iver, who came with several stout serving men and took the lord of Wulfborn from the hall and out into the courtyard, where they set him upon his horse and led it across the drawbridge to rejoin his men-at-arms. Father Peter followed but not before he and Father Donald managed to speak privately.

"I will send to you when I know what he means to do," Father Peter said. "I am not being disloyal, but for months I have attempted to dissuade him from this path. There are at least two marriage prospects for him to choose from in his vicinity."

"Thank you," Father Donald said. "I have known Colm Scott since he was a boy. He will not give over. He loves his wife, and his heart is held captive by her. Godspeed to you, Peter."

"And God bless you, Donald" came the reply as the English priest mounted his horse and set off after his master. When he had caught up with Sir Udolf he asked him, "And now, my lord, will we return home to Wulfborn?"

"Nay, we are going to find Queen Margaret" came the surprising answer. "Did she not give me her permission to wed Alix if I gained the dispensation? Surely she will have some influence upon my wife. And I will gain her aid in petitioning the bishop of St. Andrew's. We will see if the letter I hold is false or nay."

"My lord," the priest said desperately, "let us go home, I beg you. The matter is settled for all but you. Why would you try to take her away from Dunglais?"

"Because she is mine," Sir Udolf said as if the priest were simpleminded and could not comprehend. "She is mine, Priest, and I will have what is mine."

But Margaret of Anjou had left Scotland with her son and returned home to France in the hopes of gaining aid from her family and from the French king so her husband might be restored to his throne. Henry of Lancaster remained in Scotland, moving from sanctuary to sanctuary within the borders. Some days his mind was clear, and some days it was not. While disappointed, Sir Udolf was not discouraged. He rode on to St. Andrew's to gain an audience with Bishop Kennedy. The bishop, however, was not at St. Andrew's. He was with the young king. But Father Peter was able to learn from one of the bishop's undersecretaries that the letter that was supposed to have come from St. Andrew's had not. None of the bishop's people recognized it, or the hand that wrote it. And as for the archbishop of York's dispensation, it would not be upheld by the bishop of St. Andrew's.

"We must go home, my lord," Father Peter said.

And Sir Udolf nodded. "But this matter is not over," he told his priest.

The priest said nothing. A reasonable man would have admitted his defeat, but Sir Udolf had never been a man to give up easily. Still Sir Udolf had met with failure at every turn. *It is obvious,* the priest thought, *that God is answering my prayers. Perhaps if I pray harder my lord will give over and pick a new wife from among the women of our district.* Encouraged, Father Peter turned his face south towards Wulfborn Hall.

Chapter 14

A lix had been both upset and astounded when Sir Udolf Watteson had appeared in the hall at Dunglais. She wasn't certain that he was mad. But his refusal to accept the reality of his situation was disturbing. *Perhaps I should have let Colm kill him when he rescued me from Wulfborn,* she thought guiltily. Her husband had told her if Sir Udolf ever again attempted to enter their life and disarrange it he would indeed slay the Englishman. Alix had not protested his words this time. She was angry Sir Udolf had upset Fiona, who was now having nightmares and would wake up crying out for Alix.

The laird would not allow his wife to ride from the keep without a large party of men to guard her. After midsummer Alix refrained from riding at all, pleading her belly, but it was not her pregnancy that prevented her riding out. Taking men from the keep so she might ride endangered Dunglais. And Fiona had become fearful of leaving her home lest Sir Udolf come and take Alix away. Only remaining within the keep did the little girl feel truly safe.

"Look what he has done," Alix railed to her husband. "We cannot remain boxed up forever in our home because of this man."

"I know," the laird answered. "I mean to put an end to it as soon as possible. I will go to the queen and to Bishop Kennedy about the matter. They will straighten it out." He bent and kissed Alix's sweet lips. "If I left you for a few weeks, would you be all right, lambkin? I need only two men to travel with me. Beinn will see that the keep is well defended. And you will have Iver and Fenella in the house."

"If it means this can be over, Colm, then aye! Go! But how do you mean to set the matter straight? Sir Udolf has his dispensation from York. You have seen it."

"Father Donald does not believe the dispensation is legitimate, although certainly Sir Udolf does," the laird told his wife.

"But it came from the archbishop's palace. Father Peter took the request to York himself," Alix replied.

"Monies were exchanged," Colm Scott reminded his wife.

"Monies are always exchanged where the church is concerned," Alix said scornfully. "But I cannot believe York's archbishop would condone a match between me and Sir Udolf, given our prior relationship."

"We will see, but no matter you are mine, Alix, and I am yours forever," the laird swore to his wife. And several days later, after sending a messenger ahead of him and seeing that his keep would be impregnable, Malcolm Scott rode out with two men-at-arms by his side as he headed north to find the queen and Bishop Kennedy. It was high summer when he reached Ravenscraig Castle, the queen's home and her favorite residence. He was not surprised to find Adam Hepburn there with the queen.

Queen Marie welcomed him graciously, the young king by her side. He thought she did not look as well as she had in the past. But very astute, she was taking advantage of the political confusion still existing in England and making it work to Scotland's best advantage. Bishop Kennedy, having a quarrel with the English bishop of Durham, planned to lay siege to the bishop's castle of Norham. The queen saw no point to this exercise but went along with her bishop in an effort to assuage his anger that her influence in her son's government was perhaps a bit stronger than his.

The Laird of Dunglais bowed to both the young king and his mother. James III was eleven now. He was a tall, slender boy with black hair and amber eyes who resembled his mother more than the

Stewarts. "I am pleased to see Your Highness in such good health," Malcolm Scott said to the king.

"How is Mistress Fiona?" the boy asked. "We much enjoyed her visit and hope to see her again soon."

"My daughter is well, Your Highness, though disturbed at the thought of losing her stepmother to whom she is devoted," the laird answered the king.

"Is your wife ill, my lord?" Queen Marie queried the laird.

"We have had some difficulty with her former father-in-law, Sir Udolf Watteson," Malcolm Scott said. "He holds a dispensation from Yorkminster that says he may wed her. He refuses to accept the fact Alix is my wife, the mother of my son and soon to birth a second child for me. At one point he kidnapped her, taking her back into England."

"Adam Hepburn told me," the queen said.

"He came again several weeks ago, but this time openly, to insist I turn my wife over to him as she was his. His priest traveled with him. He brought with him his dispensation from York as well as a letter he claimed came from St. Andrew's backing York and Sir Udolf's claim. My daughter became agitated at the thought of losing Alix. My son was frightened by this man. I put him from my house and warned him that if he came again I would kill him."

"And rightly so," the queen exclaimed. "Is the man mad that he continues to pursue your wife? Or is he just a fool?"

Malcolm Scott smiled slightly. The queen's outrage was oddly comforting. "Perhaps a bit of both, Your Highness," he answered her.

"You have obviously come to us for help," Queen Marie said.

"I have, madame. Sir Udolf's own priest is not certain, and we certainly are not, if this dispensation is legitimate. Monies were exchanged allegedly for the archbishop's Christian work. But did York's archbishop actually receive those monies, and did he approve such a dispensation allowing a father-in-law to wed his deceased son's wife? My own priest says the letter from St. Andrew's is a forgery. I need Bishop Kennedy to confirm that. I need Yorkminster to confirm whether the dispensation is legitimate or nay. And if it is, what action can we take? I have offered Sir Udolf an indemnity for any wrong he feels he has suffered. He will not take it. We are at a loss, Your Highness, as to what to do. But we cannot be harassed forever by this Englishman. Can you help us?"

The queen was thoughtful for several long moments, and then she said, "I can have inquiries made, my lord, through my own private channels. And Bishop Kennedy is here at Ravenscraig. He will search his memory, and also make inquiries at St. Andrew's." She looked to her son, the king. "Your Highness, will you add your name to the correspondence I will have written?"

"Mistress Fiona loves her stepmother," the boy king said. "And you say this Englishman caused her distress, my lord?"

"Aye, Your Highness, he did. So much so that my daughter attacked him, beating him with her fists," the laird responded.

"Oh! I should have liked to have seen that!" the king exclaimed, and he grinned. Then, turning to his mother, he said, "Aye, madame, I will add the weight of my kingship to this matter. If the letter from St. Andrew's was a forgery then certainly the dispensation from Yorkminster must be suspect as well."

Malcolm Scott was surprised by the boy's astuteness. He had been king only two years, and yet he already had an instinct for what was truth and what was not. "Thank you, Your Highness," the laird said, bowing deeply before the king.

"My lord Hepburn," Queen Marie spoke. "Please take the Laird of Dunglais to meet with Bishop Kennedy. We must straighten this matter out as soon as possible."

Adam Hepburn bowed and led Malcolm Scott off. "Your request comes at an ideal time," he told the laird. "The queen would do anything to deter Kennedy from this ridiculous quarrel with the bishop of Durham. But of course our good bishop thinks that since Edward of York is still busy consolidating his position, he can war in England with impunity. Norham Castle, however, is unlikely to be taken."

"What is the quarrel between these two holy men about?" the laird asked.

"Who knows?" Adam Hepburn said. "A relic, the question of who is greater. Churchmen are no less vain and ambitious than normal mortals. Kennedy's nose has been out of joint ever since the old king died. He expected to take charge of the young king to the great advantage of his family, just like the Crichtons and Livingstones did in the time of a young James II. But the queen was there before him, and her people remain in the key positions. She's a clever lass and compromises with the bishop just enough. He's not a bad fellow, but the queen is more sophisticated because of her upbringing. Between us, however, she influences her son a bit too much. This is not the civilized court of her father, Duke Arnold of Gueldres, or her uncle, Duke Philip of Burgundy. This is Scotland, where a man is expected to ride well and fight well. Our young king does neither, nor does he speak the old language still used in the Highlands. He loves the things his mother loves. Music. Art. Beautiful clothing. He speaks of bringing artists and musicians here to Scotland, of building a great hall at Stirling. This is not what his lords want to hear. I have tried to advise him, but he doesn't listen."

"You love his mother," the laird said quietly.

Adam Hepburn laughed wryly. "Aye, God help me, I do. But my love for the queen is not important, for I am no Black Knight of Lorne to sweep a widowed queen off her feet and wed her, nor is she like her predecessor, Queen Joan. My queen will not wed again, for her son's sake. If he were grown perhaps I should convince her, for while she loves the others they are not important to her as the young king is important to her. But here we are. Bishop Kennedy is housed here." Adam Hepburn rapped sharply upon the door, and it was opened by a young page who bowed and ushered the two men inside.

Bishop James Kennedy was not a young man, but neither was he in his dotage. A big, tall man, his head was tonsured, the fringe of hair snow white. His blue eyes were fathomless and offered no show of emotion. He nodded in acknowledgment of his visitors' bows, and waved them to seats opposite him by the fire. "Well, my lords, what is it that brings you here today? You are usually close by the queen, Hepburn. A bit more discretion would be appreciated, sir. And who is this with you? He looks like a borderer."

"Malcolm Scott, the Laird of Dunglais," Adam Hepburn replied, ignoring the bishop's pointed remarks about his relationship with the queen.

"And I am indeed a borderer, Your Grace," the laird said.

"Aha! The man who has as priest in his borderer's lair the best secretary I have ever had," Bishop Kennedy grumbled. "I don't suppose you would be of a mind to give him back to me, Scott of Dunglais."

"Only if he wanted to return, Your Grace," the laird answered with a small grin.

Bishop Kennedy snorted, and then he smiled sourly. "You say that because you know he doesn't. Why Donald preferred serving our Lord in a border keep to serving him here in the halls of power I will never know. He could have gone as far as Rome, Scott of Dunglais. Did you know that? *Rome!* He is intelligent and clever. And, God help us, humble! *Truly* humble. Why I was blessed briefly by his company and skills only to lose him I will never know."

"He is invaluable to us, Your Grace," the laird said.

"But do you appreciate him? Understand him?" the bishop wanted to know.

"I know he is wise and brings comfort to my Dunglais folk," the laird answered.

"Bah!" the bishop said. "I can see you deserve each other. Well, border lord, what is it you want of me? You have not come all the way from your border keep simply to pay me a visit. And you seem to have the queen's ear or Hepburn would not be accompanying you."

"My lord Hepburn is an old friend," Malcolm Scott said.

"And so was James, the second Stewart of that name," Bishop Kennedy said quietly. "I remember you now, Malcolm Scott. The boy who came from the borders, and when the others fell away, or were subverted by Crichton and Livingstone, you remained true to your king. When you had to return home after your father died I remember he was saddened by your loss. I remember how he looked forward to your visits. Well, now I do not feel quite so badly about losing Father Donald."

The Laird of Dunglais nodded his acknowledgment of the bishop of St. Andrew's words. Then he said, "I desperately need your help, Your Grace." And he went on to explain the situation affecting him and his family to the churchman.

James Kennedy listened carefully as the laird spoke. Finally he said, "I will check with my people, for the truth is few of them are so totally honest they would not accept a bribe. And a quarrel between two men over the right to marry a widowed woman would seem a small matter to them." Reaching out, he poked at his page, who was dozing by his chair. The boy immediately jumped up. "Go and bring the secretaries to me one by one, in order of precedence," the bishop said.

The boy quickly ran off.

"If they would take a bribe, would they not lie to you as well, Your Grace?" Malcolm Scott asked the prelate.

"Ah, but I know when they lie, so usually they will not dare" came the answer.

Then the door opened, and one by one the bishop's secretaries entered his privy chamber to be questioned. There were six of them, and each one of them denied having composed, signed, or sent such a missive to Yorkminster.

"Father Donald said the letter was a forgery," the laird told the bishop. "He did not recognize the hand, nor was your seal affixed."

"Then it is likely this dispensation is false as well," Bishop Kennedy declared. "I do not see York giving such a permission. I know there have been cases where a father-in-law has taken his dead son's widow to wife, but those marriages usually involved men of wealth and power who do not choose to lose the woman's large dower portion. It is a nasty business, but an unimportant English baron would be unlikely, no matter his measly bribe, to gain such consent from York."

"His own priest was at York," the laird reminded Bishop Kennedy.

"A country priest who had probably spent most of his life at this Wulfborn" came the reply. "You met him, Scott of Dunglais, did you not? Would you call him quick-witted and clever?"

The laird shook his head. "He was not a fool, but neither did I think him particularly wise. Kindly. Loyal to Sir Udolf, but deeply concerned by what was happening and becoming suspicious that perhaps his master had been misled. He was very anxious to get Sir Udolf to consider several women of respectable lineage who were capable yet of bearing children and lived in the vicinity of Wulfborn. Sir Udolf would have none of it."

"I will make inquiries for you, although I am not on the best of terms with the church in England right now. Still, my quarrel is with Durham, not York. I will send one of my people south, and we will see if we can find the answers to your questions."

"Your Grace, I thank you with all my heart," Malcolm Scott responded, and then, kneeling, he kissed the hand with the bishop's ring that was held out to him. Standing again he said, "And shall I tender your compliments to Father Donald, Your Grace?"

The bishop gave a snort of laughter. "Aye, you may. And tell him I miss him, his wry wit, and invaluable counsel." And turning to Adam Hepburn he said, "Can you do nothing with the king, Hepburn? His ability to control a horse seems to get worse, not better. Some of the lords have begun to look to his brother Alexander."

"They would do well to cease their hostility towards His Highness," Adam Hepburn said. "It is true he rides badly, but he is intelligent and civilized, unlike his brother, who is bad-mannered and prone to make foolish choices even though he rides like he was born on a horse. Is that all the earls want? Someone to ride, drink, dice, and wench with them? If that be the case, then any man might be king."

"So it has been said," Bishop Kennedy replied dryly. "You may go now, my lords. And give the queen my compliments."

"Sly old fox," Adam Hepburn muttered when they were well out of the bishop's hearing. "He plays a crafty game. If he thought he could control any of the princes without the queen's interference he would put one of them on young James's throne instead. He is a constant worry to her."

"She does not look well," the laird remarked.

"She is not, but none know it but me. She strives hard to hide it from them. She fears showing any sign of weakness will endanger the king. Her children are her life, but especially her eldest. She knows better than any what her husband would have wanted from them. She would live long enough to see young James reach his majority, where hopefully he will not be influenced by others. The boy is vulnerable, and try as she might, the queen cannot teach him the fine art of compromise. It is his greatest weakness."

"He is young yet," the laird noted.

Adam Hepburn shook his head. "He is stubborn," he answered.

That night in the great hall of Ravenscraig Castle the Laird of Dunglais sat at the first table below the high board with Adam Hepburn and observed everything. The young king had grown proud of his position. His brothers had grown more unruly. He had two younger sisters. Mary, the elder of the two, was a pretty little girl who seemed to enjoy flirting and chattering. Her younger sister, Margaret, was quiet and serious. She watched everyone and everything with sharp eyes but said little, although he could tell she understood all that went on about her. But then she was very young, he considered.

In the morning Malcolm Scott bid the queen, Adam Hepburn, and Ravenscraig Castle farewell to return home to Dunglais. Because the weather was fair and the days long, they needed no shelter at night and the three riders were able to travel more quickly. Reaching Dunglais halfway through the second day they watched as the drawbridge was lowered so they might travel across it.

Alix came out into the courtyard to greet her husband, for a man-at-arms on the wall had seen him coming and called down to a servant, who ran into the great hall to tell his mistress. She was followed by Fiona. The laird slid easily off of his horse and swept her into his arms, his lips touching hers in a hard kiss. "Welcome home, my lord," she said, and kissed him back gently.

The laird then bent down to kiss his daughter. "Have you been a good lass, Fi?"

"I have, Da!" Fiona assured him. Then she ran off, for Fenella had told her that one of the hounds had delivered a litter of pups that very morning.

Linking her hand into his arm Alix walked with her husband into the keep. "What news?" she asked him. "Can the bishop of St. Andrew's help us?"

"The letter from St. Andrew's was false, as we anticipated," the laird said as they walked into the hall. "The bishop will send an inquiry to York as to the validity of Sir Udolf's dispensation."

"Yet what if it isn't, but those who granted it see the query and tell St. Andrew's that it is valid?" Alix asked worriedly. "I am fearful to trust anyone now, Colm."

"If the dispensation is valid St. Andrew's will not uphold it, and we are married in the eyes of God, the church in Scotland, and the law. If Sir Udolf pursues this matter further, I will kill him, lambkin. I will have no other choice. We cannot spend the rest of our days living in distress over this man. Now, I must go and find Father Donald." He kissed her brow and set her down by her loom.

That night as they lay abed he realized, though they had been apart a brief time, he had missed her. He sat in their bed, the firm yet soft pillows against his back, Alix, her back to him, between his legs. His hands were filled with her delicious round breasts. He played with them, teasing at the nipples by pulling them out as far as they could go, rolling them between his thumb and forefinger. "Your belly is small yet," he noted. "You were so certain of the first. Is it a son or daughter you give me this time, lambkin?"

Alix sighed with the pleasure his hands gave her. As much as she had enjoyed nursing young James, she had relinquished those duties over to a wet nurse Bab had found in the village. The woman, Bab had said, was a veritable font of nourishment, and so she had proved. Her son was content, and Alix was able to enjoy her husband's attentions more fully. "I don't know yet," she told him. "It is too soon, and the bairn has not yet spoken to me."

He placed a kiss on her shoulder, and then his tongue traced a path to the curve of her neck. He licked up the soft column to her jaw, and then reached out with his teeth to nibble upon her earlobe. "You are a most tasty morsel, my love," he told her. And then his tongue traced the interior of her ear, tickling it. "Did you miss me?" he murmured into that small ear. His fingers tightened about her breasts, and he squeezed them gently.

Alix leaned her head back against his shoulder, looking up at him. "Did you miss me?" she countered. "Was the fair Mistress Grant there to tempt you?"

"I did not see her," the laird answered his wife. Then he bent and kissed her lips, running his tongue lightly over them. "And if I had, she would have been doomed to disappointment as she previously was, for there is only one woman in the world I want to fuck, lambkin. And you well know who that woman is."

Alix squirmed about to face him, kneeling as she did. Her small hands reached out to fondle his cock, which was already stirring restlessly in anticipation. She reached beneath him to cup his love sac, rolling it about her palm as she bent her head to take him into her mouth. "Ummmm," she murmured as her fingers teased at his sac, while her other hand caressed his length, sucking him all the while to encourage his burgeoning within the warm, wet grotto of her mouth.

Malcolm Scott closed his gray eyes and groaned with the pleasure she was giving him, remembering the first time he had taught her this skill. Shy at first, Alix had soon shown a great talent for this particular form of lovemaking, to his delight. He groaned again as she gently nipped and nibbled at the tip of his cock. "Lass," he said in a thick voice, "you'll kill me if you go much further with this delicious torture."

She released him from the captivity of her mouth. And straddling him, she sank slowly down to recapture him within her sheath. "Is that better, my lord?" Alix purred.

He grinned up at her. "This is better," he told her, rolling her over onto her back. "Much, much better," he said as he began to thrust deep.

"Ahh, Colm, my love," Alix sighed happily, letting him sweep her away. She clung to him, her nails delicately scoring his back as they pleasured each other. Their mouths fused together, and one kiss melted into another and another and another until they were bruised and swollen. Her teeth caught at his lower lip, nibbling gently. Her tongue pushed into his mouth to dance with his while the rhythmic drive of his body against hers set her head spinning as she felt herself beginning to soar. *"Mon Dieu! Mon Dieu!"* Alix cried out.

He smiled triumphantly. She always cried out in French when he particularly pleased her with his passion. He redoubled his efforts, his mighty cock flashing back and forth within the heated tightness of her womanly sheath.

"Colm! *Mon Cœur! Je t'aime! Je t'aime!* Ohh! *Je meurs! Je meurs!*" And Alix's slender body shuddered with lust fulfilled even as her husband flooded her with his love juices, his big frame shaking with pleasure.

He remembered through the haze of desire her condition, and rolled quickly to one side so he would not crush her or the bairn. "I love you, lambkin," he told her. "I have never loved any but you, nor will I ever love any but you."

"You are my life and my love, Colm Scott," Alix told him as she curled into his embrace and quickly fell asleep.

He drew the coverlet over them and lay quietly thinking. He didn't want to have to kill Sir Udolf Watteson. But if Yorkminster's dispensation turned out to be authentic then he would have no other choice. It wasn't that the Englishman loved Alix. The laird didn't believe he did. He considered Alix his by right of possession, like his sheep or his dogs or his horses. She had been his son's wife, and therefore belonged at Wulfborn. She would be the means of giving him an heir in exchange for the heir he had lost. The very thought of Sir Udolf touching his sweet lambkin, kissing her sweet lips, thrusting his cock into her, made his blood boil.

And then Malcolm Scott knew with a strong instinct that overcame him and filled his mind. In the end he would have no other choice but to kill Sir Udolf Watteson. If the dispensation was proved true, the Englishman would come for Alix, yet he would not, could not, let his wife, the mother of his children, go. But if York ruled the dispensation had been obtained by means of fraud, and was therefore not valid, the laird suspected Sir Udolf would ignore it and come for Alix anyway. Aye, he would have to kill the Englishman, for Sir Udolf would give him no other choice. He was a man obsessed by Alix Givet and could see no other woman but her.

And so they waited for word of what was to come.

The bishop of St. Andrew's was not on the best of terms with his English brethren, but one of his secretaries, a young Franciscan, had an English mother. Calling Brother George to his privy chamber, James Kennedy explained the situation to him.

"If the lady wed her laird knowing the dispensation was being sought, there may be fraud on her side," the young priest said. He was tall and slender with a tonsured head, pale skin, and fine dark eyes.

"She was honest with the laird's priest. He vouched for my word in the matter," James Kennedy said.

" 'Twas bold of him to do so," Brother George remarked.

Bishop Kennedy laughed. "Aye, it was, but Father Donald was once my chief secretary and greatest confidant. He knew how I would feel about the matter. Even if the dispensation were genuine,

I should not honor it. A man attempting to marry his late son's wife smacks of incest in my opinion. Disgusting!"

"Just what is it Your Grace requires of me, then?"

"Have you any contacts at Yorkminster, Brother George? We need to know if this Sir Udolf has a genuine claim on the Laird of Dunglais's wife. There are bairns involved in this muddled matter. The laird's son and heir chief among them. I would not have the wee lad declared bastard, nor the child the laird's wife now carries," the bishop said.

"I have a cousin who is a priest and serves at a church in York itself. He would surely know people within the cathedral precincts," Brother George replied.

"Go to York, then, for me and learn the truth of this. I do not think the archbishop would give such a dispensation. While Sir Udolf sent his own priest to disburse bribes where he could, he has not the kind of monies that would be necessary for such an enormous favor. There is some wickedness afoot here, Brother George. Root it out for me, and then return to St. Andrew's."

Brother George departed St. Andrew's and rode for Yorkminster. After several days he finally reached the walled city, entering it and seeking out St. Cuthbert's Church. There he found his cousin, Father Henry, who greeted his relation warmly.

"I had heard you were in the service of the bishop of St. Andrew's," Father Henry said. His father and Brother George's mother had been siblings.

"I am, and I have come discreetly for him in a matter that may involve Yorkminster. Queen Marie has requested of the bishop that he learn if a certain dispensation to wed had been issued by the archbishop or if said dispensation was fraudulent," Brother George explained.

"What makes you think the dispensation was fraudulent?" Father Henry asked.

"It is said to allow a minor baron to marry his son's widow," Brother George said.

"Is she rich?"

"Nay, far from it I am told" was the reply.

"I have heard rumors of bribery among the archbishop's minions," Father Henry said. "Such a thing is not unheard of. And those without means and influence are apt to fall victim to the less than honest in the minster."

"I'm certain the archbishop would not want a scandal, and the young woman involved is the goddaughter of Margaret of Anjou," Brother George murmured.

"And she has no fortune? Are you certain?" Father Henry was surprised. A goddaughter of an English queen surely was a woman of wealth.

"She was the daughter of the queen's physician. They were left behind at Wulfborn when the old king and his family fled north into Scotland. The physician died shortly after his daughter married the lord of Wulfborn's son. Then the groom died. There were no other children, and the lord took it into his head to wed his son's widow. She resisted and fled into Scotland. Her husband's people found her almost dead on the moors. Nursed back to health, she caught the laird's heart and they were wed. The laird had been a widower with one daughter. The child adores her stepmother, I have been told, and now there is a son and heir, and another child on the way."

"The archbishop would never countenance a match between a father-in-law and his son's widow," Father Henry said. "I will gladly help you, Cousin, to get to the bottom of this matter."

Brother George reached into his robes and drew out a small leather pouch. Taking a gold coin from it, he said, "My master would show his appreciation of your efforts with more than prayers. I can see your church needs certain repair, Cousin."

Father Henry did not demur. He took the gold coin. "This will repair the steps to the sanctuary and buy us a pair of silver candlesticks," he said. "I thank you, Cousin, and I thank your bishop. Come now and join me for supper."

The English priest was as good as his word. He went personally to the cathedral and began making discreet inquiries. A cousin on his mother's side was a nun and served as a housekeeper in the archbishop's household. She was a small, plump woman with a motherly face. He took Brother George to meet Sister Mary Agnes.

When she had heard his story she said, "My master, the archbishop, would never countenance such a dispensation. I have heard rumors of certain chicanery among some of the lesser priests in the archbishop's secretariat. I have a friend who can learn the truth of this matter for you," Father Henry's cousin said. "She will find out what has been going on."

"*She?* Another nun?" Father Henry asked.

"She is not a nun," Sister Mary Agnes replied. "She is a whore."

"*Cousin!*" Father Henry exclaimed, surprised. "How is it you came to know a whore? I am shocked you would be acquainted with such a woman."

"Do not be a ninny, Henry," the nun said. "Whores serve a purpose, as do we all. And as whores go, Lettice is a respectable whore, and she keeps a quiet, respectable house. She has regular visitors, among them some of the priests from the archbishop's secretariat. They come to futter her and remain to talk with her. She can ask questions without anyone being suspicious, for she is considered both damned and beneath contempt."

"I don't know," Father Henry said slowly.

"I do," Brother George spoke up. "I would be grateful for your help, Sister Mary Agnes, and for that of your friend."

"She will want to be paid something for her trouble," the nun murmured.

"If she gains me the information I need, she will be well rewarded," Brother George promised, "and, of course, there will be something for your convent too."

Sister Mary Agnes smiled, saying, "You are most generous, Brother."

The whore, Lettice, knew immediately who it was who had elicited bribes from Sir Udolf. Eager to impress the whore, he had told her, for he had never before had the monies to ride between her legs and had been desperate to do so. "His name is Father Walter," she told Brother George. "He enjoyed bragging to me how he had fooled the country priest and his master. He managed to make them pay him thrice before he wrote the document and used the archbishop's seal on it. But my testimony in the matter will not be heard, for not only am I a woman, I am a whore. I will be punished for slandering a priest and my possessions forfeit. I am not young anymore, and I have more than I ever dreamed of having. I will tell you the truth, but I will not endanger myself by accusing any priest."

"You will not have to," Sister Mary Agnes assured her friend. "They have the name of the priest now. Let them get him to confess to his misdeeds. When they have, you will be rewarded."

Lettice smiled, eying Brother George lasciviously. "Father Walter usually frequents a low tavern near the walls next to the main gate of the city," she told them. "He is there almost every evening after Vespers. He can no longer afford to lie with me, and the tavern wenches are always willing for a ha'penny or a penny to lift their skirts. He has a mighty appetite for a little man," she noted. "You'll know him right away. He is short, wiry, with dark eyes that are always darting here and there for fear of missing something."

The two priestly cousins went to the tavern in question that same evening. The tavern was dark. It stank of sour ale, urine, and puke. The wenches earned their coins in the open without shame. One girl was bent over a barrel near the tavern door, her skirt bunched up to the small of her back while a soldier thrust himself in and out of her, grunting as he moved. Father Henry swallowed hard, staring, but Brother George's eyes roamed the room seeking the man they sought. He found him quickly.

Father Walter sat in a corner of the tavern, a plump girl in his lap. His hand was beneath her skirt. After a few minutes Father Walter dumped her from his lap. She fell to her knees before him, and her hands slid beneath the priest's brown robe. Brother George could see her lips moving, and then after a moment or two the girl climbed upon the priest's lap, sheathing his cock in her lush body. She jogged up and down a few times and then fell forward briefly upon his neck. Then, getting up off of Brother Walter, she took a coin from his fingers and moved off, a bored look upon her face.

Brother George moved to the table and sat down. "Did she give you pleasure?" he asked the startled priest.

"I am a weak man," Father Walter said with a shrug, but there was no remorse in his tone.

"I am told you are a man who can get things done," Brother George murmured.

"For a price, anything in this world can be had." Father Walter chuckled.

Father Henry now joined them.

"My cousin and I have been told by Lettice the whore that you managed to gain a dispensation for a man who wished to marry his son's widow. Is this so?" Brother George asked softly. "If it is, I have a small proposition for you of a similar nature."

"Such things are expensive," Father Walter said slyly.

"My master can pay," Brother George assured him.

"What is it he desires, then?"

"For the church to dissolve his marriage to his wife of ten years. She is barren, and he needs an heir."

"Why doesn't he just kill her? By not giving him his heir, she is being disobedient. He could beat her to death, and no one would fault him as long as the stick he uses isn't any larger around then his forefinger. The law permits it."

"My master is a kind man. He simply wishes the church to dissolve his marriage to this woman. If the church will do it, then my master can keep her dower, which is *very* large," Brother George explained. "And he has already chosen a new bride. The girl's mother has birthed ten living children, six of them sons. This makes the girl a fine choice, for she is likely to be an excellent breeder. But others want her too. My master must act quickly. And too, the girl's father might be loath to give his daughter to a man who had beaten his previous wife to death."

Father Henry listened in rapt amazement as his cousin spoke to Father Walter. His story was plausible, and the mention of the *very* large dower portion had brought a light into the dishonest priest's eyes.

"Tell me," Father Walter said, "has this woman born any children at all?"

"None," Brother George replied.

"It could be said then she had refused to consummate the marriage," Father Walter suggested.

"No man would remain with a wife for ten years who would not consummate the marriage," Brother George responded. "Nay. My master wants the church to give him a divorce. His wife can end her days in a nearby convent. She is a devout woman."

"A divorce would take time," Father Walter said slowly.

"Is there any way such a matter might be speeded up?" Brother George asked innocently, and he smiled at Father Walter.

Father Walter appeared to be considering the matter. Then he said, "It is possible, but your master would have to make a rather large contribution to the archbishop's fund for Christian charity, I fear. Do you think he could afford it?"

Now Brother George appeared to be considering the matter. Finally he reached into the pocket of his robe and drew out the leather pouch. Opening it, he pulled out a gold coin and held it up in front of Father Walter's face. "Do you think," he asked, "this would begin the process for my master?"

"It would take at least five more of those coins," Father Walter said slowly, and he reached for the gold coin.

Brother George palmed the gold coin. "Three and first your guarantee you can get the process started. And I must have the documents within seven days."

"Seven days!" the dishonest priest exclaimed. "It is not possible!"

"Then I will find someone else within the precincts of Yorkminster who can supply me with what I want within the time period," Brother George said, standing up. "A pity. Lettice said she enjoyed your company greatly. But as long as there are tavern whores, your itch can be scratched, eh?" He turned to walk away.

"*Wait!* For six gold coins I can make your request possible," Father Walter said.

"Four, no more," Brother George replied in a hard voice.

"Done!" Father Walter said, and he caught the gold coin the Franciscan tossed him with a skilled hand.

"A down payment," Brother George said. "I will meet you here in seven days, Good Father. If you try to cheat my master, I will kill you."

Chapter 15

ather Walter watched as the two other priests turned without another word and departed the dark tavern. And then he realized Brother George had not given him the name of his master or the unfortunate wife. But no matter. The names could be quickly inserted. Four gold coins! He rolled the coin he had been given about his hand. He had never had a gold coin in all his life. Most of his victims paid him with silver and copper. He was rich! Or would be when he collected the other three coins. He was tempted to go and visit Lettice, but he decided it would be foolish for her to learn of his good fortune. She might want a fee for having directed Brother George to him. He was not of a mind to share his gold with a whore. Even a whore as fine as Lettice. Stuffing the coin in his pocket, he hurriedly left the tavern. He had much work to do if he was to finish the required documents within seven days.

Some minutes ahead of the dishonest priest Brother George and Father Henry walked back to St. Cuthbert's. The hour was late and the streets dark. Father Henry carried a lantern that lit their way. Thieves lingering in the shadowed alleys and doorways remained where they were as they saw the two men were clerics. Priests never had any coin or other valuables about them, and they could damn a man's soul to hell if attacked. Here in York that was a serious deterrent to robbing a man of God.

Father Henry's small house was behind his church on the other side of a garden. Entering it, the two men found a plate with cold meat, bread, and cheese, along with a pitcher of ale left by one of the women of the parish. They prayed over the food, ate it, prayed again, and went to bed. Both men arose several short hours later to say the Mass. Both heard early confessions and then broke their fast with a hot oat porridge brought in by one of the women of the parish. Then together they walked to Yorkminster to see Sister Mary Agnes. Inviting them into the archbishop's garden, she inquired as to what they had learned. "Was Lettice truthful?"

"She was indeed," Brother George replied. "This priest is a greedy fool, and the sight of gold was enough to convince him to do our bidding."

"You should have heard the tale my cousin told," Father Henry chuckled, and then went on to enlighten the nun. "At one point I almost believed him myself."

Sister Mary Agnes gave a little chuckle herself as she listened to Father Henry. "I would say you will go far in the secretariat of St. Andrew's," she observed.

"Should one not be as ambitious for God as others?" Brother George asked.

She reached out and patted his arm soothingly. "I do not criticize, Brother. I am actually admiring of your skills. In my convent we have several women like you. They will serve God in a far higher capacity than I ever will housekeeping for the archbishop. Some days I envy them, and then I pray to our Lord for his forgiveness for that sin."

"We all have our gifts," Father Henry murmured.

"You will serve God's greater good helping us to rid your master of this dishonest priest who eats like a poison at the holiness of York," Brother George said. "Can you aid us in gaining the archbishop's ear, Good Sister?"

"I can," she said, without hesitation. "Come with me."

They followed the nun through the beautiful garden, and as they rounded the corner of a tall green hedge they saw a man seated upon a small stone bench in seeming meditation. He wore a simple dark robe, but about his neck hung a large jeweled cross, the symbol of his office. Quietly they stood before him, waiting to be recognized, and then finally the archbishop of York looked up.

"Yes, Sister Mary Agnes, what is it?" he said in a quiet voice.

"Your Grace, this is Father Henry from St. Cuthbert's by the walls. And his cousin, Brother George. They need to speak privily with you."

"How is it you know these men?" the archbishop asked her.

"We are all cousins, Your Grace," the nun answered, simplifying the relationships.

The archbishop nodded his understanding, then said, "Very well, Good Fathers. What is it you need speak with me privily about?"

"There is a dishonest priest among those serving in your secretariat who has caused a great deal of difficulty for some and continues to do so," began Brother George.

The archbishop stiffened slightly. "You are a Scot," he said warily.

"I am, Your Grace, and I am in service to the bishop of St. Andrew's," Brother George responded with a polite bow. "Queen Marie requested a boon from my master, and I have been sent to York to expedite the matter."

The archbishop nodded. "Say on, Good Brother. As we all serve the same God, I will hear what you have to say. Would that James Kennedy understood that as well."

Brother George's mouth quirked briefly in a small smile, and then he went on to explain the problem between Sir Udolf Watteson of Wulfborn Hall; Malcolm Scott, the Laird of Dunglais; and Mistress Alix Givet. He concluded by saying, "My master knew you would never give such a dispensation, Your Grace. However, until Sir Udolf can be convinced otherwise, he continues to insist the laird's wife is his and causes great distress to both Malcolm Scott and his family. I have been given to understand the lady Alix does not dare to venture outside of her keep anymore for fear Sir Udolf will kidnap her again and carry her off to Wulfborn Hall. The lady is with child again, and should not be harassed so lest her offspring be harmed."

The archbishop nodded. "She has given her husband a son and now is expecting a second child?"

"Aye, Your Grace, and she is a good mother to his daughter from a first union," Brother George explained. "The lady Alix is the only mother the little lass can recall, and she lives in terror of losing her as she once lost the mother who bore her. And all of this unhappiness is being caused because a priest in your secretariat has solicited bribes from petitioners to Your Grace to issue dispensations of all sorts. This is only one case I bring to you, but there are surely others. And last night I offered this same priest a bribe to issue a declaration of divorce for a lord I claimed to represent."

"You will understand that before I act," the archbishop said, "I must be absolutely certain of this priest's guilt, Brother George. I will accuse no man without proof positive." He looked hard at the two priests.

"I would expect no less of Your Grace," Brother George said. "When this priest contacts us to turn over his false documents, we will send to you with the time and place so you may be there to see what transpires and catch this miscreant in the very act."

"Agreed," the archbishop replied. "I am disturbed by what you have told me, for who knows how many other false documents this man has issued in my name?"

"It is likely he has only preyed upon those he believed without other influence, as Sir Udolf Watteson. Men not clever enough to see through his ruse," Brother George said in an effort to calm any fears this high churchman might have regarding his office and most especially his reputation. "He is in actuality a petty thief."

"Indeed you are probably correct in your assumption, Good Brother," the archbishop replied, but his eyes still held worry. Then he gave them a brief smile and raised his hand in blessing. "Go with God, my sons, until we meet again."

Dismissed, they turned away from the great churchman and, led by Sister Mary Agnes, made their way from the cathedral gardens. She brought them to a small gate that opened onto the street.

Brother George turned to the nun to thank her. "I am most grateful for all your help in this matter. Without you my path to the archbishop would have been more difficult," he told her.

"If you are truly grateful, Brother George, then when you retrieve that gold coin you gave Father Walter, stop by St. Mary's Convent as you leave the city and donate it to my order," Sister Mary Agnes said with a small smile.

"I will, and gladly!" Brother George told her with an answering smile. "Were you a man, Good Sister, you would make a fine bishop."

"I have learned well from my master never to let an opportunity pass by," the nun told him with a little chuckle. Then, with a nod of farewell, she closed the gate behind the two priests, who walked off briskly down the narrow street.

"She would make a shrewd chatelaine for a rich man," Brother George noted to his priestly cousin. "She is a clever woman."

"She was her parents' younger daughter, and betrothed to a wealthy man," Father Henry explained. "But she always wanted to serve the church. When her betrothed husband died suddenly a month before the wedding she told her parents that it was obviously God's will that she enter the convent and not the marriage bed. Since their eldest son had been married the year before to the dead man's sister, she now became her father's heiress and nothing was lost. My cousin's elder sister was well married, and the younger brother pledged to a young woman of means. So they gave Mary Agnes her way, and let her enter the convent," Father Henry concluded.

"And yet she does for the archbishop much of what she would do as chatelaine of her own home," Brother George noted. "Nor do I find her particularly pious in her manners. How curious she should know and befriend a whore."

"I have always believed God places us where we are meant to be," Father Henry murmured quietly. "And many who claim piety do so only for others to see but in their hearts are as worldly as those outside of our calling."

Brother George thought a moment at this, and then he nodded. "True, Henry. True," he said.

Five days went by during which time the bishop of St. Andrew's messenger helped his cousin in the small church that was his domain. He celebrated the Mass. He heard confessions, and he ministered to the poor and helpless. And as he did he understood the sense of Father Henry's words, for this kind of priestly life was not at all to his liking. He far preferred being in the thick of things as he was in the bishop of St. Andrew's secretariat. And Brother George smiled to himself as this revelation unfolded itself to him. And, finally, on the sixth day a ragged urchin came into the church as the two clerics were snuffing the precious candles.

"Masters, which one of you is Brother George?" he asked.

"I am," the Scots priest said, stepping forward.

"I have a message for you," the lad said. "Didn't make sense to me, but the man who give it me said I just had to repeat it, and you'd give me a penny."

Brother George reached into his robe and drew out the pouch that held his coins. After extracting a silver penny from it, he restored the pouch and held the coin up for the boy to see. "And what is the message?" he asked.

"Same place, same time, tomorrow" the answer came.

"Same place, same time, tomorrow," Brother George repeated.

"Aye," the lad said, and his dirty hand shot out to catch the silver coin tossed to him. Then he ran from the church.

"We must notify His Grace," Father Henry said. "I will send to him."

"Send to Sister Mary Agnes lest the message is seen by the wrong eyes," Brother George suggested to his cousin, who nodded. "Tell His Grace to come here in disguise with two of his men-at-arms. We will go to the meeting together, and we will go before our dishonest friend gets there so His Grace may secret himself and listen to what is said. Father Walter will incriminate himself nicely before he is arrested."

"You are enjoying this," Father Henry said with a grin. "But then you always did like games when we were boys together."

"Indeed, and I did," Brother George admitted cheerfully with an answering grin.

Early the following evening the archbishop came with two of his men-at-arms. He was dressed in a heavy, hooded dark cloak. Together the men walked to the small disreputable tavern by the city's walls. Entering, they saw with relief that they were there before Father Walter. Brother George led them to the same table in the rear of the room where they had met first with Father Walter.

"This place is foul," the archbishop murmured, his eyes sweeping the tavern.

"It is a perfect place for a villain, Your Grace," Father Henry said quietly.

"God's foot! Is that man fornicating with the tavern wench?" the archbishop asked. He pointed discreetly across the room, where a rough-looking man was lustily fucking a barmaid he had pinned against a wall.

"Yes, Your Grace," Father Henry replied softly. "The wenches are for sale, as is the ale. But you and your men had best secret yourselves in the shadows here," he advised.

No sooner than the three men had done so a tavern maid came to ask what the two men at the table would drink. She did not notice the others. "Ale or wine?" she asked with what she assumed passed for a seductive smile. "We have both, Good Fathers."

"Ale," they answered in unison.

"And would either of you want a little futtering this evening? 'Tis only a ha'penny unless you want my asshole, and then it's a penny," the wench said. "You look like two big strong men who could give a lass a good fucking."

"Not tonight, dearie," Brother George said, reaching out to pat her bottom. "We're meeting someone on a matter of business. Bring three ales."

"Didn't I see you two the other night with Father Walter?" the wench inquired. She was not a striking girl, but pretty enough in the dimly lit room if a man was half-drunk. Her stringy hair was dark blond, but her skin was pockmarked, and she was missing one front tooth. But she had very large breasts.

"Aye, you did," Brother George said.

"If it's Father Walter you're meeting, then I'll be back later when your business is done. No one likes a good jogging like Father Walter. He's as randy as a billy goat," the wench said, and then she laughed heartily. "I'll get your ale." And then she flounced off.

"Turn your head and look," Brother George said to Father Henry. "The villain has just come in from the street. Ah, he sees us, and comes. He has papers with him."

Father Walter hurried to the table where the other two priests sat.

"I've ordered ale," Brother George said. "Let us wait to finalize our business until the wench returns and serves it."

"Agreed!" Father Walter said.

The tavern maid rejoined them, three mugs of ale in her hands. Setting them on the table, she sat down in Father Walter's lap with a giggle. "Do you want a little jog?" she asked him, provocatively wiggling her bottom in his lap.

Father Walter stuck his hand down the girl's gown and pinched her breast. "Aye." He nodded. "Come back later, Violet." Then he tipped her from his lap.

"Here, Violet," Brother George said and handed the wench a coin.

"A silver penny! 'Tis too much for just three mugs of ale, Good Father."

"It's for the ale, and for the pleasure you will give Father Walter later," Brother George said with a grin.

" 'Tis still too much," the girl said slowly.

"Then take what is left over and buy something for your child," Brother George told her quietly.

"How did you know I had a child?" Violet wanted to know.

Brother George shrugged, and the girl bobbed a curtsy before running off. He picked up his mug of ale and drank a deep draft. It was good, which surprised him, for the tavern was so low. "Now, Good Father, to business," Brother George said. "Have you brought the documents I require?"

"I have, but one thing is missing. I do not have the names of the parties involved. Will you add them? Or shall I? I have brought my quill and inkpot."

"Spread your parchments out, and I will tell you the names. You may write them into the document so there is no confusion in the matter," Brother George said. He watched as Father Walter unrolled the parchments. The work was flawless, and there at the bottom of the bill of divorcement was the seal of the archbishop of York. "Your work is excellent," he complimented. "No one will ever know it is a fraud."

"The archbishop's seal makes it quite official even if the old man hasn't authorized such a divorce. The names now?" He set his inkpot on the table and drew out his quill.

"My master's name is Sir Richard Dunn," Brother George said, watching as the priest carefully wrote the name he had been given. "His wife is Mary Anne."

Father Walter added the second name.

"Do you do all of this yourself?" Brother George answered. "The work is so fine."

"I do," Father Walter said. "I should not like to have to share my gains with anyone else. And, too, I should not like a dissatisfied client returning because the fraud was discovered. Your master should not be pleased when he remarries and gets an heir on his new wife to learn the child is a bastard. No! No! I do all my own work."

"And the archbishop's seal? Is it real?"

"His Grace has several seals. I took one once, and no one has been the wiser. No secretariat of a great man is so free from disorganization that everything can be accounted for, which allows for the more enterprising among us," Father Walter admitted. "Now, if you are satisfied, I should like payment for my work. Four gold pieces I believe we agreed upon, and you have given me one as a down payment."

Brother George drew a small pouch from his robes, and as he did Father Walter said, "You said you had also heard of my skills from another. Can you tell me who?"

"A priest named Father Peter, whose master, the lord of Wulfborn Hall, needed a dispensation to wed his son's widow," Brother George said, cupping the pouch in his hand but not yet releasing it to the dishonest priest.

"Aye! I remember him. I was able to extract three payments from his master, for the old fool lusted after his widowed daughter-in-law. It is not often I find someone as gullible as that lordling. If I had only been dealing with him I might have gotten more, but his priest began to get suspicious of the delay, so I turned over the dispensation I had written up for him to Father Peter so he might wed the woman." He laughed. Then held out his hand again. "My gold," Father Walter said.

"I think not," Brother George replied. He turned to the shadows and said, "Have you heard enough, Your Grace?"

The archbishop of York stepped from the dim recess where he had been listening to everything that was said. His two men-at-arms were by his side. "Arrest him!" the archbishop said in a cold voice, "and take him to the cathedral dungeons."

"What is this?" Father Walter cried, jumping back. "You have tricked me! And you have cheated me! A pox on you for it!"

Brother George stepped forward, and reaching out, he grasped the priest by the neckline of his robe. "Where is the gold coin I gave you the other day? You'll have it on you, I know, for you would not hide it for fear it would be stolen. Where is it?" He began to rummage in the pockets of the robe, and then he smiled. "Here it is!" Taking the coin, he stepped back, releasing Father Walter. "I promised Sister Mary Agnes to donate this coin to her convent," he told the archbishop, "and so I shall."

"Before you leave York we must have your testimony, Brother George," the archbishop said to him. "I know time is of the essence to you and so tomorrow you shall be examined by a panel of priests. And you as well, Father Henry." He turned to Father Walter. "You will be defrocked, and then you will be executed as a warning to others who consider dishonesty," he told Father Walter. "Take him away!"

"Help! Help!" the dishonest priest cried, drawing the attention of others in the tavern as he was dragged forward.

The archbishop followed, saying in a loud voice, "This is church business, my children. This unworthy priest has stolen and lied."

"Make way for His Grace, the archbishop!" Brother George said as he stepped before York's prelate. Father Henry brought up the rear. The inhabitants of the tavern looked the other way, and went back to the business of drinking and wenching. Those who knew Father Walter didn't particularly like him and saw no reason to go to his defense. His pleas for aid were in vain. The archbishop's men dragged him off down the street in the direction of the cathedral.

"An unpleasant business," the archbishop said.

"I apologize, Your Grace, if I have embarrassed you in any way by bringing this matter to your attention," Brother George said.

"None of it shall be made public," the archbishop responded. "Whatever he has done shall remain done. We cannot know how many people this affects."

"But I would beg Your Grace to settle the matter of Sir Udolf Watteson, the Laird of Dunglais, and his wife, the lady Alix," Brother George reminded the prelate. "That is why I came to York in the first place."

"Come to the cathedral in the morning to see me," the archbishop said. "You have rid me of a bad priest. In this case I will correct the fraud, for you have told me of it." Then, as they had finally reached the cathedral, he bid Brother George and Father Henry a good evening. The two cousins returned to St. Cuthbert's.

When the morning came Father Henry and Brother George said the Mass for the parishioners of St. Cuthbert's, broke their fast, and then walked to the archbishop's house on the cathedral grounds. They were admitted by Sister Mary Agnes, who whispered to them as she escorted them into her master's privy chamber, "See me before you leave."

The archbishop greeted the two priests, holding out an elegant hand so they might kiss his ring of office. Then he invited them to sit opposite him on the two chairs that faced the long oak table he used to write. There were two sealed parchments tied with black ribbon upon the table. The two priests waited for the archbishop to speak.

"Late last night," he began, "I had two of the most trusted members of my secretariat draw up these papers. They are identical. They nullify any dispensation received earlier from this bishopric by Sir Udolf Watteson in the matter of Alix Givet. This document explains the clerk writing the parchment was young, inexperienced, and misunderstood the instructions given to him. That he sent the fraudulent dispensation off to Wulfborn Hall without the proper seals. Alix Givet, being as a daughter to Sir Udolf Watteson, would not be allowed to enter into an incestuous union with him. That upon having this matter brought to our attention by the bishop of St. Andrew's we have sought to correct the misunderstanding. Sir Udolf Watteson is advised to seek another wife. He is forbidden by God's law, and the king's law, to take Alix Givet from her lawful husband and attempt to force her into an illegal union. Will this satisfy your master, Brother George?" the archbishop asked.

The Franciscan nodded, and then he said, "Two parchments?"

"Actually three," came the reply, "but the third has already been placed among the official documents. This one is for you. See that it is delivered to the Laird of Dunglais and his wife. Then tell James Kennedy he will owe me a favor eventually for this favor I have done for him." He handed a rolled parchment to Brother George. "And this last one will be delivered by one of my messengers into Sir Udolf Watteson's own hand. It is hoped this will end the matter once and for all."

Brother George arose. "I am most grateful to Your Grace for all he has done," the priest said. "I will leave for Scotland on the morrow." He kissed the hand extended to him once more, and with Father Henry left the archbishop's privy chamber.

Sister Mary Agnes was waiting for them. "You should know Father Walter is dead," she whispered to them. "They tortured him to gain any information he had, but he was naught but a greedy little man, so they garroted him to put him out of his misery."

"Thank you," Brother George said softly. "God bless you, Sister."

"Go with God, Good Brother," she responded as she ushered them through the front door of the archbishop's dwelling, closing the door firmly behind them.

"Did you notice," Father Henry said, "how neatly he solved the matter without ever accepting blame for it?"

Brother George laughed. "Such is the way of the world, Henry. You are carefully insulated in your little church with its merchants and artisans and goodwives. I live in a world of pride and power, as does your archbishop. I am rarely, if ever, surprised."

The next morning the bishop of St. Andrew's emissary rode out of York heading north to Scotland. And on a separate road the archbishop's messenger directed his horse towards Wulfborn Hall, which he reached several days later. On his master's instructions he sought out Father Peter first.

"My master, the archbishop, asked that you be with me when I deliver this parchment," the messenger said.

Ah, bad news, Father Peter thought to himself. "I will gladly accompany you," he told the messenger, and directed their footsteps to the house and the great hall.

Sir Udolf Watteson lay sprawled in a high-backed chair by the hearth, which burned low. A large goblet hung from his hand. There were no servants in sight, and the hall was rank with the smell of urine and rotting food. He did not move as the priest and the messenger entered the hall, and as they drew nearer they could hear the sound of snoring coming from the chair.

"He has not been well," the priest excused his master.

"Wake him so I may deliver the parchment," the archbishop's messenger said. He had stayed the night before at a nearby monastery and as the sun had not even reached the midheavens yet he intended returning back to York this very day. Looking about the hall, he could tell its hospitality would be scant. He wanted to be on his way as quickly as he could be. He gazed at the sleeping man. It was obvious that he was drunk.

"My lord. My lord!" The priest gently shook Sir Udolf. "Please awaken, I pray you. There is a messenger here for you from York."

Sir Udolf struggled to open his eyes, to gather his thoughts. Only one word had penetrated his foggy brain. *York.* "Give me some wine," he husked, and the priest hurried to fill the silver goblet that was held out to him. Sir Udolf gulped down half the cup. His eyes began to open. He drank the rest of the liquid and tossed the cup aside. It hit the stone floor with a clatter. Then, rising, he pissed into the hearth, thoroughly extinguishing what little fire was left. Then, turning about, he said to the messenger in a rough voice, "Who are you, and what do you want?"

"Message from His Grace, the archbishop of York," the messenger said, shoving the rolled parchment into Sir Udolf's hand. Then he moved to leave the hall.

"Wait! Are you not to remain to carry back a reply?" Sir Udolf asked.

"I was told there would be no reply, my lord," the messenger said. He could hardly wait to get out of this place.

"Go on! Get out, then!" Sir Udolf said in not particularly hospitable tones. He unrolled the parchment and began to read it. As he read his face began to flush and then grow scarlet with his outrage and his anger. Finally he flung the document towards the dead hearth, shouting, "I will not be cheated! I will not!"

"What is it, my lord?" But Father Peter suspected he already knew.

"Read it yourself!" Sir Udolf said grimly, gesturing toward the fireplace where the crumpled document now lay. "I will not be cheated of what is mine! Does that fool in York think he can cheat me?"

Father Peter picked up the parchment and, smoothing it out, read it. He had been a fool, of course, to allow his master to keep giving that priest in York—what was his name? Walter? Aye! Father Walter—monies. While he had not sensed it immediately, he had sensed later on that the priest was dishonest. And now that he recalled it, there were no seals but one on the alleged dispensation. "You have been the victim of a fraud, my lord," he said quietly to Sir Udolf. "I am sorry, my lord. But now you have been given His Grace's official ruling in the matter and must abide by it."

"*I must abide by it? Why must I abide by it?*" Sir Udolf demanded. "Alix Givet is mine, and I will have her no matter what this archbishop says!"

"My lord," Father Peter pleaded, "Do not, I beg you, persist in this folly."

"There is but one woman for me, and that is Alix Givet," Sir Udolf declared.

"My lord! The church forbids any union with Alix Givet. They have declared it incestuous! You must understand that. *You must!* Will you damn your immortal soul to everlasting hellfire, my lord? You cannot have this woman!"

Sir Udolf grabbed Father Peter by the neck of his robe, glaring down into his face. His eyes almost bulged from their sockets. "*Cannot?* Do you dare to tell me what I can and cannot do, Priest? I will do as I please!" And he flung the frail man from him. As Father Peter fell backwards, his head hit the iron ball of an andiron in the great fireplace. His neck snapped audibly as he crumpled into the now-cold ashes of the hearth, which were quickly stained with the priest's blood. He was quite dead, and Sir Udolf knew it just looking at him. "Old fool!" he muttered. Then, picking up his goblet, he went to the sideboard and refilled it. "I must go to Scotland and fetch Alix," he said aloud. He drank down the contents of the goblet. "Aye, I must go to Scotland today. I will change my garments and then be on my way. My horse!" he shouted. "I want my horse saddled immediately!" Then he hurried upstairs to find fresh clothing. Where were the servants? Lazy good-for-naughts! Alix would see they behaved when she returned home. She would see they did their duty.

An hour later Sir Udolf Watteson rode forth from Wulfborn Hall and headed north for Scotland. He knew Alix would be at Dunglais. She was a prisoner, of course. Had she been free she would have returned home to him at Wulfborn. He thought of how beautiful she was with her honey-colored curls. He thought how his foolish son had mistreated her. *I will not mistreat her,* Sir Udolf thought to himself. *I will love her, and she will give me another heir.* He rode on determinedly.

At Dunglais a different scene had played out. The bishop's Franciscan, Brother George, had come directly from York with the good news he knew the Laird of Dunglais and his wife were waiting for and would welcome. The drawbridge leading into the keep was up as he approached it in late afternoon. "Brother George from the bishop of St. Andrew's with a message for the laird," he called up to the watch. Then he sat upon his horse and waited. After a few minutes the drawbridge was lowered, and the iron portcullis raised up to allow him through. He heard both means of entry being replaced as he rode into the courtyard. A boy hurried to take his horse away, and a man was suddenly at his side, bowing respectfully.

"I am Iver, the laird's steward," the man said. "If you will come with me, Brother George, I'll bring you to the great hall. The laird has been anxiously awaiting your arrival for some weeks now." As Iver spoke, he hurried along into the house, leading Brother George into the hall.

The scene that greeted the priest brought back memories of his own childhood. The hall was not large, but it had two fireplaces now burning. Four arched windows were set high in the stone walls. The furniture was well polished. The stone floors clean. On a cushioned settle by one of the fireplaces sat a young woman who he saw was with child. She was sewing. On the floor at her feet sat two children. A lovely little girl with long dark hair and a little dark-haired boy who looked perhaps two. They were playing with a puppy. The man who had been seated next to the woman now rose and came forward, his hand outstretched.

"I am Malcolm Scott, the Laird of Dunglais," he said.

"Brother George of the bishop of St. Andrew's secretariat," the cleric replied.

"Welcome to Dunglais," the laird said.

"I have just come from York, and I believe I bring good news, my lord," Brother George said with a smile.

The laird brought him to the hearth where his family sat, introducing him to Alix and the children. He offered him a comfortable high-backed chair in which to sit. "First some wine," he said, as a servant stepped forward to offer Brother George a goblet. "Hospitality should not be neglected even when the news is of great importance."

The Franciscan took the goblet, swallowed down some wine, and then set the goblet down upon the floor next to his chair. Reaching into his robes, he withdrew the rolled parchment with its red wax seal and black ribbon binding. "With the compliments of His Grace, the archbishop of York, my lord. And the compliments of my lord, His Grace the bishop of St. Andrew's," he said, handing the document to the laird. "If you cannot read I will read it for you," Brother George offered.

"I can read, and so can my wife and daughter," the laird replied, "but I thank you." He slowly unrolled the parchment, and his eyes began to scan the words written thereon. When he had finished he handed it to Alix. There were tears in his eyes.

She took the document from him and read it. Then she began to weep.

"Mam!" The little girl sprang up from the floor and put her arms around Alix.

"It's all right, Fiona," Alix said. "Sometimes grown-ups cry when they are happy. And I am very happy by the news Brother George has brought us. Remember the wicked man who had me taken away and whose men frightened you so?"

Fiona, her blue eyes wide, nodded. "Aye, I remember."

"Well, he can no longer harm us. God has forbidden him from it, my daughter. We are now safe and may ride out again once I have birthed this new bairn who currently resides in my belly," Alix told Fiona. "We must thank Brother George for riding all this way to bring us this happy news."

Fiona turned and smiled at the priest. "Thank you," she said.

"You are most welcome, young mistress," he told her. They were a beautiful family, he thought. And he was glad for his part in lifting this burden from them.

"You will remain the night," the laird said. "I've some fine venison, and rather good whiskey we make here. You've ridden a long ways, and have more miles ahead of you, I know. When you reach St. Andrew's, tell James Kennedy I am in his debt, even though he already knows it. Ahh, Father Donald. Here is Brother George, who has ridden from York with good news. We have been freed of the lord of Wulfborn at last. Father Donald is our priest, Brother George. He once served your bishop."

"Praise God and his Blessed Mother you are now rid of that crazed lord," Father Donald said. "We are free to roam our own hills again in safety."

Chapter 16

He was near now. He sensed it. He had stopped at one of the Douglases' lairs just on the border separating England and Scotland. The Douglases populated both sides of the periphery between the two countries. He would not remain the night with them, for he did not trust them, but stayed only long enough to gain directions to Dunglais. While he had been there once before, he was not entirely certain of the way. He rode out again. Above him the sky was lowering and threatening. There was the sound of thunder in the distance, and the distant sky was filled with sheet lightning.

The Douglas chief watched him go, and his son remarked that the man was a fool to leave when the weather was turning dangerous. "What does he want at Dunglais so badly that he continues on in such a storm?" the boy asked his father.

"The laird's wife," the Douglas chief said, laughing knowingly. "He stole her once before. It's not likely he'll succeed again. The man is as mad as a rabid fox."

"Should we send word to the laird then, Da?" the boy asked.

"Nah. No need. The laird will kill him on sight. No reason for us to be involved," the Douglas chief decided as the skies opened up and the rain began to pour down. He peered through the torrent, but Sir Udolf Watteson was no longer in sight.

Indeed, he was now a distance from the Douglas house and struggling to keep his edgy horse under control as the thunder boomed and jagged lightning began to pierce the skies around him. The animal danced nervously, becoming more frightened with each clap of thunder, which seemed to be growing louder. In a rare moment of sanity, Sir Udolf began to consider that perhaps he should have remained with the Douglases at least until the rain was over with. And then, without any warning, a bolt of lightning shot almost directly into the path before them. It was so close it singed the horse and Sir Udolf smelled the scent of burning hide. His animal reared up, terrified, throwing the rider from its back and galloping off into the mists.

Sir Udolf hit the ground and his head struck a rock, rendering him unconscious. But before he lost his senses he heard a crack and a fierce pain shot through him. Around him the thunder continued to boom, now moving away with the lightning, but the rain poured down in torrents for at least another hour. Night fell, and Sir Udolf lay unconscious on the hillside. Now and again he would swim to the surface of the darkness only to fall back again.

The following day dawned fair, and two women out seeking medicinal plants came upon the injured man. One of them was young and garbed in a red jersey gown. The other, obviously a servant, older. It was she who spotted Sir Udolf first.

"Mistress, look!" She pointed to where the fallen man lay.

"Is he alive, Fyfa?" the younger woman asked, her bright blue eyes curious. "I hope he is alive. It has been some time since I have had a man to amuse me." She peered closely. "His clothing is good. See what is in his pockets. Does he carry a money pouch? It's been so long since I've had any coin of my own."

"Mistress, this is not wise," she said nervously.

"Do as I bid you, Fyfa!" the younger woman commanded in a hard voice.

The serving woman bent down and rifled through the fallen man's clothing. She found one small pouch containing some silver coins and three coppers. "Here," she said, handing them up to her mistress. "It isn't much."

The man groaned suddenly, and Fyfa jumped up with a little shriek.

"Oh, he's alive!" the young woman said. "Good! We must get him to the cottage if we are to keep him alive. You stay with him. I will go back and fetch Rafe."

"Mistress," Fyfa quavered. "I do not think this is wise."

"You never think what I do is wise, Fyfa," the younger woman replied, and then she tripped off.

The man groaned again, and his eyes opened. "Where . . . am I?"

"Do not move, sir," Fyfa responded. "You have been injured. We are getting help now. How came you here?"

"Where is my . . . horse?" Sir Udolf asked.

"There was no horse when we found you," Fyfa said.

"The storm . . ."

"Is long gone, sir. It was yesterday afternoon, and a fierce storm it was," Fyfa replied. "Did the storm frighten your beast? Did it throw you?"

Sir Udolf tried to remember, and his brow furrowed. Then he nodded. "Aye."

"When we get you safe to the cottage I'll send Rafe to seek it. If you are a fortunate man we will find your horse, sir," she told him.

"Where am I?" he asked her again.

"Near my mistress's cottage. She has gone to get help. We have a man to do heavy chores. He is simple-minded, but willing and strong of back," Fyfa said. "She is fetching him so we may get you back to the cottage in order to treat your wounds, sir. It appears that you hit your head on yon rock. See. There is blood."

He turned his head, and pain shot through him. He groaned. "I may have broken a bone," he said.

"Will you permit me to check for such an incident, sir?" Fyfa asked him.

He nodded. His head hurt him, and he was helpless. "What is your name?" he asked the woman, who, from her appearance, was a servant.

"Fyfa, sir," she responded. Her hands moved gently over him. "I believe you have dislocated a shoulder and possibly broken your left arm." Her hands moved carefully over his torso, and he winced. "Bruises, I'll wager, nothing more," she assured him, "but all in all 'tis not too bad."

"I'm hot," he said. "Have you any water?"

Fyfa put her hand on the man's forehead. He was burning up with fever, and had obviously caught an ague lying out all night in the damp. "Nay, I have nothing with me, but it will not be long, and Rafe will get you to safety. Might I know your name, sir?"

"Sir Udolf Watteson," he replied.

They waited silently then until her mistress and Rafe came for them.

"Be careful of Sir Udolf," Fyfa told the big dull-witted serving man. "His left shoulder is dislocated, and the arm may be broken. Be gentle, Rafe," she cautioned.

Rafe nodded and then picked the injured man up as gently as he could. The wounded man cried out and then fainted. Rafe trotted back to the large cottage with his burden, looking to his mistress for further directions.

"Put him in the little bedchamber," she said, licking her lips. Then she turned and looked at Fyfa. "You obtained his name?"

"He is Sir Udolf Watteson, but that is all I know," Fyfa said.

"Time enough for the rest of his story," the young woman said. "Go and tend to his wounds, Fyfa."

"I will need your help, mistress," Fyfa said. "We must get him out of his clothes to gain the true measure of his wounds."

The younger woman nodded. "Very well," she said.

Together the two women entered the little bedchamber where Sir Udolf had been set upon a small bed. There was no help for it but to cut his clothing off.

"Burn them, Fyfa. They stink. We'll have to bathe him after we've examined him. Pull his right boot off. I'll remove the other."

Fyfa threw Sir Udolf's soiled garments into the hearth. Rafe had been told to take a horse and see if he could find Sir Udolf's own animal. Perhaps there would be a change of clothing in his saddle-bags. If not, they would have to find something for him. For now the unconscious man needed to be washed and tucked beneath the coverlet. And then Fyfa thought she would have to make some kind of a brew to take down his fever, get his shoulder relocated, and put a splint on his arm.

"His manhood is quite nicely proportioned," the young woman noted. "When he is well enough I shall avail myself of it." Reaching out, she fondled Sir Udolf, her elegant fingers sliding up and down its length. Her dainty hand slipped beneath the man to cup his balls in her palm. "They are a bit smaller than I would have anticipated, but then he is injured, and his cock shows promise." She chuck-led, releasing her hold on the now stiff fleshy rod. "Let us heal him quickly, Fyfa. I will leave him to you now," she said, and departed the tiny chamber.

The serving woman fetched a warmed cauldron of water from the cottage's hearth, some rags, several jars, and two pieces of wood. She set to work bathing Sir Udolf as best she could. When she had finished she put her knee into his shoulder and pressed down hard, and to her relief it snapped back into place. She poulticed the arm to help it heal before binding the two short pieces of wood to it. For-tunately the bone had not come through the skin of his arm, but she had been able to see the damage before she bandaged it. It was not likely the arm would be of much use to him again even if it did heal. Then she managed by pulling and rolling him to get him beneath the coverlet. He stirred and opened his eyes as she began to draw the curtains about the bed to keep the draft from him.

"Where am I?" he rasped.

"You fell from your horse, Sir Udolf, but you are now safe in my mistress's cottage. I have bathed and tended to your injuries. I am going to get you a soothing draft to drink now. It will help you to sleep, and sleep will heal you."

"Fyfa," he said. "Your name is Fyfa."

"Yes, my lord," she said, and then she left the small chamber.

She had left the curtains half-open. He scanned his surroundings. A cottage, but not a servant's or peasant's cottage. That kind of cot would have had just one or two rooms. There would not have been a chamber, however small, for a guest. Nor a bed with hangings. He became aware of himself suddenly. He was naked beneath the coverlet. His arm was poulticed and splinted and, while sore, his shoulder seemed back where it should be. He shivered beneath the coverlet and, closing his eyes, dozed fitfully until the door to the little chamber opened and Fyfa returned carrying a steaming mug.

"I've fixed you a nice cup of broth with some healing herbs mixed into it," she said and, drawing up a stool, she began to feed it to him. She didn't mention that she had also added a sleeping draft. Sleep was the best medicine for his injuries, and for the ague he had contracted out on the moor in the pouring rain.

"Whose cottage is this?" he asked her, speaking between bites.

"My mistress will tell you all you need to know on the morrow, my lord," Fyfa told him. "You are safe, and Rafe has returned. I am sorry, but he was not able to find your horse anywhere. The storm obviously sent it into a long gallop." She continued to feed him until the mug was empty and his eyes were beginning to droop.

"I am tired," Sir Udolf said.

Fyfa stood up. "Then I will leave you to sleep, my lord."

He watched her go, and while he needed to know where he was and who the mistress of this small house was, he accepted that with a broken arm he was helpless for now. He would have to wait a bit longer to claim Alix, but had he not already waited several years? He could wait a while longer, but she would be his. He could hear the faint stirrings of the household about him as he fell asleep.

"Will he live?" the mistress of the cottage asked her serving woman.

"He'll live," Fyfa said. "I've washed him, tended to his injuries, and fed him. He'll sleep until the morrow. He's got an ague, but I do not think it will trouble him too greatly, mistress."

"How quickly that lovely cock of his rose when I stroked him," the young woman murmured. "In a few days, when his healing has begun, I shall take him for a little jog," she said with a smile. "How long has it been since I have had a man to fuck? We do not see many visitors, Fyfa, do we?"

"This one is a lordling," Fyfa said. "English, by the sound of him."

"We shall have to learn what he was doing in so desolate a place," her mistress said softly. "And if anyone will miss him if he does not come home," she purred, her blue eyes narrowing in thought.

Fyfa said nothing in reply. There was no stopping her mistress when she made up her mind. It was all she and Rafe could do to keep their mistress contained to the cottage and the area around it. But that was their duty. She and her brother had been fortunate to gain this employment. They had been penniless and homeless when the laird had found them on the streets of Edinburgh. After he had questioned them and learned their circumstances, he had offered them a comfortable home in exchange for watching over a mad relation.

"Let her have her way within reason and as long as she does not harm herself," the laird had instructed them. "But she must not be allowed from the cottage unless you are with her, and she must not be permitted to roam the hills about the cottage. She is isolated for a reason. If you feel at any time you can no longer continue to mind her, you will send to me and I will see you are relieved of this duty. You will not be sent off penniless. I will provide that you and your brother receive coins enough for a fresh start wherever you choose to go."

But where would they go? Fyfa thought to herself. They were country folk driven from their father's farm by their elder half brother, who had inherited. He didn't want an unmarried sister and half-witted brother about when he married shortly. And so Fyfa had taken Rafe to Edinburgh seeking employment, but there had been none. She had taken to begging on the streets to sustain them, and then the laird had come along. He had carefully questioned them. Fyfa was gentle-spoken and Rafe simple-minded but obedient to his sister. And so the laird had brought them to this isolated place in the borders to look after the mistress.

They lived comfortably. The house was a large cottage with several rooms. Rafe slept in the loft of the little barn with the animals. They had a cow and several chickens for which he was responsible. There was a small brown and white hound and several cats. Every few months a large fellow would come from the laird with the supplies necessary to keep them well fed. If they needed something, Fyfa would request it of the big man. The mistress was always kept in her own chamber when the man came. Fyfa grew a kitchen garden in which there was an apple tree. And she was skilled in the making of herbal drafts and cures. It was a pleasant life but for one thing. Her brother had had the task of burying several men over the almost seven years they had been here. They were hapless creatures, young and fair, who had stumbled upon the cottage, been ensorcelled by the mistress, and then killed by her when their usefulness ceased. Fyfa knew she should have told the laird's man the first time it had happened, but then what would happen to her and her poor brother? Although she had no reason to distrust the laird, she could not be sure he would keep his word. He might even blame her for these terrible things that had occurred. And then they would be homeless once again, at the mercy of who knew what. Rafe could not manage on his own. He was content now in the life he had. Fyfa remembered how difficult it had been for him in particular when their brother had cast them from the only home they knew. So she kept silent.

And Fyfa had remained quiet, keeping a careful watch for any who might happen upon their isolated cottage that she might drive them away before the mistress could see them and work her wicked wiles. For over a year now there had been no victim for her mistress until they had found Sir Udolf Watteson on the moor. But he was neither young nor handsome. Oh, he was pleasant-looking enough, but the mistress liked them young, fair, and lusty. Sir Udolf certainly didn't meet that criteria, yet when the mistress had seen the sick man's cock her interest had been piqued. It was a fine cock too, Fyfa admitted to herself. God obviously had compensated Sir Udolf for his other deficiencies.

Several days passed, and it appeared that good food and good nursing were beginning to show results. The ague that Sir Udolf had caught out on the moor faded, leaving him with just his physical injuries. The soreness in his shoulder began to fade away. But he grew impatient and anxious to be on his way again.

"Give me the loan of a horse," he said to Fyfa.

"We have no horse," she replied. "We must walk wherever we go, sir." Learning of her guest's restlessness, the mistress of the cottage decided to pay him a visit. Fyfa prayed that Sir Udolf's years and ordinary demeanor would keep him safe, but she was doomed to disappointment and grew fearful of what was to come.

"Fyfa tells me you are making progress towards good health again, my lord," the beautiful woman said as she came into the chamber, closing the door behind her.

"I am indeed feeling better, madame," he answered her. "Your kindness is most appreciated. May I have the honor of knowing your name?"

"My name is Robena Ramsay, my lord," she answered him. "You are restless, however, I am told."

"I am an active man, Mistress Ramsay," he told her. "And I must be on my way again. I have business that cannot wait any longer. Fyfa tells me you do not keep a mount of any kind, and I must walk."

"That is so, my lord," Robena replied. "What is so important that you would leave us? I could make your stay with us quite pleasant." She smiled seductively at him. "I think I can cure some of your restlessness, my lord," she said, coming to sit upon his bed. "Would you like me to do so?" Her bright blue eyes bored into him.

Sir Udolf Watteson suddenly felt more a prisoner than a guest. He did not quite know what to answer this bold woman, but, drawing in a deep breath, he finally said, "Madame, while I am grateful for your kindness and your hospitality, I require nothing more from you but directions to Dunglais Keep and the loan of some clothing."

Robena Ramsay stiffened at his words. "Why do you seek to go to Dunglais?" she inquired of him, her blue eyes narrowing.

"I have business with its laird."

"What business?" she demanded to know.

The question and the tone of her voice surprised him. But if an answer would gain him what he needed, directions and clothing, then he would give her an answer.

"My son, my only child died, and I decided that his widow being an orphan would make me a good wife, as I had no other heir. I sent to York for a dispensation, and it was granted. But Alix was frightened of the honor I was doing her. She ran away from me and crossed into Scotland. There she was captured by the Laird of Dunglais, a wicked man, I can tell you. He forced her to his bed. When I finally found her, this man claimed she was his wife. They already had a child and claimed another was coming." Sir Udolf was abbreviating his tale and telling Robena the story as he wanted her to know it so he might gain her sympathy and her help. It was really not her business. A woman living alone but for servants out on the moor would not know the laird. "The laird's daughter from another union attacked me, madame. The brat screamed I should not take her mother from her. But my Alix was not her mother. She was her stepmother."

"If this wench had become the laird's whore then why did you not just leave her?" Robena asked him. At the look upon his face she laughed, although she found herself suddenly filled with jealousy. "Ahh, she did not want to go with you, my lord, did she? She had made herself a new life, hadn't she?"

"I had my dispensation from York saying that she was *my* wife!" Sir Udolf said angrily, and then his eyes grew teary. "But recently the archbishop sent to me to say that the dispensation given me was fraudulent. The priest who gave it to me was dishonest. I was told that the archbishop would have never given me permission to wed my daughter-in-law, and there was but one seal of his office on the document instead of two. I was told one seal was not official. But Alix Givet is mine! *Mine!* I shall go and fetch her from the Laird of Dunglais. He shall not keep my wife and claim she is his. The bastard she birthed him, the one she now carries in her womb, he may keep them. But Alix is mine, and I shall have her!"

Robena Ramsay had listened and as she listened she was filled with a burning fury. The bastard! Malcolm Scott had taken some little English girl and was calling her his wife? The bitch had probably given him a son. That was it. It had to be! He had gotten a son on his whore, and he wanted everyone to believe this Alix was his wife so the brat would be his legitimate heir. "You say this laird claims your woman is his wife?" she asked slowly. "Where is the mother of his daughter?"

"Dead, he says. And not only does he claim my Alix as his wife, he says that the bishop of St. Andrew's sanctioned his marriage to her," Sir Udolf said. "I must go to her, madame. I must bring her back to Wulfborn. Tomorrow, with your help, I will leave here. You have but to clothe me and give me directions to Dunglais."

"Of course you must," Robena said slowly, and in what she hoped passed for a calm voice. "And I will most certainly help you, my lord." Her mind raced with her thoughts. How could Malcolm Scott wed another when he was married to her? He couldn't! Aye, his whore had given him a son, and her belly was big again, was it? *And she has the temerity to mother my daughter while trying to displace her as Dunglais's legitimate heiress with her bastard? She will not have my bairn,* Robena decided. Then she focused on her guest again. "We will have a celebratory supper tonight, my lord, as you do indeed seem healthy enough to continue on your mission."

"You are most gracious, madame," Sir Udolf said.

"And I shall see you are properly clothed for your trip. Fyfa will cut down a pair of her brother's breeks, and I may have a sherte that will fit you." She smiled.

"I am assuaged that you understand why I must go so hastily," Sir Udolf said, sounding relieved. When she had offered herself to him—or had he misunderstood?—he had been very troubled by such boldness in a woman. But then a female living alone on the moor with but two servants was probably not very respectable, he decided.

"Of course I understand," Robena murmured in dulcet tones. "You must do what you must, my lord." *And so will I.* She arose from his bedside. "I shall go and instruct my servants to prepare us a good supper and find you some garments, my lord." Then she departed the little chamber. Aye, she would find him some clothing. There had to be something one of her other unfortunate lovers had left behind that would fit him. She would lie and say they belonged to a distant relation who visited now and again. She hurried to find Fyfa.

"Well?" her serving woman asked as her mistress entered the tiny kitchen.

"I want a *special* meal prepared for tonight," Robena told her.

Fyfa cocked her head to one side. "You mean to kill him before you have used him? What has happened to change your wicked mind, my lady?"

Robena was pacing the small space irritably. "It is what he has told me, Fyfa. Do you know the destination he sought? Dunglais! My husband, it seems, has taken a mistress and is attempting to pass her off as his wife. She's already birthed one bastard son, and is big of belly again! But my husband's whore is"—and here Robena laughed almost insanely—"the wench Sir Udolf means to marry! And even after the fact she has been more than well fucked by my husband, the old fool still wants her!"

"Perhaps he loves her," Fyfa said quietly.

"Pah! Love is for fools, but, then, Sir Udolf is one, isn't he?" Robena remarked scornfully. "Now to the supper. A capon if we have one to kill, and with a sauce. I smell bread baking. Serve it with that cheese I like."

"I will see if there is any left," Fyfa told her.

"And a custard with plum jam for the after," Robena said thoughtfully. "I always like a sweet with these meals. It adds a certain piquancy to the occasion." She chuckled.

"What about the wine?" Fyfa asked meaningfully.

"Prepare two pitchers as usual, but use small pitchers so the need for a second is not suspicious. The second will contain the sleeping draft and the poison. And make certain your brother does not mix the pitchers as he did that one time. If I had not made myself immune to the poison by ingesting a bit of it daily over the years, he would have killed me. As it was my head ached for several days from the sleeping potion."

"I'll see there is no problem, my lady," Fyfa promised. Then she said, "Will any come seeking Sir Udolf?"

"I am certain he has no one as his only child is dead. He mentioned none other to me but for my husband's whore," Robena replied. "You have been with him more than I. Has he said aught to you, Fyfa? Sisters? Bastards?"

Fyfa shook her head in the negative. "Nay. I believe he is all alone, poor man."

"So much the better for me," Robena said. "Have Rafe dig his grave while it is still light. But out of sight of the house. We do not want our guest becoming suspicious. Now tell me. Do we have any male garments that would fit him? I must allow him to believe that on the morrow he will depart from here to continue on to Dunglais," Robena told her serving woman.

"Aye," Fyfa responded. "The small chest in the hall contains a number of garments from your past lovers."

"Find something to fit him," Robena instructed the woman. "Choose the best there is so his pride is not too damaged. As I recall, that merchant's son was about his height, and his garments were particularly fine. If he asks, tell him that I have a cousin who sometimes visits now and again. And have Rafe polish up his boots. But remember to remove it all, including the boots, before we bury him," Robena said. "Now I must go and attempt to rest myself. You know how excited I become before the kill, and I know I shall not sleep a wink this night afterwards." And she was quickly gone from the little kitchen.

Fyfa heard her footsteps as Robena almost danced up the stairs, and she shuddered. The mistress was a terrible woman, but Fyfa knew she and her brother were safe. The lady needed them. She called to Rafe, and when he came Fyfa gave him his instructions, watching through the little kitchen door as he shambled off to dig the grave. The day was fair, and she wondered as she looked out over the gently rolling moor how long their lives would go on like this. Eventually a mistake would be made, and Robena's wickedness exposed. What would happen to her servants then? Would they be held accountable too? Whatever happened, Fyfa thought to herself, their fate was already sealed. If they left the mistress alone and to her own devices, she would certainly attempt to return to Dunglais and then the laird would know of their betrayal and he would certainly seek them out to punish them. She and Rafe were caught as surely as two poor rabbits in a trap. There was no help for them now but to continue on and pray when the lady was finally found out the laird would have mercy on them. Then, as she looked out over the late-summer landscape, her eye caught a sudden movement on the hillside. Pray whatever it was it did not come this way. At least not today.

The horse grazing the hillside looked up as the rider approached. It did not resist as its reins, which had been hanging, were taken up, and it was led away. It trotted along obediently until it was led into the courtyard at Dunglais. The rider dismounted, giving the lad who ran forth instructions not to take the beast into the stables until the laird had come and seen it. Then Beinn hurried into the keep, making his way immediately to the hall, where the laird was eating his morning meal.

"I found a horse, saddled, without a rider, grazing out on the moor," the captain informed his master. "I think you had better come and take a look, my lord. It's saddlebag contains papers, but I do not read. It could be important, and there may be a rider injured somewhere nearby, though I saw no one, nor heard any cries for help."

Malcolm Scott arose from his high board and followed his captain. As Alix was not in the hall, there was no need for an explanation. "How long do you think the horse has been out there alone?" he asked Beinn.

"Difficult to say, my lord. A few days, a few weeks. Its coat is roughened and it has not been curried in some while, yet the beast is sound, so someone once cared for it."

The laird grunted. "Hmmm." The creature before him was vaguely familiar. He reached into the saddlebag, pushing past the few garments, and drawing out several papers. His eye scanned the documents and then he swore aloud. "Christ's bloody wounds! The man is mad! Totally mad!"

"My lord?" Beinn looked puzzled.

"The horse belongs to Sir Udolf Watteson. He has obviously decided to ignore the archbishop of York and the bishop of St. Andrew's. He has come to claim my wife as his, Beinn. You did not see him?"

"Nay, my lord. There was no one near the horse out on the moor. Of course, if he were dead and lying in the heather I could have easily missed him. But I saw no carrion birds or beasts about at all. There would have been even if he had been killed a few weeks ago. His bones would not have been quite picked clean yet."

"We must search for him, Beinn. I need to know where that damned Englishman has got to, and I need to know if he is dead or alive." Malcolm Scott sighed. "God forgive me, but I hope the fellow dead. I will not have Alix distressed again by the man, and especially as she is now with bairn. Say nothing, Beinn. Gather a few of the men, and we shall go hunting this day for a sick old fox."

"And if you find him, my lord?" the captain asked quietly.

"I will have no choice but to put him out of his misery," the Laird of Dunglais said with a deep sigh. "It is a sad thing when you must kill a man not in honorable combat."

"You must do what you must do to protect your wife and bairns, my lord. There can be neither dishonor nor sin in that," the big man responded. "The priest will surely grant you absolution for such a deed. I would seek him out now."

The laird nodded, and without another word hurried off to find Father Donald. He discovered him in the little churchyard seated upon a stone bench in prayer. Malcolm Scott cleared his throat softly, and the priest looked up.

"Ah, my lord, is there some way I may be of help to you this fine day?" Father Donald said with a smile.

"Aye, Father," the laird replied, and then he told the priest of the discovery Beinn had made out on the moor and what must be done should Sir Udolf be found. "I would seek absolution for any sin I must commit, Good Priest, but I see no other choice open to me in this matter. My wife and bairns must not again be distressed by this man."

Father Donald did not hesitate. "Kneel," he said to the laird, and when Malcolm Scott knelt before him he absolved him of the sin of killing, signing him with the cross as he finished, and his lord arose to his feet once again. "There is no choice for you, my lord. I see that, but pray God the man is already dead and in purgatory so your conscience need never trouble you again in this matter. You go with my personal blessing as well. Does the lady know?" Father Donald asked.

"Nay, and I would not tell her. She was so relieved when the matter was finally settled that I have not the heart to distress her, especially now."

"Then the fewer who know the better. Let the men with you and Beinn believe that they are indeed out hunting game in preparation for the winter to come," the priest advised his master. "If any learn the truth, it is certain to come to the ears of another, and another, until finally some serving wench hears it and tells Fenella or Iver."

The laird couldn't help but chuckle at Father Donald's observation. "You're right, and I will heed your wisdom," he agreed. "Thank you." And the laird hurried off again to tell his wife that he was going hunting.

" 'Tis early," Alix said. She was now seated in the hall at her loom, weaving a new tapestry. "Now even autumn yet."

"But the day is fair," he told her. "And who knows what kind of a winter it will be? I should sooner have too much than not enough game hanging in the larder. And if we cannot eat it all ourselves, we will share it with the village."

"Oh, you are just restless." Alix laughed, and then she waved him off with a smile. "I envy you, for I should enjoy a good gallop myself."

He put a big hand on her rounded belly. "Birth the bairn first, my love," he said, and gently patted the mound beneath his fingers.

"Don't wake it," she cautioned him.

"You are still not certain, as you were with our lad?"

Alix shook her head. "This bairn keeps its own counsel, my lord. I think perhaps I carry a future bishop," she said with another smile.

He bent and kissed her lips. "If I find a pheasant, you shall have a fine feather or two for your blue velvet cap, my sweet Alix." Then he was gone from the hall.

Alix watched him go, considering how fortunate she was in her husband. Then her attention was drawn to Fiona, who came skipping into the hall. "Are your lessons done?" she asked her young stepdaughter.

"Aye," Fiona said. "May I put some of my own stitches in your tapestry, Alix?"

"How would you enjoy learning to make one of your own?" her stepmother asked.

"Oh, could I?" Fiona squealed, delighted.

"I will have Iver find another frame and set it up here in the hall near me," Alix said. "Then we will stretch the fabric and fit it to the frame and begin." She heard the sound of horses in the courtyard. "Your da has gone hunting," she told Fiona.

"Oh," Fiona said, sounding disappointed. "I should have liked to have gone with him." But then she brightened. "But if I had I would not learn how to make a tapestry."

"I would have liked to have gone with them too," Alix said, and then she called to Iver to help them.

Outside, the laird and his men departed. As the point of the excursion was to hunt they did so while Beinn and the laird carefully scoured the hillsides they rode looking for any sign of Sir Udolf Watteson. Finally, as the two men traveled a bit apart from the main troop, Beinn spied something in the grass and, riding over, he reached down to pick it up. It was a dark velvet bag cap trimmed in rabbit fur, somewhat the worse for wear at this point, but the small tarnished silver broach with a little ruby proclaimed its owner as a man of rank or means or possibly both. He handed it to the laird.

Malcolm Scott examined the cap. "I couldn't say if it is Sir Udolf's or not," he told his captain, "but it probably is. We can find no body. There are no carrion creatures about. Therefore I must assume the man lives. He obviously fell from his horse. Perhaps he was injured. But where could he be?"

"He could have been found," Beinn said slowly.

"By whom?" the laird wanted to know. "And if he was found, why was he not brought to Dunglais? These are my lands, and there is no keep nearer."

Beinn hesitated, and then he said, "*Her* cottage is nearby, my lord."

"Jesu! Mary!" the laird swore softly. "I had forgotten. I think not of her anymore, Beinn. Not since my sweet Alix came into my life to show me that love truly exists."

"Her servants are decent folk, my lord. If they found Sir Udolf injured they would have brought him back to heal his wounds," Beinn said.

"And if he spoke with them he would have told them why he is here, and she will have learned of Alix and our bairns. Jesu! Mary!" Malcolm Scott swore again. "The bitch was always jealous even when there was no cause."

"Shall I go, my lord, and investigate the matter?" Beinn asked.

"Not now, for the others would wonder where you have gone, and I am not of a mind to make explanations. If I do not, they will be even more curious. Tomorrow is time enough, Beinn. Ride out at first light. Reconnoiter, and see what you can find. Then report back to me when you have. Take a few days. Be in no hurry. If Sir Udolf is injured he will be within the house. I do not want us to tip our hand. If the bitch has learned of Alix, I will take care of the matter quickly. And this time I will show her no mercy. I should not have to begin with, but killing a woman, even one like Robena Ramsay, goes against my grain," Malcolm Scott said.

"Aye, my lord, I understand. I will watch carefully," Beinn told his master. And then together the two men rejoined the hunting party returning home to Dunglais late in the afternoon with half a dozen grouse, a pheasant, and a duck.

Chapter 17

obena Ramsay came down from her own bedchamber in late afternoon to the kitchen. She was dressed in a burnt-orange jersey gown with a low neckline, her long black hair contained by a simple copper caul. "Is the meal near to ready?" she asked her serving woman. "The day grows late." She sighed. "I shall lament the loss of that fine cock of his. I had so wanted to enjoy it. It has been months since I enjoyed a good fucking. I am almost desperate enough to take your brother to my bed."

"Mistress!" Fyfa looked both horrified and distressed.

Robena laughed. "Do not fret yourself," she told her servant. "I know his mind is that of a lad, though he is long grown. One taste of my cunt and he would be lost to me forever. I certainly do not want a jealous, half-witted lover mooning about me. Especially when the next fine lad comes upon our little cottage. I can be patient, but I do hope we will have a lusty visitor or two before the winter arrives and we are snowed in for several months. Do you never get hungry for a sturdy cock, Fyfa?"

"I planned to go to the church, but when our da died, our brother would not give the nunnery my dower portion," she answered. "But I do not have to be within a convent's walls to maintain my virtue, mistress," Fyfa said quietly.

Robena shrugged. Then she said, "Did you take him some garments?"

"I found breeks, a sherte, and jerkin to fit him, but I thought it would be better if you brought them to him. That way he could not flee us this afternoon," Fyfa responded.

"Well considered, Fyfa," Robena approved. "Give them to me. And serve the supper in a few minutes. I want him buried before moonrise."

Fyfa took the clothing from the table where they lay and handed them to her mistress. Receiving them, Robena departed the kitchen and made her way to the small bedroom down the narrow hall behind the stairs. Entering, she found Sir Udolf standing by the single window staring out. "My lord, I have brought you some garments to wear. They belong to my cousin who comes to visit now and again. They are sturdy and they are serviceable though not, I fear, quite as elegant as a man of your rank should possess. But I was fortunate to have them. I had quite forgotten he left them, but Fyfa reminded me."

"I am grateful to you, madame," Sir Udolf replied. "The Laird of Dunglais will know who I am without my fine feathers, as will my dear Alix." He pulled the breeks on beneath the simple chemise he had been wearing and then the sherte. He found the materials of both garments rough against his skin, but as she had said, they were serviceable. A leather jerkin completed his outfit. It had horn buttons. Clothed he felt stronger and more in control of himself again.

"Ahh, how well you look," Robena complimented him with a small smile. "Now, come into what I refer to as my hall," she invited him. "I did not always live in a cottage on the moor. Fyfa has prepared us a good supper. And in the morning I shall direct you to Dunglais, which is not very far." She led him from the little bedchamber down the corridor and into a small rectangular room with a large hearth.

"It is still light," he said. "Could I not reach Dunglais if I departed now?"

"If you had a horse, perhaps," Robena replied. "But on foot? Nay, my lord. You will need much of tomorrow, and after your illness you should not overnight on the moor. Dunglais is several long miles, and if you will but gaze out my cottage door you will see the sun will soon set. It is no longer high summer, my lord. But come and have supper with me. Then you will tell me of your home and your woman." She could see he was actually debating with himself as to whether to remain or set out. Robena quickly looked for the pitcher of wine and, after finding it, poured him a small goblet. "Here, my lord," she said, handing it to him.

He took it from her almost absently, sipped, and then said, "I suppose you are right, madame. I do not really know the countryside, and might easily become lost again. And as I am now unarmed, there are wild beasts to consider."

"Indeed, my lord, you are wise to remain but a few hours more," she almost purred at him. "Ah, here are Fyfa and Rafe with our supper." She led him to a table already set with a linen cloth where their meal was now being set out. "Let me serve you, my lord," Robena said. "Thank you, Fyfa. Rafe, wait outside the door. If I need you I will call you." She waved them from the room, and then proceeded to fill a bread trencher with capon, trout, and a potage of vegetables consisting of onions, peas, and carrots in a creamed sauce. Putting it before him, she served herself. She buttered some bread for him, adding a wedge of cheese.

They ate, and when he had finished, looking more relaxed than he had since they had brought him to the cottage, Robena served him a plate of Fyfa's custard with plum jam. The first pitcher of wine was already emptied, and so she called to Rafe to bring another. "I find wine helps me sleep," she remarked. "And you will want to sleep well tonight so you may start your journey early, my lord."

"How far are you from Dunglais?" he wanted to know.

"About eight miles," she told him. "You must go north and just slightly east from my cottage, my lord." She filled his now-empty wine cup.

He shoved a piece of bread and cheese into his mouth and drank it down. The cup was filled again, and he sipped it thoughtfully. "I suppose I could not travel so far now with the sun set," Sir Udolf remarked. "So I shall accept your hospitality for another night, but no more. A pity my horse could not be found." He stood, clutching the cup, and walked to the door of the cottage to gaze out at the darkening skies.

From his place in the heather where he lay observing the cottage Beinn saw the man shadowed in the doorway. It was not the lack-witted Rafe, for Rafe was a big man. This fellow was of medium height, and stocky. So the bitch had found herself a lover to scratch that unquenchable itch of hers. Beinn thought back several years when Robena had been in residence at the keep and his master's wife.

Several times while working in the stables he had thought that someone was watching him. It always amused him, for he knew that the serving wenches considered him a fine man. With his sherte off as he pitched hay or curried a horse, his muscles rippling, he could arouse their lust, and he was never above a quick tumble in an empty stall. Sometimes he even heard them giggling, and he would stop, pretending to be tired and, turning about as he rubbed the sweat from his forehead, give them a good glimpse of his brawny, hairy chest.

One day as he worked, a lass came up behind him, putting her arms about him, one hand reaching about and down to fondle his cock. He was easily aroused, and let the wench have her way. She'd pay for her boldness in a few minutes when he put her on her back and gave her a good fucking. Reaching about, he turned her around so that her back was to him. She giggled as he pulled her gown down from her shoulders to her waist so he might feel up her breasts. They were large and filled his big hands. He pulled her gown up after a few minutes, one hand cupping her mons. She was already so wet, her juices were running down the insides of her plump thighs. His finger found her little love button, and she squealed with pleasure.

"By Christ, you're an eager little wench," he growled in her ear. "Give us a kiss then, and you'll have a good long fucking for your reward, lass." He turned her about, and found himself staring into the dancing blue eyes of the laird's wife. Horrified, he had shoved her away. She fell into a pile of hay, laughing at his surprise. He had stepped back away from her, shocked, as she spread her bare legs to him.

"Lady . . ." He could say no more.

"Come, Beinn," she invited him, her fingers parting her nether lips wide. "You want to fuck me. I know it. Your cock is bursting forth from your breeks, and a fine cock it is too. And I want to be fucked by that beautiful cock of yours. Come, don't be shy. I am your mistress, and I command you to fuck me. *Now!*"

He had undone his breeks in his eagerness, and indeed his cock was thrusting forth from them. He was as hard as a rock, and it was painful. But he pushed himself back into his garment, fastening it as quickly as his shaking hands could, and retreating from the woman lying on that pile of hay.

Robena's face had grown dark with her anger as his refusal became apparent. Her voice was low and measured, but deadly as she spoke. "Do you think your master is the only man to have ever ridden between my thighs, you dolt? My brothers broke me in before I married, although my stupid husband believed me a virgin because I screamed when he first had me. And of course there was the skin of chicken's blood for the sheets." She laughed. "The king even lusted after me when we were at court, but forbore my company for his friendship with my husband. Fortunately the Earl of Huntley was not so scrupulous. He was a vigorous, if uninspired, lover. But now I am home again, and your master bores me. I must have a lover, and you could please me, Beinn. Come now, and lie with me. Fuck me hard and deep. I will not tell if you won't." She smiled seductively at him, beckoning with her finger.

He had turned and left the stables. He was at first confused as to what to do. He had had his hands on his lord's wife, fondled her breasts, stroked her cunny. Should he go to Father Donald and confess this monumental sin? He was close to weeping with his shame and the dishonor. He sought out the priest, who listened quietly and then spoke the words of comfort that Beinn had needed to hear.

"You are not to blame, my son, for this transgression. The woman tricked and entrapped you, and while you may have fondled her while her identity was unknown to you, you left off upon seeing her face. I have long suspected that the lady was not the wife our laird deserves, but until he learns the truth they are joined under God's law. For the sin of your unbridled lust, however, I must punish you. You will be present at the early Mass for a month, and at Vespers as well, Beinn. And you will keep your own counsel, saying naught to the laird."

"What if she accuses me of assaulting her?" Beinn asked Father Donald, still frightened by his encounter with Robena.

"She will say nothing, Beinn, for she does not want her husband suspicious of her, and she is obviously seeking a lover to amuse her. She chose you because among the laird's men you hold a small rank. She will bother with none of the rest of them, for the lady believes them beneath her even as you are," Father Donald had told him.

And of course, Beinn thought as he lay watching the cottage, she had indeed sought out a lover, who had turned out to be her husband's wicked half brother. When he had caught them he had killed his sibling. Many thought he had killed Robena too, but Beinn knew better, for he had helped his master. After the laird had buried his half brother he had taken his captain into his confidence. They had ridden out, found Robena, and transported her to a convent, where she was incarcerated while the laird made other arrangements for his adulterous wife.

The evil bitch had murdered some poor beggar woman she had found on the moor, and was exchanging clothes with her when they had caught up with her. They had half hidden the body to decompose and be found at a later date when the laird would identify it as Robena's and the matter would end. Then the laird had installed Robena in the cottage below with the two servants he had found in Edinburgh. His master had not wanted any other of his people to know Robena still lived. He had cleverly avoided any feud with the Ramsays in this way, and only Beinn knew his secret.

It was a confidence the big captain wished he did not carry. But then he considered that was the real punishment for his sins. The darkness set in, and he stood up, no longer fearful of being seen. The lights from the cottage twinkled invitingly. He wondered who the man in the door had been. Was it Sir Udolf? He would watch for another day or two and then return to Dunglais to report to his master. He worried that if it was the Englishman he would have told Robena things it was better she not know. And if Beinn knew Robena Ramsay he knew she would be seeking revenge. The lights in the cottage began to go out but for the main room.

Sir Udolf Watteson came to stand in the door once more. His belly hurt, and he was feeling very sleepy.

"What is it, my lord?" Robena asked, coming to stand near him.

"Suddenly I am not well," he told her. "Was the capon fresh, madame?"

"The food was all quite fresh, my lord, and as you can see I am suffering no ill effects. Drink a bit more of your wine," she encouraged him. "Perhaps it will help."

He gulped down the bit remaining in his cup and, holding it out to her, said, "More!"

"Alas, my lord, you have had more than enough," Robena told him. "You drank the second pitcher all by yourself. Soon you will sleep, but it is a sleep from which you will not awaken, I fear. If you believe in God, Sir Udolf, make your peace with him now before it is too late." And she smiled at him sweetly.

"What have you done?" he gasped.

"Killed you," Robena replied sanguinely.

"Why? What have I done to you?"

"You poor old fool," Robena said, rubbing his balding pate in an oddly comforting gesture. "You have done nothing to me. But I cannot have you going to Dunglais. By telling me of my husband, his whore, and their bastards, you have done me a great service. Now I shall have the revenge on Malcolm Scott I have been seeking all these years since he incarcerated me out here on this lonely moor. I will not let you take that from me. Say your prayers, my lord, for you will be shortly dead."

The darkness was reaching up to claim him. Sir Udolf could actually feel his heart slowing. He was overcome by a sudden weakness and fell to his knees, struggling for breath, and finding it a final time, he grated out, "God curse you, lady?" Then he collapsed and died on her doorsill.

"Rafe! Come and bury the fellow before he begins to release his bowels and stink," Robena Ramsay said. She yawned, and turned back into the cottage.

On his hillside Beinn had watched the pair as they stood in the door. He had been very surprised when the man had collapsed. Robena had shown no signs of distress, nor had she cried out. Instead she had turned away and disappeared back into her home. A moment later the light in her second-story chamber had flickered brightly. A shadow of another man, Rafe, came into the cottage entry. He picked up the body and threw it over his shoulder. Beinn could see the shadow of something in his other hand. A shovel?

The moon was beginning to rise over the hills, but it was not yet bright enough to light the region. Keeping to the shadows, Beinn slipped down the hill so he might more closely observe Rafe. The lack-wit shambled up a small rise near the dwelling and, laying the body down, he stripped it of boots and clothing. Then, with a foot he pushed it, and it disappeared. There was obviously a predug grave there, Beinn realized as Rafe began filling it in with his shovel. Finished with his task, Rafe walked upon the grave several times in order to tamp down the earth. Then, shovel over his shoulder, he returned down the rise and went into the little barn where Beinn knew he slept with the beasts.

The Dunglais captain sat down in the heather and waited. All the lights in the cottage were now extinguished. He waited. The moon rose slowly, slowly, and then it was filling the sky. About him Beinn could see everything with clarity. He arose now and found his way to the new grave. Then he began digging with his big hands.

Once he was past the top layer than Rafe had stamped down it was easy if tedious work. He did not seek to open the whole grave. He just wished to see the face of the man who had been so unceremoniously buried there this night. Eventually he was able to make a place for himself to stand and then kneel. Carefully he pulled the earth away, going deeper and deeper into the dirt until finally his fingers reached the body. Brushing the dirt away with his hands, he was at last able to see the face of the unfortunate man. It was Sir Udolf Watteson. Beinn nodded to himself. Poor devil, he thought, and crossed himself.

Then he climbed from the grave and began filling it in again. This was more tedious work, especially without a shovel. But when the dawn came the grave could not look like it had been tampered with or suspicions would be aroused. His horse awaited him on the hillside, and when he had finished he would begin his return to Dunglais. There was no reason to remain observing the cottage any longer, and the laird should know what had transpired. Sir Udolf's lips had been a bright purple and swollen. It was obvious he had been poisoned. How many others had the bitch Robena Ramsay murdered? Were there other graves here on this little rise? He bent to smooth the last bit of earth into place, and as he did he felt a sharp pain touch the back of his head and a bright white light flashed before his eyes as his legs gave way and he fell to the earth.

When Beinn awoke once more he found himself in a small chamber upon a bed to which he seemed to be manacled hand and foot. And he was shocked to see he was completely naked. His head hurt fiercely, and he was very thirsty. As his eyes focused more clearly he saw Rafe sitting in a corner staring blankly at nothing. "Oi!" he called out to the man. "I need water, and undo these damned chains!"

Rafe shambled to his feet and picked up a leather water bag. He pushed the spout into Beinn's mouth so he might drink. "Mistress says you must stay," he told the other man. Then he grinned. "Mistress has been wanting a fine cock for her cunny for many weeks now. She says you have a fine cock," he chuckled.

Beinn swallowed down the water. It tasted bitter, but it was drinkable. When he had finished he pulled his head away. "Your mistress is a murderous bitch," he said.

"Aye," Rafe agreed, "she is. But she is the mistress. I will go and tell her you are awake. I'm glad I did not kill you, Beinn. The mistress is much happier to have you alive than dead. She gave me sweets as a reward." Then he departed the chamber.

"Christ's bones!" Beinn swore softly. Somehow the lack-wit had come upon him just as he was finishing refilling the grave and hit him with something hard. He was no fool. The bitch meant to use him, and then she would kill him as she had obviously been doing to all her lovers. He tested the strength of the chains attached to the manacles about his ankles and wrists. There was no weakness in them. He had to find a way to free himself so he might defend himself. As for pleasuring her, he thought grimly, he had refused her once. What made her believe he would change his mind now?

The door to the chamber opened, and Robena stepped into the room. "Ah, Beinn, how good of you to visit. You usually do not remain when you bring us our supplies." Walking to the bed, she knelt down and took his cock in her hand. "I have always wanted this," she said. "It is such a large weapon for a big man." She drew the foreskin down, and then, bending her head, licked the tip of it. "Ummm," she purred. "It is even tastier than I imagined, Beinn. And I see it is beginning to awaken from its slumbers even as you have. We shall have such fun together, darling."

"I'll not fuck you, you evil bitch!" he said angrily.

"Nay, but I will fuck you, Beinn. And you will come for me, and you will sob like a lad with his first whore. And you will keep pleasuring me until I grow tired of you, darling," Robena told him with a smile.

"The laird will come looking for me," he warned her.

Robena laughed. "I hope he does," she said. "And when he comes he will find us together in this bed. Whatever you choose to tell him, he will believe you betrayed him. My servants and I shall confirm it. I shall tell him you bedded me at Dunglais, and afterwards here each time you came. I shall swear you have been my lover for years." She laughed cruelly. "Do you think I have forgotten how you insulted me in that stable? I offered myself to you, and you refused me! Well, you shall not refuse me now, Beinn."

"I do refuse you!" he snarled at her.

"Nay, you will not," Robena told him. She bent her head, took his cock into her mouth, and began to suck lustily upon it. She licked him and nibbled upon the tender column of flesh. It began to thicken and lengthen without her mouth as she played with him. She heard him gasp with his surprise. He had no idea the water he had swilled so eagerly was well laced with aphrodisiacs that would keep him aroused for the next few hours in spite of himself. He would yield to her desires because he would have no other choice. But eventually he would come to her willingly. For now, however, it excited her greatly to force this big man to her will. She sucked him hard, and he finally came with a cry of anger as she eagerly drew every bit of his seed from his cock and swallowed it down. "That is a fine start," she said, licking her lips and smiling down into his face.

Beinn could not believe what had just happened. A woman did not assault a man and force his seed from him. Yet Robena had done just that, and his cock still stood tall. What sorcery was this? Was she a witch as well as a whore? "What have you done to me that you can use my body in such a lewd fashion?" he said to her.

"Oh, come, Beinn. Do men not force women?" Robena replied. Her delicate long fingers played with his stiff length thoughtfully.

"That is different," he replied.

"Not really," she told him. "When a man's cock is engaged by lust, he does not ask the woman in his bed if she is also lustful. He just mounts her and has his way because he believes it is his right."

"Have you never loved?" Beinn asked her.

"Love is for fools, darling. Now I need a taste of that fine cock of yours, and I am not of a mind to wait," she said as she arose and then mounted him. Positioning herself over his great length, she lowered her body to take him in, sighing gustily as he filled her. "Ahh, God, that is good," she murmured as she sheathed him entirely. Then, leaning forward, she took his face in her two hands and kissed him hard. "Tell me it feels good," she purred at him, and then, leaning back, she began to ride him hard.

He fought with himself to deny her what she wanted, but he could not. Whatever had been in the water, and he was now certain something had been, his manly lusts were well aroused and beyond his own control. Unable to help himself he rose up and fastened his mouth about the nipple of one of her large breasts. He sucked on it hard, and then his teeth clamped down on the tender flesh. She spasmed around his throbbing cock and screamed with her own pleasure as she fell forward.

"Ah, you devil! That was very good," Robena praised him as she finally sat up again. "I can see we shall have a fine time together."

Beinn closed his eyes, ashamed. What had made him do that? And then he realized that she was still mounted and he was still hard as iron.

Robena leaned forward and rubbed a breast against his lips. "Open your mouth again, darling, and suck me sweetly," she ordered him.

Mutinously, he clamped his lips tightly together, and she laughed. "If you persist in being a bad boy, Beinn, I shall have to whip you into obedience. Yes, I think I shall have to give you just a little taste of punishment so you understand that I am the mistress here, my captain. It is your duty to serve me as I wish to be served. Rafe! To me!" she called to her serving man. Then she climbed off of him and, to his surprise, put the pointed tip of a dirk to his throat. "Rafe must move you, and while I know thoughts of escape are already in your mind, do not attempt to be foolish. My dirk's tip is poisoned. The slightest cut, and you will die a most painful and swift death, darling. So be a good boy, and let Rafe do what he must."

Go to the devil, bitch, Beinn thought as Rafe came to unfasten the manacles about his wrists. But as he sat up he was overwhelmed by a terrible wave of dizziness. Before he might consider a struggle, the wiry Rafe yanked him forward over the end of the bed and fastened his wrists into clamps that were set into the floor of the chamber. His ankles remained manacled to the bedposts. Beinn had never in his life felt so helpless. Or so angry and frustrated. Sweet Jesu! What did she do in this place that it was so equipped for torture of this nature? The laird should have killed her when he had the chance, Beinn thought. It was his right to slay an adulterous wife. The Ramsays' pride could have been assuaged in some manner. Then her hand smoothed over his buttocks.

"Round and tight," she said softly. "And so ready for my strap and my switch. Leave us, Rafe! I will call you when I want you." Then she waited until her servant had departed the room before speaking to him. "I want you to understand, darling Beinn, that I am your mistress. You are a hard man. A difficult man. You lack discipline, but I shall teach you that fine art this day. First you will receive ten strokes of my rod. It will be painful, but pain can lead to pleasure. My leather tawse will warm your buttocks after the rod has punished them. Then your cheeks will be burnished to a fine glow with a bunch of switches. And finally . . ." She paused and laughed. "I shall let the last be a surprise. Now, are you ready for the rod, darling?"

"Go to hell, bitch!" he growled at her.

She laughed, and the first blow fell upon his helpless flesh. He sucked in his breath, but remained silent. By the sixth blow he could no longer deny the pain, and he howled with it. Robena laughed again as she laid the last four blows upon him. "I have never had a man last so long before crying out," she told him in a delighted tone. "You obviously have a goodly capacity for punishment. I shall render you two more blows of the rod," and he yelped in pain as she did. Tossing the rod aside, she took up her tawse—a strip of leather several inches wide, its ends cut into narrow fingers that had been knotted. "Now to heat up your bottom," she said as she began to flog him.

Oddly, the leather beating him hurt less than the hard rod had, but he was still, to his shame, unable to restrain his cries.

"I like the sound the strap makes when it meets your lovely rump," Robena said. "Your white flesh is becoming quite pink. Soon the shade will deepen until the pink turns a most delightful shade of red." She wielded her tawse to deliver several more smacks to his flesh. "Beg me to cease, Beinn," she taunted him.

"Go to the devil!" he cried.

She laid several more spanks upon his hapless flesh. "Do you want me to stop, darling? But oh, I must, for your bottom is quite scarlet. Now I must burnish it with my switches," she told him.

The switches stung and irritated until he thought he could stand no more. She seemed to sense it and ceased the punishment, rubbing her hand gently over his wounded flesh. Her fingers playfully drew the twin halves of his buttocks aside, and she ran a finger about his anus.

"God in his heaven, bitch, what are you doing?" Beinn demanded of her.

"I am curious," she murmured softly. "Have you ever taken another cock there, Beinn, my darling?" The finger rubbed him suggestively.

"Are you daft?" he shouted at her. "Do you think I am a sodomite to copulate with other men, bitch?"

Her finger circled the sensitive little aperture over and over again. "You were not even curious of such things as a boy?" she persisted. "My brothers said all lads were."

"Never!" he denied vehemently. "*Never!* Your brothers were surely as depraved as you are, lady."

"Tell me you want me to put my finger in your ass," Robena said softly. Her finger pressed against the opening and it began to give way.

"Nay! Nay! And again, nay!" Beinn roared.

"But I want to do it," Robena said, "and I will. You cannot stop me!" Then, wetting her finger with her own juices, which were already flowing, she pushed her middle finger into him as far as it would go. "There now, darling," she crooned at him. "That is not so terrible, is it, Beinn?" She began to simulate the actions of his cock with her finger. "Do you liked being fucked this way, darling? Is it nice?" Robena purred. "Shall I let you do it to me when you are a little more amenable?"

The Dunglais captain was outraged by her actions, but he was also horrified by his own reaction to the finger moving back and forth in his ass. It actually excited him when it should have repelled him. Yet that wicked finger in concert with whatever potions she had fed him was stoking his lusts. He could feel his cock swelling painfully beneath him, and he groaned, helpless to this shameful arousal.

"Shall I make you come, Beinn?" she asked him. She bent and slipped her other hand beneath him to feel his swollen cock. "Ohh, how hard you are," she cried, excited. "I must have that great cock of yours again! *I must!* Rafe, quickly!"

The serving man burst into the room. "Mistress?"

"I must feel his weight atop me," Robena said, and she was almost weeping in her eagerness to have him in that manner. "Get him back on the bed, facedown. Leave his legs free, but keep his arms chained. Hurry! Hurry!" She began to play with herself in her great need as she scrambled to get on the bed.

The serving man did as he was bid, and again Beinn was overcome with dizziness as he was yanked about. Then he was kneeling between Robena's thighs, and there was no help for him. He had to fuck her or he would die. Without release, he would be crippled for hours, and he believed now that he might break the chains that held his arms fastened to the bedposts. He had been more tightly constrained when his legs were bound. "Get out!" he growled at Rafe, and to his surprise the man obeyed him. "Now, bitch," he said to her, and he drove himself to his hilt as hard and as deep as he could go.

Robena screamed, but it was a sound of pleasure, of satisfaction. "Fuck me, you great brute!" she said to him. "I want to come thrice, and if you fail me I shall beat you again, and this time it will be the worse for you."

Beinn said nothing to her, but instead set to work to do as she bid him. She came quickly for him the first time and again the second time. But as his cock throbbed with its own need, she withheld herself from him a third time. He was not certain he could contain his juices much longer, but then he felt the tremors within her beginning, and Robena began to moan and cry as a great pleasure overcame her.

"Yes!" she screamed. "Yes! Yes! *Yes!* Oh, you beast, I cannot stop coming! You have killed me with your passion as I knew you could all those years ago!" She shuddered and fell into a deep swoon.

He had seen this happen to a woman once before. She would not regain consciousness for some time, so great had her sexual excitement been. Able to kneel, he looked at the chain attached to the manacle. Then he examined the bedposts. They were solid oak, but now he saw they were carved so that the middle of the post was thinner than the rest of it. He slid the iron ring at the end of the short chain down to that narrow spot, and then he began to yank against it. After several hard tugs the bedpost gave way, and Beinn was able to slide the ring off of it. There was no way to remove the manacle and chain from his wrist, but he would in effect be free once he snapped the other post, which he quickly did.

Beinn slid off of the bed quietly and looked about the chamber. Against a wall was a small trunk. Opening it, he discovered his breeks, sherte, and boots. He quickly dressed himself despite the disadvantage of the manacles and chains he bore. Then he went to the small window and squeezed himself through it. He immediately headed for the hill where his horse had been tethered. But the animal was not there. Had Rafe found it and stabled it? Had it wandered off? Beinn decided he had no time to go back or even consider where the horse might be. He had to reach the keep. It was not quite evening and he began to run. When darkness settled in he slowed to a walk.

With luck the bitch would not awaken for another few hours. Rafe had been taught not to disturb his lady, nor would Fyfa. Beinn trudged on. He was furious with himself for having been so careless as to be put at a disadvantage by the lack-wit Rafe. The man walked like a damned cat, for he hadn't heard him at all when he came up behind Beinn. As for the beating and sexual torture the bitch had inflicted upon him, he had wanted to kill her when he got free, but then he had realized that that was his master's right and not his. He felt no guilt for what had happened between them this time. She had forced him, and he knew better now, though he would confess the sordid hours spent in the cottage to poor Father Donald. It wasn't something he wanted to keep to himself, and it was the priest's business to listen. Though he had been bound and impelled to her will, Beinn knew his lust had also been responsible, especially when Robena lay beneath him, clawing at his back and howling with her satisfaction.

The moon rose, and while on the wane it still gave him more than enough light to travel. He began to run carefully and after several hours the tower of Dunglais Keep came into view. He stopped and listened carefully. The moor was silent but for the soft rustle of a few night creatures out hunting in the grass. None pursued him, he realized to his great relief. He moved swiftly across the moor, down a hillock, through Dunglais village, and finally up to the closed gates of the keep. He knocked softly.

"Who goes there?" a young voice quavered.

"Beinn, your captain," he replied.

The little grate in the door was opened and a face peered out at him. It was quickly shut, and the small privy gate was unbarred for him. Beinn hurried through, saying as he did to one of the several men on duty, "Wake the blacksmith! Wake Iver, and find the priest for me if he's in the keep tonight. If not, fetch him at first light." Then he directed his footsteps to the smithy.

The blacksmith came, looking irritable until he saw the manacles and chains about Beinn's thick wrists.

"Get them off," the captain instructed, "and ask no questions of me."

"Aye," the smith said with a nod of his head. He was by nature a taciturn man.

Iver arrived as the first manacle and chain fell from Beinn's wrist. He cocked an eyebrow with curiosity, but did not ask. If Beinn wished to tell him, he would.

"Fetch the laird, but be careful not to frighten the lady," the captain said. "She should know nothing of this."

Iver nodded silently and disappeared back into the building. The second manacle and chain fell loose. Beinn was rubbing his wrists as Iver returned.

"He'll see you in his privy chamber," Iver said. "Can I go back to bed now?"

"Aye, and say naught to Fenella," Beinn responded.

"Fenella?"

"She's in your bed, isn't she?" the captain said with a small grin.

Iver neither denied nor confirmed Beinn's query.

The two men entered the house, Iver going one way and Beinn the other. Reaching his master's privy chamber, he knocked and then entered.

The laird shoved a goblet of wine in his hand. "What happened?" he asked. "Why did you not remain watching longer?"

"There was no need. Sir Udolf was there. She's killed him, and he's buried. I would have been back a day sooner but that her lack-wit somehow heard me and hit me with something, probably a shovel. When I awoke I found myself restrained. It took me several hours to break free from the wooden posts I was chained to, and then several more hours traversing the moor home in the darkness."

"Your horse?"

"Probably wandered off. I didn't want to waste the time searching for it. While all in the house were sleeping when I broke free,

I feared discovery. I was fortunate the dog did not hear me and set up barking as I went through the window. There is a chance they have the horse though," Beinn admitted honestly. "I was already up the hill to fetch it when I found it gone. I thought it better I not go back, my lord. It was more important I reach you. I think *she* meant to kill me."

The laird nodded. "Aye, she is not afraid to murder, as we know. You've done well, Beinn."

"What will you do, my lord?" he asked the laird.

"I am not certain I will do anything," Malcolm Scott said. "Sir Udolf is dead and so Alix will not be harassed again by him. As for Robena, let her wonder what I will do. But why did she kill him? And did he tell her of Alix and our bairns? I am curious as to what she will do, but then there is little she dare outside of her own cottage."

"I do not know if she knows of your wife and bairns, my lord," Beinn said honestly. "But I believe she may be waylaying those who stumble upon her cottage and robbing them of whatever they have."

"And probably taking the hapless men who fall into her web as lovers," the laird said dryly. "I hate the thought of imprisoning her in the old tower by Dunglais Water, but I suppose I must think on it. It would not do for either Alix or Fiona to stumble upon Robena's dwelling one day. I know I have been lenient with her. Another man would have slain her where he caught her that day, Beinn."

"Aye, my lord, they would have. But this new murder cannot go unpunished. It is true that Sir Udolf Watteson has no family to come seeking his fate. But if there have been others in the past, if there are others in the future, the bitch may not have such good fortune. You have done your best to protect her from herself, my lord, but now I fear you must protect others from her. Fyfa and Rafe are good souls, and they do their best by her, but you know that she dominates them by virtue of her position as their mistress. They can do so much. She is dangerous, and grows more so, I fear."

The laird nodded. "I do not disagree with you, Beinn," he said. "But autumn and winter are upon us. My lady will birth another bairn soon. I would not have her learn of Robena and her situation, for it will certainly distress her. And I most surely do not want Fiona ever knowing that the mother who birthed her is yet alive. The pain that woman caused my daughter has been wiped away by Alix's love for her."

"You cannot wait, my lord," Beinn pressed the laird as gently as he dared.

"I know, I know. Before the winter we will settle the matter. I would speak with Father Donald before I make any decisions about Robena. The secret must remain only with the three of us, old friend."

"Agreed, my lord," Beinn said.

"You look weary, as well you should," Malcolm Scott noted. "I know it is almost dawn, but go and find your bed for a few hours."

"Aye," Beinn responded. "I am weary, my lord." *Wearier than you can imagine*, he thought to himself as he left his master's privy chamber and went to his own space. As captain of the laird's men he had a little chamber of his own. His buttocks were sore with the beating he had received, but at least she had been careful and not drawn blood. He washed in the cold water from his pitcher as best he could, trying to rid the stench of the woman's sex from his body.

God's bones! Had the laird smelled it on him? He prayed not. But then his long walk in the night air should have helped to dissipate the stink of her. The priest had not come. He would see him later though, and tell him all that had happened. Then he would make his confession to Father Donald. The priest would agree with him. Robena Ramsay needed to be caged like the wild beast she was. Malcolm Scott's heart was much too good, but if he did not act soon his indecision could very easily lead to a tragedy.

Chapter 18

‾‿◝

*I*n the half-light of an early dawn Fyfa shook her mistress roughly awake.

Opening her eyes, Robena Ramsay snarled, "What is it? The sun is not even up yet, and you waken me?"

"He's gone!" Fyfa said.

"Gone? Who is gone?" And then Robena's blue eyes snapped fully open. "What the hell do you mean? How could he be gone? He was chained to the bedstead. He cannot be gone."

"Well, he is," Fyfa said bluntly.

Robena's eyes narrowed speculatively. "Did you or your brother . . ." she began.

"Of course not!" Fyfa snapped.

"Then how?" Robena demanded to know. "*How?*"

"The bedposts were not as sturdy as you might have supposed," Fyfa said. "He snapped them in two, took his clothing and boots from the chest, and fled."

"You put his garments in the same room where I had him imprisoned?" Robena jumped up from her bed and hit Fyfa a blow.

" 'Twas not me," Fyfa said, rubbing her cheek. " 'Twas you, mistress. You had my brother disrobe Beinn when he had dragged him into the house. I was not there. I suspect in your eagerness to see him naked you stuffed his clothing in the nearest chest, giving no thought to the possibility he might escape."

"None have ever escaped me before," Robena said, sitting heavily upon her bed.

"The laird will know now," Fyfa said, and her voice shook.

"Perhaps," Robena mused. "Or perhaps not."

"Beinn is loyal to his master," Fyfa reminded her mistress.

"But he is also a proud man," Robena replied. "I wonder if he will be willing to admit that I beat him and forced him to my will. Ahh, and I had such fine plans for him for today," she sighed.

"But why was he here in the first place?" Fyfa wondered aloud. "It was not his time to come with supplies. And Rafe found him at the new grave."

"I don't know why he was here," Robena said. "It doesn't matter to me. He knows nothing of Sir Udolf. Why would he? It is not his concern."

"Perhaps the laird's men found Sir Udolf's horse," Fyfa suggested.

"More likely some traveler on foot found it and claimed it for himself," Robena said cynically. "You fret too much, Fyfa. Aye, Beinn has probably returned to Dunglais, and he will have found a way to explain the manacles and chains, but I doubt he has told my husband the truth. How could he, and keep his position? Everyone knows that Colm was always very jealous of me, of the men who admired me. Do you really think he would believe the truth if Beinn had the courage to tell him? Nay. My husband's captain will want to keep his position at Dunglais. Do not men always wish to keep what is theirs, Fyfa? We are still safe, for my husband would not want known what he has done to me. I am not pleased, however, by a dreary, lonely winter."

"It is only September, mistress," Fyfa said dryly. "Time enough yet to catch some unsuspecting traveler in your web."

Robena brightened. "Aye," she said. "And I have other plans to execute as well. I have decided that I want my daughter. Sir Udolf told me that my husband's whore is raising Fiona and that the brat even addresses her as her mother. I will not have another woman mothering *my* child, nor will I reason with him in this matter. If he does not wish his bigamy revealed, nor his bastard rendered publicly illegitimate, he will give me *my* child. I shall take her, and he will keep his mouth shut or I will expose him, expose his bastards to the world. He will have no legitimate heir then."

"Mistress," Fyfa said, "this is no place for a little maid gently reared."

"She will be a help to you," Robena said carelessly. "And if she is pretty she will help me to lure travelers to our cottage. There are men in this world, Fyfa, who prefer very young lovers." And Robena laughed.

Fyfa shuddered at the cruel sound. While she did not wish to find herself and her helpless brother once again without a home, she almost wished that the laird would come and put an end to her mistress's cruel debauchery. "I'll get your meal," she said, and hurried from the bedchamber.

The autumn came to the borders. It was now October, and the weather had been beautiful and unusual for so late in the year. Her instincts had been right. No one came from Dunglais. She had set Rafe to watching the keep. Certainly at this age her daughter rode out regularly. Once she learned Fiona's habits, she would ride out on Beinn's horse, which Rafe had found the day he had brought Beinn to her, and she would take the child herself. Robena smiled. Aye, it was a far better plan. She would gain Fiona almost immediately, and Fyfa would then have someone to help her with the chores.

The brat would quickly learn that she was no longer her father's pet. Robena wondered if her daughter had ever been whipped. Well, let her disobey her mother's wishes and Fiona's bottom would soon be introduced to the hazel switch. A good beating never hurt a child. He own father had whipped her with great regularity until she had grown breasts, and then her mother would not permit it. Robena arose from her bed and began to prepare for the day ahead.

She had lost a lover, but there would be another eventually, and in the meantime there would be Fiona to amuse her.

Fyfa, of course, did not think her mistress's plan a sound one. "You are safe and comfortable here," she said. "You have the opportunity to enjoy a lover now and again. Even if you manage to take your daughter from your husband, he will certainly come after her. And this time he will kill you. When he hired my brother and me he was quite honest about you and what you had done. He did not kill you then because he wanted to be able to say with complete truth to your family that he had not slain you even though it was his right to do so. He identified the body of that poor beggar woman you killed out on the moor and exchanged clothing with as your body. He let her lay there for months in the open so that she would be unrecognizable but for the clothing she wore, in order to give truth to the lie that you were dead, mistress. He protected you and kept your father's family from further embarrassment, thereby preventing a feud."

"I would have liked a feud between the Ramsays and the Scotts," Robena said. "Perhaps I shall cause one by letting my da know I am alive and how ill treated I have been by Colm." She giggled. "Imagine all those clansmen fighting and dying over me!"

"If you keep on like this, mistress," Fyfa warned, "the laird will indeed kill you, and he has every right to do so. And if he kills you then he can in truth wed his mistress. Do you want that? Isn't is better for you to have this hold over him that you now have?"

"But he doesn't know I have a hold over him," Robena said irritably.

"He will when you take his daughter," Fyfa said. "Even if he comes and takes her back he will know that you know his secrets. You are fortunate that he does not know yours. Do not bait him. You would be wise to leave the child with him and not be bothered. Then you can live your life as you will, and he will never be the wiser. Knowing what you know, there is always time to expose his bigamy. Wouldn't you gain more satisfaction exposing his bastards after his death? Then your child should inherit."

"I want my daughter now!" Robena said. "I do not want her calling another woman her mother. I am her mother. She belongs to *me* and not to this Englishwoman. He can have his whore, but I will have my bairn."

"You haven't seen her since she was two years old," Fyfa reminded her mistress. "And the laird told me you rejected her from birth."

"But she is *mine*," Robena responded, "and I want what is mine."

Fyfa shook her head. There was no reasoning with her mistress when she got into a mood like this. Robena Ramsay was a woman who always needed something to do and now, bereft of her recent lover, she was looking about for that something. *She will bring trouble down on us all,* Fyfa thought unhappily, but there was nothing she could do. She was a servant. A favored servant to be sure, but a servant nonetheless. "Sit down at the table," she said. "You need to eat." And when she had finished cooking and serving Robena, Fyfa stepped outside of her kitchen to work in her little garden.

The day was fair and the air still held a hint of warmth. The trees and the hills were now bright with color. Fyfa watched with trepidation as her brother Rafe set off on Beinn's horse towards Dunglais. She had a very dark premonition about what was to come, but short of going to the laird herself there was nothing to be done. She couldn't risk losing their place. While Fyfa knew that she could always fend for herself, there was her poor lack-witted brother to consider. She saw how people treated folk like Rafe. Their own elder half brother had been cruel to him. Fyfa sighed. What was going to happen was going to happen.

At Dunglais the beautiful autumn weather and the knowledge that the church had lifted the threat of Sir Udolf from the laird and his wife brought about a happy change. Alix could no longer ride, but now that she was free to move outside of the keep's walls she would sometimes take her son in the pony cart while Fiona rode by her side. On other days Alix would walk with Fiona on the moors. They treasured these days, as winter was certain to set in sooner than later. One early November afternoon Alix and her stepdaughter walked out of sight of the keep picking late flowers that had escaped a recent frost and gathering small plants that had medicinal value, which they carefully put in a willow basket.

"I have to stop a moment," Alix said. She was breathing hard, and her belly was very big. "I shall be glad to have his child born. I so dislike being encumbered."

"Will you sit, Mam?" Fiona asked her.

Alix laughed wryly. "Oh, Fi, if I sit I shall not be able to get up again unless someone comes to winch me onto my feet."

Fiona giggled. "He's going to be a big lad, Mam," she said.

"You keep saying *he*," her stepmother noted.

" 'Tis a lad, Mam. I just know it. And James will have a playmate," Fiona said.

"You don't want a little sister?" Alix asked her.

"I am too big now to enjoy a little sister," Fiona said. "Remember, I am to be nine. But you must be sure my brother is not born on my birthday. I do not wish to share."

"I have already told him, but we shall see if he is an obedient lad," Alix replied, smiling at Fiona. How she loved her, Alix thought. Fiona was starting to look less like a young child and more like young girl. And with order and peace in her life now, Fiona was less and less prone to mood swings. She was learning self-control. "I think I have walked far enough today," Alix decided.

"I told you you should have taken the cart," Fiona responded. "Your burden is great now, and the bairn due to be born in another few weeks."

"You sound like Fenella," Alix teased the girl.

They turned together to walk back, Alix moving slowly, Fiona carrying the basket with their treasures. And then behind them they heard hoofbeats. A rider came up beside them and blocked their path. Alix moved to protect her stepdaughter. Then she realized that the horse's rider was a woman.

"Is this girl Fiona Scott?" the woman asked in a hard voice.

"Who wishes to know?" Alix said quietly. She was less frightened now that she saw the horse's rider was a woman.

"Who are you?" the woman now demanded.

"I am the Laird of Dunglais's wife," Alix said.

"His whore, you mean," the woman declared. "Is this the laird's daughter?"

Fiona stepped forward. "Do not dare speak to my mam like that!" she cried.

The woman laughed scornfully. *"Your mam?"* she said derisively. "She is not your mother. I am your mother, you little brat!"

"The mother who birthed me is dead," Fiona said heatedly.

"I am not dead, brat! Your father imprisoned me in a cottage out on the moor with two servants when I refused to give him another child. 'Tis true you were a disappointment to us both, but there it was. When I wanted to go back to court your father refused to allow it unless I gave him a son. I tried to run away from him, and when he caught me he put me in that cottage." She moved her horse between Alix and Fiona. Robena looked down at Alix. "Did you give him a son, whore? And I see your belly is big again. But know that you are *not* his wife. *I am!* Your bastards will inherit nothing from their father." She leaned down from her saddle and, gripping Fiona by her long black hair, so much like her own, she yanked her roughly up and over her saddle. "Tell *my* husband that I have taken *my* daughter. No whore will raise her or be called her mam whilst I live." Then, turning her horse about, she rode off with the girl, who had begun to scream and kick in an attempt to escape her captor.

Alix had teetered dangerously when Robena had drawn her mount around, for the creature's nose just brushed her. She struggled to remain on her feet, and when she had finally regained a firm footing she stood stock-still in shock for a moment or two. That the woman who had just stolen Fiona was who she said she was Alex had not even the slightest doubt. While Fiona did favor her handsome father, she also had some of her mother in her, and Alix had recognized it. Not just the silky black hair, but the bright blue eyes and the slight slant of those eyes. Robena Ramsay lived, and Alix Givet was indeed the laird's whore and her sons his bastards.

How could he have done this to her? Alix asked herself as she attempted to run back toward the keep. Did he really love her? Or was he just so desperate for sons that he did what he felt he had to do? Either way it didn't matter. She was shamed, and her children were stained with the mark of bastardy. She would never forgive him. But for now, alerting her hus—the laird—that Robena had kidnapped Fiona was more important than her outrage and her sense of betrayal. Her breath coming in short pants, she gained the lowered drawbridge and stumbled across it, crying loudly, "Fetch the laird! Saddle his horse! To horse, men of Dunglais! To horse!"

Beinn came running, and Alix collapsed against him. "My lady, my lady! What is the matter?" He looked past her. "Where is Mistress Fiona?"

"The laird's wife has her," Alix gasped.

Beinn stiffened. "My lady, you are the laird's wife," he said.

Alix looked up into his big, honest face. "Nay, I am his whore, and the wife who he married ten years ago has come out of whatever private hell she inhabits and stolen Fiona away. Get my—his daughter—back!"

Malcolm Scott ran from the house. "What has happened?" he asked her.

Alix looked up at him with angry eyes. She wanted to slay him where he stood, but now was not the time to give way to her fury. Fiona must be rescued from that horrible woman and brought home to Dunglais. "Your wife accosted us on the moor and took Fiona away," she told him.

He didn't bother to deny or explain. Ignoring her, he said to Beinn, "The bitch can't have gotten far on foot."

"She was a-horse," Alix said stonily. Then she turned on her heel and left them.

Beinn shrugged fatalistically. It was obviously his horse.

"We'll go alone," Malcolm Scott said. "We can't have this getting out of hand, or the Ramsays will be at my door spoiling for a fight. Damn!"

A stable boy ran up with the laird's big stallion and Beinn's new large gelding. The two men mounted. When they approached the gate, the laird gave instructions that the drawbridge should be drawn up after them and the gates closed until he and Beinn returned.

"Robbers have stolen Mistress Fiona," he explained. "Beinn and I will go after them and fetch my daughter home again, but the keep must be secured." Then he and his captain rode across the oak drawbridge and out onto the moor. "She'll be heading for her cottage in all likelihood," Malcolm Scott said.

Beinn nodded in agreement.

"She knows the penalty of exposing herself. I warned her that if she could not settle herself peaceably I would intern her in the dungeon of the old tower by Dunglais Water. I probably should have done it in the first place, but I could not bear to think of anyone living in that dark and damp pile of rock," the laird said.

"You should have strangled her when you caught her with Black Ian," Beinn said bluntly. "She had already been tainted by him, and I'm not so certain the Ramsays didn't cheat you when they gave you their daughter to wife. I never knew such a high-strung lass as the lady Robena. But until now she has been content to abide in her confinement."

"I couldn't kill her, Beinn. Even when I saw what she had done to that poor creature she killed in order to hide her tracks. She was a woman, and she had given me my daughter. But now I will kill her when I catch her. I have no other choice. I did not lie to the Ramsays seven years ago. Thank God they will never know of this incident."

"What will you do with Fyfa and her half-wit of a brother?" Beinn wanted to know. "You have been candid with her all along. But if you kill the lady she will know."

"They will have a choice of either remaining in the cottage, or leaving. If they leave, I will see they have the means to begin anew wherever they go," the laird said. "I will not kill Robena in their sight, so they will never know what has happened to her, and I suspect that will suit Fyfa well. She is a practical woman."

"And pretty too," Beinn said with a small smile.

The laird laughed. " 'Tis not often you speak of a woman, old friend."

"She's a good woman, my lord. When her father's heir sent them away, she remained with Rafe to look after him, for he could not fend for himself. She might have found employment alone, but who would have cared for him? I admire her."

The laird chuckled. "You're a good man yourself, Beinn," he said.

Am I? Beinn wondered, remembering his hours as Robena Ramsay's captive. At the last, when he had had her on her back, he had found a certain enjoyment in fucking the vicious little bitch. He would not be sorry to see her dead.

The two men galloped their horses across the moor in the direction of Robena's cottage. Finally they saw a horse ahead of them and they spurred the mounts to catch up.

She heard them coming. She did not bother to even turn. The young girl across her saddle had ceased to struggle and was half-conscious. But her horse began to slow its gait, limping, and she cursed volubly, finally drawing to a stop. There was no help for it. She couldn't have the damned animal collapsing beneath her.

Fiona whimpered. "Da! Mam!" she sobbed.

"Shut your mouth, you little brat. I'm your mother, and if I have to beat you to death to understand that, I will!" She dug her fingers into the girl's scalp and yanked cruelly on the dark hair so like her own.

Fiona cried out softly.

The laird and his captain had finally reached her. Malcolm Scott looked at the woman who had once been his wife. She was still beautiful, but there was something dissolute about the shape of her mouth he had never before noticed, and her beautiful bright blue eyes were hard and merciless. "You will return my daughter to me, Robena," Malcolm Scott said in a quiet but firm voice.

"*Our daughter*, Colm," she answered him.

"You rejected her at birth, and when you deserted her at two you relinquished your right to call her yours," he replied. "Fiona is my daughter."

"She calls your whore *Mam*. Do you think I will let her be raised by that whey-faced English bitch, Colm? Do you think I will let her call that woman Mother?"

"Alix has been more of a mother to Fiona than you ever were," the laird told her, "and she has spent more time with her than you ever did. Beinn, get Fiona."

Robena backed her horse away. "Stay where you are!" she cried.

"I spared your life seven years ago, Robena," the laird said. "I will not spare you again. I warned you then if you defied me I would put you in the tower dungeon."

"You will never put me there, Colm, and you shall not have Fiona back!" Robena Ramsay screamed at him. And then, pulling her horse about, she kicked the injured beast, who leaped forward, startled, and disappeared from sight with its shrieking rider and Fiona.

"What the hell . . ." the laird cried out.

"Wait, my lord, wait!" Beinn shouted, and jumping from his own horse he walked carefully forward. "Dear God," he said, for the moorland disappeared suddenly and unexpectedly at the point where they were standing, giving way to a steep drop down into a fast-running water that tumbled over its rocky streambed. "We must go on foot, my lord. Hurry! Hurry!" And he immediately began the descent downward.

Malcolm Scott swiftly joined him, and together the two men made the climb down to where Robena Ramsay's horse lay in a crumpled heap, its rider and passengers beneath it. Quickly the two men struggled to move the dead animal enough so they might get to the child. The angle of Robena's neck indicated that she had been killed in the fall. They both crossed themselves at the realization. A little groan from Fiona increased their sense of urgency as they reached her. Carefully Beinn extricated the girl from the tangle, and they climbed the steep incline once again. Gaining the top, the laird mounted his horse and reached out for his child. Cradled in his arms she opened her eyes, smiled, and said, "Da!" Then her eyes closed again. Her breathing was labored. Her little face pale.

Malcolm Scott sent his captain on ahead to alert the keep and see it was opened to him. Then he slowly and carefully made his way back to Dunglais, his injured daughter in his arms. As he clopped across the lowered drawbridge into the keep's courtyard he saw Alix and Fenella waiting. Beinn took Fiona from his master and, following instructions from the women, brought the child into the dwelling. When the laird finally reached the hall it was empty. "Where is my daughter?" he asked a pale-faced Iver.

"They have taken the little mistress to her bedchamber, my lord." Tears sprang into the steward's eyes. "She is grievously injured, I fear. I have sent for the priest."

Malcolm Scott felt as if an icy hand had clutched his heart. He ran up the staircase to the upper hall and into Fiona's room. His daughter, white as snow, lay upon her bed. Alix sat on one side of her, holding her small hand, Fenella on the other. Her gown was wet and streaked with dirt. Her small face was dirty from her tears. "Why is she not clean and dry?" he demanded in a fierce voice.

Alix looked up at him but said nothing.

"We dare not move her, my lord. It is too painful for her," Fenella said. What she did not say was apparent.

Fiona Scott was dying. Her little body had been crushed by the weight of Robena and Robena's horse. Her bones were fractured and broken. Her innards were shattered beyond any repair that might be done had they had a physician to aid them. But at the sound of her father's voice she opened her eyes and whispered, "Da!"

He was at her side in a moment, taking the little hand that Fenella relinquished. "I am here, my sweet bairn," he told her, fighting to hold back his own tears. "I am so sorry, Fi. I am so sorry I could not protect you better."

"Love . . . each other," Fiona whispered to him. "Love . . . my . . . mam. I . . . love her."

"I love Alix, my bairn," he told Fiona. "I love your mam."

Fiona turned her head slowly, painfully so she might look at Alix. "Tell . . . my . . . brothers . . . that I . . . loved . . . them," and then she died with a small shudder.

He looked across at Alix. "I do love you," he told her.

Alix arose from the dead child's side. "I will never forgive you for what you have done to all of our bairns," she told him. Then she walked slowly from the death chamber.

Malcolm Scott put his head down and began to cry. Shocked to see her master so distraught, Fenella crept from the room. Her own heart was filled with sorrow, but her head was clearer than either her master or her mistress. Going to the hall, she found Iver waiting. "The little mistress is dead," she said to him even as Father Donald ran into the hall and heard her tragic words.

The priest crossed himself. "Where is she?" he said.

"I'll take you," Fenella said, and led Father Donald upstairs to the bedchamber where the young girl lay. As she could hear the laird still sobbing over his daughter, Fenella pointed to the door and retreated.

Father Donald entered the room. Without a word he took out his holy oil and anointed Fiona with it. Then he knelt by her bedside and prayed. When he had finished he arose and went to the still-weeping laird. "Come, my lord, we need to speak," he said. "Fiona will be taken care of by the women." He led the laird from his daughter's chamber downstairs and into Malcolm Scott's own privy chamber. He seated his master, and pouring them both a dram cup of the laird's own smoky peat whiskey, he sat opposite him. "Now, my lord, tell me what has happened."

"I am responsible for my own daughter's death," the laird said bleakly. "I should have killed Robena when I first found her with my half brother."

"But we settled this matter with Robena Ramsay years ago," Father Donald said. "Did you not send her away? Why was she still on your lands?"

"I sent her from the keep," Malcolm Scott replied. "If I had sent her back to her family it would have caused all manner of difficulty. Her behavior shamed them, and they would not have accepted her back. It would have made ill will between our clans. Are there not enough feuds in the borders that I would start another over a woman like that? And where would she have gone? I had not the heart despite all she did, despite her character, to send her into the world. She would have ended up God knows where."

Father Donald sighed, shaking his head. "Your heart is too good, my lord. So you isolated her in a cottage with two servants and only Beinn went with supplies several times a year. Did he know she was there?"

"Aye. I had to tell him, but he kept my secret."

"Did he know that St. Andrew's had given you a bill of divorcement dissolving your marriage to Robena Ramsay?" the priest queried the laird.

"Aye, that too. He knew my marriage to Alix was true and not bigamous," Malcolm Scott responded.

"Yet I am puzzled why Robena chose this moment to attempt to take Fiona from you," Father Donald said.

"She has lived out on the moor peaceably for seven years. Why did she suddenly want the daughter she had always rejected? I am totally confused by it," the laird admitted. "I know she had learned of Alix, and Robena was always a jealous woman."

"You will have to go and speak with Fyfa, for she may be able to shed light on this matter. What will you do with her and Rafe now?"

"They may have a lifetime tenancy in the cottage," Malcolm Scott told the priest. "They did their duty and cared for her. She was not an easy woman. But to kill Fiona . . ." He struggled to keep the tears pricking at his eyelids from falling. Men did not weep like women, but Blessed Mother! This was his child. He had lost his daughter and would never again see her laughing face, hear her giggle, receive her sweet kiss on his cheek.

"Where is Robena's body?" the priest asked. He felt like weeping too.

"Where she died," the laird replied stonily. "Let her rot where she fell!"

Beinn and I will bury her," Father Donald said. "No one else should be involved. And tomorrow you will go to the cottage and speak with Fyfa and Rafe. It is possible they will know what happened to bring this mood upon her. Now go to your wife and comfort her, for Fiona was as much a daughter to her as she was to you. It must have been quite a shock to her to meet up with Robena."

"More than you can know, Good Father. There never seemed to be a reason to tell Alix the whole truth." He flushed guiltily. "And I never told Robena about the bill of divorcement. She would not have accepted it. So she believed herself still my wife. I can but imagine what Robena said to Alix. Now she believes I have made a bigamous marriage with her, and that her children are stained with the shame of bastardy."

"Jesu! Mother Mary and Joseph!" Father Donald swore, unable to contain himself. "I cannot believe you were so imprudent as to not tell Robena that she was no longer your wife! Aye, I can well imagine what she said to Alix. You are a fool, Malcolm Scott," the priest scolded. "Go and find your wife at once so her mind may be put to rest! And when this matter is finally all over and done with you will come to me for a penance. Aye, I must think upon what God would want you to suffer in order to expunge your cruel thoughtlessness to that sweet faithful young woman who is your wife. Go now!"

Malcolm Scott arose, leaving his little privy chamber to seek out Alix. He found her in the hall where the body of his daughter had now been brought. His wife and Fenella were bathing the small corpse. Unable to help himself, he stood watching them, tears pouring down his face. And then he saw that they too wept as they cleansed and dressed Fiona in her finest gown. It was a new one of scarlet velvet that Alix had made to give to the girl on her ninth birthday, which she would now never see. He watched as the two women plaited Fiona's long black hair, weaving red ribbons into the braids as they worked. When they had finished, they made to lift the girl's body into a plain wood coffin Beinn had carried into the hall.

The laird stepped forward then, taking his daughter's broken body and gently setting it into the plain wooden box. Then he lifted it up and placed it on the high board. Wordlessly Fenella brought four brass candlesticks to set on either side of the coffin and at each end of it. Alix lay the late flowers they had been gathering earlier around the simple box. She looked upon the child she had come to love as her own and gently caressed her face.

"Lambkin," he said softly to her.

Alix turned to look at him, and seeing his face so filled with sorrow, her own anger suddenly left her. She knew how much Colm loved his daughter, and when he held out his arms to her she went into them without hesitation. He had lied to her and bastardized their children, but they had both loved Fiona. It was time for mourning and not for recriminations.

"I have not betrayed you, lambkin, nor shamed our son, or the bairn now in your belly preparing to be born," Malcolm Scott told his wife. "Come and sit by the fire with me, and I will explain it all to you." Taking her by the hand, he led her to the settle and they sat together. "After Robena's betrayal of me I wanted to kill her, but I could not. I put her from the keep into an isolated cottage out on the moor. And then Father Donald applied to the bishop of St. Andrew's to obtain a bill of divorcement for me. And the late king, my friend, spoke up on my behalf. The divorce was granted. I did not tell Robena because I did not ever want to see her again. It took me two years before I could excise from my mind the picture of her and my brother together in each other's arms. I saw she was properly cared for and unable to leave her confinement. The horse she rode today she stole. I did not wed you under false pretenses, Alix. I was free to wed you. Did you truly believe that I could be so dishonorable, lambkin? You are my beloved wife, and our son is no bastard, nor will any of the bairns you give me be bastards."

"I forgive you, Colm," Alix sniffled softly.

"You forgive me?" Her words astonished him. "For *what* am I being forgiven?"

"When you did not tell me all of this before we wed, you committed a sin of omission, my lord," she told him. "Did you think me so silly a creature that I could not bear to hear the truth from you?" When she looked up at him he saw her dark lashes, so in contrast with her honey-blond hair, had clumped with her weeping.

"I did not think it was necessary to burden you with the whole sordid tale," he said feebly. "I never thought you would meet up with Robena Ramsay. I saw her sequestered and cut off from decent folk. This should not have happened."

"But it did happen," Alix said. "Now, is there anything else you have *neglected* to tell me about yourself and your life, my lord? Are there any other surprises you have for me that I must face? I am but a frail female after all."

"You are the strongest woman I have ever known or am likely to know," he told her. "Do you truly forgive me, lambkin, for my *sin of omission?*" And he smiled down into her face, brushing her lips gently with his own.

"I do, Colm. I do!" Alix said to him, wrapping her arms about him and kissing him back. "You are my love and my life." And then she laughed softly as the child in her womb stirred strongly. Alix put her hand upon her belly. "He is almost ready to be born," she said to her husband.

"*He?* Until now you have not been certain," the laird replied.

"Fiona said it was another son for you. I believe she somehow knew," Alix said, kissing him again.

And Fiona's intuition indeed proved correct when her second brother, Andrew Donald, was born on the last day of November. A gentleman from the beginning, he had not taken his sister's birthday for his own.

And when the spring came the Laird of Dunglais, his wife, and sons visited the little churchyard in Dunglais Village where Fiona was buried and discovered that flowers springing from the warm earth had covered the girl's grave, yet nowhere else in the little church graveyard did flowers bloom.

"Our daughter is safe and well," Malcolm Scott declared, his voice catching.

"She will always be with us, Colm. Her last wish for us was that we live and love happily in her memory," Alix said as James clung to her skirt and Andrew babbled in her arms contentedly.

"We shall, lambkin," the Laird of Dunglais promised his wife. *"We shall!"*

And two years later on the first day of May, Alix bore her husband a daughter, whom they named Fiona after the child they had lost. And eventually girlish laughter was once again heard in the keep at Dunglais as Scotland enjoyed peace in the borders for a brief time.

Author's Note

*M*arie of Gueldres, wife of James II and the mother of King James III, died before her son was grown, leaving him in the competent hands of James Kennedy, the venerable bishop of St. Andrew's. Unfortunately the bishop himself died two years later, leaving the teenaged king at the mercy of Scotland's lords: the Kennedy family and the Boyd family, both struggling for supremacy. The Boyds won the day when they kidnapped the young king as he was out hunting on a summer's afternoon.

The young king was not unfamiliar with the Boyds, as his weapons instructor was Sir Alexander Boyd, who, in league with his brother, Lord Robert Boyd, had led the coup d'état forcing James to issue a statement saying he approved of their actions. Lord Robert had his eldest son created Earl of Arran, and arranged a marriage between him and the king's little sister, Mary. Lord Robert saw his daughter, Elizabeth, married to the powerful Earl of Angus.

Though the major offices in the royal household and government were retained by those not in the Boyd family, their greed still managed to make them extremely unpopular. The young king's dislike and resentment of them grew with each passing day. However, one thing was not interfered with, and that was the king's marriage to Margaret of Denmark, King Christian's daughter. It came about when James III was seventeen. With his bride's encouragement, James III took control of his own government at last. The Boyd family lost both their lands and political influence. Lord Robert and his son fled Scotland. The unfortunate Sir Alexander, least guilty of the Boyds, was executed.

As for poor Henry VI of England, he became a pawn in the power struggle between the Lancaster and Yorkist factions. Returning to England in late 1464 to regain his throne, he was caught and imprisoned in the Tower of London, where he remained until 1470, when he was briefly restored to reign under the careful supervision of the Earl of Warwick, known as the Kingmaker.

But Edward of York would not be denied the throne. Returning to England from Burgundy, where he had been in brief exile, he won the battle of Tewkesbury on May 4, 1471. Henry VI and Margaret of Anjou's son, also Edward, was said to have been killed in that battle, although there were rumors of a murder done to the prince. He was seventeen. Less than three weeks later, Henry VI's death was announced. His body was conveyed via barge up the Thames at night to Chesney Abbey, where he was first buried. He was eventually moved to St. George's Chapel at Windsor Castle, where his simple tomb can be found today near that of his successor.

Margaret of Anjou was captured by the Yorkists and sent to the Tower, where she was shown the body of her newly dead husband as it was being taken away for burial. With her husband and son both dead, she wished for nothing more than to return home to her father in Anjou. Finally in 1475 a ransom of fifty thousand marks was raised when her father sold some of his holdings in Provence to King Louis of France. And in January 1476, after crossing a stormy English Channel, Margaret arrived in Rouen, where she was forced to suffer a final humiliation by signing away her dower rights to the English.

Rejoining her father at his country home in Reculée, near Angers, she remained until his death in 1480. She then went to live at Château de Dampierre, near Saumur, with François de la Vignolles, a distant relation who had served in her father's court. It was there that this most tragic of England's queens died, on August 25, 1482.

There is no memorial to be seen at her grave site, but she is buried with her parents in Angers Cathedral. She was fifty-three.

In 1485 Lancaster and York were finally united with the marriage of Henry of Lancaster, who ruled as Henry VII, and Elizabeth of York. So ended the War of the Roses.

About the Author

$\mathcal{B}$ertrice Small is a *New York Times* bestselling author and the recipient of numerous awards, including the 2008 Pioneer of Romance Award from *Romantic Times* magazine. In keeping with her profession, Bertrice Small lives in the oldest English-speaking town in the state of New York, founded in 1640. Her light-filled studio includes the paintings of her favorite cover artist, Elaine Duillo, and a large library. Because she believes in happy endings, Bertrice Small has been married to the same man, her hero, George, for forty-five years. They have a son, Thomas; a daughter-in-law, Megan; and four wonderful grandchildren. Long-time readers will be happy to know that Nicki the cockatiel flourishes, along with his fellow housemates: Pookie, the long-haired greige-and-white cat; Finnegan, the long-haired bad black kitty; and Sylvester, the black-and-white tuxedo cat, who is now the official family bedcat.